The Rebellion

S. L. SCOTT

The Rebellion
First Edition

Copyright © S. L. Scott 2017

Paperback ISBN: 978-1-940071-51-0

Cover design: Sarah Hansen of Okay Creations

Interior Design: Angela McLaurin, Fictional Formats

Cover Image Photographer: Scott Hoover

Editing:
Becca Mysoor, Evident Ink
Marion Archer, Making Manuscripts
Marla Esposito, Proofing Style
Virginia Carey, Proofreading
Kristen Johnson, Proofreader

For the music lovers and the shower singers,
the late night writers, and the believers,
Dreams Can Come True.

The Rebellion

Prologue

Derrick

CLIMBING IN THE back of the SUV with the rest of the band, I slam the door shut behind me. "Go."

The vehicle makes it around the corner before the fans even realize we left through a different exit. Somewhere along this tour, we've developed a drive-away habit with Johnny in the third row, Kaz and Dex in the middle, I'm in the first row, and Tommy is upfront with the driver. The best thing about this arrangement is that I can spread out and lie down, which is exactly what I do. Scrubbing my hands over my face, I close my eyes and remember when this used to be fun.

Running from rabid fans builds an ego fast. But after two years of sneaking away through back exits, finding groupies in hotel bathrooms, and getting mail with locks of hair and proclamations of eternal devotion, the illusion I once lived in has been destroyed. *All hail the life of a rock star.* My rose-colored glasses have been traded for scratched designer shades that shield me from the normalcies of everyday life. The lap of luxury has replaced simple pleasures. The lifestyle of the rich and famous is *and was* intoxicating for a while.

Now I just wish I could walk down the street without being harassed for an autograph or a picture.

The ride from the arena to the hotel doesn't take long, but the adrenaline from the concert is draining, leaving me lifeless on this seat, and a little annoyed. "Did you see that couple in the front row?"

Johnny asks, "What couple?"

"The one face-fucking the entire fucking concert."

He laughs. Once. "What about them?"

"They should be coming for the music."

Kaz says, "They were."

"If they were, they should be listening to it."

Now Dex is laughing. "What the fuck's gotten into you, Derrick? What do you care if some couple is getting off to our music?"

I sound like a lunatic, and a prude at that. Why do I care? They paid their thousands for those seats. If they want to strip naked and fuck for real it shouldn't bother me. But it does and I don't know why.

Maybe it's because I haven't kissed a woman like that in a long fucking time. Not a real kiss—one with more meaning behind it than getting laid for the night. The last time I kissed someone like that... I stop myself from going there because every time I do, it's a downward spiral from there. But when I think of a kiss, she's the only woman who comes to mind, the only woman that when our lips embraced, a part of our souls were exchanged.

Did she keep all the pieces I'm missing? The holes I'm still searching to fill that she left behind?

The door slides open and I sit up to get out. The guys pile out behind me and we go in the back entrance to the private elevators. One helluva good-looking brunette catches my eye while the guys brush by quietly. It's always quiet after a show. We're exhausted and tired of being "on" for everyone.

She hands me a card key and her business card, and says, "We've upgraded you to one of our suites. I'd be happy to give you a private tour, Mr. Masters."

Tempting. *So damn tempting.* I could fuck all night, but it's not going to change the fact that my head's already fucked up over a girl I can't seem to stop thinking about lately. There's no reason for me to give her a second thought. She *should* be nothing but a ghost from my past—part of a past I left behind.

I just wish I hadn't left her behind with it. I slip my shades back on as flashes from the lobby start going off in the distance. "Thank you for the upgrade. I'll take a rain check on the tour."

"My pleasure, and my number's on the card if you need anything at all."

Funny how life works.

The one thing I need is the only thing I can't have. *The only person I can't have.*

"Get the fuck in here." My shirt is grabbed and I'm yanked into the elevator by Dex.

The brass doors close behind me and I stand there facing the band, this band of dreamers who live their dream every day. "I should have taken her up on the tour."

Kaz leans against the corner. "I'm surprised you didn't."

Music is piped in and it takes a second, but we all hear it. With our heads tilted toward the speaker, one of our most popular songs has been turned into classical elevator music. Johnny shakes his head. "Fuck me." Turning his attention down, he starts texting.

Dex is drumming his fingers beside him on the railing. "Now I feel fucking old."

Kaz is laughing and hits me in the chest. "Can't blame us. It's classic Resistance. A song put out before our time."

Tommy asks, "Anyone up for drinks later?"

Everyone ignores him. Kicking my shoe, he says, "Derrick?"

"Going out? Nah."

"Staying in?" Tommy asks in disbelief.

"Yeah."

"Don't leave me going solo. What's gotten into you, Moody?"

"We've played six cities in six days," I complain, catching a glimpse of myself in the metal doors. I look exhausted, my dark hair

3

a mess and my eyes bloodshot. "I need sleep."

"You're twenty-three. These are the best years of your life. Don't waste them sleeping. Right, Johnny?"

Johnny's phone rings, and a wide smile cuts across his world-famous face. The elevator doors open just as he says, "Hey baby," and walks off.

Dex and I follow suit and get off. Holding my key in the air, I wave to Tommy and Kaz who remain on the elevator. "It's good to be me," I tease.

Kaz flips me off and Tommy is cut off by the doors closing, "Fucke—"

Dex walks past me and says, "At twenty-three, I would have taken the tour."

"Maybe I still will."

I slip my key card into the door and enter the suite. My luggage is in the middle of the living room. A bottle of Jack Daniels and a fruit tray are on the table by the window. I toss the business and key cards down next to the bottle and open it. I don't bother with the glasses or the fruit tray. I drink straight from the bottle, stand at the window, and stare at the neon lights of the street below. The room is too quiet, the lingering buzz from performing live still rings in my ears. Another sold out show for The Resistance is behind us and I'm left with the silence of a hotel room. Sometimes I love it, when I'm at home, but the road gets lonely. I pick up the phone and call downstairs. When the pretty brunette answers, I say, "About that tour..."

1

Derrick

SITTING UP IN bed, I watch the back of her bent forward while she clasps the straps of her heels around her ankles. She looks back, and says, "If you need any—"

"Yeah, I'll call you."

A sleek smile slides into place and suddenly I don't feel like my "tour" was a one-time thing for her. She stands and straightens her skirt. "You've got my number."

I reach for the card on the nightstand, and hold it up. "I do. Thanks for—"

"My pleasure."

I'm relieved she cut me off. This is the awkward part I dislike the most. Thanking her for sex would up the weirdness factor. She grabs her hotel manager's jacket and slips it on over her shirt. One last wave, and she says, "It was great meeting you."

"Yeah, you too."

When she disappears, I take her business card in hand again and read out loudly, "Brenda." The door to the suite shuts and I hear the distinct sound of the lock clicking into place.

Another city, another—*meaningless*—distraction. Physically I'm sated, but now what? I pick up my phone and text Tommy Rhodes, the band's manager and my wingman since Kaz abandoned his post: **When do we leave?**

A return text comes fast: **One hour.**

I text again: **Where are we going?**

Tommy: **Nashville.**

Me: **Where are we now?**

Tommy: **Miami.**

Nashville. Miami. East Coast. We're a damn long way from home in LA. It shouldn't bother me. It's not like I've got anything or anyone back home waiting.

I slide my sunglasses over my eyes and lie back down. I'm a rock star, damn it. This is probably why I used to do drugs in the first place. I could leave my own mind for a while and live in the euphoria of fame. But being in the band means being clean. Sure, they don't give a shit about marijuana or booze, but with the history of the band, anything harder breaks my contract. That contract is all I ever fucking dreamed about so I'm not going to screw it up for a temporary high. Anyway, I may not have anyone back home that gives a shit about me, but on the road I can have a Brenda in every city.

Life can be pretty damn sweet if I look at the bright side.

The only problem with my bright side these days is that my head is overrun with memories of a girl I left with a broken heart and out of tune guitar. I meant to fix that before I left—the guitar. There was no fixing the heart unless I stayed, and I couldn't. Good reasons at the time, but hell if I can remember what they are now.

I TOSS MY carry-on in the seat next to me and open the shade. Sunny

Miami. I'm leaving before I even had time to experience the city. Other than the arena we played last night, I didn't see anything beyond the inside of the hotel and an SUV. Releasing a hard breath, I slam the shade back down and close my eyes.

"Rough night?"

I don't have to open my eyes to recognize the voice—Kaz. My best friend, my former roommate, and the bassist for The Resistance aka the best band in the world, moved on. I know I'm lucky. I was chosen from guitarists vying for this spot from around the world to join this band, along with Kaz. It was a quick and easy fix to a spot they had open. At the time, it was a two-for-one kind of deal.

It took the man behind the brand, Johnny Outlaw—lead singer, former rock star bad boy, and the face of the band—two minutes to decide. As a guitarist himself, he knew what he was looking for. We continued to play through three more songs for the other surviving band member, Dex Caggiano—drummer extraordinaire—to decide. He said he actually didn't need to hear more, but liked watching us sweat our hearts out through every chord we played. It was an asshole move. So basically he's my idol now.

The trial period ended a long time ago and we've been officially part of the band for years now. Our dreams came true. Dreams and goals, bucket lists and accomplishments, but once those goals are reached, *what then?*

Before I can say anything to Kaz, Johnny sits across from me and buckles in. Fuck. This can only mean one of two things—I fucked up something in the show last night or he's firing me. The dude never sits by me. He actually sleeps in the bedroom of the private plane most flights. Or is stuck in interviews and doing PR shit. Having him sitting across from me right now is worrisome to say the least. He's not talking at me. He's talking to me. I like this shift in our relationship, this new dynamic.

He stares at me until I remove my sunglasses, then he says, "We all burn out at some point or another. Some take longer to get there. Some sooner. It's how you handle it that determines your future.

How do you plan to handle it?"

Sitting back, my leg begins to bounce and I scoff defensively. "I'm not burned out."

"Bullshit."

"There's nothing to handle. I'm happy as a clam."

His jaw tics. That usually only happens when he's pissed, but his eyes don't show any anger. Blowing out a deep breath, he looks out the window as the plane starts down the tarmac. He says, "Mine was Germany."

"Your what?"

"My bottom." When he turns back to me he says, "The fallout from partying, drugs, booze, women, the whole fucking cliché was a year earlier. Sure, I still did a lot of shit after, but no more hard drugs. As for the women, it was entertaining for a while, but there was no substance. No one I wanted to call the next day or even get their number. Some of the time... a lot of the time I didn't even bother with their names."

Brenda comes to mind. I caught that one as she was walking out the door this morning.

"Look," he says, leaning forward and resting his elbows on his knees. "It happens to all of us. Not many relate, or ever will understand this life on the road, the demands of being in a band that's as successful as The Resistance. But we do. All five of us do. Tommy's given up his life to put us first without the fame or notoriety we have. The rest of us, we're doing the best we can in an extraordinary situation. But I'm telling you. I see the signs. I see it destroying you. Slowly. Meticulously, almost to where you don't notice you're not you anymore." We haven't reached altitude yet, but Johnny stands. "It's great to be a rock star, but not at the expense of having a life. Two tours in two years wears on you. When we get back to LA, find a life again, Derrick. It's the only way you'll survive when you're on the road." I watch as he walks down the aisle to the bedroom and disappears inside. *What the hell?*

As soon as the door shuts, Kaz pops into the chair Johnny

vacated. "Shit, man. What'd he say?"

Find a life.

> *Get a life.*

>> *Live my life.*

"Find myself again."

"I didn't know you were lost."

"Neither did I. Until now."

WE LAND A few hours later to fans screaming behind the metal fence at the private airport. I wave while coming down the stairs and then slide into the first SUV. Dex slides in after me and shuts the door. Tommy, Kaz, and Johnny take up the next black SUV parked beside the plane.

My head pivots in Dex's direction. "What up?"

He nods while staring at his phone, reading something on the screen.

I look out the window next to me already forgetting which city we're in.

"I'm not going to lecture you," he starts. "I leave that to Tommy and Johnny. This band is their baby, hence why we're still hitting the road so hard with each new album."

I'm actually surprised he's talking to me about this. Dex is reserved. Most would say he's not, but over time I've learned he rarely instigates trouble despite his bad reputation. He's more of a reactionary man. "It's fine." I'm not sure what to say. "It's smart to support the record."

"I heard what Outlaw said on the plane. He's right. We see the signs."

"What are they?"

"You're fucking up, not on stage. You're incredible on stage. But you don't have anything keeping you grounded."

"I'm not gonna float away."

"We've had that happen. I fucking did it. You know my story. I think you're a lot like me, Derrick."

"And this is a bad thing?"

"Nah." He chuckles humorlessly. "I just liked to party. There's nothing wrong with that, but the thrill is fading for you. After the show tonight we're home for a few weeks. Take it off. *Really off*, like out of the limelight, and regroup if you can. Well, don't take off from the band sessions, but the other stuff. Hang out with your friends, get laid by a girl you want to have breakfast with, and get some fucking sun. You're pale as a ghost these days."

If only I could have breakfast with the only girl that I'd want to. "What are you gonna do when you get back?"

"See my woman, play with the family. Just live a real life." He drops his head back on the seat and closes his eyes. "I've been given a damn good life, but it comes with sacrifices. That I'm here today, has been no easy feat, and I bow down at the feet of those who got me here. That's who I'll be spending time with. The people who make it possible for me to do this. The people who are there for me when I fall, which as you know, I still do. But these days, I don't fall as far."

"Am I in that bad of shape that everyone is concerned?" I chuckle.

"No." He looks at me. "Just that, I know sometimes it feels like you and Kaz versus me and Johnny. It's not." He holds his hand out to me. "Johnny once told me that being bandmates makes us brothers. I'm always here for you, brother."

We do our handshake that the band adopted soon after we joined. There's comfort in knowing what I'm feeling is normal... as normal as a rock star can be. A new perspective is loaded, the trigger cocked, and hits me right on target.

Another day. Another hotel. Another back entrance. We're shuffled through quickly and into our rooms before the fans realize where we're staying. Or so I thought. Five stories below, "Johnny" is chanted, the hum of fans outside penetrating not just the walls, but my head. I peek out the window before swallowing ibuprofen and lying down. Six hours before sound check. Time to settle my mind and try to get some sleep.

2

Derrick

I'm WOKEN UP by Tom Petty singing about his girl. It's been my ringtone for years and never gets old. 'Cuz Tom Petty rocks.

Grabbing my phone, I answer, "Yeah?"

"Hi, dear, it's Mom."

"Hi, Mom." My voice is gruff and I rub my eyes before checking the time.

"You're sleeping?"

"Yeah, I'm tired. We have a show tonight, so I want to rest while I can."

"I'm sorry. Do you want to call me back?"

I push the button on the remote and the curtains begin to open, letting the setting sun in. "No, I need to get up. How are you?"

"I'm good. It's been a little chaotic today. I finally had someone come fix the cracked window in the kitchen. They had to replace it in the end."

"That's good. It will keep your electric bill down. Did you have them send me the bill?"

"No, son. I took care of it. You do too much as it is."

"I want to and I can afford it. You did more than you should have when I was younger. I've got money now, Mom, let me repay you."

I hear the sigh. The one that reveals the battle between not wanting to accept money from her son and that strong independent woman who raised me when she had nothing but love to give. Even though she worked three jobs, she made sure there was dinner on the table every night. She only missed one of my soccer games because her boss refused her the time off. She had another parent record the entire game and watched it that night with me, cheering like it was live. We lost, even though I scored twice. She treated me to ice cream and a consoling hug while praising what a great job I did. She is literally the best woman I know.

Bringing me back to the present conversation, my mom says, "Having a kid isn't a debt owed to me. I chose to have you because I wanted you. I love you, but keep your money this time."

"I love you."

"I love you too, Derrick. You don't sound good. Talk to me."

"I'm just tired." I scrub my free hand over my face.

"Where are you?"

I know. This time I know. "Nashville. I'm sorry I need to cut this short, Mom, but I need to hop in the shower. Everything else good?"

"Yes. Great. Will you come over for dinner when you get back?"

"Of course. We come home tomorrow, I think. How's the day after that?"

"Perfect. Have fun."

It cracks me up that she said the same thing to me when I was eight years old and going outside to play, when I was sixteen and hanging out with the guys, and now as a twenty-three-year-old who performs in front of twenty thousand people. I hope she never stops. I kind of like that I'm her baby boy.

Fuck. What is going on with me? Baby boy?

I need to pull it together.

"I will. See you Thursday."

"Bye, son."

I hang up and toss the phone on the bed, lying prone a few minutes before I finally drag my lazy ass into the bathroom and shower the tiredness away.

If only showering was a cure that would last.

SITTING ON THE couch in Kaz's room, I scarf the last of the pizza, and finish a can of energy drink that tastes awful, but it's necessary.

Kaz leans back, rubbing his stomach. "I'm stuffed. The rest is yours."

"I'm good." I sit back and kick my feet up. "Remember eating pizza at three a.m. and passing out on the floor?"

"That sucked so hard, but five years ago isn't as long ago as it feels."

"We did what we had to, to survive. If that meant eating pizza about to be thrown out and sleeping on the floor until we got mattresses, we did it."

He's quiet, so I go quiet too. Looking around the suite, he comes back around and I know what he's thinking.

Keeping my voice low, I say, "I think about it all the time."

"We're damn lucky."

"Nah, we made our luck. We wouldn't be here if we hadn't played clubs every night and restaurants during happy hour. We gave up our lives in pursuit of our dreams."

"And it paid off. Are you happy?"

I shake my head and sigh. "Not you, too." I stand up, ready to grab my stuff and go.

"I wasn't talking about you."

Stopping in front of the door, I turn back. "Are *you* happy?"

"I'm happy we're going home in the morning. Playing the shows are great, but I might be ready to have *more*."

"Luxuries a few years ago wouldn't have afforded us. Well,

maybe you, Prince Kaz."

He laughs, but it fades and he eyes me. "I worry about you."

"Don't. We're not chicks."

"As your bandmate, I can say that. As your best friend, I can admit that the guys are right. You look like shit."

What the hell? I open the door. "I'm going to sleep for a week when we get back, let my liver dry out, and do nothing."

"Sounds like a good plan." Grabbing his phone, he gets up and follows me out.

"What about you?"

"I think I'll move up the wedding and start working on that *more* I mentioned."

The old me would have ragged on him so bad for even mentioning a future with a wife and kids, teasing him relentlessly for giving up his manhood.

The *new* me, if he actually exists? Having watched Outlaw and Kaz lately, how they have a stillness about them that's linked to the women at their sides, I am starting to want the same thing. The *same* thing I'd been so set against in my youth. What's more confusing is that it seems to have happened overnight. And having just spoken to my mom, who I love more than life itself, I'm reminded of the girl I let go. The one who has owned my heart for years, but until recently had been pushed to the periphery of my brain. Why can't I stop thinking about her now though? Why does she own so many of my thoughts lately? *It's torture if I'm honest.*

Walking into the bright lights of the parking garage a few minutes later, I realize I miss the sun, and fresh air. I miss my freedom. I climb to the back of the SUV and kick my legs up on the seat. It's too small to stretch out, but it's good to have the space. Now I see why Johnny likes sitting back here. It's less crowded. More room to think.

The guys pile into the van. Johnny stops when he sees me, but then gives me a nod and an understanding grin before he takes the seat closest to the door.

I should have known better. Living in my head for twenty

minutes isn't really an option before a concert. Pre-gaming for a show is much louder than after. We're pumped, keeping the energy high. By the time we reach Vanderbilt Stadium, we're wired. We tour the stage for sound check and I pluck a few chords, tighten some strings, and test them again. I'm not feeling it. Last minute, I decide to change out guitars altogether. "Tommy, get me Jaymes."

He returns with my most treasured guitar. I usually don't bring her on the road with me, but I found myself carrying her on to the plane when we left LA. Maybe that's why the woman behind the guitar has been monopolizing my thoughts. I strum and tune and then sit on the edge at the front of the stage and let my fingers play the song they can play in their sleep. *She* used to say I did.

Our song, the one we wrote together sitting by a fire pit made from old bricks we stole from a construction site, runs through my fingers onto the guitar. The nights were chilly, but that fire felt just right. Just like the girl. She would play along with me and sing like a little songbird, hitting all the right notes, hitting me in the heart. I remember the night I gave Jaymes her first guitar...

"Two hundred. I can't take a dollar less."

"I've got one seventy-six. C'mon, Tank, cut me the deal. It's Jaymes's birthday present."

Tank doesn't usually negotiate. Given his size, there was no need to explain his name, but under the wall of muscle and bad attitude, he is a softie at heart. He sold my mom my first guitar five years earlier. He claims he got the full hundred out of her. She once told me she paid fifty. I don't blow his cover. I think he just wants to help us local kids find something better to do with our time than sell drugs or pretend to be badasses with real guns.

"I'll do the deal for Jamie, but on one condition."

"Name it," I reply with a wide, winner's grin.

"You both play my grandmother's ninetieth next weekend."

"What?" I'm offended to even be offered the gig, much less be told I'm playing at a grandmother's birthday party. "Fuck, man, really?" He grabs the neck of the guitar roughly and lifts it from

17

the pawnshop counter. "No. No, that's cool. We'll be there. Just tell me the time and place."

The guitar is set back down and his open palm waits as I slap every dollar I have left after buying groceries, paying some bills, and passing some cash to my mom. Six months of savings and my goal of saving to fix up the truck went out the window. My girl is worth it. Every penny. Every minute of hard labor on that construction site. All worth it. If I can't follow my dream, I'll sure as hell do everything to help her achieve hers.

Three hours later, I've picked Jaymes up from her job at the sandwich shop. Our dinner wrapped neatly in the wax paper between us. Two Cokes in the cup holders clipped to the window sill. Tom Petty playing on the CD player. A sky full of stars and a truck cab full of dreams. We make our way to what feels like another land, a land where wishes come true. Through the Los Feliz neighborhood, we drive to Griffith Park, and closer to the Observatory.

Parking off by a trail entrance, we hop out. I don't have much time. She'll spot her present when we climb in the back. So I say, "Close your eyes."

On the other side of the truck, she smiles, knowing she can trust me. Always trust me. Her hair is the color of night. Her eyes sparkle under the moonlight—looking more gray than green in the dark. "What are you up to, Derrick?"

"No good. Just the way you like me."

"I like you good. You're good through and through, Masters, and you're so good to me."

Leaning on the opposite side of the truck from her, I reach out until she follows my lead and reaches for me. The tips of our fingers touch and I say, "I'm good because of you."

She's emotional, always wearing her heart on her sleeve for the whole world to see. I tell her people will notice and take advantage of her kind heart if she's not careful. Deep down, it's one of the things that drew me to her. She's soft when the world we live in is hard. She loves openly and had somehow reached in even though I had closed myself off. My songbird sings of hope and impossible things when the rest of us struggle to keep faith. "Close your eyes," I whisper again.

This time she does, our hands falling away. I remove the blanket and pick up the guitar with the deep pink bow. Her favorite color. Coming around the back of the truck, I hold the guitar and say, "Happy birthday, baby."

Her mouth falls open, but her hand is quick to cover it as her eyes go wide. "You did not."

"I did." I move closer. "Do you like it?"

"Derrick." She says my name like it's a warning, which makes me laugh.

"Don't worry about the money."

"How can I not worry about the money?"

I move until she has the guitar in hand and I have mine wrapped around the back of her as she strums. "Just promise me you'll always sing."

"I do." Her vow echoes through my soul and I hold her closer. "Thank you. It's the most beautiful gift I've ever been given."

"I feel the same about you."

...Damn, I loved her.

Last I heard, she had shacked up with my *ex*-friend. I moved my mom out of that dump of an area and told her to never speak of her again. Curiosity is starting to get the best of me.

What does she look like now?

How has time changed her? Age? Life?

Me leaving?

Does she still hate me or can she forgive me?

Does she still like The Resistance, still listen to the songs, listen to me playing them?

They used to be her favorite band.

What does she think of me being a part of the band? Is she happy for me? Or does she hate that I got out and she didn't?

Maybe I should look her up when I get back home? Or maybe it was good I left. Maybe we were never meant to be. Or maybe—Nah, no use dragging old feelings into my current life. If there's one thing I've learned, it's that leaving that life behind is the only reason I have the life I lead now. It may be lonely, but I don't wake up ready to hit the floor and hide from cops. I don't worry about being pulled over and the police finding a gun under the seat or drugs in the trunk. I don't go to bed thanking God for letting me survive another day, but maybe I should.

I push up off the stage and walk to Tommy. Handing him the guitar, I say, "Save her for another day. I'll use the Stratocaster."

"You got it."

He hands it off to a roadie, and I add, "Careful."

Another roadie runs on stage with Old Faithful. I stroke the sleek design when I take it in hand, plug in the cord, and tap my effects pedal when Kaz and Johnny walk on stage with their guitars. We work as a well-oiled machine, so sound check never takes long. Two songs for the crew to work out the kinks and we're done.

Backstage I spy some hotties lingering around near the exit doors. I smile. They wave. I wink. They giggle. I head their way. They stand straighter, their lips are licked, and whispers exchanged between them.

"Hey."

Tommy's hand anchors my shoulder. "Hello, ladies."

"Hi," they reply in unison with an expression that is more than a little friendly. The redhead holds her hand out. "I'm Cherry."

"Did you know my favorite pie is cherry?" I take her hand and kiss it.

"I'm glad to hear you like pie."

The euphemism isn't lost.

Tommy's already scoring a phone number when I hear Dex down by the dressing room yell, "Get down here, fuckers."

The girls look anxious, their opportunity slipping away. I take a step back. Cherry steps forward. "Let's hook up after the show."

Her phone is out and I glance down to it, then back up to her. "I'll find you."

As I'm heading to the dressing room, she says, "Promise?"

I look back, give her my best *sure, sweetheart* smile, but keep going. How is it that girls willingly beg a stranger for a random hookup? To promise they'll bang them later. *I hate that I've never been good at keeping promises.* I sure as fuck ain't keeping one to a stranger looking to score with any celeb that glances her way.

The door to the dressing room closes behind Tommy and I head for the couch next to Kaz who's fixing a broken guitar string. I grab the yo-yo from the table on the way and sit down. The toy is spinning down and back up before my ass hits the vinyl. It's a substitute, a distraction from a craving that hits me every now and again. It's not the drugs I want. I was in deep, but got out before I went deeper, before they controlled me. It's the habit. The smoking. Jaymes. The nerves I try to suppress. The habit of having something in my hand to occupy it when I'm not playing my guitar. In my old life, I'd raise hell to burn off this restlessness. In my new life, I do tricks with a yo-yo while hanging out with my best friend. My how times change.

When Dex, Johnny, and Tommy leave to eat dinner, Kaz and I hang back, still full from the pizza we ate before leaving the hotel. I work on a new song, fleshing out the second stanza while he plays Word Wobble on his phone. He gruffs out loud, "Damn it."

I look over.

"Ignore me."

"It's hard to ignore you when you're shouting about a word puzzle game on your damn phone."

"I missed an easy one."

Trying to block him out, I strum the next chord, but he pipes in again, "How's your mom? My mom wanted to invite her over soon."

Not able to concentrate, I toss the pencil down and lean back with my guitar over my lap. Strumming softly, I reply, "She's good. Hey, I've been meaning to ask you about Lara and if maybe she'd consider helping my mom finish decorating her place."

Kaz smiles, that goofy grin he sports anytime his fiancée's name is mentioned. "I'm sure she wouldn't mind."

"I'll pay her. I don't want my mom spending a dime."

"I'll make sure she charges you double," he replies, going back to his game.

That sixth sense kicks in and a text comes through from my mom as if she knows we're talking about her. I tap the screen and read: *Having lunch on Thursday with Nita. She's picking me up since my car is going into the shop. Can you pick me up from her house?*

What? Nita?

I reply: *Nita Grenier? Jaymes's mom?*

The dots are flashing and I'm losing patience, along with my shit. Finally her text arrives: *Yes.*

Damn. Coincidence or irony?

She hasn't seen Nita Grenier in years. Fuck, it's been, what, three years? Nita had once been someone special to me, someone, who like my mom, had wanted more for me. *More for us.* Why is Mom going to have lunch with her now? They went through a lot together, as did most moms of that neighborhood. But few emerged from its smothering darkness. My mom being one of the few. Not everyone was so lucky. Some of her friends lost kids to gunfire. Some to drugs. A few escaped. Mom and I are the lucky ones.

I was given a second chance, a new beginning, but not everyone was that lucky. *Jaymes.* Whether she chose to stay for her mother, or chose to let me leave alone, she remained behind. From the rumors I heard before I forbid her name mentioned, she has paid the price.

I type: *No problem. Why is your car going into the shop?*

Mom: *It has a recall and now they need it in to fix it.*

Oh. Me: *Let me know what they say.*

Mom: *Okay, dear. Love you.*

Me: *Love you.*

22

A lump forms in my throat. Jaymes doesn't live with her mother, Nita, like she once did, but if I happen to run into her while picking Mom up, do I really want to take that risk of seeing her again? *Stupid question, Masters.* You know you *need* to see her again. To somehow put all these memories to bed once and for all.

Or reopen old wounds.

Hell, they've already reopened.

Maybe this time they'll heal.

3

Jaymes Grenier

I DON'T THINK I've ever bolted from bed so fast. That's what bad memories do to you. All it takes is one riff from "Here Comes My Girl" by Tom Petty to send me flying toward my alarm. Everything about that song reminds me of one person, and *that* person is the last one I intend to ever give any of my time to again. He just stole my usual five-minute bonus snooze.

Damn him.

The alarm clock is whacked and the song that reminds me of a life I let go of years ago is silenced. *Tried* to let go of...

Sometimes thoughts of that life still linger along with my girlhood dreams of marrying someone who loves me unconditionally, reminding me of what has become a fantasy. Disappointment sets in for like the billionth time. I know with all my heart that I'd never trade Ace for fulfilled dreams. Often I just wish fulfilled dreams *and* Ace could have gone together.

I flick my bedroom light as I walk into the hall and pad quietly past his room. Sneaking into the bathroom, I turn the light on and squint as I work my way to the shower and start the water. Stripping my pajamas off, I step in before the water heats up. The reality is it's never going to get hot enough to make that much of a difference. I'm just hoping for lukewarm this morning. I tilt my head under the spray, keeping my body angled away. I'd rather deal with cold air than ice-cold water.

Five minutes later I'm out and drying off. Cold showers have taught me to be quick. It's funny what we get used to when we're out of options. While scrubbing the towel over my head I realize this applies to more than cold showers. I don't dwell. It's a trait I embraced wholeheartedly when I decided I would—*and could*—face whatever life threw my way. I'm not making lemonade out of my lemons quite yet, but I strive for it every day. For Ace. *He* deserves better than this life has given us.

A soft knock pushes the door open. As a single mom, I never use locks inside the house, but the bathroom one is broken anyway, so any pressure opens the door. I pull it open the rest of the way and smile when I see my sleepy little baby. "Good morning," I say, leaning down and kissing the top of his head.

My sweet five-year-old rubs his eyes, the light from the bathroom blinding compared to the dark room he came from—*from the darkness he came from.* He's good. So good. My light. My purpose. I would trade my dreams any day for him. No matter the circumstances, I've been blessed to be given this purpose, blessed to be his mom.

"Good morning, Mommy."

The best name I've ever been called. "Good morning, buddy. You hungry?"

"Yes. Pancakes?" He looks up with all the hope I used to have. It's contagious. Big brown eyes that don't match mine, but I can't help loving. Bright. Happy. I put that there. I'd give him everything if I could.

"I think we have just enough mix to make some."

He jumps up with excitement. "Yay!"

"Go get dressed and I'll start making breakfast."

He runs off just as I bring our small apartment to life, switching lights on as I make my way to the kitchen. With a towel wrapped around my body, I start making the pancakes. I see the TV flick on a few minutes later and Ace sitting on the loveseat with the remote in his hand. The news is on, and he looks frustrated the way he's handling the remote. The pancakes aren't bubbling yet, so I take a piece of tape from the drawer and go to sit down next to him. Taking the remote, I flip it over and tape down the battery door. When it's loose, it won't work. I hand it back and he smiles when it works as if I just performed a magic trick.

Running back into the kitchen, I flip the pancakes and a few minutes later, I mentally add syrup to the shopping list in my head while serving the pancakes and the last of the syrup. It's the simple things kids love and appreciate. I've become the hero of my son's world just for making pancakes. Like being his mother, pancake hero is another title I adore. I relish. It's good to feel loved without conditions, loved for just *being.* I treat him the same. This world will do its job and cause enough damage, so I'll work hard to do mine and try to protect him from it.

With my hair dried and my skirt on, but unzipped, I pull my blouse on and give the warning, "Five minutes, buddy. Brush your teeth and hair and get your shoes on."

"'K, Mommy."

Ten minutes later, we're heading out the door. I've learned to build in extra time. With a kid, it's inevitable we're going to be late. I don't have that luxury though. I can't be late to work or I'll be fired.

The car starts with a gruff and a puff of black smoke kicked out the back, but it starts and that feels like a victory in and of itself. After dropping Ace off at kindergarten with a kiss and a lunchbox, I drive the twenty minutes to work. My backpack is slung over my shoulder and I head inside.

Leah, the office manager and one of my closest friends, greets me, "Good Morning, Jamie."

"Morning." I drop my pack to the floor behind the reception desk and take the chair.

She leans against the wall with a cup of coffee in her hands. "How are you? You look tired."

My head tilts. "Geez, thanks."

Shrugging, she laughs. "Sorry. I've seen you look better."

I push my hair back away from my face and sigh. "I am tired. My classes are tough this semester. I'm not getting much sleep. I was up until three studying for a test I have tonight. Six a.m. was painful."

"Oh no. You should have told me. I could have talked to David."

"You know he doesn't allow anybody to be late, so it wasn't even an option to ask."

She sighs, standing back up. After glancing at the clock on the wall, she says, "True. Well, if I can help out this weekend with Ace, let me know. Roger's on the road through Wednesday. So I'll be around."

"Thanks. I might take you up on that offer. I have to go to the library at some point and do some research. It would be easier not having to keep one eye on Ace the whole time."

"You got it."

Through the windows to the side, we both spot the king of used cars—at least in a two-mile radius—also known as our boss, parking his very shiny new car. "Off to work we go."

She hurries to her desk, both of us at our stations for the day, exactly how he likes us. The door swings wide and he grumbles until he sees me. It's only eight in the morning, but his balding head is already beading with sweat. Traffic is hell when you drive in from a fancy neighborhood like Brentwood each day to slum it with us on the south side. Five graying hairs cling to his brow before he brushes them to the side. The only thing he's missing is the beer belly. He may not have a lot of hair, but he's relatively fit, so he can catch a woman's eye. It's his personality where he falls flat. Recently divorced, he has become a man on the prowl for his next ex-wife. I've managed to say no despite the very attractive drunken proposals I've received. I mean, I'm still surprised I was able to resist his lecherous hands cupping my ass when I was changing the

28

toner on the printer last week. He told me I was missing the opportunity of a lifetime. I kept my eye-rolls in check until he left the room. I also added another shot of bourbon to his coffee the way he likes it. The thought of his hands on me still makes me cringe. With the smile I know he expects to see on my face, I say, "Good morning, David."

"Mornin', Jamie. Any calls?"

I covertly click the after-hours voicemail system off, and reply, "None so far."

"Good. I'll be busy most of the day." When he says this, it means he'll be playing poker online. He has a nasty gambling habit. "So only disturb me if it's absolutely necessary or to close a deal."

"Gotcha."

He stops in front of my desk, and his eyes seem to have problems focusing on mine. He talks to my breasts regularly. Even though I'm buttoned practically to my chin, he still stares, and then disappointingly sighs. "You're very dressed up. You're not interviewing somewhere else, are you?"

No. I'm keeping your eyes from molesting my chest. With a plastered smile still on my face, I don't say what I really think because I need this job. "Nope. Just thought I'd look nice."

"Well, you do," he replies somewhere between giving a compliment and feeling left out of the party. The phone rings. *Thank God.* "I'll leave you to it."

Turning away to start my day, I answer with fake enthusiasm, "It's a wonderful day to buy a Calvert Car. How may I direct your call?"

And so it begins...

I'M STARTLED AWAKE and turn to the window. Jose, our top salesman this month, is just outside my car. I wipe the drool from the side of my mouth and check my watch. *Shoot.* The door flies open and I'm already dreading going inside. "Gracias, Jose."

"Mr. Calvert's looking for you," he replies in a thick accent. His smile is gentle, leaning toward sympathetic. He knows David can be an asshole.

"Thanks," I say, dashing for the door. I undo my top two buttons, needing to use any ammunition I have, before reaching the door. It swings open and I step into the air conditioning. It feels good against my heated skin. My lunchtime nap in the car wasn't long, but I can't afford to leave it running. The afternoon sun is strong through the cracked windshield, so I feel a little sweaty, the cotton sticking to my back.

David is sitting at my desk. "The phone rang."

"I'm sorry," I say, rushing toward him to take my place. "I fell as—"

His hand goes up, stopping me before I can finish. "I'll let it slide this time, but you can stay late on Thursday to make up for it."

Not a question, though he likes to hide behind the ambiguity of it. "Sure." I have no choice. I've tried to argue before, but to no avail. I'll just be reminded how he's done me a favor and if I don't appreciate it, I can find work elsewhere.

He stands. I sit, and then ask, "Did the call get taken care of?"

"No. I can't be answering my own phone. How would that look to customers? Small time." He knocks on my desk. "That's how."

Small time. That's how I feel. *Small.*

I'm left to do my small job, in my small life, and my even smaller future. "I've got to graduate next semester," I mumble under my breath. So much hinges on that one thing. Graduation. With my degree, I'll finally dictate where and who I work for. I'm not wishing for the stars. I'm not dreaming above who I am. But I will be more than a glorified customer service operator working for someone who hired me in hopes of sleeping with me.

I'll never be anything more than someone else's employee, but at least I'll be respected. *At least I'll have that.*

4

Jaymes

FIVE MINUTES OVER on my lunch the other day and I'm stuck doing
an extra hour in penance. I'm well aware that David does this on
purpose to ensure I'll be alone. It's the only way I'll *voluntarily*
spend time with him—forced atonement.

Leah did me another favor and picked Ace up since my mom is
working until six. I owe her a mountain of favors in return. Another
debt I'll never be able to pay off. At least my mom feeds her. She
loves that, and Ace.

David saunters in after the last employee has left. I smell the
bourbon before he even gets near the desk. I keep my headset on as
a deterrent. I'm a great actress when I need to be. My mom says I
missed my calling, but really it wasn't the big screen calling. It was
the stage. That call just never came through like I once dreamed it
would.

With papers shaking in the air, he says, "Jamie, I need you to—"

With my hand pressed to my headset, I hold my finger up, and
mouth, "Hold on."

Looking impatient, he waits, standing closer to me than I like.

31

He won't dare interrupt a potential customer or sale though, so I know I'm good for a minute or so, hoping he gets bored and goes back to his office. The problem is, ever since his divorce last year he spends a lot more time hanging around here, and especially around me. Beyond the inappropriate proposals, he has asked me out more than a dozen times, offered to make my life easier, and to, and I quote "help take care of that kid of yours. He needs a father in his life." After swallowing down the bile that filled my mouth after that offer, I politely told him to fuck off. Though my exact words escape me, they were more along the lines of me wanting to do this on my own.

What a lie.

This was never how I planned to live my life. Having a kid out of wedlock wasn't a big deal. Not in this day and age, or any other. I can defend my decision if need be. What I can't defend are the actions of Ace's father.

David leaves in a huff and I stop jabbering like someone is actually at the other end of this fake call.

By seven, I'm out the door and driving to my mom's house. I park out front and am welcomed with open arms from Ace. "Hey, you," I say, cupping his face and smiling. "How's it going?"

"Missed you, Mommy."

Bringing him to me, I hold his small body in my arms, close my eyes, and breathe easier now that I'm here. "Missed you too, buddy." I stand and take his hand, walking to the house. "Did you eat all your dinner?"

"Yes, Grandma said I did good and made me brownies."

My smile grows. "She's the best like that."

Leah is on the front porch, waiting. "We need to talk." If she said that to me without the big smile on her face, I would have been worried.

"Now or in a few?"

"It can wait, but not long."

Laughing from her mysterious, but excited secret holding reaction, I ask, "Do I need wine for this?"

"Most definitely."

We go inside just as my mom calls from the kitchen, "Brownies are ready."

"Hey, Mom. I'm here."

Her head pops around the corner, and a smile that has seen more than its fair share of tragedy to dampen it, still shines bright for Ace and me. "Jamie, you're here. I saved you a plate. You hungry?"

"Always for your cooking."

When we enter the kitchen she's pouring three glasses of white wine from the box spout. Not the expensive stuff, but it gets the job done and I can't complain. I also like the taste. "Did Leah already tell you?"

"No, but she's bursting at the seams. What happened?"

"C'mon, you. The grown-ups are going to talk." My mom ushers Ace out and sets him up in the living room with a cartoon, a brownie, and a glass of milk. She returns and picks up her cup and takes a sip. A plate of food is set down at the table and we sit around it. "I had lunch with an old friend today."

"Oh? That's nice. Who was it?" I take my first bite of broccoli.

"Diane Masters."

I start to choke, coughing furiously until the food dislodges from my throat.

Before I can react with more than the wide eyes and a sore throat, Leah says, "Derrick came by to pick her up."

Derrick.

Derrick Masters.

How can she say his name so casually? His name rolls off her tongue in a way that reminds me of many nights confiding in her through tears and wine and support. My heart even now, fracturing inside.

The fork slips from my hand and clatters off the side of the plate. I watch the metal as it bounces across the table. I shake my head as the name Masters makes my heart start aching. My mom picks up the fork and hands it to me. Softly, she asks, "Are you okay?"

"Yeah, I um." Two sips of wine and then a big gulp to empty the glass follows.

Leah takes my empty glass and stands. "Let me get you another."

"No, it's okay. I have to drive home, and I have studying to do." This time I stand, push back from the table, hoping my legs will hold me. The metal feet of the chair grind against the linoleum. Somehow the screech of the chair feels like the noise of hearing *his* name. Later I'll try to get my head around the fact that my mom had lunch with Diane. *Much later.*

"I'll get Ace."

My mom grabs the plate. "I'll wrap this up for you." I hear the nervous tone. "You can eat later."

"Mom." I reach for her before she turns her back. "I'm fine. I am."

"You don't seem it."

"I." Swallowing down the lump in my throat, I close my eyes. I'm about to speak, but I'm struggling to share my real feelings. *Or rather, I'm terrified to share my real feelings.* "I think I'm just tired."

My mom carries on and grabs the foil to cover the plate, but Leah is living the high life on this whole mess. "He sure is cute. I can't believe you once date—"

"Leah!" My mom and I stop her from going further in unison.

Her mouth closes quickly. I shake my head. "No, please not tonight."

"Okay," she replies gently. "Sorry."

"You don't have to be. Just... I'll tell you everything soon. Just not tonight. Ace? Come on. We need to get home."

Ace runs into the kitchen with chocolate all over his face. "Did any make it to your belly?" I tease, reaching for the wet wipes.

"I want another."

"I'm sure you do, but that's enough for tonight." When I stand my mother hands me two plates. My dinner on one. Brownies on the other. I kiss her cheek. "Thank you."

"You're welcome. I know you have to study, but I don't want you up all night. I see the dark circles under your eyes. You're not getting enough sleep."

"I'm doing the best I can."

"You're doing a great job. Just be kind to yourself too. You're everything to everyone else, Jamie. Be good to *you* every once in a while."

We walk out the front door and I'm about to walk down the steps, but I stop and turn back. "I'll try." Her brown hair is pulled back with a few strands flying free. The lines she earned worrying about me, but maybe they were destined to be there from living. I like to think I contributed more to the lines that create her smile. If you were to ask her, I did. She's always been there for me, even when I had no one else. Hugging my mom, I whisper, "How did he look?"

Her arms wrap around me and I feel enveloped by her love. *I needed this hug.* "Disappointed."

My smile comes easy. "Thank you."

"I'm only speaking the truth."

I step back and turn to hug Leah. "Thank you for picking Ace up and bringing him over here."

"No problem. You know I love hanging out with him. And your mom."

"She loves it too." I look between the two of them and point my finger. "You two are trouble together."

Wiggling her hips with her hands on them, my mom replies, "I think I'm due a little trouble."

"Oh, good grief. Ace and I are leaving before you get any sassier. Love you both. Thanks again."

We load in and I turn back and look at my son as he buckles into his car seat. "All ready to go?"

"Yep."

Ace tells me every detail of his day, including who got yellows and notes sent home to their parents in their folders, and who got an extra turn to read from the book during their story time. I got a whole earful about Francisco stealing grapes from the cafeteria line and getting caught. I gave my usual response of knowing what's right and wrong and stealing is wrong. It's a hard lesson to teach in an environment that encourages it. The other kids in the apartment complex where we live have already approached Ace several times. His father's reputation protects him, but for how long? They're scared of what might happen now, but shortly those kids will be turning eleven, twelve, and thirteen and recruited by gangs sooner than they know. The cycle will repeat itself, as it so often does.

Six months. That's all I need until I'll have the tools to move us out of here to somewhere safe, somewhere my child won't be the target of rival hate. I'll get him out, just like Derrick got out.

It's possible.

Derrick.

I go through the motions of getting Ace to bed and spreading my books across the coffee table, preparing for another long night. I have a test tomorrow and I'm behind two chapters. I start the coffeepot, but don't worry with heating my dinner. It's good cold. So I eat, and read, take notes, but my mind still wanders back to what my mother said.

Disappointed.

Derrick Masters looked disappointed.

Of all the things she could have said about him, I hadn't expected that. *Who would?*

What could he possibly be disappointed about? He has everything he ever dreamed of. Everything he ever wanted. Easy Street came so easy to him, practically dragging him away from me without a second glance.

Seeing him this many years later and the only word my mom chose to describe him with is disappointed.

Fascinating.

I click over and open a new search tab on my clunker of a laptop. It's slow. I think dial up back in the day was faster. But as soon as it pops open, I type in Derrick Masters. I pause before pressing enter though. It's not like I've not searched him before. My browser history would be the first to bust me. This time is different though. This time I'm trying to figure out why he looked disappointed. Is it because I wasn't there? That's a flattering thought, but I hardly think after all this time, he'd be disappointed not to see me. Relieved was probably more like it when it comes to me.

My mom has great intuition though, so what if he was disappointed he didn't see me? Or worse? What if he saw Ace? Oh God. Disappointment wouldn't be the only thought he'd have. I quickly press enter and watch my screen suddenly fill like lightning struck it. "Oh now, you're in a hurry." I roll my eyes. Even my computer is a traitor when it comes to Derrick.

Scanning the news page, I read that The Resistance just wrapped the East Coast leg of The Rebellion World Tour. Livin' the life. I smile. Even my residual anger and pain can't keep a little pride from seeping in. He did what he set out to do. I click on the top article.

The band arrived back in Burbank on their private plane to a crowd of cheering fans... Johnny... Dex... band manager... I scan farther down the page until I see Derrick's name. *Derrick Masters, the band's lead guitarist didn't have a comment at this time.* His head is down in the photo next to the text, and I find my fingertips tracing along his jaw and my heart beating for him, just like years ago. "Oh Derrick. What has become of you?"

That's when I see it. The truth is found in a video.

I click the video of the reporter hounding him as he cuts through the crowd of paparazzi. "We've been hitting the road pretty hard. It was great to be out there, but I'm happy to be home for a while. I think I'll sleep for the next week."

My mom had it all wrong. He wasn't disappointed.

He was exhausted.

A lot like me these days.

Just for *very* different reasons.

Unlike me, he still looks damn good. Square jaw that I used to caress. Broad shoulders that have widened with age. He looks taller, if that's possible. Darker hair than I remember. Familiar in so many ways and foreign in others.

Damn him.

Damn me and this stupid lovesick heart. And there it is. The splintering in my heart. I close the window. That's enough of that for one night. Because when it comes down to it, it doesn't matter if he's tired or disappointed. It's only momentary. He's not mine to worry about. My heart doesn't matter.

Hopefully, these feelings will subside one day. All I need to worry about is asleep in the back bedroom. I don't need anyone else or anything. All I need is my son. We'll get by just like we have the last five years. Just the two of us.

"We've been hitting the road pretty hard. It was great to be out there, but I'm happy to be home for a while."

Lucky him. Home for him is respite, rest, and parties, whereas home for me is constant responsibility, studying, and fatigue.

You have all you need, Jamie.

You have all you need.

5

Jaymes

SITTING ON THE bench, I watch Ace run around with a girl playing tag. The park isn't busy considering it's a Sunday. I like it. It's peaceful. Looking down at the textbook next to me, I feel instant guilt. I should be studying, but I don't want to. I'd rather be distracted by birds singing in the trees above or the sound of giggles from happy children playing. Even the cars driving by on the other side of the playground seem to garner my attention.

I think I'll give myself the morning. It's too beautiful a day to waste not appreciating it. Anyway, I always have this evening to bury my nose back in the books.

The sound of a thumping bass interrupts the tranquility of the park a few minutes later. I watch the shiny royal-blue car with sparkling silver rims roll by and know it's going slow to keep an eye on me, and Ace.

My heart thuds in my chest louder than the music could ever be blared. A guy I don't recognize hangs out of the window of the vehicle just far enough for me to worry. When he falls back into the shadows of the interior and the car drives off, I feel the breath I refused to breathe release. And just like that, the little peace I had found is gone.

I toss my textbook back into my backpack and shove our water bottles into the side pockets. I'm ready to flee this park, wishing we were in another part of the city altogether. When Ace comes running up with his new friend, the mother of the other child looks over concerned. I wave. "It's okay," I reassure her. I'm sure she lives with the same fears I feel. The same fears our mothers once held for our futures. Maybe they still do since we're still here. Since we haven't gotten out yet. I'm going to change that. I'm going to make good on everything I swore I would. I'll show Mom a better life. I'll make sure that Ace doesn't have to fight the same battles I fight. I'll sleep at night knowing we're safe, instead of living in perpetual fear.

One day I'll even get the puppy Ace so desperately wants. I may not be able to afford an extra mouth to feed now, but one day I will.

Ace asks, "Can we stay longer, Mommy? Tegan wants to play on the swing. I said I would push her first if she pushed me second."

My smile grows. This is the biggest concern I wish my son to ever have. "Of course. It's good you're taking turns and helping each other out."

Ace shrugs. "That's what friends do."

They run off and I repeat, "Yeah, that's what friends do." Maybe not loves of your life, but friends.

I decide I should study before my mind drifts to a sexy guitarist that looks disappointed when I'm not around... I mean *tired*.

NOT SURE HOW long I've pushed my peas around my plate, but Mom is. She says, "Just put the poor things out of their misery and stop toying with their emotions."

I start laughing and set my fork down. "Dinner was good, Mom. Thank you." Ace jumps up, but I correct, "Sit down please."

"Can I go?"

"Not *can I go*. You need to ask, 'May I please be excused?' "

"May I please be 'scused?"

"Yes." He's running before I can ask where he's going. The back door squeaks from its rusty hinges and then slams closed. He's safe in the backyard, one of the few places I never have to worry about him. It's small and tidy with just enough room for a growing boy to burn off some excess energy. "He starts soccer next week. Will you still be able to help out?"

My mom sits her elbow on the table and I know a heart-to-heart is coming. "I'm always here for you and Ace. My job, not so much. I just had my hours cut back—"

"Again?"

Resting her chin in the palm of her hand, she nods. "I was thinking maybe you and Ace could move in. I know you like your independence and I like mine—we're similar in that way, but I love you two more. With less money, I'm not sure I can keep the house, and I know it would help ease some of your expenses by splitting the bills."

"Mom—"

"Just hear me out, Jamie. You're busy. He's over here all the time already—"

I reach over and take her hand. She sits up and I hold tight. "You don't have to sell me on it. I think this is a good idea."

"You do?" she asks, surprised.

"I do." I breathe out and it feels like some of my load has lightened. "I'm tired of fighting this war, trying to prove to God only knows, that I can be super mom. I'm exhausted—mentally, physically, and financially. You're right. This way we can keep the house and help ease some of the financial burdens. Then next year, we're moving away anyway."

"Jamie, you work so hard. It will pay off for you and Ace."

"And you. We're all going to get out of this part of the city. I promise you. No more worrying about *him*, or his guys."

I try to never say *his* name. Not ever unless I'm being forced to, which has happened before. Once to the police who sent me right back to face him on my own. Once when he forced his name on Ace's birth certificate just like he forced himself on me.

That pain in my chest comes back with a vengeance, the tears that blur my vision come quicker. I hate feeling weak. I hate being weak. My mom is up and her arms are wrapped around me before I have time to turn away. I close my eyes and the tears are squeezed and fall to the table. "It's okay, honey. Everything you said, we'll do."

Nodding against her, I'm too choked up to speak. I finally pull myself together and she sits back down. "I promise you. I'll get us all out of here. If I give my notice by morning, I won't have to pay another month. The sooner I'm out of that place the better."

The tightness of her lips would indicate otherwise, but the look of determination in her eyes matches mine. "I know." She stands and smiles, her sunshine smothering the heavy, and bringing back the light. "Can I get my pretty daughter a bowl of ice cream? Oops, I mean *may* I?"

We laugh while I stand. "I'm good, but I could bet my paycheck that the little guy out back wants some."

"That's a sucker's bet. You go out and I'll bring the ice cream."

Sitting under the stars, I look up. They're hard to see in the city, but I manage to make a few out. Ace has finished his ice cream and had another burst of energy from the sugar rush. My mom has a glass of wine and is in the chair next to me. "Diane says hello."

I turn her way. *Diane Masters.* "We never did get to talk about your visit. How was it?"

A thoughtful smile appears. "It was so much fun. We talked for hours. Just like old times."

"It has been a few years since you've seen each other, right? Why is that?"

She sips her wine and then watches Ace make a divot into her lawn with his play shovel—an imaginary game of Whack-A-Mole happening. "I guess we just drifted apart after she moved a few years ago."

"I'm sorry."

"For what?"

"You guys were good friends and the breakup—"

"You and Derrick had nothing to do with Diane and me not seeing each other. We are grown women. We let life get in the way of our friendship, but we're going to change that. Lunch last Thursday was a renewal. We're actually going to see each other again this week."

"Really?"

"Really. So if you want to come a few minutes early on Wednesday we might get to see something other than disappointment on a certain someone's face."

"No, don't even go there. That ship has long sailed."

"Maybe there's a port nearby?"

I give her the look, the one that warns her not to even contemplate whatever she's already plotting.

"He sure is handsome."

"Mom. No."

"I'm just saying."

Tilting my head back, I look for the stars Derrick used to say only shined for us. In my darkest hours, I would search for the fated couple, wondering if Derrick was searching for them wherever he was in the world. The stars seem to align better when we were together, the memories from back then still too vivid...

The tailgate was pulled down and a blanket was spread out. I stood by waiting until it was ready. Derrick had gone to so much trouble that I didn't want to ruin it by taking over, but the giggles still came.

"Fuck it," he says, then looks back at me. His expression responds to mine, and he smiles. "I tried."

"It's perfect."

"It's not. I want it to be for you, but it will have to do."

"It doesn't matter. We're together."

He nods and then lifts me by the waist and sets me on the

tailgate. I scoot to the back and take my guitar before settling on the pillows and stretching my legs out.

With ease, he jumps into the back of the truck bed. Grabbing his guitar, he sits across from me and starts strumming. His fingers move from memory as he looks up. "Perseus." I follow his line of sight to the dark night above. "Perseus. Poor but determined to live a better life."

"Is life so bad with me?" I tease, but like the tides, Derrick's mood has shifted.

"I'm moving to Hollywood."

My hand stops, the chords crashing together in an unsoundly catastrophe. "You're leaving?" Me?

"I want us to leave. It's time. Six more months max. I've already started looking for places. I found a cheap—"

"I can't leave my mother. My father died not even a year ago. I can't leave her now."

"We'll leave. We'll pack our moms and just go."

"Derrick, you're talking crazy."

"No, I'm not." His voice falters to anger. "I can't keep Reggie off my back much longer. You know what that means?" I do. He continues, "I've been busted for possession once. Reggie twice. He's not going to go down. He'll pin it all on me. And then what happens to you? What happens to my mom if I go to jail?" His fingers run through his hair. "What happens to me?"

I set the guitar down and crawl over next to him. The cool air chills my legs exposed by the short skirt, but I settle on his lap, his guitar discarded to the side. With his strong, warm arms around me, I lean against his chest. "Tell me about Perseus again." I know the story of the boy who became a man when he cut off Medusa's head and fulfilled a destiny predicted long before his birth, but I like hearing him tell the ending.

Derrick's hand rubs over my thigh, the veins more prominent as he grows bigger and stronger, becoming a man. "Jaymes, my beautiful Andromeda," he whispers against my neck. "Together we'll forever live in the heavens."

I tighten my arms around his neck. "Forever in the heavens together."

...I was naïve enough at seventeen to believe we could be together forever here on Earth. Seventeen feels like a long way from twenty-three these days. So much life has happened I don't think he'd recognize me now. I barely recognize myself. "Hey Mom?"

"Yes?"

"Don't get your hopes up, okay? Sometimes we've got to let the ones we love the most go so *they* can live their dreams."

She doesn't say anything, but I can feel her sadness through the air between us. Or maybe it's mine I feel. Either way, hope isn't a luxury I can have these days. I deal in reality. Always reality. I peek back up at the sky and there they are shining brightly despite the haze of the surrounding lights. Perseus and Andromeda.

Together forever.

But only in the stars.

6

Derrick

The can I toss hits the side of the bucket and bounces onto Kaz's stone patio. My heels press against the fire pit and I lean back, balancing on the back two legs of the chair. "The stars betrayed the raven night. Two lovers caught in the shining light. Each held a dream to believe. Their love, like their hope, stolen by thieves. Winter now shuddered and spring lay nigh. What was once forever became a dreadful goodbye."

"We should record that with the band."

I don't move anything but my eyes when I swing my gaze to Kaz. "It's written in a past that pulls me back too often to admit."

"You used to sing it. One of our more popular songs. We played it every night whether we had a gig or not. It's when we lived in that first apartment down on Sunset. Remember? The one with the broken air conditioner and no fridge."

"We lived out of a cooler for drinks and leftovers foraged from the great wild hills of Hollywood."

Kaz laughs. "How many couches do you think we slept on?"

"Too many to recall." I look at him. Really look at him. He's different these days. Still my same friend always looking to the sunny side of life. Talented. So damn good with a guitar, and any instrument you put in front of him. But in the last year he's had his own form of evolution. He's changed. He's at peace with the war he was waging inside. "How's Lara?" There's that damn smile again, just from the mention of her name. I roll my eyes, but find myself smiling too. "I want that."

He tosses his empty beer can and makes it into the bucket, his arms flying up in victory. "What do you want?"

"That feeling."

Kaz rarely shows all of his cards, but we know each other well enough for him to lay down his weapons. "We don't have just one shot. The beauty of living is that we get better. Every day is a new start. But nothing is gonna change if you don't. Toss me another."

I reach into the cooler, like old times, and toss him a cold one. He takes a long drag before belching operatic style.

"Like I was saying, tomorrow's a new day. You going to live the same as today?"

My gut twists as disappointment sets in. "I was hoping to see her. Was that an asshole move to show up like that?"

"Not when your mom asked you to. The asshole move was waiting all these years to see her, and then *only* go because your mother wanted you to."

After popping the top on another for me, I swig and swallow. I grab my guitar and he grabs his. We start a song we've played in front of thousands, but keep it acoustic and just for us tonight. I stop halfway through and add, "The guy I trusted with my life growing up is the same one who stabbed me in the back the second I was out of sight. She's been with him ever since."

His hand stills and he turns his baseball cap around, bill backward. "You sure about that?"

"It took a lot to get out of that shithole. I owe him. He won't forget or let it slide."

"You owe him what? Your girl? He got her. There. Done deal. What else do you think you owe him that keeps you from getting the life you deserve?"

I'm still not sure I deserve what I have now, or ever will. "Why do I deserve *this* life, Kaz?"

"Because you worked for it. Your fingers bled for this job. It's not about being hired players. We're part of the band. A permanent part. We're not gonna get fired. We're contributors. The band is where they are now because of us. Own it. You deserve that recognition. So whatever the fuck those guys back home think you owe them, you don't owe them shit. But you do owe a lot to yourself." He shrugs. "Some people are just born into greatness. Others work their asses off for it."

Jaymes was born with the most perfect voice I'd ever heard. Add in her guitar-playing brilliance, and she was also meant for more than the life she's living. Choosing to stay for the right reasons killed her chance of getting out. She should be reaping the rewards in a music career. She is *that* talented. *She* deserves the recognition. But there was no talking her into leaving...

"Come with me, baby. Just pack and leave."

Her tears cover her lap, her head hanging low. "I can't. I can't leave her."

"I'll come back for your mom. I promise, but I have to go tonight."

As if I've injected hope straight into her veins, she looks up—bright, but pleading eyes on me. "Okay. Tonight. That means we have a few hours to figure things out. We can go inside and talk to my mom." She reaches for the truck door to open it, but I stop her.

"No. I don't have hours." I take her face between my hands, my anxiety making them shake when I touch her. "You've got to listen to me, Jaymes. They'll come here—"

"Who? Reggie?"

"Yes."

"Good. He can help us."

"No. He won't help us. Please. Just pack—"

Her hands wrap around my wrist. "I need more time. I can't just leave because you want me to." The air thins in the cab of the truck, our eyes lock together, until I blink, realizing this is it. The feel of her skin becomes a memory keeping my palms warm as I pull away.

"I love you."

Tears flood her eyes as her hands still hold tight like a vise around my wrists. "Don't leave me," she whispers.

My voice matches hers; so quiet I can't hear it in my heart. "Please. Come with me."

"I ca—"

"I'm begging you. Please come with me."

I once swore I'd never beg anyone for anything again. That sick feeling that settled in the back of my mind at ten telling me I was less, not worthy of even food some days comes back like a bolt of lightning. For her. For Jaymes. For love, I'll beg. "I'm begging you."

She sits back and looks away from me, solidifying that emotion in my gut. "I love you."

I reach for her again, touching her hand and bringing it to my lips. As soon as I kiss her delicate skin, she looks my way. The tears overcome the barrier of her lower lids and fall in streams down her cheeks. "I will always love you."

"Come back for me. Don't leave me here forever. Promise you'll come back for me."

My heart hurts, so much that I struggle to look beyond the pain. I say the words, although I'm not sure I can back them. Not right now. Not under the circumstances that have driven me to make this rash decision. I understand she can't leave her mom. I really do. I'm leaving mine too. But I want her with me. Need her with me. But I won't force her. I love her too much to do that. "I promise."

The door opens and I close my eyes. I can't watch her leave me. She steps out, but looks in. "Derrick?" I loosen my hold on the steering wheel and look her way. The quiver in her tone is heard when she says, "I know I just made you promise, but I changed my mind."

Confusion sets in quickening like the beat of my heart. "Don't come back. Not for me. Not for anything. Go do great things and don't let anyone stand in your way. Not even me." The door slams closed and she turns and runs inside her house.

She meant every word. There were no tears in her eyes. All I saw was the strong determination of the stubborn girl I love more than life. "Don't come back. Not even for me." Oh, Jaymes...

But my time's run out. Reggie's probably already left my house. He'll come here next, so I can't be here when he arrives.

He'll stay away from Jaymes as long as I stay away.

The only way to protect her is to stay as far away.

Until I can come back for her.

That's a promise I can keep.

Shifting the truck into drive, I pull away from the curb and head into the heart of LA.

..."I didn't know it was goodbye for good."

"It doesn't have to be. You don't know what's going on in her life. Maybe you should put some feelers out."

"My mom knows, but I told her not to tell me."

"So she won't? Even if you want to know now?"

Sitting up, I say, "I need Lara."

Kaz's head jerks back. "Whoa. Whoa. Slow up there."

Shaking my head and rolling my eyes, I say, "Not in that way."

MY MOM NUDGES me. "I don't need a professional to help me."

"You've talked about having friends and family over for meals and parties. You need a table to do that. You hate shopping, so let Lara help you out."

"Have you seen the prices? That's why I hate shopping."

"Stop worrying about money and let Lara and me worry about that. You just pick out stuff you like. Then you can start hosting your friends over here."

She stops and turns toward me. "Friends like Nita?"

"Exactly," I reply with a smirk that gives it all away because she's onto me.

"Maybe this *is* a good idea." She pats me on the arm and walks away. "Lara?"

I sit on the couch and open the photos on my phone. Scrolling back to the first few I ever uploaded to this phone dated back to the night Jaymes and I celebrated four years of dating. On a whim, we drove down to the Hollywood Bowl. Her favorite band was playing and I wanted to surprise her. I didn't have tickets, but I planned to get us in any way I could. I scored two tickets in the parking lot thirty minutes after it started, but we got them for a discount. I brought binoculars. We needed them, but she loved every minute and sang every song. She danced, her skirt blowing in the wind as her legs swayed to every note of the greatest band in the world's music. All three original members of The Resistance were on fire that night. That's when I knew what I had to do.

I'd get us out. I would be the one that took dreams and made it happen. Watching the band on stage, I knew that's what I wanted to do and nothing would stop me.

I flip to the next photo. Jaymes's hair was wild that night, a flurry of dark hair flying around in the wind. Pink lips puckered for a kiss that was just blown my way. God, she was so gorgeous. I'm reminded of what Kaz said the other night. *Feelers.* "Hey Ma?" She and Lara are looking at an iPad on the kitchen counter. They both stop and look my way. "When are you seeing Nita next?" There's no point pretending. The woman always could see right through me.

"Wednesday. Maybe you can pick me up again? Say a half hour later?"

"That works." I look back at the phone. *Feelers.* That's all it is. Just a quick *hi, how are you?* Nothing more.

Unless there's a chance for more and maybe feelers can turn into a conversation. I turn off my phone. My imagination is getting the best of me, but I can't help feel that I might finally get the chance to keep the most important promise I once made.

7

Jaymes

THREE TEXT MESSAGES later, it's confirmed. Diane Masters is at my mom's house. This wasn't anything but good news last week. I was simply happy my mother had reconnected with her long-time friend. Diane got out. Derrick fulfilled that promise. He never owed me anything, but when Diane moved it felt like that last remnant of the glue was gone. There would never be any reason left for Derrick to come back.

I didn't just miss him. I envied him.

He did it.

He chased his dreams. Made them happen. I was both proud he made it and sad that I didn't. When we were together, I never thought it had to be one or the other. I have no ill will that he found fame, or has made money. It's quite the opposite. I still care. I still cheer. I still smile if I see him on a billboard or hear him on the radio. He was always confident, so damn confident. The irony from the night we went to the Hollywood Bowl still plays in my mind sometimes...

"I'm going to play that stage one day. Just you wait, baby." His arm wraps around my shoulders and he pulls me to his side, one of my most favorite places to be. His six-foot-one frame towers over my five-foot-three body so I fit snuggly against him. I feel loved. I feel safe. His smile is contagious when he looks down at me. "You and me and the whole wide world will be ours to see. To own. Hollywood won't know what hit them."

"You think—"

"I don't think, Jaymes. I know. That's gonna be me. And you, my songbird, are going to sing for the world. Every station is going to be playing your songs. Maybe even our songs."

"You dream big."

"As big as the universe. What's the point if any schmuck can do it?"

He's got a point. I close my eyes and lean my head against him. We sway to a ballad that breaks my heart and heals me again. The lyrics of this song remind me of Derrick's. There's a haunting quality that rolls through my soul like a fog creeping out to sea.

...A few years later, Derrick Masters joined *The Resistance*. The announcement spread like wildfire; he was now lead guitarist. The news was received on shaky grounds. Some were thrilled and proud of a local making good. Others, like Reggie, were wound so tight I thought he might go after Derrick just to bring him down again. It took a lot of convincing, calming, and negotiating to keep him from pursuing the vendetta he had, but I did it for Derrick, and for Ace's safety.

I listened to him complain. A man with a wounded ego is dangerous and nobody hurt him more than being betrayed by Derrick. It's the only time Reggie ever treated me like a human with feelings. Might have been my face of disgust when he touched me or that he knew deep down what I was really up to—trading myself for Derrick—but either way, mercy was shown. Now I carry the debt Derrick once owed Reggie. I just wish I knew what that debt was.

When I pull up and park, I pack my memories away and look

over at the house. My headlights shine on a shiny blue Lincoln. I cut the engine and take a deep breath. That's not my mom's car. Diane is driving nice wheels these days. Inside my rusting Corolla, that David gave me a *great* deal on, I stare into the front window of the house for signs of life. If I thought my hands were shaking before, that was nothing. Even my lip is trembling, so I bite down on it to keep it steady.

Leah picked up Ace from his after-school program and was supposed to drop him off here while I went to night school. But her car is still in the driveway. I was so tempted to ask David if he needed me to come back and work late. "What am I doing?" I whisper, leaning my head against the steering wheel. My stomach has been full of butterflies all day. Over what? He's probably not even here. She obviously drove herself this time.

I always adored Diane. She was like a second mother to me and that our moms were best friends, it just made our lives so much easier to spend time together. But now, years later, I'm a nervous wreck over seeing her again. I know damn well it's not just her I'm nervous to see. Taking my gloss from my purse, I swipe over my lips quickly and rub them together. Flipping my visor down, I look in the mirror. I pull my hair from the messy topknot and then twist it back up when I see it looks worse down. "Shoot." He might not be here, I remind myself.

A knock on the window startles me and I jump a mile, my heart beating right out of my chest. When I look over through the passenger door window, I see Ace. "Oh, thank God."

"Hi, Mommy."

My world calms when I look at his face. "Hi, baby." I get out and walk around the front of the car. "How was your day, buddy?" I ask, just as I catch something out of the corner of my eyes.

On the front porch, leaning against the wood column in all his newfound glory, stands the most breathtaking man I've ever seen. As a teenager, I thought he was the best-looking *boy* I'd ever seen, and based on how I'm struggling to breathe just from looking at him now, I think he still holds the title. *But now he's a man.*

Ace is talking about what some kid named Shiloh got in trouble for today at school, but I'm still staring at Derrick Masters.

Derrick Masters.

My very own Perseus, though right now I'm thinking he was more my Achilles heel in the grand scheme of things.

Derrick Masters is standing on my mother's front porch like he belongs there. A smile that shines like the star he's become appears and he waves. Not sure if it was the grin on his face or the wave that sends me tripping flat on my face into the grassy lawn, but I'm cursing the curb when I lift up and look right into the dark blue eyes I've tried to despise.

"Are you okay?" he asks, trying to help me up. His voice is deep, the timbre the same one that always made my heart beat a little faster. It's not that thought that runs through my mind. It's his hands on me, grappling to help me to my feet.

He's touching me.

Derrick Masters is touching me and I consider lying there longer just to savor the feel of his calloused fingers again. Ace tugs at my ankle like that will help me up. "Mommy, you fell."

Mommy.

Mommy.

Derrick knows I'm a mommy.

Oh my God. *What does he think?*

Does he hate me? Disappointed in me? Happy for me? Or not care at all?

I would care if I found out he has kids.

Maybe he already knew...

Maybe I'll just lie here as long as I can until he goes away.

Ace lies down next to me and rests his face on my hand. Looking at me with wide eyes, he asks, "Are we playing a game? This is fun."

"Yes, I quite like it here."

I hear Derrick chuckling just above me, enough to feel his warmth covering my body like sunshine as I lie in the cool grass. I might be mistaken but it sounds like he's behind me now. On the ground with me.

Ace's eyes look over my head. "My friend is here too." He giggles. "See? Right there."

Lying like a dead fish, I smile at my cute son not quite ready to face Derrick Masters. "What's your new friend's name?"

"Derrick. He plays a guitar like you, Mommy."

After a tap on the back, Ace's new friend speaks, "Hi."

I miss Derrick's hands on me, even if it was just helping me up. Ace is a ball of laughter and gets up. I watch until he runs behind me. "I'm here now. We're all here. This is fun. Oh look, the moon."

I can't avoid him forever and the grass is grounding, literally, and settles my anxiety over just this kind of thing happening. I've embarrassed myself and he's found out I'm a mother in the course of one sexy smile and a wave. I shake my head and close my eyes annoyed with myself for acting so foolishly in front of him. *He was once my everything.* When I roll onto my back, the top of our hands meet in an innocent touch that neither of us bothers to retreat. Finally building enough nerve, I turn my head and look straight into his eyes again. "Hi," I whisper.

That devastatingly charming smile reappears, and he says, "It's good to see you, Jaymes."

Lying on the other side of Derrick, Ace pipes in, "Everyone calls my mom Jamie."

"It's okay, buddy. He can call me Jaymes." Just like old times. My gaze goes to the evening sky. I can't see our fated lovers, but I can feel them, their presence mingled with ours.

My mom's voice slices through the feelings threatening to arise. "What are you guys doing out here?"

Tilting my head, I catch another glimpse of Derrick on my way to looking at the three women who have congregated on the porch. All three with wry grins that will eventually mortify me with their teasing and taunting. "We were just coming in."

Ace runs to the house and I look at Derrick, not sure why I'm feeling so emotional. Fortunately, joy overrides the rest. "It's good to see you, too."

He sits up and then he's on his feet offering me a hand up. "That was quite a trip you took."

"I didn't even bring a carry-on."

"No," he says, chuckling, "but you played the whole thing off really well if that makes a difference."

I take his hand and he pulls me to my feet. In one fell swoop, my body is against his. The questions will come. I'll answer. His piqued curiosity will be sated and then he'll be off for good this time. I like this quiet before the storm I know is coming. Taking the few extra seconds I have before this bubble is burst, I let my gaze wander over his broad shoulders and higher. His chiseled jaw is shadowed in light stubble. His hair messed in ways that remind me of the mornings after we spent all night making love. Is it possible for him to be even more handsome than when we were younger? Because he is. He so is. It's unnerving. I feel I've aged thirty years in the time we've been apart. He's aged just right.

Standing in front of him, pressed to him like this, and looking into those dazzling eyes that match the LA night skies, I feel myself melt. It's not just that he's even more gorgeous. It's his eyes. His warm, caring eyes haven't changed, and I'm a little in awe.

"I have pie," my mom says, receiving cheers from Ace. "Come on inside."

Seconds later the screen door slams closed and I know we're alone. I mean, the whole city is revolving around us, but none of that matters.

It's us.

The emerging stars above.

And the man I once thought I would be with forever. We're now standing in the same place where he left me. I don't know what to say to him, except, "Rebel finally returns."

8

Jaymes

DERRICK TAKES A step, his hands falling to his side, and his tongue running over his bottom lip. I think he's unsure what to say, so I fill in the silence, "Come on. You always did like her pie." The first steps I take are the hardest, but I keep going and it gets easier this time to walk away.

His footsteps are heard behind me with each step up the stairs and across the porch. With the door in my hand, wide open, I turn back. "Don't say anything about us in front of Ace. Okay?"

"Nothing's been said yet."

"Thank you." I slip inside and walk into the kitchen where everyone's gathered.

Leah hands me a plate. Her eyes dart between me and the man I know is standing probably too close.

I sit at the table as he's handed a plate and fork. He sits down across from me and even though I'm doing everything not to look at him, I know he's looking at me. The kitchen is too quiet. Ace is the only one oblivious to what's really happening. He's just thrilled to be eating dessert. If only my life were that simple. These days it

61

takes a lot more than blueberry pie to make things better, though I can admit as I take another delectable bite, it's helping.

My gaze finally works its way across the lightwood tabletop and higher when Derrick says, "I've missed your pie, Mrs. Grenier."

I think he catches it as soon as I do, my mouth falling open. As my mom revels under the spotlight of compliments, I stare at him with wide eyes. He looks down and I see his chest puff with a hard breath. When he looks up, we share the silent joke together and smile. For a brief second it almost feels natural.

I'm quickly reminded that we aren't those people anymore. "Mommy?" Ace bumps into me and wriggles onto my lap, causing me to scoot the chair back to make room.

"Yeah?"

"May I leave the table? I want to go." I smile. He is just the cutest little person.

"Are you tired?"

"I want to see my show."

Leaning my forehead against the side of his, I nod. "Okay, buddy. Go pack up your stuff."

He dashes off and that's when I realize the room had gone quiet watching us, including the man across me. My knee begins to bounce and I tap the table twice. "Well, I should go. He's going through a Curious George stage. I don't know if I should be worried that he loves a troublemaking monkey or that the man only wears yellow."

"The yellow."

All of us look at Derrick when he speaks, but Ace walks in with his backpack and says, "I like yellow."

Derrick smiles, breaking whatever tension was building. "Me too, buddy."

My heart clenches hearing him call Ace by that name, but when he rubs the top of his head, I rush from the room. "Come on, Ace." It wasn't tension that was building. It was pain, regret, shattered dreams, and lost love. That's what Derrick is to me now, and to see him be so sweet to my son breaks me.

I don't know if Ace has ever seen me move so fast. I'm halfway to the door before my arm is caught and I'm brought to a stop. "Hey." I rip my arm away when I turn back. "Don't touch me."

His hands fly up in surrender. "I'm sorry. Don't leave, bab— Don't go. I'll go. You stay." He corrects himself, but some habits die hard. I should know.

"Don't tell me what to do. I've got to get my son home."

Slowly lowering his hands, Ace comes up next to him. Right there before me is the future I thought I'd once have. Blueberry pie isn't going to fix the tangled mess my life became. Taking Ace by the backpack strap, I pull him closer until he's in front of me with my arms protectively around his shoulders. And maybe I'm reading too much into Derrick's expression, but it looks a lot like how mine felt moments earlier. He nods and steps around me as the ladies enter the living room. The door is opened and slams closed and my heart deflates when he leaves.

Their three fallen faces kind of express everything. I swallow and say, "Thanks, Leah, for everything with Ace."

"No problem. Do you need me on Friday?"

"No, class is online that night. My professor is out of town. Thanks though." She hugs my mom and tells her she'll see her next week. I'm given a sympathetic side hug. I'm sure I'll hear more in the morning at the dealership, but she's kind enough to let it go tonight. The door opens and I hear their muffled voices on the porch.

Ace says, "I'm going to see Derrick." I let him, too tired to worry about the *what could have beens*.

"It's good to see you, Diane." Her whole face brightens and I'm instantly soothed by the smile I used to find comfort in. She comes to me and takes me by the hands. "Your mother has bragged about all of your accomplishments with school and Ace, your work. I'm so proud of you, Jamie."

The tears I denied in the kitchen come this time. Just two. I only allow two, but I let them fall. I've had an exhausting day and my emotions are paying the price. "Thank you. That means a lot to me."

It does. Her approval and support mean so much more than I ever thought they would.

"You've grown from a beautiful girl into a stunning woman."

I look down from her gaze, feeling self-conscious. I don't feel stunning. I feel harried and exhausted. "Thank you," I reply tugging at the loose strands of hair hanging down over my neck.

When I look back up, she says, "Well, you have a sweet little boy to get home and…" She stops to laugh. "I do too."

Now we all laugh. *Sweet little boy? He hasn't been that for a long time.* She was always a role model when it came to parenting. The man out front is a testament to her efforts. I hope my son will see me the same way one day. Diane and I walk outside and she gives me a warm hug. "I would love to see you again and spend some time catching up. Maybe you and your mother can meet me out for brunch this weekend?"

Mom mode kicks in automatically. "I'd love that, but I have Ace. It's only mom and me. Leah helps when she can, but I hate to ask too much of her." It's not until I stop talking that I remember Derrick is standing nearby, listening to everything I've just said. I dare look his way. Like the day I met him, I'm drawn into the ocean-blue of his eyes as the storm brews inside.

Diane draws my attention back, and says, "You can bring Ace. He's so delightful. It will be good to have a kid around. I'll call your mom with details. Bye, Nita. Thank you for the tea and pie, and the company." She squeezes my hand and walks down the steps to the sidewalk. "Are you ready to go, son, or do you need a few minutes?"

Derrick looks from his mother to me. When I give him the smallest of head shakes, he replies, "No, I'm ready." He steps past me and my mom embraces him. "Thank you, Mrs. Grenier."

"Please call me Nita. I think you're old enough now." When they part, she says, "Maybe you can join us again—"

I interrupt in a flash, "Mom."

She smiles and shrugs. "I want to hear about the band. You're not the only one who listens to them, you know."

My huff of annoyance comes louder than I intend, but Derrick

64

ignores it, and says, "Next time then."

He doesn't stop to hug me or even say goodbye. He's quick to turn and rush down the steps, but he gets about halfway to the car and stops. I follow his line of sight. Ace comes running to him and Derrick kneels down so he's eye level. I can't hear what he says, but Ace bumps knuckles with him and giggles, making me smile.

Before he stands, his eyes meet mine, and he waves. "Good seeing you, Jaymes."

"You too," I reply with no regard to my crushing heart because it is. It's so good to see him again, even though I'm fairly sure it will be the last time.

I hug my mom and she then walks me to my car just as Derrick is turning his car around. His mom waves to us with a broad smile on her face, but Derrick doesn't and just that little lack of acknowledgement feels a lot like rejection. I hate it. I swore I would never let a man control my emotions again. I fought for it. I fought for my sanity. I had to so I could be everything my baby needed me to be. But I guess when it comes to first love, emotions don't play by the rules.

I get in the car, make sure Ace is buckled in the back. When I roll the side window down, my mom leans in, and says, "You are an astonishing young woman and an even better mother."

Wanting to wipe the tears that have surfaced, I reply, "What brought that on?"

"Sometimes when we're caught in the crazy that is life it's good to hear something positive, something we're doing right. I don't tell you enough. Tonight was a good reminder. You make me proud every day, Jamie." She reaches into the back and tickles Ace. In a kid tone, she teases him, "You do too, big guy. Take care of your mommy. All right?"

"I've got it covered."

My heads turns to the side as laughter boils up from his surprise comment. "I don't even know what that means."

He winks, and says, "I've got your back, Mommy."

I'm not sure how much time he and Derrick actually spent

together, but it's apparent that it was enough to rub off on him. "And I've got yours, buddy. Say goodbye to Grandma."

When we get home, Ace is bathed and is now watching his show. He's curled on the loveseat while I sit on the floor with my legs under the coffee table. A toy guitar was dragged out of the hall closet the minute we got home and he sat plucking the strings until his show started. The guitar was discarded, but for minutes after, I stared at the empty stand in the corner that used to hold mine. The pain over having it stolen still hurts. Even with the out-of-tune sounds of Ace's toy, the room feels warmer with music filling it.

Now I find myself with my laptop open, and although I do have my test material open in Word, I've also got a new browser open with four words sitting in the box ready to search as soon as I hit enter.

Is Derrick Masters single?

Right when I'm about to push enter, worry filling every second that ticks by, I hear the soft slumber of my little boy and look behind me.

Smiling, I lean back and kiss his head, stand up, and then lift him into my arms. He's growing fast. I'm not sure I'll be able to carry him much longer, but while I can, I savor holding my baby in my arms. Before I take him to his room, I click the X and close the tab.

It doesn't matter what Derrick's dating status is. My life is full of everything from raising my kid to work to school to finding a way to a better life at the end of the day. I don't have time for love, or lust, or whatever that little ball of messy feelings is that's growing. I just need to stop feeding it so it goes away. Just like Derrick did. *Our* dreams died the day he left. But I will achieve my dreams. My new dreams.

He got the life he deserved, the rewards he'd worked so hard for. I never regretted the tactic I used. He would have stayed otherwise. I know it. He'd have driven off but he would have been back the next day. Breaking his heart meant breaking mine, but I'd do it again if it had the same outcome. Better to save his life than for both of us to suffer and eventually blame each other. Our love would have turned to hate, dreams stomped out like a cigarette. Hating the only man I ever loved wasn't an option. It wasn't the ending either of us deserved. It wouldn't be living. That would be hell.

It didn't feel like a sacrifice despite the pain that consumed me. It was the only option we had. He just didn't know it at the time. Hopefully he never will.

Derrick looked good tonight. Healthy. That's what telling him to never look back that day did—gave him a chance at a happy life.

9

Derrick

WHAT JUST HAPPENED?

Jaymes Grenier.

That's what just happened.

"...pie recipe. What do you think?"

Taking my mom's exit, I brake when we come to a light and look at her. "Huh?"

"I can't put my finger on it and it's driving me nuts. Cinnamon makes no sense with blueberries."

What the fuck is she talking about? "What?"

"The pie." She looks annoyed. "Nita's pie. The secret ingredient. Have you not been listening at all, Derrick?" Her annoyance quickly turns into an all-knowing smile. "*Ahhh.* You haven't been listening. Got something on your mind, or should I say *someone*?"

"No."

"I say yes."

I glower. "I'm not ready."

A hand reaches over to comfort. "It was a lot to take in."

And Ace... *Grenier? Rogers?* Damn, she has a kid. "Did you

69

know she had a kid?"

Mom sits up properly in her seat as if she's just taken the stand. "I did. I'm sorry, but you told me not to say anything about her."

My betrayed heart speaks for me, "A kid kind of overrules that, don't you think?"

"Don't be mad, Derrick—"

"I'm not mad at you. I just... I don't know." I deserved to know that she started a family with that asshole. But I'm not sure it's the anger that I was betrayed by her, lied to by my mother, or the jealousy that she has a family with another man that gets me more upset. "Deep down I thought maybe we'd find a way back."

"You still can. She has a child. She's not married."

"Why isn't she married to Rogers? That's Reggie's kid, right?" Some friend he was. *Fucker.* Moved right in the second I moved out. They wasted no time. I don't fully blame him for it. I knew he always had a boner for my girl. I guess screwing him over gave him the right to screw me over. She fell for it. She didn't have to go there, but she did anyway and it felt like everything we had been through together, everything we were to each other meant nothing. *She'd told me she loved me.* The timeline is obvious. Did they even wait a day? Fuck me. The years apart were a waste of regret, making me regret every time I ever thought of her and for coming back.

When my mom doesn't respond, I check on her. "What's up?"

"You don't want to hear it."

"One minute you're going on about pie, the next I'm having to drag information out of you. I want to know. Tell me. What's on your mind?" I turn down her street.

"He's a cute kid."

He is, kind of ridiculously so and I'm not a kid guy. He's also cool for a five-year-old. The kind I could probably tell a secret to and he wouldn't tell anyone. None of this surprises me though. Jaymes is his mom.

Jaymes.

Damn.

Just as I pull up to the gate of her complex, she says, "She's had a hard time, Derrick. I know you're upset and hurt right now. It was a lot to take in, which is why I thought it better for you to experience it more than just hear things and let your mind wander. She's a good mother who is working so hard to give not just Ace a better life, but her mom."

I pull into a spot in front of her townhome and park. "Mom—"

"No, I want you to listen to me. You're caught in your emotions. I get it. I do, but you need to cut her some slack." The car door opens and she gets out. When I get out, I glance her way over the roof. "She's not married to him. She's single. I think you should know that, but from my perspective, it wasn't easy for me either. You know I loved you two together. Maybe your soul mate is still out there, or maybe she's right where you left her. I don't know, Derrick. I know I look at that little boy and think of you. You were such a sweet and innocent kid before..." She doesn't have to say more than that. You either survive this part of the city or it destroys you. There is no in-between. "I look at them both and think of what could have been. How he could be my grandson."

Dropping my head down on my arm, I lean against the car. When I lift up, I try to hide the anger. What is usually an emptiness inside me fills with rage. I love her, but I can't be buried by what she needs when I'm barely holding on these days. "I can't do this. I can't live with both my regrets and your disappointments."

"I'm not disappointed, son. I'm so proud of you. Look at what you've accomplished. You've made something from nothing. You did that." She walks to the sidewalk and waits for me. When I hand her the keys, she adds, "You have both changed. I'm not saying you should give it a second chance, but I'm not saying you shouldn't either." I roll my eyes, but give in and give her the smile she's earned for all her efforts. I receive a poke in the stomach in return. "Are you staying or going?"

She's given me a lot to think about. Jaymes even more. "I should get going."

"Thank you for driving me. I know Nita was so happy to see you again." I walk her to her door. With her key in the lock, and her back to me, she says, "I'll text you the details for Sunday."

"What's Sunday?"

"The brunch." She steps inside. "Love you," comes rushing out of her mouth as the door starts to close.

My hand slams against the wood of the door stopping it from closing. She peeks out the crack all wide-eyed and innocent. "Nice try, Mom."

"What?" She shrugs, willing to keep the act going.

"Brunch with Jaymes."

"Oh, yes, she'll be there, but you can come with me."

"I know what you're doing."

She opens the door back up and puts her hand on her hip. "What am I doing?"

"Jaymes is off limits. She has a life. You said it yourself. She made that very clear to me too. She's got no time for any of the bullshit that distracts her from her kid." I roll my eyes, knowing the romantic soul that is my mother.

"I want you to be happy. Why do you think it can't be with Jamie?"

"She made it clear she didn't want to see me again."

"She told you that?" she asks, suspiciously.

"She didn't have to. She has a life now, one without me and doesn't need me intruding on her life."

A self-satisfied smile appears. "If she didn't say it, you shouldn't assume it." The door starts to close again, but she stops to say, "You're leaving on the tour again soon, so you're coming to brunch and I'm not hearing otherwise. Be safe on your drive home."

This time I let the door close. I don't know what's worse—an encounter with your ex-girlfriend that knocks your life out of its regular rotation or a mother determined to nag you to death over said girlfriend. I mean ex-girlfriend. Either way, I know I'm not getting out of brunch on Sunday, and I'm not so sure I want to.

JAYMES ANNE-MARIE GRENIER.

She once told me her mother named her Anne-Marie to go with the traditional French last name she acquired once she married Jimmy Grenier, James. He moved her here once they got married and promptly left her when she became pregnant. Upon hearing of Nita going into labor, he sobered up enough to make an appearance just as his daughter was born into the world. Nita saw the man she fell in love with that night as he made promises to take care of them. With tears in his eyes, he apologized for leaving her and said he'd never make that mistake again.

To honor her husband's commitment to their family she signed the birth certificate—Jaymes Anne-Marie Grenier—after her husband.

They made it a month before his gambling and alcohol addiction kicked back in and they ran out of money. He was gone the next day, leaving Nita with no savings and a newborn to raise on her own. Jaymes said she only saw her mother cry once when it came to her father. I never told her I saw her cry too, or that I had also met her father.

Jaymes was scheduled to close the sandwich shop that night, but needed to study for a biology test the next day. She had forgotten her book at home because she'd been running late. I went by her house to grab it so I could bring it up to her. Her house was like my second home. I had a key and all. So when I was about to leave, and saw a man walking up the path, I didn't think much of it. He did.

He wailed into me about this being his wife's house and asked if I was fucking her. I was seventeen at the time. It was as if he wasn't even aware that he had a daughter a few months younger than me. I was not as big as I am now, but I was growing. I'd already been hazed into Reggie's gang, got the tat and all to prove it, so he didn't scare me. But he did cross a line. Especially when he spit on me.

With poor timing, Nita came outside, and defended me. I didn't need her to. I don't even know why she did other than maybe it was her mama bear protective instincts kicking in. When he shoved her to the ground, I beat him to damn near death.

Sometimes I think about him, and wonder what happened. Is he dead or alive? I didn't kill him. He walked away that day, but he never came back either. He wasn't a man bent on changing his ways, so he was smart enough to stay gone for good.

Sometimes I think about Nita, and wonder why she never told Jaymes what happened. Was she protecting Jaymes or me? I'm not sure. I never thought it right to question her decisions when it came to how she ran her family. I wouldn't want my family questioned. Things are the way they are now because choices were made along the way that set things in motion. Good or bad, things were set in motion that day. A pact was made with her mom. I vowed I would always protect Nita and Jaymes.

Yet, I drove away, leaving both of them a year later.

Another promise I didn't deliver on.

Sometimes I think about Jaymes, and wonder how she looked at me like I made the sun shine just for her. When I brought the book to her that night, she sat next to me and smiled like she didn't have the shittiest misfortune to have James Grenier as a father and a mom who was fighting a battle her daughter never knew about. As I stretched and fisted my fingers under the table, she never saw the pain I was in or how sad I felt for her. She never saw because when I looked into her green eyes, I did what her mother did. I put on a smile and gave her enough love to make her feel whole, to keep that smile on her face, and to give her hope. She may share a name with that fucker, but she would never suffer again because of him, or any other man.

Except me.

"Fuck, Derrick. Get your shit together." Tommy's voice floods my internal thoughts. Tilting my head up, Tommy is flipping me off from the sound booth.

Kaz kicks a leg on the stool where I'm propped with my guitar.

"You need a break, or what?"

"No, I'm good."

Johnny doesn't look convinced when I catch of glimpse of his reflection in the glass, but he lets it slide. "That was too fucked up to fix. Let's go from the top."

This time I don't think about James or Nita. I push away all thoughts of Jaymes and Ace, and play the damn song perfectly. This is my life. My future. My focus. *This.*

It's not until I leave the studio that night that I realize how much I've hidden behind the bright lights of stardom. Yes, The Resistance is my life, my future. But in my heart of hearts, I know it's Jaymes I've been thinking about for all these years. *The biggest regret. The most important dream I've yet to fulfill.*

I slip into the custom leather seat of my refurbed 1972 Gran Torino Sport and wait for my Bluetooth to connect.

"Well to what do I owe the pleasure?" My mom sounds chipper.

"I'll come to brunch on Sunday." I hear her giggles of excitement and shake my head. "Happy?"

"Very," she says. "It will be fun."

"Yeah, guess we'll see."

10

Jaymes

I WALK INTO the kitchen and my mom's mouth falls open. Holding my finger up, I think I catch her in time. "Don't say a word." Her mouth closes and swerves into a smile, so I call her out, "I can see right through you."

"And yet, you still came."

Shrugging, I reapply my gloss. "Call me curious."

"Curious."

Ace skips through the kitchen and out the other door. I don't think I've ever welcomed an interruption so much. "We should go or we'll be late. You know how bad traffic gets with the Sunday brunch crowd."

"Californians brunch like it's their business." She grabs her purse just as Ace runs by. "Go potty and we're leaving."

In the car, my mom tells me how she picked a small restaurant that was out of the way to avoid paparazzi. That is something I never thought would be a concern, but here we are at a quaint café.

"I'll pay for valet, Jamie."

"No, don't waste your money. I'll drop you guys off and park down the street. It's fine." I pull to the curb and they get out. I can't stop from doing a quick scan for any sign of Derrick or Diane. The place looks fancy though. As soon as I find a spot two blocks down and around the corner, I apply my gloss one more time. I think it's a nervous tic I'm developing because of a certain hot ex-boyfriend. I grab my bag and head back to the restaurant. I start to get nervous as I approach the little café, tugging at the hem of my shirt. My flats are scuffed at the toe and my jeans are old, but they fit. I drag a large section of my hair around to the front of my shoulder and play with the ends nervously. I reach the door just as it opens. Derrick is there and smiles. "Hi."

"Hi."

He holds his phone up and says, "I've got to take this. I'll be right back."

The door is open wide so I move around him, but my arm brushes against his middle. I just keep walking hoping he didn't mind the bonus of my bony elbow to his abs. "Sorry."

"It's okay. They're out back." The phone is to his ear and he walks outside and down the sidewalk.

I survived. In the courtyard out back, I sit in one of the two open seats that are conveniently together at one end of the table. The moms dote on Ace as he scribbles on the kids' menu. Diane looks my way and says, "You always had such pretty hair, Jamie."

Looking down, I grab at it again. "It's a mess," I lie. I spent over an hour styling it and putting it up only to let it come down at the last minute.

I'm alerted to his presence just from his proximity, the heat of his body warming my whole soul. "It always looked lovely any way she wore it, but particularly down and loose around her shoulders."

Lovely. He just said my hair is lovely. I look up as he sits down next to me and my cheeks actually heat. "Thank you... Diane." I turn my attention to her, but she's pretending to be engrossed in Ace's art. When I look into the eyes that once only shined for me, I reply, "Thank you. That is very sweet of you to say."

"I struggled picking my favorite way you wear your hair. You

78

had it up on your head in a rubber band the other day and that looked good too."

Resting my chin on my hand, I lean in. "Was this a difficult struggle, thinking about how I wear it? One that kept you up nights or just a passing fancy?"

"Up all night thinking about you."

Our eyes lock, and I'm unaware of the magic that must be happening to have me here. I'm surely in fantasyland in my best blouse sitting next to a world-famous musician who's insisting on complimenting me as if I can live up to the celebrities he's used to dating. I sit up and take my napkin, the perfect distraction, and place it across my lap. "What are you doing, Derrick?"

"I'm drinking coffee and making small talk."

"Your small talk feels awfully large in the scheme of things."

"I don't need to lie to you and I don't want to hide behind some charade like we're supposed to be on a blind date or something. That's not us." He stops and says, "Look at me, Jaymes." When I do, he lowers his voice and whispers, "I would really like to spend some time with you alone and catch up, instead of brunch under the watchful eye of our moms."

The moms are up and scooping Ace from his seat. The crayons roll off the table and flustered, Diane says, "We forgot our... our... um—"

"Bicycles," my mom shouts.

Diane nods. "Yes, our um bicycles?" Turning to Nita, she asks, "Right?"

Ace looks between them. "What are umbicycles? Can I have one?"

"Yes, let's go get you one. You two stay and talk. We'll be back in a few minutes."

Derrick and I watch them weave through the tables like they've actually got somewhere better to go. When I turn to the man who once owned my heart, I sigh. "That was subtle."

"Not at all."

"Nope. Not at all."

Picking up where he left off, he says, "I don't even know if you want to talk to me, but I would love a second chance."

"Dating?" I ask, stunned.

"No, talking. Well, um... what?"

He takes a large gulp of water and I cut him some slack. "Sorry. I don't know why my mind went there. You meant a chance to talk. We can do that. We're here. Apparently alone. What do you want to talk about?"

"Should we start with Ace?"

Tension fills my shoulders as my defenses go up. I twist the napkin in my lap and look down at the splintering wood of the table. "Sure." I hate how meek I sound, but when it comes to my son, I shouldn't have to explain anything to anyone.

"He's great, Jaymes."

Surprised, I look back up. "What?"

"He's a great kid. I haven't been around either of you much, but I can tell what a great mom you are just by the little time I've spent with him."

My smile grows. "Thank you. That means a lot to me."

Taking my hand, another surprise on his part, he says, "I'm not going to pretend I know what's gone on in your life, but I'd like to know. Even more so, I'd like to know what's happening in your life now."

"What do you want to know?"

"I want to know if anyone's going to be upset about you having brunch with me."

Reggie. My heart quickens like any other time I think of him. Fear does that to you. I'm not sure it will ever change. Not until I know Ace and I are safe from him forever. I pull my hand back slowly despite how much I like Derrick holding it. "I can't answer that. I'm sorry." This time I don't look away.

His disappointment is seen and he lowers his hands to his lap. "That seems like an odd question to dodge."

"I'm not dodging. I just can't give you the answer you want to hear."

"So you're seeing someone?" He's annoyingly handsome even when his brow furrows.

Despite his good looks, I have to look deeper because of the complicated situation I'm in. "Please, Derrick. Let's not do this. It's too—"

"Too what? Soon? Invasive? Close for comfort? Backstabbing?"

"Backstabbing? What? No. Me?"

"Yeah." He moves away from me by leaning back in his chair. His gaze casts down and his arms cross over his chest. He looks genuinely hurt.

By me? "You left, not me."

"Why didn't you, Jaymes? Tell me. You've got to tell me why you chose Reggie over me."

I'm standing, my bag in hand before he even finishes that question. Staring at him, I search his face for the guy I once knew. Instead I'm met with a man I don't recognize. I swing my bag over my shoulder and leave. Searching the inside for the moms and Ace, I don't find them, so I push through the door and walk out to the sidewalk. I look both directions with no luck.

I reach for my phone in my bag when Derrick comes barreling out of the café. "No. You don't get to walk away like that."

"You can't stop me like I'm one of your roadies."

His head goes back. "What are you talking about? First off, I don't control the roadies. They're there to do a job. Secondly, why are you talking to me like you don't know me?"

"Because I don't. I don't know you anymore. As much as I thought I should come today, I see I made a big mistake."

"Why?"

The moms and Ace come around the corner, but as soon as they see us they scurry back, disappearing again. Turning my attention back to Derrick, I take a breath. "Look," I start, then readjust the bag on my shoulder. Ace's books are starting to weigh me down. Or maybe it's my emotions. Either way, I'm ready to go. "This was a fun little attempt by our moms. I don't know why they thought this was a good idea, but it clearly wasn't. I'm in no position to offer you anything more than friendship—"

"I'll take it."

"I was going to say we used to be friends but now we're better off acquaintances. You don't want that."

"I want anything I can get with you."

Without realizing it, our voices have gone from strong-willed to barely above a whisper, our proximity closer, almost touching. "It's not just me not knowing you anymore. You don't know me either." Looking down the street, I say, "So much has changed. I've changed. I'm not the same girl you once knew."

He takes my hand in his, his fingers lightly manipulating mine as if I were strings on his guitar. My chin is touched, so delicately, but with enough pressure to turn me his way. Our eyes meet, and he whispers, "Then let me get to know the woman you are now."

"Why are you so insistent on this? You're as bad as the moms."

"If I tell you that you're more beautiful now than ever would it kill any chance we have of reconnecting? Or that when I look at you, my heart hurts just enough to remind me I'm still alive? What about that when I play certain songs I still think of you? What if I told you those things, opening myself up in a way that I never do? Will you walk away or will you stay?"

There's no logical reason for me to stay. Ace. Reggie. My job. School. My life. I can't fit another thing in without sacrificing more of myself, but here he is more open than he ever was when we were together. His heart is open and his words are an elixir, tasting sweeter the second time. I'm in dangerous territory that could cost me more than my heart. It could cost me Ace. "I'm sorry. So sorry."

I walk away. Inside, I am running. I can't lose Ace. *I won't lose the most precious gift I have.*

I hate myself for doing it, for hurting Derrick, but it's not just him I worry about anymore. Despite my desperate need to look back, to go back, to run into his arms and find the comfort I once felt in his arms, I can't. I can't think about anything but protecting my son. *Just keep walking. Don't look back. Just go.*

"Wait."

Pulling my emotions under control, I gnaw on my bottom lip before turning around. My heart is pounding. I know I should have listened to myself seconds earlier. When I see him running toward me, my better senses fall away and I force my arms to stay at my sides instead of opening wide.

He says, "I forgot something."

"What?"

"You."

I'm about to ask what he means, but then I don't have to because his hands are on me, holding my face, and angling me up as he bends down. My heart pounds against my chest and this time I don't have the strength to deny him.

Or me.

11

Jaymes

WITH HIS LIPS pressed to the side of my mouth, he kisses me so sweetly that I almost pressure him for more. I ease into the feeling of us again, but then he whispers, "You. God, Jaymes, I missed you."

My heart is racing, my emotions rampant as the consequences of feeling something, feeling everything for this man again pulses through me. I push him back, and stumble out of his grasp to get away. With a good ten feet distance keeping him safely away, I shake my head. "No. You don't get to say that."

"I did. I said it, Jaymes. I'm sorry if that upsets you, but I've missed you."

"No." I start pacing, my hands going into my hair. "No. You can't do this."

"I'm doing it."

Stopping, I look at him confused. "I don't understand. It's been a long time, Derrick. Nothing about what you're saying makes any sense."

"That's because you're trying to make sense of how I feel. Sometimes we just feel and that should be enough. Like love."

"Oh no, no. You don't get to drag love into this. You drove off that day. Were you thinking of love then? Were you thinking of me? For years I've had to live with the sound of your tires as you drove away like you couldn't get out of there fast enough."

"You know why you remember the tires instead of me? Because you ran away. A lot like you're doing now."

"Accusations are easy to throw around—"

"Two-way street, baby."

"Mommy?"

When Derrick turns his body to look behind him, Ace is there, our moms keeping their distance. I bend down and put on a smile for my son. "Hey, buddy. You ready to go?"

"I'm hungry."

"I'll make you pancakes at home." Holding my hand out, he takes it. I glance to Derrick who looks as gutted as I feel. "Goodbye."

"Bye," he says, tucking his hands in his pockets. "See ya, Ace."

"See you, Big D."

Squeezing his hand, I quickly correct him, "No, we aren't going to call him that."

"Why not?"

Good Lord. I need to get out of here. "Just no, Ace. Call him by his name Derrick, or Mr. Masters. It's more respectful."

"Okay, Mommy. Why are we walking so fast?"

I tap his nose. "'Cuz Mommy's hungry, too." I doubt I'll be able to eat anything by the way my stomach's twisted in knots, but I need to, just like I need to leave Derrick Masters in the past. Just before I turn the corner, I sneak one peek back. Damn him. Why did he come today? What was his agenda? To try and pick up where we left off? *"I want anything I can get with you." Why?*

Why does he have to look so damn good when I'm a complete mess?

Or maybe he's a mess inside just like me, but wrapped up in one hell of an enticing package. Either way that man's off limits. Not only for me, but there's no way I can let Reggie find out or I'll have hell to pay.

I start the car and make sure Ace is buckled in. My mom comes around the corner and gets in. When the door shuts, her mouth opens, but I'm getting quicker, "Not now. Not in front of Ace."

"What not in front of me?" he asks, pouting in the back seat.

"Don't worry about it," my mom and I say in unison and then turn to each other.

I break first and start laughing. The reprieve needed. Exhaling loudly, I grip the steering wheel and then look back. "In-N-Out Burger?"

Ace's arms fly into the air. "Yay!"

Shifting the car into drive, I avoid looking at my mother. I feel her thoughts spanning across the console. I don't need to see her disappointment too. When Ace is happily distracted naming the color of every car that drives past us, I say, "The boat can't be rocked."

"He has too much control."

Reggie.

"I have no choice."

"You do. You're just choosing not to use the power you have."

Glancing into the rearview mirror, I see my son and his smile. I will do anything that protects the light that shines bright for his future. "He'll take him. I can't let that happen."

She reaches over and rubs my arm. "Maybe Derrick can help."

"It's complicated."

Resolved, she breathes out. "It always is."

"I'm not having this fight with you. There are things you don't know that I can't tell you."

"Can't or won't? I don't understand his hold on you. I know you don't love him."

"Enough." I shoot her a look that this conversation is over. I hate being curt with her, but I cannot do this again.

Ace pipes in, "Love who?"

"Whom." Catching a glimpse of him in the mirror again, I say, "Nothing, sweetie. The big question is—animal style?"

"Yes please," he replies joyously.

When Ace and I get home, I drop my bag by the door and hang my keys on the hook. I'm anxious. My skin crawls from the thought of the depths Reggie is willing to go to hurt Derrick. He never loved me. I'm just a pawn in his game of revenge. I deserve some of the blame. I knew what I was doing when I made that deal, but Ace and his innocence are now and forever caught in the middle. Kids weren't part of the bargain. Why Reggie still shows such interest when he never wanted to be a father is beyond my rationale. My nightmares are based on the reality of his words, his threats, to take my son away. To turn him into the prince he wants him to be. His legacy.

I will die before I let that happen. I'll do anything it takes to make sure Ace gets out like Derrick did.

THE SUN HAS set and Ace is snug in his bed when the banging begins as if his ears were burning today. Ace runs into the living room and grabs hold of my leg. "Who is it, Mommy?"

"Go back to bed and don't come out for anything, okay?" I shuffle him back to his room as the banging continues matching my heartbeats. "Get in bed. Now."

"I'm scared."

Steadying my voice, I say, "Don't be, buddy. I'm not." I put on a fake smile and blow him a kiss. "I love you."

"Love you," he replies with the covers up to his nose. I shut the door and grab my phone. Texting my mom, I hit the agreed upon letter and send. Setting my phone on the coffee table I rush to answer the door, knowing he won't go away when he knows I'm home.

One lock clicks open and the banging stops. I remove the chain and turn the knob lock before opening the door. Raising my chin, I come face to face with true evil—dark hair, eyes so light that they're hard to see at night. Just pupils black as his soul shine in the dark, like now as he stands under the porch light. I whisper, "It's late. Ace is sleeping."

Reggie's hand flattens against the dented metal door and he pushes it open. "Aren't you gonna invite me in?" He's slurring and those black as death pupils are pinpoints. Drunk and high. My fear builds and my mouth opens to deepen my breaths. I don't want him to sense how scared I am. He gets off on it.

"It's late." I try my best to wrangle even a fake smile, but can't seem to manage.

"Where've ya been lately?"

"I'm always here."

A dirty nail tipped finger runs along my jaw. I start to turn but he grabs my face and yanks me back to look at him. "Don't you ever turn away from me."

My neck aches, but the pain is overridden by the sounds of Ace's door creaking open. No. No. No. Please, God. Let him go back to bed. "I'm looking at you, Reggie," I say as calm as I can. My hand covers his and slowly lowers it back down. "I'm looking right at you."

Leaning against the doorframe, a smarmy self-pleased grin injects itself on his face. Touching his lips, he licks his finger, and then reaches for me. "So pretty. One taste will never be enough."

Blood rushes in my ears as the horror of him "tasting" me comes back. I flinch, my eyes closed tight. One. Two. Three. Four. One. Two. Three. Four. I reopen my eyes to find his, too lazy to notice, giving me an opportunity. "Shayna is a very jealous woman, Reggie. You know she doesn't share."

"Might be interesting to see what you can do—"

"Ace needs me. You know that."

Pushing me, he walks in. "Where's my boy?"

I hurry around him, a barricade he'll have to destroy to get to my son.

"He's sleeping. Remember? It's late, Reggie." My hands are against his chest. "You should go home to Shayna."

Moving me back, he demands, "I want to see my son. What's he like three now?"

"Yes, something like that. He needs his sleep. You should go home."

He stops, his gaze piercing mine. Locked in a silent standoff, neither of us moves. I don't even breathe. I've got five minutes left to call my mom back before she calls the police. I can't let this escalate. I'm about to distract him with another threat of his girlfriend, but his body goes slack and he starts laughing. "Fuck, woman. You're tougher than you look. I like that."

Just as I pretend to smile and play along, I'm grabbed by the back of my hair and brought in, my body slamming into his. I fight to silence my terror but it slips out in the form of a weak cry caught in my throat. I hate myself for not being stronger.

The smell of rotting flesh burns my nostrils as he holds me so close I feel his breath against my cheek. "Don't you ever fucking tell me what to do or I'll fucking take my son and leave your ass for fucking dead. Do you understand me?"

Tears well in my eyes. Another tight pull and I know he's pulled some out this time. My head is angled up when he pushes his mouth against my ear. "You were *his*. Now you're *mine*. Or did you forget?"

"I didn't forget."

Inhaling me, he closes his eyes as his grip on me loosens. "I give you my patience. No one else, but you receive my mercy on a regular basis. Why do I do it?"

Remaining quiet, I let him play out the fantasy in his head. He's not someone I can reason with in this state. And honestly, I don't know why he's spared me. Often, I think it's leading to something bigger. He's a showman, a lot like Derrick—probably the only thing they have in common. He's waiting for his big finale, but hopefully I'll be gone before he gets to it.

Taking a deep breath, he rubs the back of my head with his grimy hands as if that will soothe the ache of my scalp. "Rebel tried to fuck me over. Payback's a bitch. Right, Jamie?"

"Yes." That I can agree on.

"Our Rebel has lived up to his name. Wonder how we can get a cut of all that dough he's making." He walks away, but makes sure to watch my face when he asks, "You ever hear from him?"

For someone so out of touch with reality, he seems to be in the dead center of mine. "Nope."

"Oh man," he says with his hands covering his heart. "That's gotta hurt. He burned you good." Finally, he walks to the door, but turns back. "But don't worry, I'll take care of you. It's the least a friend can do for another friend. We're friends, right?"

"Yeah. Sure. Friends." Disgust fills my stomach that I am stuck dealing with this disgusting excuse for a human. Sometimes I wonder where he went wrong, what happened to fill him with the hate that he breeds now. Sure he was stabbed in the back by a friend, but that wouldn't lead to this. He was well on his way to who he is now long before Derrick left. How did he turn out so bad? What led this kid who once won a ribbon for his poetry into the gang leader he's become now? Life means nothing to him, except for his own. Yet he fills his with nothing but hate, killing himself slowly.

Does it make me a horrible person that I've prayed for him to overdose? Looking at him now, threatening my son and me like our lives mean nothing, I want him dead.

"If you hear from our famous friend, you let me know. One step back in my hood and his ass is capped. If he even comes within two miles of you or my son, everyone will die."

A wadded-up twenty-dollar bill hits me on the chest. "You remember who lets you go to school. It's me who lets you have a job. You have this place because I allow it." Then he says what he always says, "Don't ever lie to me and don't go gettin' crazy ideas in that pretty head of yours about skipping town. You know what I do to people who betray me?"

I do, so I nod. People go missing, or get shot, or hurt. He destroys lives. Coming back over, he pats me on the head. "Good. Make sure to buy my kid some fuckin' toys." He leaves, slamming the door behind him. I scramble to my feet, lock the door, and grab my phone to text my mom: ***Okay. I'm okay.***

If she only knew the full truth. Shame works its way in and I start to cry.

She's quick to reply: *I love you.*

Through blurry, tear-filled eyes, I type: *I love you too. Night.*

I rub the back of my head, strands tangling between my fingers, a clump. I don't know how long I stand there with the phone and my hair in my hand. Pulling them close to my chest, I realize I don't have anyone I can call. With my back to the wall, I slide down slowly, still holding on to the phone like I'm holding on for dear life. Maybe I am.

When my ass hits the carpet, I look down. What is this life I'm leading? How many lives do I have left before he kills me, or worse... I can't even think it. I'll do anything for Ace. I will do *anything* to protect him. And against my better judgment, I'll continue to protect the man I once gave my heart to, even if he did leave it behind for lights brighter than the ones that once shined in my eyes just for him.

I wasn't enough to keep him here and there wasn't enough time for me to go with him.

But I told him to go and never look back.

What was I thinking going today and seeing him?

The touch of his lips to my lips.

That can't happen again. No. It's not worth the risk.

Derrick Masters needs to stay in the past. That's the only way I can make sure I stay on track with my plan. *I will take Ace out of this hellhole and get him away from that dangerous, vile monster.*

The only plan that matters—saving my son from being taken.

That connection I felt stretching across the table, the one that once had me head over heels for that man, needs to go away. Five minutes more and my heart would have been his all over again. That can't happen. Not ever.

Ace. My sweet son. How will Derrick look at him, or treat him when he will always know that he's Reggie's. And my mom. I need to make sure they're safe. Love can wait. My heart will have to bear the brunt of more time.

Destiny sure does have a screwed up sense of humor.

12

Derrick

TWENTY MINUTES. I was granted twenty minutes with Jaymes and not only did I completely blow it, but she was even more amazing than I remember. "If I start writing fucking happy-go-lucky love songs like some sixties musical sitcom, shoot me."

The expression on Kaz's face is one of horror and confusion. "I don't even know what you're talking about."

"Never mind. I forgot you're not from around here." Resting my arms behind my head, I add, "If it gets to that point, it's bad. That's all you need to know."

He leans back on the lounge chair of my deck and drops his sunglasses over his eyes. "You named a guitar after her. That was already crossing a line if you were trying to get her off your mind, don't you think?"

"There was no other name for it. That guitar was created in her likeness—sleek, black wood to match her hair. The inlays on the face of the fretboard match the unique green of her eyes. The strings are taut and I've never seen such a well-crafted guitar. Jaymes."

"I think you've already crossed it." He pulls his fingers into a gun and shoots me. I don't tell him that shit is dangerous even in jest. He knows almost everything about my past. He knows my history with gangs, but he never judged me. Kaz is a stand-up guy. He took me at face value instead of nosing around the baggage I was carrying. I've left a lot of it behind, but that guitar, like the girl—there's no getting over her.

"...one week. Lara's not happy."

The tour. Like the rest of us, he's been bitching about the time we'll be gone. We got our new schedules yesterday. Instead of two weeks on and two off, we're filling in the gap and adding shows to our sold-out tour. "One month on the road. How many shows is that?"

"Twenty."

Joking, I say, "They're going easy on us."

"We have a few days off I guess, but I've never felt older than I have in the last two years."

"That shit will age you, but I don't know. These days I prefer the stage. For a show built on dramatics and performance there's less drama there than in real life."

He looks my way. "Brunch didn't go well?"

The mocking tone can be heard in the way he says brunch. I would have been mocking him for that shit, so it's only fair to get it in return. "No. Not well at all."

Sitting up, his body angles in my direction. "You haven't talked about her in a long time and now she seems to be back in play. What gives?"

I keep my shades over my eyes to hide what I'm feeling inside. When I don't respond, he stands. "Since you're not going to tell me why you're suddenly thinking about your ex again, beer?"

"Nah, but help yourself. Grab me a Topo Chico while you're in there though."

"Fuck you and your imported water."

"Let me enjoy the perks that I have enough money to splurge on mineral water." Flipping him off, I laugh. "Thanks, brah."

He laughs in response and goes inside.

My phone chirps with a text. Mom comes on the screen. Usually I'd be annoyed by all the extra texts I've been getting lately, but I'm not. Not when they involve a raven-haired beauty. I read what she's sent: ***You didn't want to talk about what happened yesterday, but I'm here if you ever need me.***

I respond: ***I know. Thanks.***

Mom: ***Nita said Jamie was in a foul mood.***

Foul mood? Fascinating, and I need more information on this bad mood. Speed dialing my mom the next second, her phone rings. "Hello, son, how are you?"

"Tell me about the mood."

"I thought you might find that interesting."

Jaymes is never... I should say *was never* in a foul mood unless she was really bothered by something. She should have been pissed off at me more than she ever was, so to hear she was bothered yesterday, kind of inserts a little hope in my day.

"What happened? I know she told you, so spill it."

"She said you would have thought your name was Satan's himself." There goes that hope. She continues, "But I guess she mumbled something about not just how handsome you are, which you are—"

"Okay, Mom, just say it."

"Nita said she was drinking a strawberry shake and cursing some connection that has never gone away. And that seeing you has stirred up a whole slew of emotions that she doesn't have time for." Did my mom just giggle? "I think you should ask her out."

My lips curve up. She always did like anything strawberry. "Wait, what? No. She told me no." *Did she mean yes?*

"Derrick, listen to me. I didn't think I had to tell you about women. I mean, you seemed to know quite a bit too soon for your age, but Jamie Grenier is showing all the signs."

"Signs of what? That she hates me?"

"She doesn't hate you. Quite the opposite according to Nita."

Although I like that apparently Jaymes is thinking about me and might not hate me, I shouldn't encourage this route to her heart.

"Mom, you and Nita are trouble together. Stop the matchmaking. It's not going to happen."

"We're not matchmaking. We're simply pointing out the obvious."

"No," I say, standing and walking to the edge of the deck. Staring out over LA, I run my hand through my hair. "You're so busy hoping for this to happen that you haven't heard what she's saying. Well, I did. It wasn't pleasant, neither was her reaction to me. That's not usually a good sign."

"It's because she likes you. Still."

"God, Mom. Listen, we're not ten and hitting each other on the playground because secretly we like each other. She has a kid, a kid who comes before me or any other guy. That's her priority and I don't blame her. I commend her for it."

"I do too, honey, but—"

"No buts. Not this time. You gave it a valiant effort, but I can't see Jaymes again unless it's on her terms." The silence on the other end of the phone starts to worry me. "Mom, you there?"

"I am. I'm just thinking about what you're saying."

"Good." Kaz comes out of the house with my water and his beer. "I've got to go. Kaz is hanging out."

"We'll talk later."

We'll talk about Jaymes some more and run this topic into the ground is what she really means. "Fine. Later, Mom."

"Bye, Mrs. Masters," Kaz yells just before I disconnect.

"Back off my mom."

An eyebrow lifts, along with a half smile. "She was a young mom. I hear the roadies talking about her."

"Fuck me, no. Just no on this."

"She's what? Forty-five?"

"Fuck you. She's my mom. And she's older than that."

He laughs. "What, forty-seven?"

"Maybe. Now shut up about it and if you ever hear anyone talking about my mom other than her being my mom, tell me so I can kick their ass."

Reclining back on the lounge chair, he goes on as if this is the funniest shit he's ever thought about, "Whoa. You said your ex has a son who's five. Damn, brah. Crazy thought, but what if you were his father. The cycle would have continued. You would have been a dad at like eighteen or something. Can you imagine that?"

Yeah, imagine that. "Drink your beer and let's play some music. I'm tired of talking." I don't know if it's sad or crazy, but I can imagine it. Ace is a good kid. As for Jaymes... fuck, she was right. I felt it too. That damn years-old "thing" that was always there is still intact like it had never gone away.

I PARK AND get out, but then get back in the car. "What the fuck am I doing?" Knocking my head against the steering wheel a few times, I hope to knock some sense into myself. I can have any girl. Shit, I've got a phone full of numbers and texts full of tits. I can have anyone.

But I'm sitting outside a used-car dealership with sandwiches from the same place where she once worked in one hand and a melting strawberry shake in the other. "What the fuck am I doing?" Just go, I force myself out of the car.

Stop thinking. Just go.

A guy in a tie, which means I already don't trust him, fast approaches. "Good day, sir." He eyes the food in my hands. "Are you stopping by shopping for a car on your lunch break?"

My pace never slows as I head for the door. "No. Is Jaymes here?"

He hurries next to me and opens the door. "We don't have a James here."

Shit. "Jamie. Jamie Grenier?"

"Oh. Yes," he replies with a *too happy to be thinking about my girl* grin. Narrowing my eyes at this guy, I cross my arms to intimidate. He better not be thinking about my girl, or worse, have his eyes on her. I remind myself that she's not mine. Yet. So I attempt to tamp down the emotions that rhyme with hellousy. The ones I have no right to be having much less acting on. I take a deep breath and walk inside. I recognize Leah from Nita's house. She stands, her mouth open. Her eyes wide. I can see her tapping the desk next to her. My gaze shifts right and there she is—*my girl*. I keep going until I'm right in front of them. Jaymes has her back to me as she types away on the ancient desktop computer anchored on her desk.

I smile at Leah and she stutters, "Ja-Ja-mie."

"Hold on," Jaymes replies making me smile even wider.

"No," Leah says, "You need to see this."

In pure annoyance she swivels around in her chair. "What?"

When her eyes land on me, her mouth hangs open, and I say, "Hi."

She's standing. Straight up. Her palms run down the front of her gray skirt. I've never seen her dress like a "professional" but she makes that skirt look damn sexy. "What are you doing here?"

Holding the food out for her, I say, "I thought you might be hungry." Her mouth opens. Her sweet pink lips part and I'm tempted to toss the food and devour her instead. When she doesn't seem to find any words, I stretch my arms toward her. "I brought sandwiches."

"From Ernie's?"

"Yeah."

"We should go to the back for more privacy." She scoots around her desk, glances at Leah, and has completely managed to avoid any eye contact with me. Her skills are impressive. She's honed them over the years. I follow her to the back break room that has no window, a large vending machine with dusty candy bars, and smells of rotten cheese, or a guy's locker room. Kind of the same smell.

"What are you doing here, Derrick?"

"Like I said, I brought food."

Her hands go to her hips. "No, for real." She finally looks directly into my eyes. "Why are you here?"

"We didn't get a chance to break bread the other day. I wanted a second chance."

"You keep talking about second chances like I'll change my mind."

I set the food on the table and sit down in the metal chair. "Why are you so adamant about hating me? Can't we lower our weapons and just eat a sandwich together?"

"Hating you? Is that what you think?" Her voice raises like her anger by looking at the red flooding her cheeks. "You think I hate you?"

"Sure feels like it."

"Then why would you come around? Why would you bring food for someone you think hates you?"

"To make amends."

Her fingers entwine behind her head and she takes a deep breath as if to calm herself. When she opens her eyes, she says, "No amends need to be made." She maneuvers around the table, heading for the door, but I catch her by the wrist.

Her breath catches and it's quick, but I also see the terror that crosses her face. My hands are off her and I'm standing. "I'm sorry."

Her eyes snap back to me, but she seems to be focused on her breathing. In the quiet of the room, both of us stand there motionless, but I hear the faintest, "...three. Four," from her.

Holy shit. What the fuck? "Are you counting?"

"I um," she says, shifting back, away from me. "It's just something I do. Sorry."

"Why are you sorry?"

"You looked worried. I'm sorry for worrying you."

"What?" I move closer, but her back hits the wall, causing me to freeze to the spot. "Are you afraid of me? Did I scare you?"

"No," she whispers, looking at the door ready to escape. "You should go. Thank you for the food, but I don't have a break today."

I stare at her. Where's the feisty girl I once knew? Where's the fierce woman from Sunday? "What the fuck is going on here, Jaymes?"

The salesman from earlier comes to the door and peeks in. "Everything okay in here?"

When's it more than apparent that she's not going to say anything after a few seconds that feel like a time bomb's about to go off if she answers, I reply, "Fine. I should get going."

I move past him and walk through the car showroom. Pushing the door open, the sun is blinding, so I pull my sunglasses from the neck of my shirt and slip them on. They don't just shield the sun, but they're damn good at hiding the emotions I'm struggling to hide.

Angry.

Confused.

Defeated.

Hungry.

Hurt.

Concern.

Fuck.

Just seeing her—I feel everything all at once. Is there a name for that fucked-up emotion?

Yes. It's Jaymes Grenier.

13

Jaymes

MY HEART SINKS. I close my eyes and mentally beat myself up. How can I let him leave when he came here so sweetly searching for me? Damn it. I open my eyes and see Jose staring back at me. "You okay?" he asks.

He's not nearly as interesting to look at as Derrick. "I am. I'm good. Really good."

Jose shrugs. "Cool."

I run past him, through the showroom, and around a Hyundai. Shoving the entrance door open I run out into the daylight. Derrick is getting in his car when I shout, "Hey!"

When he looks my way I suddenly feel like one of those girls on the tarmac when The Beatles came to America for the first time. Another fan vying for the great musician's attention. My arms lower... ah, screw it. I run to him, wishing I were in sneakers instead of these high heels. Coming to a stop right in front of him, he stands still, door still open, sunglasses covering his eyes, hair lightened by the sun, and just enough stubble to make me wonder if he shaved for me today. "Hey," he says.

But I'm still caught up wondering if he was always this gloriously handsome. "You're tall."

"You're kind of short." He looks down, but takes his time working that gaze back up. "Even in those shoes."

"There are two sandwiches."

"Thought you might be hungry."

I can't stop my smile listening to him try to act like what he did was no big deal at all. "That's a lot of food. Maybe you might stay and eat one with me? And was that strawberry shake for me?"

Although he fills out the rock-star status nicely, I see the boy I once loved so easily when his shoulders shift down and he relaxes. "Yeah."

"Come back with me. Please?" I hold out my hand, needing to give him those few minutes he asked for. I owe him that. I owe him more, but I start with this peace offering, "I'm sorry."

The twitch in his neck isn't exaggerated, but I see it. I know him. I know this man before me, like no other. He always hated apologies, even more so when they were mine...

The pads of his thumbs wipe away my tears. His lips caress my cheek, and then he whispers, "Lovers. Soul mates. Friends. Those three words come with three others—trust, love, and forgiveness. They're not given. They already exist between us, baby."

Looking up into his indigo eyes I get lost in my love for him. It's deeper than the ocean and vaster than the universe, but it keeps me here, gravitationally pulled to him. I don't know when it happened or why we fell like we did, but I cling to it, to him. "I don't deserve you."

He chuckles. "You're right. You deserve better."

"Don't say that." I run my hands over his chest, underneath the leather jacket and around his middle until I'm fully pressed to him with my ear over his heart. The beat is strong like his arms around me.

"It's true, but guess what?"

"What?" I tilt my head up and wait.

"You're kind of stuck with me."

The smile on my lips feels good, like him. "Why do you love me, Derrick?"

Reaching down, he grabs my ass. "Because you're hot."

I giggle. "That's it? You like the way I look?"

He leans against the side of his truck and crosses his legs at the ankle. Scanning me down and then back up, he runs his thumb over his bottom lip. When he finally speaks, he says, "It's a nice package, but it's your heart I'm after."

"Such a charmer."

"Maybe that will be my next tattoo."

The glare is instant. "I can't believe you did that."

"It was inevitable."

"I know," I reply, the disappointment engulfed by the sadness I feel for our situation. "We're never getting out, are we?"

Taking my hands, he parts his feet and pulls me close. The warmth of his hands cradles my face. "I promise I'll get us out of here and I'll always take care you." The heavy breath tasting of peppermint fills my mouth as he kisses me. He's always so gentle, but not now. Desperation fills our kiss, but we part, panting and searching each other's eyes. "If anything ever happens to me—"

"Stop saying stuff like that. We'll leave before it gets worse."

Worse. He'll be killed and where will that leave me? A body without a soul? "You're marked for life, branded to them."

"Branded to me. It's only a tattoo."

"It's across your whole back."

"Good. We won't have to look at it much." Rubbing my arms, he asks, "What was your plan anyway?"

"I wanted to stop them. I wanted you to stay you."

Taking my hand to his lips, he kisses it and brings me back to him. "I'm me. As long as I'm with you, I'm me. No tattoo is gonna change that unless you hate Rebel."

"I don't hate Rebel. I hate what the nickname represents. I love you."

The questions are seen in his eyes when he asks, "You'd leave with me, right?"

"Any day. Anything to leave this hell behind."

"What if we never make it to heaven?"

"We'll always have each other."

"I love you, Jaymes."

Though the air is heavy with our circumstance, I manage to smile. "Why do you always call me Jaymes?"

"Because everyone else calls you Jamie."

"But I'll always be your baby." I spin away from him.

"That you will." I'm promptly pulled back in, dipped, and kissed like in the movies. Deep. Real. Raw. Passion. Love. Forever. He says it all without saying a word.

...He asks, "What are you sorry for?"

"Brunch and how abruptly it ended." Looking down, I whisper, "Us and how abruptly we ended."

"So, you do have a lunch break?

Glancing over my shoulder, I see David leaving out the side door. He'll be gone to lunch at least an hour if not more. "No, but I'm taking one anyway." My eyes meet his again.

"Look, we don't have to dwell on the past, not right now. How about we just enjoy your lunch break?"

"I'd like that." As we walk back in, I don't tell him I don't have an official lunch break today because I have to leave early for class. I also don't tell him that I've missed him so much that my heart still aches for him. Or that when I dream, I dream of him holding me again. We sit across from each other and I do tell him what I should have told him years earlier. "I'm sorry for embarrassing you in front of the guys when you got the Rebel tattoo."

"Why did you cry?"

"I think I was crying for our lost youth. Sounds silly to say that at twenty-three, but I feel much older than my years these days. Anyway, at the time, I thought I lost you to Reggie and the... guys."

"Call it what it is—a gang. But to be clear on one thing, you never lost me, Jaymes. I was across town, not across the country. I should've checked on you. I should have done more, but I was hurt. That's silly, not that you mourned for youth. I get it. I sucked it up that day because I had to. There was no more stalling and I wasn't ready to leave you. At eighteen, I knew you wouldn't come."

"I couldn't. I wish I would have though."

"You're doing so good, Jaymes. You really are. You don't have much school left either. You'll have a degree, something I never got. My smart girl. Always so damn smart."

Hearing him call me his girl is like an arrow to my heart. I take a deep breath, inhaling his words deep into my soul where only he's allowed to visit.

"You're making me blush, Derrick."

"I like you blushing. If you're blushing, you've lowered those walls that you carry like a fortress around you."

"I know you so well, but sometimes I forget that someone out there knows me just as well." Leaning in, I whisper, "Don't tell anyone I let you in or they'll all want in." I laugh.

"Your secret's safe with me."

"Can I ask you something?"

"You just did."

"Ha!"

"Ask away."

"You're not seeing anyone, are you?"

"No."

"Is that why you started coming around?"

"No." A playful smirk appears.

I take a sip of the shake when he seems to be intent on keeping his secret. "This is delish. Thank you."

"You're welcome."

"Are you going to eat?"

Unwrapping the sandwich, he laughs. "Sure." It's a carefree laugh, and one I remember from years ago. He was always easy to be with, and if the tension weren't here because of our past, or he wasn't a rock star and loved by the world, I know I'd feel just as comfortable now.

But things have changed.

Reggie.

His threat from last night comes racing back. Derrick takes his first bite, and I say what I have to say, "It's been good seeing you again—"

"It's been good seeing you again, too."

"Please. Stop being so nice."

That makes him gut chuckle. "Now I'm too nice? That might be a first, Jaymes."

"No," I say, sighing. "Just let me get this out."

His sandwich is discarded and I get his full attention. "It's good to see you again, but I can't keep seeing you."

"You said that the other day. Something about no time for any relationships."

"Unfortunately, that's where I am in life. I'm sorry. I don't mean to hurt you."

"I think that's like your fourth sorry in less than fifteen minutes."

Setting my sandwich down, I say, "I am though. So sorry for so many things."

"I don't want you to be sorry. I want to know what's going on."

"Life, Derrick."

"Life? Like I'm not living one?"

"You're living a big one and I'm just trying to survive while raising my son."

"It's not bigger than yours. You're a mother. God, Jaymes. You're a mother. That's amazing. *You* are amazing."

I turn away from him. His pride feels unwarranted. I've failed in so many ways. If only I could change the past. "I'm not. I'm barely getting by." My life feels so little compared to his.

"Don't believe the lies in your head. What you're doing, raising Ace, is the most important job ever."

Peeking back up at the attractive, passionate man across from me, I say, "It's not glamorous like yours."

108

"I can't lie. I love performing live. The energy. The excitement."

"You were born to be on that stage."

"You always believed in me, even when I didn't. I just want you to know that all the success you see, it's yin and yang. Life balances itself. With the good, you get the bad. I like recording in the studio. I dig the travel. But it's wearing me down. It's hard sometimes... or maybe it's just lonely."

"Why are you lonely? You're surrounded by thousands of people who adore you every day."

"But I'm only looking for one." He pauses and I think it's the first time I see him a little unsteady. I know I am from the turn this conversation has taken. He fills the seconds, breaking my heart a little more by saying, "Despite the house I own, I feel lost, homeless at times. My north star has moved and I can't seem to find it."

"You have a home—"

"No, I have a house." Leaning in, he glances to the door, then back to me. "I can't stop thinking about you."

I lean back, away from him. "You shouldn't think about me at all."

"I shouldn't?"

Standing up, I grab my sandwich, my appetite gone anyway, and toss it. "I have to get back to work."

"What are you doing?"

"I have to go before I get in trouble by my boss."

He meets me by the door, throwing his uneaten food away. "No. What. Are. You. Doing?"

I know what he means, but with last night's encounter too fresh in my mind, I know what I need to do. My heart be damned. "You've got to stop this. No more coming around. No more meet-ups with the moms." I look away from him, not wanting for him to see how hard this is for me. "No, nothing. Whatever this is between us can't turn into more." My eyes go wide and I point at his mouth. "No. No. Whatever you're thinking, stop. Whatever that smirky smirk thing you're doing, don't."

"What am I thinking?" His body presses to mine and my back

hits the wall, knocking the light switch. The room is dark, but the light from the showroom reveals his every bad intention. Tempting my body, his lips entice when he leans down and whispers, "What am I doing?"

I know I shouldn't. Everything that matters is now at risk, but my soul misses him in ways that I can't let go. My fight weakens. I can almost remember the life I once shared with him. The beat of my heart quickens. "We shouldn't."

"We should."

"This is bad." My breath comes short.

"I'll make you feel so good." His counteroffer is so tempting.

My arms wrap around his neck. "Derrick?"

He takes me in his arms. "Jaymes?"

"One kiss and that's it."

"Or two or three," he replies, cutting a deal. His nose slides along the bridge of mine. "Then I'll go. I promise."

"Swear?"

Our lips come together and my body gives in, molding to his as if we were never apart. He speaks of performing on stage in the same way I feel about this kiss—the energy, the excitement. I was born to kiss this man and I wish I could spend my life doing it.

Large hands rub along my middle and soft moans escape him. I inhale him and his sweet sounds, loving this... *loving him* too much.

14

Derrick

"Damn you and your seductive kisses," she says, pushing her hands against me to put distance between us. "We can't do this."

"We just did." Moving in again, I whisper, "Now let's do it again."

"No, Derrick."

But I see the smile that belies her words. She liked that kiss. I loved it. I lo—nope. Not going there. I steal another quick kiss and leave before she gets in trouble. The gasp is heard as I walk away. "Damn you," she whisper yells.

I can only imagine she's shaking her little fists me. Turning back, I have to see her. She was always incredibly sexy when she was mad. If she was mad at me that meant one thing—make-up sex. Fuck. She was a vixen in the sheets.

"You're impossible," she adds, full volume.

"See you around, babe."

I pass Leah, and cock a smirk with my nod. She says, "Byyye."

The salesman opens the door and says, "If you're ever in the market for a quality used car, Mr. Masters, let me know. My name's Jose."

"Thanks. I'll let you know."

My alarm chirps and I open the driver's door. Slipping into the sleek leather seat, I start the car, and back out before that ball of fucking sexy fire makes its way outside. I like her feisty. That means she won't give up. It also means I'll get another shot at wooing that woman. Yep, I said woo. Now that I know what I'm missing, I don't want to miss anymore. It's as if just from my lips touching hers, that I can forgive how quickly she was with Reggie. How quickly she *moved on.* How much I want her still.

This car dealership is a long way from the Hollywood Hills, but I don't even make it five minutes before I get a call. I don't recognize the number, but I'm glad I don't send it to voicemail once I hear Jayme's voice ring out through the speakers. "You're a bastard, you know that, Derrick?"

"I do. I also remember how much you loved it."

"Your rebel ways. You still got that tattoo?" She sounds mighty pleased with that zinger. Bringing up sore subjects is used like ammo for her defensiveness.

"Come over and find out."

She laughs, annoyance in every note. "Like I said, impossible."

"Let's make possible together."

"Do you ever give up?"

"You know me, right?"

"Right. Stupid me. I almost forgot who I was talking to."

"Speaking of me, come over."

A loud sigh punctuates the debate I know she's having, probably sitting at that messy desk of hers with the ancient computer sputtering shit she doesn't even care about in front of her. But the fun we were having seems to dissipate and her voice goes quieter, "I can't. I'm sorry."

"Again with the *sorrys.* When did our conversations just become a bunch of apologies? No, don't answer that. I have a feeling I don't want to know the truth."

"There's lots you don't want to know, so we need to make this goodbye for good."

"So a goodbye versus a *bad* bye. That's progress, I think."

"No, they both end the same with bye."

"Wait," the word rushes out. She doesn't hang up. Thank God. Her breath remains light as it dances through the line. "I leave in four days. Please. Come over. I just want to see you again. I won't even ask how you got my number... though I'm curious." She hmms. So I continue, "You said whatever this is between us can't turn into more. You, yourself, admitted not only is there something here, but it could be more. Come explore that more, baby."

"You shouldn't call me that."

"I know, but I can't seem to stop myself. I'm not giving up. One date."

"Now it's a date you want?"

"I want more," I say, chuckling. "But how about we start with a date."

"Your honesty is almost endearing."

I laugh. "The girls got jokes."

"Not many these days. Look—"

Taking a left, I'm already onto her emotional tides that change her mind. "I know what you're going to say. I'm asking you, Jaymes, for your time. Just a little. One-on-one without interruption. We'll walk away putting this, whatever it is between us, to bed, or maybe it will turn into seeing each other again. I don't know. I just know it feels good being around you again."

"It does," she admits, which feels like a victory of epic proportions.

"One meal. One date. One hour of your time?"

"Okay. But will you promise not to tell anyone?"

"Are you that ashamed of me?" I tease.

Finally a laugh, and it's the sweetest music to my ears. I'm tempted to record it and listen to it on replay or drop it into a song. "Not at all. It's complicated, like I said. I don't want anything affecting Ace in anyway."

"My lips are sealed unless you want to make out and then I'll totally give it up for ya."

"Like I said, you're impossible. I've got to get back to work before I'm fired."

"How's tomorrow night at seven?"

"You're not going to give up, are you?"

"You know it."

"So if I hang up now, you're gonna bug me about this, aren't you?"

"I'll text you my address and see you at seven."

The silence starts to extend. I can imagine her face, pursed lips, brows pushed toward the middle. Then resolve. "Eight works better."

Gotcha! "Eight it is."

"Fine. Oh, and my mother gave me the number. She programmed it into my phone after spending time with Diane. I think the moms are conspiring to get us together."

"There could be worse things."

"I'm not so sure about that."

It's probably best to hang up before she changes her mind. "See you tomorrow, baby."

"Stop calling me that, Derrick."

"Habit, baby." *Not sorry.* I know how she used to love when I called her that.

I don't have to see her to know she's rolling her eyes. "Tomorrow, Romeo."

WHAT CONSTITUTES OVERBOARD? When it comes to ordering food, I don't know what Jaymes likes anymore. She used to love Mexican food. What if she loves Chinese or Japanese or Italian? Thai? Mongolian? Fuck. American?

"It's too much," my mom says looking at the delivery bags.

"Help me," I reply.

A smile tickles her lips. "You like her."

"I used to love her. Of course I like her." I push the Chinese food down the kitchen counter. "I think we'll eliminate this one. Your turn."

She grabs the Italian. "I'll take this one with me."

"Dude. Not the Italian. I ordered the spinach manicotti. Do you know how amazing their manicotti is?"

"No," she says, shaking her head, "but I look forward to finding out."

"Take it. Take the Japanese too. I have a feeling the woman is similar to the girl. I'm going with the cheese enchiladas, rice, and beans."

"You can't go wrong with that."

"Fingers crossed. So, wine or beer?"

"Wine. I brought two bottles of white. Perfect for Mexican."

"I was thinking tequila."

Her glare hits hard. "No tequila."

"I reach for the bottle of Patron. "What's one shot?"

"Trouble, that's what. No tequila, Derrick. I want you on your best behavior."

"No one ever complains about my behavior when it comes to dating."

"I'm your mother. I don't want to hear about your so-called dating. And this is Jaymes. Remember that."

She puts the Chinese and Japanese food in the fridge and takes the Italian. "I'm going. You be good." Her finger goes up. "Don't reply to that."

I laugh. "Be safe driving home."

"I want some details tomorrow."

She knows me too well. Hearing about sex when it comes to her son's activities is not something she wants the gory details on, so I always edit, edit, edit for her. In the last two years though, nothing... or should I say no one has even been worth mentioning much less edit-worthy.

Maybe tonight will change all that.

SHE'S LATE, BUT it's LA, so instead of giving her a hard time, I give her a pass. I also receive two texts when she enters the neighborhood that went a little like: **You're kidding me, right?** And then another that said, **Really?**

Hope she likes the house.

The doorbell chimes and I wipe my hands on a dishtowel and run to answer it while tucking the edge of the towel into my jeans. When I swing the door open, I about choke on the comment I had prepared to welcome her with, but I manage. "You take this *hot for the teacher* thing to a whole new level."

A quick roll of her eyes and she says, "I went from work to class. I didn't have time to go home and change."

"Glad you didn't. Come on in."

"Nice towel by the way."

"Thanks. My mom gave it to me as a housewarming present."

She's scanning the entryway and beyond into the living room. "This house is the most amazing house I've ever been in."

"It's not all that fancy, but I like it."

"You live in the Hollywood Hills. It's fancy, all right."

I take her bag and set it on the table in the entryway. Taking her hand this time, I lead her through the living room and into the kitchen. When we're well within the confines of the room, and time when it would be perfectly acceptable for her to release my hand or vice versa, neither of us does. We stand there in front of the oven, and she asks, "You cooked for me?"

"No. But I bought it and can reheat like nobody's business."

There's that smile that makes me want to commit a crime or at least a sin worth confessing every time I see it. I pour her a glass of wine and I toast, "To feeling like old times." One clink and we both drink.

She leans against the counter and asks, "What's it like to not worry about money? And to live in a place like this?"

It's hard not to feel guilty when you're living in a castle compared to the shacks you grew up in. "It feels like what we dreamed about."

Taking another sip, she says, "I bet it's wonderful."

"Where's Ace tonight?"

"With my mom. Sometimes he'll stay with her if I'm out late."

"Are you out late often?"

"I'm not seeing anyone if that's what you're asking. I have school, work, and Ace. That's enough." She walks around the bar and sits on a stool. "I'm not trying to ruin dinner but I need to be open with you. If you want me to go, I will without question. I understand that most men won't want to take on my mess."

"Do we need tequila for this?" I half-joke.

"We might." She swirls the wine around in her glass, then looks at me. "You know Reggie is Ace's father, right?"

"I didn't know for sure, but I assumed."

"It wasn't planned."

"I hope not since I had just left."

The wine settles in the glass and she closes her eyes briefly. When they reopen she says, "I've apologized for a lot of things, but I won't ever apologize for Ace."

"I would never want you to. Years ago I made the best and worst decisions of my life. I'm still paying the price for losing you."

"Reaping the rewards of leaving me."

"You told me to go."

"I lied. That was the worst decision *I* made and it's one I've had to live with for years."

"How about we clean our slates and start over?"

She smiles. "I'd like that, but I also think you might have questions. Hit me with them now."

"Do you love him?"

"No. I never did."

She never loved him but had sex with him. "Were you ever a couple?"

"Nope." She sips her wine. "You're circling around that night, so I might as well tell you that it was only one time. Ace was just determined to exist."

"Why was it only one time?"

"We're not on good terms. Tumultuous is the only word that comes to mind right now when I think of him."

"Does he help with Ace at all?"

I think my line of questioning is making her uncomfortable. I'm sure it is, so I stop. She shifts and finishes the wine in her glass. "I have a confession, Derrick."

Resting my hands on the counter in front of her, I ask, "Sure you want to share more?"

"Let's blame it on the wine."

"Okay."

Biting her lip, she inwardly debates, but when our eyes connect, she confesses, "You're the only man I've ever loved."

I reach out and take her hand, holding it in mine as I savor her admission. *"You're the only man I've ever loved."* I never knew how much I needed to hear those words. It had hurt when I found out she'd been with Reggie. I can tell I don't know all the details, and probably it's better I never do.

But those words? Knowing she's never loved anyone but me? It's as if a switch has been turned on. I know with absolute certainty that I'm the same. *She's* the only one I've ever loved. We used to complete each other, but having her in this house, knowing where she lives and the life she struggles in daily, I know she feels the disparity of all things material. But she has Ace, and I can tell the love she has for him sustains and pushes her. *You're the only girl I've ever loved, Jaymes.*

Maybe by the end of dinner, I'll confess my secret too.

15

Jaymes

THERE'S SO MUCH familiarity wrapped in this man; so much that makes me feel content around him. I see the way he looks at me like love only exists for us. A longing found deep in his eyes that comforts, forcing my walls down with the simple act of a smile.

Our reality was never simple and it definitely wasn't easy. Two kids from a part of town stuck in the life the generation before ours couldn't escape. What made us think it would be any different? But here I am near the giant Hollywood sign that sparkles like a star, allowing average people to become one.

He did it.

Derrick said he would and he did. I may have sacrificed my own well-being to enable his escape, but I'm still envious of his outcome.

He tops off my wine.

"Is this glass made of crystal?" I ask, dabbing the very tip of my finger in the wine and then run it along the rim.

The beautiful sound rings just as he says, "I guess so. I didn't buy them."

"Who did?"

"I don't know. Maybe my friend's fiancée? She helped me find the place and decorated it."

My mouth falls open, but like a fish gulping for air, I say, "Huh? Um... Wow... I don't even know what to say to that."

"I know what you're thinking, Jaymes. Get out of your head and just be here with me. You know me. You know who I am inside. Don't let all this make you think otherwise. It's money. Nothing more." His words are as casual as his body language. His muscles never tense, the most relaxed I've ever seen him.

Is that what money does? Gives you peace? "It's money. Nothing more," I repeat, trying to see if the feeling can be transferred just by saying them out loud. Relief doesn't come. My body doesn't ease. My worries are too big for a simple solution. No magic is going to save us. Everything I know about my situation and his means this can't happen. I can't throw words out like that, like they have no repercussions. My son's life hangs on the basic thread of me working as much as I can to earn money. I won't ever earn money of this magnitude or live in a house in The Hills or drink from crystal wine glasses that a personal shopper bought for me without a second thought. But if I can get Ace and my mom out of that neighborhood, I'm winning in life. My perspective is way different from Derrick Masters' these days.

His life is actresses and stardom, fancy events, and fans falling at his feet.

My life is nine-hour days at a used-car lot and hours of night school, *triple*-checking my locks every night, and hoping I can pay the electricity bill each month.

The ache of a shattering heart throbs and I share another confession, "I'm here, but I can't stay." Derrick's eyes track mine for lies. He used to be able to see right through me. It's not a lie I'm telling, but it is a betrayal, even if just to myself. "I shouldn't have come. Call me curious. I wanted to see how the other half lives."

Coming around to my side of the counter, he comes just close enough to trap me, but stays far enough away to make me wish he were closer. "Why do you keep insisting you shouldn't be here, you can't see me again, this is all wrong?" He rests his hands on my thighs and leans in. I like his proximity. Too much. "What if this is all right? What if we're right?"

I turn away so he stops looking at me like... like time hasn't passed and we haven't changed. "It's different now."

"What are you scared of, Jaymes?"

"You." It's true, but I can't tell him the whole truth. I'm scared for him as well as well as scared of my feelings for him and how strong they are. But I'm really scared of Reggie.

"Bullshit. You're not scared of me. You never were. So tell me what keeps you running away from me when I can see how curious you are? And it's not just the house you're curious about. You're curious about me just like I am about you. So, what do you want to really know?"

"How many girlfriends have you had?"

"One."

"Since me, I mean."

"None."

One heartbeat.

Two.

Three heartbeats.

Four.

I whisper, "I've seen articles."

"But not the truth."

"How is that possible?"

"How many boyfriends have you had since me?"

"None."

That lady-killer smile is in full force and I can't deny the effects it has on me. "That's how it's possible. Riddle me this. How did two really fucking attractive, if I do say so myself, people not find love again in the last five years?"

"Because they never got over it the first time?"

"It's not a question, baby. That's the truth the articles don't tell you." Moving to the side of my chair, he's just about to kiss me. I'm just about to kiss him. The oven timer goes off.

Closing his eyes, he sighs. "Not sure about that timing. What do you think? Saved by the timer or unwanted interruption?"

A trick question that I could easily say in one answer, but that would encourage him in ways I shouldn't. "I just think it means the food is ready."

"Yeah," he says, chuckling. Turning away, he gets oven gloves and pulls the dish out, setting it on top of the stove. He takes the oven mitts off and tosses them on the opposite counter. "You staying?"

My stomach growls. I only had a granola bar at lunch. It's the end of the month and funds are low, so it was my lunch or Ace's that had to go and I'll never deprive my kid of something healthy to eat. It smells so good. I bite my lip, trying to resist, trying to tamp down the hunger pangs. I'm starving though. "One meal."

"AT SOME POINT, I'm going to have to leave." I close my eyes while resting my head on the arm of his couch. Maybe just a quick catnap to help this food coma I'm slipping into.

"You can stay."

A lazy smile rolls over my lips. When I open my eyes, his are on me. "I think that's your answer for everything, but it's much too complicated to make it that easy."

With a foot on the coffee table, he leans back in the chair, settling in. "You sure do hold a lot of secrets. You know, I'm a good listener, and maybe I can help in some way."

I sit back up, well aware that this night shouldn't have happened at all much less continue so blissfully. We've talked about his touring, what it's like to sing with The Resistance, whether or not it's as good as he dreamed it would be. We've talked about Kaz, and how he quickly became such a good friend to Derrick. We've even laughed together about some of the funny backstage antics. Even how it's always been hard to juggle school, being a mom, and work, but I've enjoyed the challenge. *Sometimes. Well, rarely.* But talking with Derrick? Relaxing with him? It's been *easy.* "Is this what our life would have been like together?"

"Our life... Things weren't always good, but they weren't always bad."

"I hate that I'm part of your bad."

"You're always part of the good to me."

"I stayed away because I couldn't risk seeing you and being rejected again."

And there it is. My heart hurts, my soul sad from what could have been. "For two teenagers, life sure was complicated back then."

"I also thought Reggie would be gunning for me, but I was in LA. He knows I'm still here. He's never come after me. He's weak. He likes being a big dog in a small yard. More bark than bite." Sitting forward, he lowers his foot and rests his forearms on his knees. "I want to help you."

"With what?"

"Life. You and Ace."

I stand. "No." Still shaking my head I walk around the couch and repeat myself, "No."

He beats me to the doorway of the entry before I reach my purse. "No. I'm not letting you leave like this. We're just now getting somewhere and you want to walk away?"

"You're just going to have to trust me. It's best this way. We can't get attached again."

"Attached again? I think the problem is I never detached."

"You leaving was a pretty damn big detachment." I hate that I say it, but it's out there resting between us now. I dare look up, but find only hurt in his eyes. I hate that more.

Stepping aside, he lets me by. No arguing. No stopping me. No charming quips or slick compliments. I take my purse and move toward the door, but this time, I stop. When I turn around, his back is still to me. He's standing exactly how I left him. "Derrick?"

His head drops down. "Yeah?"

"Thank you for dinner."

"You're welcome."

This is for the best, even if he's hurt now. At least he won't be hurt in the long run. At least I'll know that I had more of a choice in closing the future from any possibilities with him. Yes, I told him to go years ago, but this time... This time I'm making the wisest decision for me. For my future. For my heart.

I open the door, but then I hear, "Jaymes?"

"Yeah?"

Turning around, he says, "I think you're right."

"About?" My knees are feeling weak. *Please don't tell me you agree. Please.* I don't want this dreadful goodbye.

"I don't think we should see each other."

Why does doing the right thing hurt so much? "Probably best," I whisper, trying desperately to be strong.

"When you leave here tonight, do you think you'll detach from me? Find love this time?"

I should go, but my feet, maybe my heart, keeps me there, standing in place. "Do you think that's really possible?"

"I'm starting to think not so much."

Whispering, I say, "Me too."

Our eyes stay connected, much like our love. We seem to be caught in a cycle that neither of us cares to break. "You know," he starts, the bravado gone, his vulnerable side revealed, "maybe we can make the impossible possible?"

I allow myself the one thing I hadn't—to feel everything with him again. Adrenaline fills my veins and for the first time in forever, hope grows. Want and need take precedence, my better judgment buried under a good meal. Just one more time with him to settle the reignited fascination I have with him. We will both be able to put us in the past for good. "It's a challenge I think I'm ready to take. Just one more kiss."

"Or more."

Taking a step back into the house, I ask, "What if I kissed

you this time?"

One step closer for him, and he says, "What if I kissed you back?"

I know better, but all that *better* seems to fly out the window when I take two more steps. "Kiss me, Derrick."

The good thing about him is when it comes to making out I never had to ask him twice. One deep, love-filled impossible kiss later, and I can't hide my feelings. My body gives me away. It's just so easy to feel so much for him. In the second kiss, I realize everything we had before, still exists between us.

The third has me against the wall.

The fourth on the couch.

By the fifth kiss, I'm underneath him.

The sixth—my skirt is pushed high on my hips.

The seventh—he's situated between my legs.

His body has changed. Gone is the boy I fell in love with, replaced by the man I now lust for. *Lust.* Such a dirty word. Sinful. A sin I commit regularly just looking at him. But this time, he's here. This time, he's touching me. This time he's loving my body as if he never gave up.

The calloused fingertips remember my body, and he strikes a chord with the firm pressure at my hip. My breath is ripped away as soon as he touches me like he still knows my inner desires, the ones my body never expresses anymore. My nails press into his broad shoulders. The expanse of his muscles angle down to his carved waist and across his abdomen. I slide my hands over the hard muscles and into his hair, holding him close because I need that eighth, ninth, and tenth kiss.

Patience isn't a virtue either of us ever aspired to have. No, Derrick Masters was no angel and never took his time. He took everything he wanted from me, including my heart. Back then I never noticed it was gone until it was too late. I feel alive, my body awakened by his desire for me. *I've missed being touched. Being desired. Loved.*

I can't confuse what this is. This isn't about love, despite how careful, how caring he's handling me. It's about that other four-letter word that starts with L.

Lust.

But, God. It feels so good.

16

Derrick

"OH MY GOD."

"What?" I ask, lifting up just enough to see Jaymes's face. Her stunningly beautiful face—flushed cheeks, ruby-red lips, emerald eyes alight with fire burning on the inside.

"Make me stop."

Surprised by the request, I ask, "Why would I ever do something so stupid?" Because there is nothing I'd rather be doing than this right here. I touch her over the lace fabric between her legs.

"Because I'm not strong enough to stop, especially when you're doin—Oh, good God, that feels amazing." I slow my pace and add a little pressure. "Don't stop that—"

Dropping her head back on the cushion, she runs her hands through her hair. "It's been so long. So good. You feel too good."

"Too good," I repeat, chuckling. "Never, but you feel damn amazing, woman."

I find her lips when I move up higher on her body, and kiss her. Our tongues meet in a heated embrace, and I'm transported back to a time when we would spend our free hours in bed. Love, we always made love like it was going to be taken away one day. We didn't know it would be, but damn I loved her. Being with her now, the pounding in my chest and the erection in my jeans, I'm going to struggle to keep it cool with her.

After untucking her shirt, I slide my hands under it, feeling her silky skin beneath. "Can I take this off?"

She nods and starts on the buttons. I'm about to fucking rip the rest off, but I don't want to upset her and I have a feeling ripping her shirt might do that. I slip it down her arms and toss it to the other end of the couch. "The skirt." I don't ask this time. I stand up and pull her to her feet as we both start stripping down.

Her eyes linger over my chest. When her skirt comes down, her hands are on my biceps. "You're hot, you know that?" She laughs. "I'm sure you're told that all the time."

I don't have to guess what she really means. She's probably seen the gossip all over from the tabloids to the shows to the online blogs who have nothing better to do than stalk the band and me and print whatever shit they dig up. I bring her warm body against mine. "Hey, I like that you think you I'm hot. I think you're gorgeous."

Her hands run over my chest and so quietly, she asks, "Can I see it?"

I know what she means and I suddenly feel self-conscious, but I turn anyway. The tips of her finger trace each letter of the ink. R. E. B. E. L. Her lips press to my back and her head leans against me momentarily. Coming around, she whispers, "I've missed you."

The air between us thickens and I kiss her. "I missed you so much." We lean our heads together, taking the seconds to slow things down. She's about to take off her bra, but I cover her hands. "Let me."

This time it's not just a part of the process, it's a fucking gift I've been given. "I can't believe Jaymes Anne-Marie Grenier is standing in front of me." I say it because fuck it all. I'm not sure why I expected her to be so different, and she is in ways, but all for the better, if that is even possible. But one thing is for sure. She still owns me.

With a soft smile resting on her lips, she tries to hide her eyes from me. I'm not having it. I tilt her chin up and say, "Watch me while I watch you." I tuck one finger under the left strap and another under the right before I pull them up and around her shoulders until they're hanging down.

She's not comfortable under my heavy gaze, but I want her to experience being cherished again, being loved, being treated like the goddamn queen she is. Reaching around her, I unclasp the bra at her back and let the pink lace fall between us.

Standing there, her arms start to move, start to reach up and cover herself. "No, you're beautiful. Don't hide from me."

The pink in her cheeks darkens and she nods. I pick her up and toss her over my shoulder. "You're mine now."

Through fits of giggles, I traverse the stairs and run down the hall to my room. She lifts her head up and says, "Nice room, playboy."

The name doesn't bother me. It motivates me to prove her wrong. When I lay her down, dark hair fans over the white sheets. My heart beats faster in awe that I have this woman in my bed again.

"You're staring at me," she says, pulling the sheets up to her nose.

I gulp, the weight of this very moment hitting me. "I can't believe you're here."

"Me either. Now join me before you make me regret staying. You're making me feel self-conscious."

Lying down next to her, I pull the sheet low enough to expose the perfection of her tits. Fuck me. "Every part of you is gorgeous. I'm just the lucky bastard that gets to appreciate it." I lower just enough to kiss her neck until she relaxes again. She molds to my body, every soft part of her fits to my hard ridges. "You feel that, baby?"

Her answer comes on the tail end of a heaving breath, "What?"

"This. How perfect our bodies fit together. We were made for each other." I run the tips of my fingers under the lace that keeps us apart. I slide down to take a nipple that matches the natural pink of her lips after I've kissed her for hours into my mouth. Lightly teasing with my teeth, her back arches, and a harsh intake of air fills her lungs. Slowly, I move her underwear to the side and slip my fingers through her lower lips. "You're so wet for me, baby. Just like you always were."

"Derrick?"

Running my tongue over her breast, I then move to the other and bite just hard enough to illicit another of her sweet gasps before looking up. For someone virtually naked under me right now, she looks shy all of a sudden. "Yeah?"

"It's been a while," she starts, then wraps her arms over my shoulders. "I'm nervous."

The frenzy that was twisting inside loosens just a little and I smile. Positioning myself between her legs, I make sure I'm eye level, and run my hands through her hair. "I want you to enjoy this. If we need to slow down, we can."

"I think I need that." She turns away from me and stares out the window.

I whisper, "Okay," then lean down and kiss her cheek because I feel her slipping away from me emotionally. Something in her gaze is leaving the here and now and disappearing into her thoughts. Taking her chin, I turn her back so she's looking at me. "Hey, you want to talk about it?"

Her head is shaking before she even replies, "No. I want to just feel. I don't want to think or talk at all. Kiss me. Make love to me. Just make me forget."

"I don't want you to forget this. I won't, that's for damn sure."

"Not *this*. *This* I want. I want you. I just don't want to think about anything but this right now, *us*."

"Okay." I kiss her. My desire to be everything this beautiful creature needs overwhelms any needs of my own. Our bodies tangle and soon our legs are twisted and moving together. "You're so beautiful." Her breath responds when she can't. "I've missed you." I'm rewarded with her nails digging into my skin, urging me for more. "I want you so fucking much."

"Take me, Derrick. Like you used to."

No way will I fuck this woman. We fucked a lot but we made love more. That's what she needs—love. That's what she has—all of mine. Going lower, I leave wet kisses down her body and blow on her skin creating goosebumps across her tan, smooth skin.

Toying with her underwear between my teeth, I finally decide *fuck it* and take the fuckers off. I'm keeping them though. I tuck them under the covers where I know I'll find them later. Returning back to her pretty pussy, I inhale. Her desire is intoxicating. Like a recovering Jaymes addict, being given a hit after so long makes me feel drunk. My thoughts are lucid as I devour her, and then tease, flicking her clit with my tongue until her hips buck. I hold her down and fuck her with my tongue. The way she pulls my hair sends the blood right to my cock. Hard as Fort Knox, I want to fuck, but I remind myself that it's love we're making tonight. Like I teased her nipples earlier, I tug lightly on her clit between my teeth and insert a finger just below. Speaking of Fort Knox. She's not lying. She's tight as fuck.

Holy shit.

The hold on one finger makes it damn hard to add another. And if I can't add another or more, there's no way my dick's going to fit. "Relax, baby. I'll go slow."

She nods and takes a deep breath. I feel her viselike grip on me loosen and I kiss her lips like I'd kiss her mouth—slowly, appreciatively. This is my chance to make things right. I'll do anything for her. Anything.

I carefully add another finger and pause. Her ribs expand and her breath is heard as she adjusts to the new size. "You okay?" I ask just to make sure.

"Fine. I want you in me."

"I will be, but I want it to feel good too."

Her body relaxes even more after that and I ease all the way in, spreading my fingers and pulling out and then pushing back in. With my lips still on her clit, I suck lightly and add pressure. I can hear her breathing change from air to soft mewls as her fingers twist in my hair. She's getting close so I pick up the speed and go deeper. I'm rewarded with tremors ripping through her body as she releases so hard that my fingers are squeezed tight. "Oh my... Derrick!" she cries and I continue to fuck her into her oblivion of ecstasy until her body calms and her eyes open. Emotions race across her face, but the bliss still sits on her lips and grows when she smiles. "Now, babe. I need you now. So badly."

Babe.

Finally. Fucking finally. I haven't heard it since the day I left and I've missed it every day since. To be rewarded with her orgasm and the moniker, I'm hard as a fucking rock. I almost sink into her, but remember protection. Fuck. I reach over into my nightstand drawer, causing her to watch me—reality setting back in. I don't want to lose this feeling between us so I'm fast with the condom and repositioned between her legs in seconds. And for good measure, I kiss her because that's all I want to do with her when I'm not making love to her.

Just as our tongues touch, I push in and she moans.

Pause.

Acclimate.

Pause.

Acclimate.

I lift up. She says, "I want you. All of you. You feel so good. Don't make me beg, babe."

"You're so fucking sexy." I'm buried to the hips with adept speed. I'm tempted to pause again but she starts wiggling for me to move, so I give the woman what she wants.

So fucking tight. Two fingers don't prepare her, but she takes me like she owns me.

She does.

The thought sends me on a high I haven't had in forever. I thrust and pull, fuck, and love her, making up for every goddamn minute I wasn't with her doing exactly this right here.

It doesn't take much—it's Jaymes. I'm in heaven again. Her

body mine. Her mind mine. Her soul mine to keep forever. My orgasm hits hard and fast taking punches along the way. My body collapses, drained of years of the pent-up need and want I held in a locked box now set free again.

I love her.

I still love her so fucking much.

She was always meant to be in my arms. I roll over and settle her on top of me. She's mine. Only and always fucking mine. I wrap my arms around her and hold her tight to my chest.

"I've always been yours."

My body stills when I realize I said that out loud for her to hear. I relax back just as fast. I don't care if she knows. She should, but then I feel it. It's subtle at first; her body trembles. At first I think she's cold, so I grab the sheet and pull it over us. Even with it covering us completely, I feel it again. That's when I lean back to get a better look. "Hey?"

Not looking up, she answers on a shaky breath, "What?"

"Look at me."

"No, let me rest." She tries for lighthearted, but I can see through the quiver in her voice.

"Jaymes?" I hate how demanding I sound. When she finally looks up, I see it. Watery eyes blurring the bright green that had just been there. Sage and moss instead of brilliance and emeralds. When she blinks, tears slip down her cheeks and land on my chest. "Why are you crying?"

"I'm not," she replies, sitting up, and swiping under her eyes.

I can tell she's about to bolt, so I grab her wrist. "Talk to me."

"I need a minute. All right?" Her tone has turned, so I release her, and let her go. Rolling to my side, I watch as she disappears into the bathroom and shuts the door behind her.

Staring at the door, I debate if I should check on her not. I don't remember her having moods after we had sex. This is new territory. Maybe this is what happens when two pasts collide in the present. For me, it feels right. I feel that I've found the missing piece of my life. Of my heart. Of me. But for her? Even though my life has been going full throttle for years now, it's as though in reality I've stood still. Waiting for her. Waiting for us to be together again. But she's made a completely new life. *Literally.* Maybe I'm deluding myself that she could still love me. She didn't say *I'd loved* earlier, and I had heard that as a possible *I still love you.* Maybe we're only colliding momentarily.

Maybe this is what we are now—shifting tides under the evening sky.

No. That is not what I want.

Fuck it. I toss the sheet off and go to the bathroom. Knocking lightly, I call to her, "Jaymes, can I come in?"

"Yes."

Her response makes me glad I made the effort. If I can make her smile again, I'll do the best I fucking can. I open the door and see her small frame wrapped in my large black robe. Sitting on the edge of the whirlpool tub, her face contrasts the darkness that surrounds her from her hair to the robe to the dark night in the window behind her. I keep my tone low, the vibe feeling like I should, when I ask, "You okay?"

"Your bathroom is the same size as my bedroom."

Looking around, I smile. "Yeah. It's big."

"Who cleans it?"

"Not me."

"Thought as much."

"Can I sit?"

"Sure. It's your house." I might be wrong, but that sounded like there was a little disdain in the way she said it. Letting it slide, I don't worry about that shit. This is new. I once had to adjust too. I owe her more than just an expectation of acceptance. Grabbing the other robe from my closet, I put it on before sitting down on the tub next to her. "You have two of these robes? What are you the king of England these days?"

Chuckling, I reply, "Something like that. I actually didn't buy them, but I do dig them."

Running her fingers over the gold embroidered initials over her heart, she says, "I dig them too. This is the softest material. What is it?"

"I have no fucking clue."

"Thank God some things don't change. I'd be worried if you cared enough to know. That's never been who you are."

"Who am I, Jaymes? To you, who do you see when you look at me?"

"A dream I once had."

Nodding, I look down and pick at the soft threads. That's a lot of heavy considering what I just said in bed. "Why did you cry?"

"I have a feeling you're not going to let that one slide."

Putting my arm around her back, I hold her to my side. "Is that what you want?"

"For the time being I do."

As much as I want to know, I need to give her the space she needs or I'll lose her again. "I'll respect your wishes."

That brings a smile to her face. "Just like a great king would. Granting wishes." She stands up and moves between my legs. This time she takes my face in her hands. Runs the tip of her finger over my lips and then drags her gaze up to my eyes. "Thank you," she says and it sounds like she means more than not badgering her about the tears.

"You're welcome."

Her lips meet mine and just like we started, we end our night with a gentle kiss that feels like more than any casual caress. It feels like us. *Again.*

17

Jaymes

"WELL, THAT DIDN'T go as planned."

I roll my eyes while sitting at a stoplight. I haven't even hit the freeway and I'm already regretting what I just did. My phone rings, plucking me out of my head right before I tailspin. "Hello?"

"Hi, beautiful."

Smiling, I say, "I thought you'd be asleep by now. You wore me out. I was hoping I did the same for you."

"I've never felt better. I feel like I could conquer the world right now."

"You can. You even have the robes for it."

"Robe. Singular."

I run my hand over the plush material draped across my lap again, for like the two hundredth time since I left. "Thank you for giving me the robe."

"Promise me you'll wear it and think of me."

"I don't have to be wearing a robe to think of you. Tonight..." I pause. I want to say was perfect. Amazing. Incredible. I should be telling him that it can't happen again, but somehow, after saying the words and then going back on them physically, I feel like it would be a bitchy thing to tell him. Instead, I struggle for what I need to say over what I want to say. *I love you. I've never stopped loving you. I wish I could live in your dream.* "I'm—"

"Sorry. Yes, I know, although I was hoping you wouldn't go there again. I don't believe you're playing games with me, but I do wonder if you went with your feelings instead of your head if you'd arrive at the same outcome."

"Derrick, please."

"No, hear me out because I've been thinking about this. There is no good reason your head should be denying me either. We come together so easy, so quickly—"

"That's just sex." *I hate the lie. I hate that I just said that to the man I've loved forever.* The line goes quiet for several discomforting seconds, so I ask, "Are you still there?"

"Yeah. I'm here." His silence becomes deafening and I feel sick to my stomach. "Okay, Jaymes. Thanks for coming over."

"Derrick, wait—"

The call goes quiet and I know he's hung up. *Shoot.*

I immediately call him back, although it's probably best if he chooses not to answer. Just when I think I'm going to be sent to voicemail, he answers, "Don't do that."

"What?" I ask.

"Don't destroy something that was good. Tonight was good. Tonight was fucking great. Let's not ruin it in the aftermath. Fine, you don't want to come over again. That I can work with, but you throwing a verbal grenade into our conversations does more than end them. It destroys them." *It destroys me too.*

I'm about to apologize because I feel like shit for being mean to him, but also because he's right. When it comes to him, I'm leaving a destructive path in my trail while trying to find a better life. He won't understand why, but that's still not an excuse.

"It doesn't matter how much you push me away, and yes, I know that's what you're doing. I don't know why, but I see it. I see the conflict in your eyes when you look at me and say words you don't mean. I let you walk out my door tonight without a fight. That is the only regret I have. If you have regrets, I hope when you look back they don't damage what we did, what we mean to each other, or what we are when we're together, because that would be a damn shame."

"I liked it." *No, I loved it.*

"What was that?"

I know he heard me, but repeating myself is the least I owe him. "I liked being with you again. Everything you said is true for me too. I didn't mean to sound otherwise." I have to choose my words carefully. If he gets any whiff of bad times, he'll feel the need to swoop in and save me. I know him well enough to know that. He already offered to help Ace and me, but I can't accept anything. Not from him. His death could come from the goodness of his heart. Reggie can never find out about him being in my life again and Derrick can't know what's really going on.

I have to keep him safe. He's another person I'm responsible for. "I'm drowning in all the things I have to do, the stuff I have to worry about, the lives that depend on me." Tonight I put my son and mom at risk, and for what? An emotional and physical attraction that could end us all? "I keep saying this, but I need you to hear me. There is nothing wrong with us. I agree. It's just so easy to slip into the old us that we almost forgot that there's a new us. An us that moved on from the other. You're leaving. I'm staying. We both just keep moving."

"Let me help you, Jaym—"

"It's not charity when it comes to you and me. You know that." His voice is deep, his tone as comforting as his words. And for a brief second I consider the offer—what if he could save us? Just one friend helping another. Maybe we could be more and live that happily ever after all...

Despite the hands around my throat, I can hear Ace crying for me in the back room. I don't think Reggie does. I pray he doesn't. He will have to kill me before I let him near my son.

At two years old, Ace can sense my distress when Reggie visits. He hides like I taught him to and usually is very quiet until I retrieve him. Reggie swears he will hunt me down like a dog, kill me, and take my son under his wing if I ever betray him. I don't have to lie when it comes to Derrick. I don't know anything about him these days. It makes me wonder if I ever did. Some days I wonder if our relationship was simply a part of my imagination and less a part of my memories the more time passes between us.

I fear Reggie. I fear what he represents in my life. Control.

"We used to be friends, Jamie. Real friends. Friends who had fun together. Friends... friends... I don't think I have any friends anymore. Rebel fucking loved you. But I wanted you first."

I don't know why that popped into my head. Pieces that didn't make sense then, now do. Reggie liked me. And Derrick knew. So has my life really been controlled by his jealousy all this time? I've been thinking it was because Derrick sold Reggie out to the police over that deal. I think I've sorely underestimated Reggie's ego and how far he'll go for revenge. *Over me.*

At the end of all the days, he's still Ace's father. No matter how many times I cried for it not to be true, that fact is never going to change.

"What do you want me to do, Derrick? Take your money and what?"

"Get the fuck out of that part of the city. Buy a house—"

A house? I scoff. "You're going to give me enough to buy a house?"

"If you'd take it."

"I won't," I reply too quickly, the response automatic.

"Without thought, you answer. Without even considering the possibility, you respond so quickly." I've been on the freeway for a few minutes and the quiet hum of the road under the tires is the only sound heard until he adds, "I owe you so much. A house is one thank you I can give you."

"You owe me nothing. Don't let guilt override your better

140

judgment. You've done so well for yourself. Get out on that stage and play your heart out. Music is in your blood and it's a gift you can share. Share it, Derrick. Then meet a girl who treats you well and have a family. Forget about me. Tonight wasn't a coming together. It was the goodbye we never got."

"It was the goodbye I never wanted."

Despite the verbal punch to the gut, I continue, not letting my pain show, or at least not all of it. It would be impossible to hide. "Circles. We're still spinning in circles, but I can't ride this merry-go-round with you. You might not know it, but I'm so happy for you and your success. I smile when I hear your songs on the radio and remember the good times when I see you perform on TV. It's time for you to let go of the past that's dragging you down and move into that light that shines brightly just for you."

"And for you." *No, there is no bright light for me. Not yet.*

"No," I say, "In another life, I'll live out that dream. In this one, I just need to keep moving. Goodbye."

"Good night works better for me."

"Good night? Fine. If that's what you have to tell yourself to sleep at night. Good night." I disconnect before he can talk me out of it and before he talks me into coming back to his fancy house. I arrive at my mom's just before midnight. She's waiting up for me and hugs me when she sees me. Getting a good look at me, she says, "Why didn't you stay?"

I close the door behind me and lock it. "Why would I stay?"

"Ace fell asleep at eight. He's not woken up." Relief is found that he sleeps so well over here. She walks to the kitchen and starts the coffeepot. "You're a grown woman, Jamie, but if you want to continue acting like a lovesick teenager, I'll play along a little longer." Staring at her, I can tell she knows. She says, "Well, at least you had a good time."

My eyes go wide. She really does know. "Mom."

"Don't *Mom* me. You look a mess, but you look happy, so I'm happy." Leaning against the counter, I watch as she gets two mugs from the cabinet and pours in creamer. She knows exactly how I like my coffee, even when we drink decaf at midnight. "How was his house?"

The most incredible place I've ever seen. I think about the robe I'm going to be sleeping in later and how even something so basic like a robe can be that luxurious. "I can't even imagine living in a place like that. Even the wine glasses were crystal." She smiles and pours the hot liquid into our mugs and stirs, mixing it up. The dark brown turns to a tawny and she hands me mine. I take a sip and goodness fills me. "I can't fall in love with him."

"But you want to?"

"I don't think there's ever been a choice when it comes to me and him."

Her happiness really does shine right through her smile and the creases around her eyes that only deepen when she's happy. "You're going to be moving in here in a week. Once you're under this roof, Reggie loses power. I won't allow him to continue his tyranny over you or Ace." She comes to me and sets my mug down. Holding my hands, she says, "I will protect you and Ace always, however I can. Together, we can figure out how to stop him."

Moving to the small rickety table, I drop my head in my heads. "He will never let Ace go, even if he let me and that seems unlikely. I'm stuck. He's holding all the cards. He doesn't care about him. He never sees him. He's just waiting for Ace to hit double digits, so he can step in and play a part in his life. Him not being around now works to my advantage. If I don't make some money, we're going to be stuck here forever."

She sits next to me and rubs my arm. "For now. Only stuck for now."

Instead of coffee, I opt for bed. Since Ace sleeps in my old room, I pull out the foldout couch and make it up with my mom. She tucks me in and kisses my head. "Things will get better. I promise you." *I hope so. I hate the despair I live with daily.*

"I love you."

"I love you too."

The lights are out, the curtains closed. I lie on the couch wide awake. Thinking about everything from the night I was raped to tonight. I hate that I can even have those thoughts in the same night. For every harsh and violent thing Reggie did to me, Derrick covered me in love and kisses, soothing the damage that was left behind.

One day I'll only have a highlights reel of memories to remind me of my life, and like he is now to the rest of the world, he'll always be one of the stars in mine.

18

Derrick

THE BAND HAS been jamming all afternoon. We stopped for food and then started up on a few of the new songs. We've been playing them on the tour, but there have been a few kinks we're still working out.

"Fucking hell, Derrick!" A drumstick flies by. When I look at Dex, he says, "If you fucking miss that lead-in one more time, I'm going to play my solo and then come fucking play your part right after."

I call them kinks. They call them screw-ups. Whatever. It's all the same. "I'm fixing it. Next time I'll nail it."

The other drumstick flies across the room and slams into the padded wall of the studio. He picks his stool up and raises it above his head. Right when he's about to slam it to the floor, he stops, and turns his back to us. The stool is set down again and he walks through the room toward the door. "I'm getting a Coke."

Johnny checks his watch, a watch that probably cost more than—well, that analogy doesn't work since my first and second cars were pieces of shit. He looks up and says, "I have forty-five minutes until I need to get home, dressed, and ready to take my wife out on a date I've been promising to do during this tour break. I can't be late. Holliday threatened me already."

"Why do you even want to go out?" I ask. "Aren't you just harassed the whole time?"

"I don't need it, but every couple of months she likes to see if we can go out and do regular stuff like shop for watermelon water at Whole Foods or see a movie at Grauman's and then walk around after seeing if my feet were as big as John Wayne's. Other times it's The Pier in Santa Monica or shopping at The Grove." He sets his guitar down and grabs his phone from a chair next to him.

"Does it work?" I ask.

"No, it doesn't work. It never works, but Holliday is determined to lead as normal a life as she can and she likes to think we can do that together. It's supposed to keep us grounded."

He's the most grounded person I know in the band. He could legit walk away from all the fame, the band, and everything and be happy living out his life in Ojai Valley. I've heard the stories, read the shit published about him, but he's changed. I think that's what is happening to me.

Change.

It can't be that fucking bad if Johnny Outlaw chose to do it. He's my idol. Everything he went through, where he came from, the work he puts into the music—he's a legend for a reason. "You once talked about a crisis you went through."

He sits down and then leans back in the chair like he's going to be there a while. "I spent half my twenties burning through life, fucking angry at everything, my dad, a girl named Patty O'Toole who dumped me in high school when I got injured. I was mad at the whole world and I was hell-bent on destroying myself."

Slumping down into a chair, I pretend to tighten and tune my guitar while taking his story in. It's familiar, hitting close to home. Very close. "So what changed?"

"Me. I met a woman."

I don't fail to notice the Patty chick was called a girl, his wife a woman. What if the woman is the same as the girl? I can't say she

146

dumped me for Reggie, but the hookup still surprises me. Tumultuous. That's what she called their relationship. I've treaded carefully when it comes to the topic. My ego took more than a wallop over that bombshell, but I can tell it's a sensitive subject for her. She has a kid she has to put first.

Johnny adds, "I met the right woman at the right time. I was over groupies and drugs. I wanted a clear mind and clear conscience. The only way to get where I needed to be was to take a step back. I wanted it to be about the music, the art, the fans, the rhyme, the rhythm. I was lonely though. It's strange how you can be surrounded by twenty thousand people, but at night you still walk into an empty hotel room and nothing. Silence. It plays tricks on you." He sits forward and rests his arms on his legs. "I was sitting at a bar in Vegas pretending to be someone I wasn't. That's when I met her. She knew exactly who she was and what she wanted."

"What was that?"

Shrugging, he cocks a smile. "That night? A hotel security manager, but she got a rock star instead. It was a win-win situation for both of us." He reaches over and cracks the lid off of a bottle of water and drinks. "You guys," he says, looking between Kaz and me, "find who you want to be and fight for it. Everyone outside this room is looking to tear you down or replace you."

Kaz says, "Dex and Tommy are outside this room."

Johnny chuckles. "Like I said... Anyway." After making his joke, he stands and blows out a big breath. "We've been there or gone through it, so if you are or are going to, we're here. The five of us, no matter where we are in the world or in our lives, we've got your back." Before he walks out the door, he says, "Go after the woman, Derrick. You'll find out fast as fuck if she's into you or not. If she is, you're gonna score for the romance. If she's not, eh, you'll get your ass kicked to the curb, but we leave tomorrow anyway. There's always a groupie waiting in every city ready to heal your broken heart." *They're not there for my heart.*

Before Johnny leaves, Kaz asks, "The burning question is, are your feet bigger or smaller than John Wayne's?"

"Bigger, but I wouldn't say otherwise." He laughs and signals to Tommy in the other room with the producer.

Tommy gets up and makes his way in. Taking Johnny's guitar and picking up Dex's drumsticks, he looks at me, and says, "Buy ya a beer?"

"You got it. Kaz, you coming?"

"Yeah, but only for one."

KAZ AND TOMMY are drunk.

Man, Kaz's tolerance has gone downhill since we moved into our own places. He says he has Russian mafia ties if I ever need something taken care of. I'm not in a good mental state because I actually start considering this option in regard to Reggie. Tommy's been whining about love for forty-five minutes and Kaz has his arm wrapped around him agreeing wholeheartedly about Tommy getting older and needing to settle down. Have some kids.

The last part drags me back into their inebriated bromance of self-help. That's when it dawns on me. I whack Kaz in the chest. Oops. I didn't mean to knock him off the stool. Reaching down, I give him a solid hand and pull his ass up. "What the fuck was that for?" he slurs.

"Accident. Sorry." It was all him, but I'll take the blame. His balance is as drunk as he is. "You told Tommy he should have kids."

He stares at me blankly. So I say, "That he should settle down and have kids."

Still nothing. "Is that what you want?"

"Of course," he says, shrugging like this is common knowledge.

"What do you mean *of course?*"

"Don't you? Isn't that what living the dream really means?"

"No," I say, shaking my head. "Living the dream means we are literally living out our dreams. Playing to sold-out shows, millions of fans, traveling the world, making money doing what we love."

"Sure, there's that answer." I can practically see the beer slosh in his eyes when he rolls them. "But like Outlaw said, what do we come home to? That's up to us. When the tours stop and the records aren't gold anymore, what do we have? I'll tell you what we have. A warm bed with a hot woman. Family. Friends. People who love you because of who you are on the inside, not because we're famous or slept with a bevy of princesses. No. We'll have a home where they leave the light on for you."

"Dude, I think you're confusing your argument with a motel commercial."

"Whatever. What were we talking about?"

"Lara and how you need to get home to her."

"Yup. I do. I'll see you chaps tomorrow." He pats my back and grabs Tommy by the shirt. "Come on, Tommy. Your ass can sleep at mine."

I look down at the beer in front of me. I don't think I even finished a pint.

The guys are right. This is bullshit. The emotions and Jaymes are messing with my head. I'm a fucking rock star. I can have any girl I want.

While I wait for valet to pull my car around like the fucking LA pussy I've become, I drop the act. Being a rock star is awesome, better than any dream I ever had. But I don't want just any girl. Nope. Now that I've spent time with Jaymes again, she's the only woman I want.

I get in my car and use my not-so-secret weapon. The phone rings and before she can speak, I say, "Mom, I need a favor."

THE LIGHTS ARE still on inside, but it's almost ten at night, so I knock lightly. The creak of the floor signals someone is looking through the peephole. One lock and then another. The door opens and Jaymes is there looking like an angel in her nightgown. It's not sexy, but it's cotton and a little see-through. She looks younger, almost like I remember, with her hair down and loose around her shoulders. The deep color a stark contrast to the nightgown. I'm starting to think she can't look anything but stunning every time I see her.

"Hi." She gazes up at me, and asks, "What are you doing here?"

"I wanted to see you before I left."

"You leave tomorrow?"

"Yeah."

A pink tongue dips out and wets her bottom lip before it's dragged under her top teeth. The war is waging. Her nightgown blowing in the gentle breeze signals her surrender. "I'm glad you came by." The door is opened and I walk on in.

She closes the curtains, but then peeks out before tugging hard in the middle for privacy. When she turns around, she asks, "Would you like something to drink?"

"Water would be great."

That makes her smile for some reason. I follow her into the kitchen and watch as she gets the glass and fills it with ice and then water from a container in the fridge. "Thanks."

Leaning against the other counter, her arms are crossed, but not hiding her chest or body from me. More just waiting to hear why I'm there. "So what really brings you by this late?"

"The other night. It was great. I wanted you to know how much it meant to me that you came over."

"It's sex, Derrick. You get it all the time," she says, walking back to the living room.

"It wasn't just sex for me. It was more. I think it was for you too, but you're just stubborn enough to not give in when you see a good thing."

Sitting down on the opposite end of the couch that I do, she scoffs. "You think I want to deny myself pleasure? Why would I do that?"

"I haven't figured that out yet, but I can tell how determined you are to deny yourself having me."

"Oh God." She stands. "There it is. Rebel and his infamous ego return. I'm so glad you felt the need to stop by and share this, but if you'll excuse me, I have an early start tomorrow."

I stand too. "That's not what I meant."

"What did you mean then?"

"You keep acting like there's nothing between us. There is. I know I can't be the only one to feel it."

Her sighs feel put on, like a show just for me, not something she truly feels when she looks into my eyes. It's an act to resist what I can tell deep down she doesn't want to. "If you're feeling it, how long did you wait once you were gone last time to be with someone else?"

"Don't ask me that."

"That bad, huh?" Her laugh is sardonic, and then she rolls her eyes, causing my blood to start to boil.

Fuck that. I'm not letting her sidetrack this conversation. "What you're doing is a distraction of what's happening between us and you know it."

"I'm just a distraction, a temporary one at that." There's that sigh again.

"You're not a distraction, you're the main attraction. C'mon, baby, say it."

I move to her end of the couch and sit down. Taking her by the hips I coax her to sit on my lap. When she does, it feels like a win. When she wraps her arm around my neck, it feels like a victory of epic proportions. But when she relaxes into me and says, "I feel it," I feel like a fucking rock star.

19

Jaymes

"WHAT ARE YOU doing to me?" I ask as if Derrick will actually answer with complete honesty.

"I decided since I can't get you to fall madly in love with me, I'll go for wearing you down."

That's pretty darn honest. Laughing, I lean my head against his. "It's working."

His smile grows. He may not be looking right at me, but I can see the lift in his cheeks. "Which is working?"

While damning my heart to hell for being so honest with him, I whisper, "Both."

Strong, caring arms tighten around me and I close my eyes. The smell of his hair is clean, soapy, but his neck has a subtle hint of sweat. I'm reminded how he used to smell and how protected I felt being with him. My body finds peace while inhaling the masculinity of everything about him again. He was always so alpha without knowing how much it turned me on.

He's grown patience over the years, something that's come with age, I suppose. Like me, there are things that have changed and some that remain. For better, and I'm sure in some ways, for worse. I'm not in a position to judge. I just know that I like the way he smells. "Why did you really come over?"

Sliding me to the side, my ass hits the couch cushion, but my upper body is left balancing in his arms. Madly in love—him or me or both? I'm starting to feel it strongly. He says, "I want you to come see me on tour. I've left two tickets at the Virgin Airlines counter. Open ended. For any city. First class. One in your name and one in Ace's."

The surprises never seem to cease with him, my lack of any response other than shock is my initial reaction. He lifts my jaw and kisses my lips lightly. "It will be fun. You can stay as long as you want or a night or two. Whatever works best for your life. A month is too damn long to go without seeing you."

"We just went years."

"Exactly. I'm not losing any more time with you."

There's nothing to argue. There's just this amazing man holding me like I'm the most precious thing he's ever held in his hands.

I kiss him.

I kiss him.

I kiss him.

And for the next few minutes, I forget about my daily struggles and making ends meet. I forget about all the bad and just feel the good. Running my hand down his cheek, I caress it, and lean my forehead against his. "It feels so good to be with you again."

"I've missed you. I've missed this, and your lips. Come see me on tour."

"I don't kn—"

Leaning back, and looking me in the eyes, he says, "I know you will have a million good reasons to say no or to not come. I respect every last one of them. Just please, when I leave here, I want you to remember this—*us*—and how we're a good reason too." He kisses me, then adds, "The other night wasn't a one-off kind of night. We're just getting started, baby. We were always meant to have this second chance. You don't have to answer tonight. You can look at your schedule and see if there's a free weekend or whenever, but consider us when deciding. If you decide against the trip or us, I won't come back and pressure you. I'll want to, but I won't."

"That's disappointing."

That brings a smile, even if it lacks true happiness, back to his handsome face. "Tell me about it." The pile of blankets and pillow on the chair catches his eyes. "Are you sleeping out here on the couch?"

"Yes. I sold our stuff and threw most of the rest away. We really didn't have much worth keeping and I knew we'd only have my old bedroom to store it in. Ace sleeps in there."

"Why did you move home?"

"To save money. You've come back into my life in the middle of so much upheaval. I'm sure it's hard for you to understand."

"No, what I don't understand is why you won't let me help you."

"Because that would only be a temporary fix. I can't just be given a house and then expected to take it at face value. There's always more to it."

"What if there's not?"

"Derrick, don't kid yourself. How can I say no to a date if you buy me a house? Or what if we do date and you bought me a house and then we break up. It leaves me helpless and in the same situation I'm already in. I have to do this on my own."

The palms of his hands scrub his eyes as he sighs. When he looks back at me, he doesn't rush his words. They come with that patience and empathy he's developed. "Maybe we're not the same people anymore, though I hate that you think I would ever ask for something I gave you as a gift back."

"It's not that I think you would. It just complicates things."

"I don't want to be another burden in your life, Jaymes. I care about you. I want to make things better. If I'm not, then just tell me and I'll go."

"You don't listen very well." I tap his nose once. "When I'm with you, I want to be with you. That's easy for me to see and feel. You feel good. I see the possibility of an *us* again. But when we're apart, I

155

see my reality. I'm not sure I want to drag you back down into it again." *Back here to this world.*

"We'll take it slow."

"How about we start now?" I grab the remote and flick on a home improvements show. "Want to watch some TV with me?"

"Absolutely."

My smile goes wide and goofy and my bones almost feel soft like my heart for this man. We rearrange so I'm snuggled against him. His arm comes around my shoulders and the smile I don't bother hiding anymore brings one to his face. "Please tell me it's me and not the DIY show that's making you smile like a loon."

Rubbing his leg, I reply, "It's you. All you."

"Good. I like that."

"I like this. Thank you."

He kisses the top of my head and we watch the show and another after this one.

SNIFFLING, I WIPE my tears from my cheeks. His arm is around me, but I find no comfort. Something is off. Reggie is tense, his tone fake. I take a deep breath and decide I'd rather be alone. "I'm sorry I called you. I thought—"

"It's okay, Jamie. I'm glad you did. He's been my best friend since I was ten. I can't believe he left like this. Your mom home?"

"No, she's still at work." His hand is on my leg and I cover it like I'm killing a bug. My brows knit in confusion. "What are you doing?"

"He's gone. Rebel left you."

My heart screams for relief from the sting of his words, but I know I won't get any because he's right. Derrick left me. I might have told him to go, but he still left.

"Guess you didn't mean as much to him as you thought."

"You're cruel." His hand is still on my leg, so I try to scoot down the couch away from him, but his arm around me tightens, his fingers digging into my upper arm. His other holds my wrist. "I think you should go."

"Did you know that Rebel stole from me?"

Reggie's pupils are wide with evil darkness centering in them. My heart starts pounding in my chest, my breathing becoming uneven as panic sets in. He knows we're alone. He knows my mom won't be home anytime soon. Oh fuck. In one swift move I pull away and say, "You should go now, I remembered my mom will be home early—"

I don't get the chance to finish my sentence. A hand is slapped over my mouth and I'm shoved back into the couch, my head hitting the threadbare arm. I'm dazed for a moment, spots clouding my vision. His rough hands are under my skirt when I come to. Scrambling to push him off, I yell, "Get off me, Reggie. What are you doing?"

But my questions, my plea fall on deaf ears. His focus is on one thing. "He owes me. Rebel owes me."

I land on my feet and run to the other side of the room. "Go! I mean it. I don't know what has gotten into you, but you need to go. Now."

"What has gotten into me?" The grin he tries for turns into a snarl as he stands. The only thing dividing us is a coffee table. "Your fucking boyfriend stole from me. Didn't you know? That's why he skipped town. Fucking loser. He used to be great. He was in line to lead this fucking gang, until he met you. You made him weak."

"I'm not going to ask you again. Leave, Reggie."

"I thought we were friends, Jamie. I thought you cared about me." His tone is mocking. "Isn't that what friends do? Take care of one another? Let me take care of you. You can be my main bitch."

My head is shaking, my thoughts running around the kitchen trying to remember if I put the knife in the sink after I used it earlier or if it's still on the counter. Shit. "No. Derrick's not gone for *good. You know he'll be back. Then what will he do to you if you touch me again? He'll kill you."*

His laughter rings out, echoing through the pit in my stomach. That's when I know. There is no out. He's not going to leave. He's come here to collect. I run for my bedroom. I can be out the window in seconds, a skill I mastered when I would meet Derrick late at night. The door, I make it to the door before I'm tackled to the hard floor, his weight crushing my soul as much as my body.

My tears come, but I fight.

I hit.

I kick.

I try to escape. There is none.

I'm hit.

I'm kicked.

My arms are held to the side, pain shooting through my veins. My underwear is ripped. My cries don't matter. Reggie is muttering how I am his payment for Rebel fucking him over.

Collateral damage.

"Jaymes, wake up."

My body shakes, my stomach turning. I scream, but no sound comes out. My heart lands in my throat when I'm grabbed. Like a bolt, I'm out of Reggie's arms and land on the floor. My eyes flying open. I scatter across heading for the kitchen. Knife. I must get the knife. I won't make the same mistake twice.

"Jaymes!"

I stop, knowing that voice. It's the voice of the one I love and trust. It's security wrapped in a velvet tone. *Derrick.* Looking back over my shoulder, he's standing, a look of horror on his face, matching the humiliation inside me thicker than blood. I turn back and look down at the floor and my whitened knuckles as I piece together the full picture. Crawling. I am crawling. I sit up and try to steady my thundering heart. My back is too him. I can't bear to see that look on his face again.

"Are you okay?" he asks. I hear the caution in his question. I've revealed myself in ways I never wanted, especially not to him. He tries again, "Please tell me you're all right."

Staring into the kitchen, I suddenly remember the knife was on the counter that night. I should have gone for the knife, not my bedroom. It's a choice that changed everything, that changed me forever. "I'm not all right."

I'm not scared. Not with Derrick. Mortified that I let it happen, but not scared of him now. Footfalls trail up to my back and he sits down in front of me, his back against the doorway to the kitchen. Despite my revelation, the expression of horror is gone, wiped clean and replaced not by sympathy, but empathy.

My mom's door opens and she looks out. "Jamie, are you okay? I heard you yell."

I put on the brave face I wear so often I have it down to a science and reply, "I'm okay. Derrick's here."

"Oh. Hi, Derrick. Well, if you need anything, honey, just call."

"I don't. Go to sleep. I'm fine. You have an early morning."

"Okay. Good night."

"Night," Derrick replies.

We wait, listening for the door to close. When it does, he says, "That was one hell of a nightmare you had there. Want to talk about it?" *Being completely honest with myself, my answer is no. I don't want to talk about it. I don't want to dredge up that pain again.* But now I know Derrick wants more from me, possibly a future, I don't think it's right to hold back. I hope he will still want me when I'm done.

"I guess it's time."

20

Derrick

THERE ARE ALWAYS two options.

Two roads.

Two paths.

Right and wrong.

Left and right.

Yin and yang.

Good and evil.

Choices.

Decisions.

Outcomes.

So much goes into deciding where this life leads. Some fate. Some destiny. Some great. Some bad. But we have to learn from those bad decisions, learn from our mistakes and hope we don't make them again.

Devastation should never exist in Jaymes Grenier's world, but it does. I control my expressions—my eyes, my mouth, my breathing, my whole body—except for my hands. As I stare into her mossy-green eyes, watch her tears fall to the floor, I can't control my hands. Tightening. Loosening. Fisting to the point of my bones aching.

"Blink, Derrick."

I blink.

She says, "Breathe."

I fill my lungs and then blow slowly out.

"Say something. Please. You're scaring me."

I blink and breathe, then ask, "I'm scaring you?"

Sucking in a jagged breath, she whips it out in a flurry of words. "I didn't mean it like that. You don't scare me. Not like that. I meant I was worried. By your silence. By your hands. I can see you're upset."

"Upset? Yes, Jaymes. I'm upset because you're upset."

Inching closer to me, she says, "If I tell you this, I need you to make me a promise."

"I can't do that and you're going to tell me anyway."

She stands, and I get up off the floor. Hugging me, she tilts her head down against my chest. When I bring my arms around her, she whispers, "You need to keep your voice down. Ace is sleeping and I don't want to worry my mom." She looks up, resting her chin on me. "Can you do that for me?"

For you? Anything for you. "Okay."

She leads me back to the couch and we sit down. I don't know if I'm blinking or breathing or what I'm doing. I know I'm imagining the worst. Her tears have dried and I failed to be the one to dry them. I failed. I failed her.

"I got away. I thought I could make it to my bedroom." She stops to reflect or to remember. "I made the wrong choice. I should have gone for the knife in the kitchen, but he was high, so I thought maybe he would be slow."

The beat of my heart rumbles through my ears.

What the fuck?

What the fuck?

What the fuck?

She continues, her eyes focused on me, her voice not trembling or upset, but matter-of-fact. No emotion, just retelling the facts of the night. I touch her arm, which seems to shake her into the present. "Hey," I say, "you only have to tell me if you want to. If you can't, I'll understand."

"I've carried this a long time. Too long. I'm tired. I'm tired of the power it has over me. I'm tired of the power *he* has over me."

"Jaymes, you need to tell me what happened."

"He was fast. He caught me before I could get the door closed. Tackled me to the floor and pinned me." She peeks over at me with shame filling her eyes. "I fought, Derrick. I promise you. I fought."

What the fuck is happening? What the fuck happened to my girl? A sickening fills me, bile rising until the taste of metal replaces it. "Are you telling me he raped you?"

I. Will. Fucking. Kill. Him.

"Keep your voice low. Please calm—"

"I never promised to stay calm," I whisper-fucking-yell. I'm on my feet and pacing, but I want to punch the fucking wall or better yet, Reggie.

"Please don't wake Ace. He has nightmares sometimes. Tonight he's sleeping. He needs it."

In my anger, I find clarity.

Ace.

My eyes flash to hers. The air stalls around us, the truth suffocating. When she looks down, I know. "Don't say it, Derrick." It's not a threat, but it's a warning.

We're in uncharted territory. I don't say a word. I can't for fear my voice will crack under the heartbreak.

She was violated, violated by someone she should have never trusted. Violated because I left. Fuck.

She didn't betray me by sleeping with him. I should have known better the minute I heard the news. "I should have come back for you. I should have called. I should hav—"

"You wouldn't be here if you had, so despite all I've been through, you're safe."

"I could have handled him."

163

"He doesn't play with toy guns, Derrick. He's shot people. He just hasn't been caught. Fortunately, they lived, but he's made everyone well aware that he's got a bullet with your name on it." When she continues, she says, "I know you're blaming yourself, but don't. We all played a part, made decisions—good or bad—that got us here today."

Four steps divide us, but not for long. I walk right over and sit next to her, pull her against me, and hold her. "We can change the future, Jaymes. Leave your job. Let me help you."

"No. You're not giving me your money or buying me a house. I'm still considering the plane tickets." She looks up and a small smile is there.

"Get away from this place for just one weekend."

"What about us?"

"Give me one weekend. That's all I ask."

"You make it very tempting."

"Just say yes. Come away with me. You and Ace."

Leaning back, she looks tired. Her eyes are on mine but she's drained emotionally, the weight of this conversation dragging her under. She lifts her legs and sets them across my lap. Gravitating to her, I rub up and down her soft skin a few times before lifting her right up and settling next to her with her back to my chest. Her hands are cold when she covers mine, but her words are warm. "We'll come see you."

I kiss the back of her head. "I'm happy about that, but I need you to know that I'm sorry for leaving like I did. I'm more sorry for what happened. If I would have stayed—"

Spinning around in my arms, her finger covers my mouth. "He would have killed you. And how would I have gone on after that?"

She's letting me off the hook, but I know what I did was wrong, even if what I did to him was right. My eyes home in on hers. "Just like you did. You're the strongest person I know."

"Your mother is a strong woman."

"So is yours, but you, you're special. Ace is so lucky to have you."

A gentle smile sweeps across her lips. "I'm lucky to have him.

He's the best result one could ever get from what I went through."
The tips of her fingers run along my jaw. "Promise me you'll never
see him again."

I don't have to ask whom. I know who she's talking about and I
can't make that promise. "It's not a promise I can keep. Not now."

Sitting up, she angles toward me. "Derrick, don't go starting
trouble on my behalf. I've got enough as it is. Things are mostly
peaceful. We rarely see him."

"Tumultuous. That's how you described your relationship with
him. Has he ever touched you again?" The memories scroll through
her thoughts. I see the hesitation in her eyes. "You don't have to
answer. Your silence says enough."

"I don't want you involved."

"Too late."

"Because I told you?"

"No, because you didn't. You've been fighting that fucker for five
years. You don't have to fight him alone. How does he even have any
visitation much less custody rights? He's a fucking gang leader. A
known criminal."

"I'm tired. I stayed up until three a.m. last night working
on a paper due tomorrow. Please. Can we please not do this
tonight?"

She's tough. Damn tougher than I am. I'm all about the physical,
but she's got inner strength. I relent and let it go for tonight. For
her. As for Reggie Rogers, he's about to have his world flipped
upside down. Again.

LEAVING JAYMES LAST night was pure bullshit. I don't think I slept at
all after she sent me home. It's now catching up with me on the
plane. I'm out before we even take off.

I'm awoken by Tommy calling us sorry fucks for partying so

hard the night before a tour. Kaz laughs. "I think you might be responsible for that."

Tommy joins in, laughing. "I can't help that the girls love me."

I've missed a part of this conversation, but don't care to catch up. Looking at the time, it's late enough for me to text Jaymes. ***Hey, we left, but if you have a chance, maybe you can call me sometime.***

Okay, I'm officially a pussy because when she texts me back right away, I'm rereading every word over and over and smiling from ear to ear. ***I'll call you on my break.***

She'll call me on her break. Yes!

I fist-pump, but when I look up, Kaz is shaking his head and laughing to himself. "I'm not going to say a word."

"Good."

"Except I told you so."

"Go ahead."

"I already did. My work here is done."

Leaning forward, I say, "Hey."

He looks up from his phone. "What?"

"If I tell you some shit, will you keep it between us?"

Kaz looks half-offended that I even preface my question like that. The other half has to be curious. His hand comes out and we shake. "You know you can tell me anything. We're friends. You're my best friend. You've always had my back. I'll always have yours."

"Thanks." Scanning the plane, I spot Tommy with his eyes closed and his earbuds in. Dex is asleep on the couch. Johnny is in the bedroom. When I feel it's sufficiently safe to open up, I say, "I used to be in a gang."

Staring at me, he asks, "Like a band gang?"

Annoyed, I lean back in my chair. "What the fuck is a band gang?"

He shrugs and chuckles. "I have no idea. What do you mean?"

"Drugs and guns and shit like that."

"You sold drugs?"

"No, but the others did." My defenses go up. They shouldn't, but

I feel judged. "Look, we can't all be fucking princes."

"Don't be an asshole. I was trying to understand. You've never mentioned this before." I look out the window. We're stuck in the clouds, lost in the gray. "Why are you telling me this?" he asks. "And why now?"

"I saw Jaymes last night and found out some stuff that drudged up old feelings."

"Gang feelings?"

"Fuck you," I say, laughing. "Yes, my delicate gang feelings."

He drinks his Gatorade as soon as it's served. When the flight attendant returns to the front of the plane, he says, "Whatever nest has been disturbed, you better hope the snakes stay put. Don't get the band mixed up in some old mess."

"That's what I'm trying to keep in mind."

"Don't keep it in mind, man. Stay focused. The band is all that matters."

"Bullshit. Lara matters to you. Jaymes matters to me. The band matters."

He nods, and I continue, "But what would you do if Lara was being threatened?"

"You know what Lara and I have been through, so I've been there. How is Jaymes being threatened?"

"I can't say."

"What can you say?"

"Not much. I just need to get her out of the situation she's in."

"And what does she say?"

"She doesn't want my charity."

"One thing I learned with Lara was the more patience I showed, the more she opened up. Trust is huge. You need it or you're sunk before you even have a chance." He starts putting his headphones on, but stops and says, "Really, I just fought for her and she was worth it."

So is Jaymes. I didn't fight for her before, but now I'll do whatever I have to do for her and Ace. Despite what happened to her, that kid is like his mother—a fighter, and a hugger. He hugged me twice the first day I met him. We were instant buds. I'm glad they have each other. I still don't know how she does everything she does with such grace, not asking for a thing. She's got her life together way more than me. I've just been luckier in a few ways.

When we're landing, Kaz looks around like we're part of some secret agent shit, then says, "So the tattoo... Rebel—"

"It was an initiation, hazing kind of thing."

"And here I thought you were just that badass."

"It was the tattoo or lose the second finger on my left hand." I unsnap my seatbelt and stand. "There was no fucking way I was going to lose that finger."

"You wouldn't have been able to play guitar."

"Oh I'd figure out a way to play. It's my ring finger though. Once I'm married, that shit is getting shown off."

His eyes go wide. "The burn out is getting to you, man. You realize you're talking about long-term commitment, right? You definitely need a few days off."

Laughing, I reply, "Just had the best break of my life. I'm good." Better than I've been in ages. As soon as I'm in the SUV heading to the hotel in Sacramento, I get the text I've been waiting for.

I can't wait to see you again.

If I thought I was lucky before, finding fame and fortune, I know I'm the damn luckiest guy in the world now.

21

Derrick

THE LIGHTS ARE out.

Dex is center stage.

His solo starts and the spotlight hits him.

Johnny looks back at Kaz and me while we wait on the stairs that lead to the stage. It feels like we've done this a million times, but the excitement and nerves never go away. It always feels like the first time. "Break a leg."

"Break a leg," we repeat.

The arena goes dark and we head up, following the small lights hidden behind the equipment that lead to our places. I swing the strap over my head and tap the pedal twice. My fingers find their position on the fretboard of my guitar and we wait again. Live shows are about more than the music. It's about the performance, the entertainment, the showmanship.

A single spotlight hits Johnny, who is standing at the front of the stage behind his microphone. He sings without music or instruments to back him up. The crowd falls silent, every last fan taking in the song and his haunting voice. Even the band stands there in awe. He pulls emotion from deep within in every note. Watching a legend live is awe-inspiring. Watching him perform at this level of talent night after night is a privilege.

Four.

Three.

Two.

One.

I kick into the chorus, singing back up as I play my guitar. Glancing over, Kaz is leaning back, his bass guitar settled over his hips as he joins in. The audience goes wild and the show begins.

Three songs in, I'm already starting to sweat. I change guitars and plug in before tapping the pedal. Tommy stands just off stage with his arms crossed, his eyes analyzing each of us. Kaz moves to my side and we kick into the riff Dex has been bitching about, and nail it.

Exhilarating.

The thrill of it hits me and I look out at the audience. It's dark, but if I squint, I can see fans forever. *How is this my life?* Kaz and I sing before popping back and challenging each other. It's a long-standing argument—bass or rhythm guitar. He knows I win when I'm on lead.

Best damn job in the world.

After the twelfth song, Johnny tells the audience we're having technical difficulty with three speakers down front and we'll be back for the encore when they're fixed. We leave the stage and head for the dressing room. Tommy calls out, "Twenty-minutes."

The guys filter around the large room—Johnny sits on the counter, the Hollywood lights surrounding him as he calls his woman. Dex is smiling as he FaceTimes with Rochelle. Tommy is dragging Kaz to the table full of posters and paraphernalia. Kaz sits with a sharpie in hand and starts autographing everything from hats to posters.

I probably shouldn't bother her, but I do it anyway. Jaymes answers after one ring, and whispers, "Hey, I'm in class right now. Can I call you later?"

"Yeah, call me when you can."

I'm about to hang up, but she adds, "How's the show?"

"Issues with speakers, but we'll be going back out soon for the encore."

There's a pause before she says, "I haven't expressed this enough, but I want you to know that I'm so proud of you."

The emotion heard in her words catches me off-guard, the softness of her tone. I think she's caught a little off-guard too. "Thanks. Hey Jaymes?"

"Yeah?"

"I'm proud of you, too."

"Thanks, Dare. I've gotta go. I'll call you later."

Smiling from hearing the nickname she used to call me sometimes, I feel like there's a chance for this to happen—me and her—again. "Bye."

Last night we broke through some tall-as-the-sky barriers I don't think she believed we could. With the truth out there, she trusts me. Like Kaz said, that's the basis. Now we can move forward together. I'm high as that sky now and I haven't even had a sip of alcohol.

We kill the encore, the energy rising and the crowd whipped into a frenzy. Then the darkness comes. The arena goes black and we run down the stairs. I grab my phone as soon as we enter the dressing room. *One missed call.*

With the guys hollering about the awesome show, I call Jaymes back and plug one ear. When I can't even hear the ringing, I walk into the bathroom and lock the door. Sitting on the back of the toilet with my Doc Martens propped on the seat, I smile when she answers, "Hello?"

"Hi."

"Hi. Is the concert over?"

"No. I just thought I'd call you from stage."

"No you aren't," she replies in a panic.

Laughing, I shake my head. "No, I'm not. We just finished. We'll be leaving shortly. I need to sign some stuff and then we'll go back to the hotel."

"Not out?"

"I'm not sure. I don't think so. We were up late last night. I'm gonna crash."

"Sorry about everything last night. I know you didn't need all that dumped on your lap like that."

"Don't. Don't apologize. I'm glad you trusted me enough to tell me. You know, I've been thinking about it. I know we said we'll take it slow, but does that feel as wrong to you as it does to me?"

"Last night was a lot." Her voice lowers. "My mom is the only other one who knows because she's the one who found me... after." My smile is gone thinking about what happened to her as she takes a moment to gather herself before adding, "I don't want to talk about this on the phone. I'm sorry. Maybe when we see each other."

"It's okay. You set the pace and I'll follow your lead."

Happiness bubbles up when she says, "I was looking at your tour dates."

"Oh yeah?"

Banging on the door makes me jump. Tommy yells, "I need the toilet, Derrick. Get out."

Jaymes laughs. "You're talking to me in the bathroom?"

"I'm not using it. I just wanted privacy."

"Well, I love that, but I think your friend might not appreciate it as much. You can call me later if you want."

This. This is what I've missed. A connection to someone who knows me well enough to not have to worry about small talk. "I do want. I'll call you from the hotel."

"I look forward to it. Talk later."

"Later."

I push the door open and push Tommy on the chest. "Fuck, there's got to be another toilet around, dude."

"Eh, you're just gabbing like a girl in there anyway."

Flipping him off, I grab a bottle of soda and a Twix. "Is the car here?"

Kaz says, "Just got here. C'mon."

"Hey, how real are those connections?"

"What connections?"

Being drunk the other night, he probably doesn't even remember the conversation. I wouldn't involve him anyway, but it's good to know it's an option.

I FLOP ON the bed, call Jaymes, and rest my arm over my eyes. When she answers, she sounds like she was sleeping. "Did I wake you?"

"It's okay. It's good to hear your voice."

"I like this change."

"What change would that be?"

Rolling over to my stomach, I whisper, "The one where you talk to me like we're friends, like there's been no time or distance separating us."

"I like it too. I know I've given you a hard time and been resistant to a lot of your kindness—"

"Don't apologize again. We could spend years searching for forgiveness for everything that's happened. Let's just skip to the present and start fresh."

"When did you become the reasonable one between us?"

"Ha. Yeah, go figure. Anyway, how was your day?"

Her breathing is deep and relaxed. "Busy. Tomorrow might be worse, so if I don't answer, you'll know why."

"Earlier, you said you were looking at tour dates. Want to elaborate?"

"A girl can dream."

"It's a dream we share."

"I need to be upfront with you on this, Dare. I don't know that I can make this happen. I have so many balls in the air that I'm afraid I'll drop them and instead of bouncing, they'll break."

I'm close to begging. I need more time with her. Selfishly, I need to explore these feelings between us. Are they lingering from the past or developing in the present? Can it be as easy as seeing her again that has calmed the inner turmoil I've had? Is all of this leading to the most obvious conclusion—it's her I've been missing all along? If I were to answer today... "Please come."

"No guarantees. Yet. I thought I would check in with you first and find out what you were thinking. We don't want to be a burden."

"You guys could never be."

She begins to whisper, "This is so fast."

And yet not fast enough.

"But—"

My breath stops waiting for her to finish this sentence. "But?"

"I want to see you again too."

Yes!

Score!

Goal!

Touchdown!

This victory feels better than when we won a Grammy.

"Is there a date you prefer? I won't know until last minute due to work and school, but I can start checking into it."

Now. I wish you were here with me now. "The soonest."

"Las Vegas next weekend? That's five days."

"Four shows."

"I'm not sure that Vegas is a place for Ace."

"It can be what we make it. If you're serious, I'll get us the best suite in the city with two bedrooms. Ace can have his own and we can have another." Too much? Too fast? "Unless you want your own private room. I can book that for you."

"No, a suite for all of us sounds amazing. Thank you."

"Thanks for coming."

"Five days. I'll get back with you, but I'm excited."

"Me too. I look forward to seeing you both."

"I should go, but thanks for always thinking of Ace."

That cute kid is hers. It doesn't matter that his dad is a fuck-up of epic proportions. Ace deserves the best chance at a future outside that neighborhood. If I can play a part in that, I will. "He's important to you, so he's important me, Jaymes."

"Thanks."

"No thanks needed. Good night."

"Good night."

Reaching over, I push the button closing the curtains and turning off the lights. Lying there, I remember so much about us when we thought we owned the world...

A rare night in LA—the stars shine above. Resting back on a pile of pillows in the bed of my truck, I stare up. Miles of universe make me feel small. Jaymes is strumming the guitar I gave her, singing softly along with the radio.

Glancing over at her, I say, "You're better."

"You only say that so you can get laid."

I laugh. "Put the guitar down."

With an all-knowing smile on her face, she passes it through the open window of the cab, setting it safely on the seat. I immediately grab her and swing her under me until I'm leaning over her. "I'm gonna get laid anyway, so when I tell you something, it's the truth, baby."

Her fingers zigzag into my hair and then stop. Full lips are licked, her eyes telling me everything she wants. I press my mouth to hers lightly at first. Running my tongue over her bottom lip, I then take it between my teeth with just enough pressure to feel her bated breath exhale. I need all of her—her breath, her kisses, her love, her soul. Our tongues touch as I rub her thigh under the little floral dress she wore to tease. I stole her innocence years ago, but the sweet little dresses she wears remind me of when I met her.

She tugs my shirt over my head and I lift up to remove my jeans. Her dress comes off next. Seeing her body highlighted in the moonlight, she's an angel here on Earth, the whole of my beating heart. Pert tits barely covered in purple lace beckon me. Dipping one cup down, I cover her nipple with my mouth, tonguing until chill bumps cover her and her fingers tighten in my hair. Peeking up, I see her eyes watching me while her mouth is open. "I want your underwear off." She lifts and I want to rip, but I pull them down instead. I can read her mood by the music she was playing and by the soft kisses.

Gentle. She wants love and romance. I can do that.

Her legs part for me and I run my fingers higher. Centered at the apex of her thighs, I rub small circles and tease until she's coming on me. Her moans echo through the trees and I lean down to devour her.

Fingers grapple with my shoulders to pull me up higher. "I need you," she says, her whisper whipped away on the wind. "Make love to me, Derrick."

When I move up, her hands push my boxers down. Moving to where we'll both feel so good, I hold myself above her. "See those stars in the sky?" She nods, her gaze heading high. "We're going to fly higher and shine brighter. Together we'll win the world over and conquer the universe."

"I'd settle for your heart."

"You already own it." I move and her head dips back. Pushing slowly in until my lips caress the underside of her jaw. My breath escapes as ecstasy takes over. Thrusting my body, my heart is pulled—all of me under her spell. I drop my head down next to hers.

Sliding her arms around me, she kisses my temple, and says, "Promise me life will always be this good."

"I promise you it will be better. I'll make sure of it."

Our lips embrace as our bodies come together in all ways.

...Wonder if we can conquer the universe this time around. I promised her a better life, and right now, I feel as though I've failed her. *I did fail her. Why did I believe she would want to be with Reggie? Why did I let my stupid pride stop me from checking the facts? Idiot.*

I promised her the world, and now I intend to give it to her.

22

Jaymes

"PACK THE PINK dress. You look so pretty in that one."

I send a glare my mom's way. "What you think is pretty and what Derrick will find sexy are two different things."

She's smiling and yes, I showed my feelings, but if I can't share my happiness with her, then who can I? She'll also help me when the time comes. The time will come when I have to deal with certain *other* people. Some guy I didn't recognize with a large lettered tattoo peeking out the back of his wife-beater was loose-lipped to Leann at the convenience store on the corner. "Reggie was picked up. He's in for the weekend. No judge will see him until Monday."

That's when I knew I had to go. I could see Derrick without fear of being caught. Two nights and I would be back before anyone noticed I was even gone. The smile hasn't left my face since I called him to confirm.

Ace has effectively taken out the four shirts I've packed for him and messed up the jeans and shorts. "Hey buddy, can you help pack your suitcase while Mommy packs hers?"

"What does sexy mean?" he asks.

My mom grabs the pink dress and throws it at me. "Pack it." Tugging on Ace's sleeve, she adds, "Come help me make dinner."

Down the hall I hear him ask, "Where is Derrick going to find sexy, Grandma?"

A laugh escapes from the relief I feel that I don't have to answer that. Looking at the pink dress, it's so pink, but when I glance over at the closet, I don't have much of a selection for sexy. I pack the dress and then decide I'll win him over with sexy lingerie, except I don't have any. I've had no reason to want to feel or look sexy for anyone in a long time. I find my best underwear instead and pack it along with two pretty bras.

"Jamie."

"Mommy!"

I dash out of the room and into the living room. "What?"

Ace points at the TV and says, "Look. It's Derrick."

Following where he's pointing, I watch the TV. The bleach-blonde reporter is wearing a skin-tight red sweater dress. She shoves the microphone toward the lead singer who ignores her question. Security rushes around clearing the paparazzi away. One of the guys with sandy-blond hair wraps his arm around Derrick's neck and drags him over to the reporter. "Single? We sure are. What's your number?"

The dark sunglasses hide Derrick's eyes but when a flash goes off, I catch a glimpse of his annoyance. And then they're escorted into waiting cars and drive away.

Ace turns back and says, "You colored the box that said single when we went to school."

"Huh?" I'm not sure what he's talking about, but then I remember. "When I registered you for kindergarten?"

He nods and smiles before pointing back to the TV. "Derrick is single too."

Laughing, I agree. "He sure is."

"Mommy, what is single?"

Oh Lordy, here we go.

MY MOM ADJUSTS Ace's backpack on his shoulders. "You be good for your mommy, okay?"

"Yes, ma'am."

She squeezes him in a tight hug while I pull our suitcases from the trunk of her car. How a carry-on for only two days weighs this much is beyond me. Oh wait, no it's not. I packed everything I could fit in there. As soon as I close the trunk, my mom is hugging me just as hard. I comfort her. "We'll be all right."

"First plane ride for you both."

I take Ace's hand. "We're gonna do this together, aren't we, bud?"

"Yup. I'll take care of her, Grandma, like I promised."

"Good boy, Ace." She kisses my cheek, and whispers, "Try to have some fun and enjoy the time away."

"I will. I promise. Thanks for driving us."

"Call me when you land."

I hug her once more and then stack Ace's small case on mine and take his hand again. When we check in we're told we can wait in a lounge. I'm not sure where she says it is. It's like trying to find a secret door in the middle of an enchanted forest and Ace is sidetracked by the pretzel place. "Please, can I have one?"

"I don't know, Ace. I have some snacks with me. Two Granola bars and two apples. Do you want one of those instead?"

"No, it's a treat on our adventure. Please?"

They do look good and it will tide him over until dinner if he eats the whole thing. "Okay. But you know we have to be careful with money. This is an adventure, but not too many treats. Deal?"

"Deal." We shake on it and I give him a five-dollar bill. He steps up to the counter and orders cinnamon pretzel bites like a big man. I rub his back as he waits for his change. Twenty-three cents. Instead of handing it to me, he drops it all in the tip jar on the counter. I say a silent prayer right there that the world never ruins the good that is my son.

We never do find that lounge, but we find our terminal and gate easily. The flight attendant calls us to the stand and greets us with a smile. "I heard you're first-time fliers?"

Ace answers, "We are."

"Well, you are going to love first class. We'll make sure to take extra special care of you." She looks at me and says, "You may board now."

"Thank you."

We find our seats and I let Ace sit by the window. I try to keep my mouth from falling open at how fancy this is. Derrick outdid himself. Ace and I are officially spoiled.

The flight is short but I'm served champagne and berries. Ace fell asleep after the orange juice and his cookies and took a quick nap. I feel like we can ask for anything and they'll have it. Flying is amazing.

I sip a cup of coffee while Ace stares out the window, excited we're landing soon. Reading my phone, I check the messages from Derrick again just to make sure I understand. *A driver will be there to greet you in baggage claim. He'll bring you to the hotel where we're staying.* Okay. I can do this.

The landing was a bit rough. Ace got scared, but so was I. I'm amazed how Derrick can fly all the time. Wonder if he gets anxious like I was?

A guy in a black suit, just like in the movies, is holding a sign up for us. He takes our carry-ons and we follow him to the private car waiting area. "Thank you," I say when he opens the door. Ace springs in and I duck in after, but am surprised. "You're here?"

Derrick melts me to the seat with his killer smile. "I couldn't wait to see you."

The door is closed and I'm brought in for a kiss, but right before we get to follow through, he peeks between us and laughs. "Hey there, Ace, my man. How's it going?"

"I got cookies on the plane and Mom bought me pretzel bites."

"Your mom's the best."

Ace nods and I laugh. "Thank you for all this. The flight was incredible. A little rough at the end, but nothing I couldn't handle." When I look back into his eyes, they darken and I realize what I just said. We used to play around, a little rough sometimes, but so comfortable with each other that we didn't have to hide any of our desires. That feels like another life. But I won't be too quick to judge.

Optimism fills the car, and while looking into those oceanic eyes, I start to believe it's possible to capture the past. *Or maybe this is not about recapturing our past. Maybe this is about finding our future. Should I think that?*

Derrick reaches his arm around the top of the seat, over Ace's head, and rests his hand on my shoulder. His fingers tap and tickle. Looking into his cheerful expression, I know it's possible.

The hotel comes into view. Gold windows and grand statues welcome us, and as soon as we step out, Ace says, "Whoa."

"Come on," Derrick says, putting his sunglasses on.

His body is tense and I feed off his reaction, taking Ace's hand. "Are we safe?"

The question seems to surprise him. "We're safe. I just don't want to draw any attention."

"Neither do I."

The left side of his lips slides up and he takes my free hand. "Elevator's this way. They'll bring the bags up."

In the elevator, he pushes the button and I stand next to him, giddy as can be to be here with him. He sneaks a hand behind my back and rubs. "You look beautiful."

Touching my cheeks, I tilt my head down, knowing I'm blushing, and whisper, "Thank you."

The doors open and he leads us down the hall and opens the door. "Hey Ace, check out that view."

Ace runs to the window and presses his nose against it. "Whoa."

"I think we're going to hear a lot of that this weekend. He's never been anywhere like this before. I haven't either for that fact."

But this is now Derrick's norm. Surreal.

Taking my hand, Derrick says, "Then let me give you a tour." We only make a few feet inside the bedroom before he tracks Ace's whereabouts and then presses me to the wall and kisses me hard. "God, I'm so glad you're here."

"Me too."

Ace runs in and we jump apart. "Mommy, you have to see the pool. It looks so small with ants around it." He grabs me and tugs me into the living room. I sneak a glance back at Derrick who's laughing and joins us at the floor-to-ceiling windows.

"Those are people, not ants." All three of us are pressed against the glass—biggest to smallest. Derrick reaches over and takes my hand. I reach over and take Ace's. *This.* This is all I ever wanted. "I don't need the view or the fancy suite."

Derrick looks over, and asks, "What?"

"That out there. Or this fancy hotel. It's nice, don't get me wrong, but this," I say, holding up our clasped hands, "is all I ever dreamed of."

The delivery of the bags interrupts a kiss to my cheek. We laugh and Derrick goes to the door. I remain while Ace points out all the things he sees, which is a lot. "I'm hungry," he says, looking up at me.

"Okay, let me grab an apple for you." I grab my purse to rummage through it until I find the Granola bars and the apples, and then set them on the table.

Derrick comes up behind me and his hands start to touch me, but he sees Ace and moves around to the other side of the table. "What's all this?"

"Ace is hungry, so I was getting him something to eat."

Holding up an apple, he asks, "You brought your own food?"

My defenses go up, but then I realize how this looks, how it appears to him. Lowering my voice and those defenses that popped up too fast for my own liking, I reply, "We don't have much money. We may be here on vacation, but I still need to be responsible."

He takes the apple and tosses it to Ace. When he turns back to me, he says, "You don't need your own food. Charge anything you want to the room and if you want anything in the hotel, just charge it to me. I've got you both covered. Anything you want, it's yours."

"This is so much. I don't want to take advantage of your generosity."

"Please. Take advantage. I have my mom. Other than that, I don't have anyone to spend all this money on. Let me spend some on you, and that guy over there."

"Were you always this charming, Derrick Masters?"

"More. You've just forgotten."

"Well, you're doing a darn good job reminding me."

"I try, sweet Jaymes. I try."

Another knock draws our attention away from each other. I join Ace by the window and we continue to look at The Strip and all the twinkling lights. I look back and see Derrick hugging a woman and welcoming a man I recognize from the band. Two kids run in and up to the windows next to us. "Hi," I say to the oldest. He's older than Ace, so I ask, "What's your name?"

"Neil." Not looking to carry on a conversation, he nudges Ace, and I smile. "This is a better view than ours. We got a parking lot. How old are you?"

Ace is shy at first, so he glances to me, but then replies, "Five."

"I'm eight. My brother's five like you. His name is CJ. Are you Uncle Derrick's kid?"

My heart sinks. This time Ace looks to me for more than a long second. He looks to me for answers. I'm about to step in and reply for him, but he beats me to it. "Yes."

23

Jaymes

SADNESS OVERTAKES HIS small frame. His shoulders sag and his sweet little brown eyes are aimed down. I want to say something, but I'm not sure what and I don't want to embarrass him by correcting him in front of the others. "Ace?"

A tiny hand rests on my knee, and when we look into each other's eyes, he whispers, "Don't be sad, Mommy."

Neil taps him on the shoulder. "Tag. You're it."

They take off running and I'm left with the shame of what I've caused him.

I fought.

I didn't fight hard enough, but if I had stopped Reggie, I wouldn't have Ace.

"Jaymes?" My attention shifts toward my name. Derrick is a few feet away with the others. All three are staring at me, expecting something from me. A hand is held out and a gentle smile welcomes me. "I want you to meet my friends."

Friends. Friends from a life I know nothing about.

I stand, and join them.

"This is Jaymes Grenier." Pride is heard in the introduction as Derrick wraps his arm around my back. "Dex Caggiano, our drummer, and this is Rochelle Floros. Rochelle keeps the band running from our brand to our image and everything in between, including helping to organize the tour."

They're holding hands, but reach to shake mine before finding each other so effortlessly again. I don't think I've ever seen two more beautiful people. Rochelle asks, "How old is Ace, Jaymes?"

"You can call me Jamie."

She glances to Derrick and smiles with a raised eyebrow. "These guys seem to have an affinity for full names. I don't know what it is, but I just kind of love it, so Dex and I will call you Jamie, and leave Jaymes for Derrick."

It's funny what you learn when you finally open your eyes. I had forgotten, it always just felt right hearing my full name from him. Derrick even called me Jaymes when he was Rebel and everyone else called me Jamie. It seems the habit is rampant among the band. Or do all rock stars prefer the formality of birth given names? It's not important, but I still like the way it feels special that only he calls me Jaymes. "Ace is five. Are those your sons?"

"Yes. Neil and CJ. Sorry for the invasion. They tend to make themselves right at home wherever we are. I guess that's what all this traveling over the years has done."

"It's fine. Neil was very nice. He introduced himself and CJ to us."

"That's good to hear. He usually does most of the talking. CJ owns being the baby of the family, from tantrums to his curiosity, so sometimes he forgets his manners. I think he's been hanging around Dex too much," she teases, wrapping her arm around him. His arm comes around her shoulders as they tease. The conversation is lost as I witness the way he holds her so casually and comfortably that it makes me wonder if Derrick and I can ever get back to that place.

Not if Reggie has his way. Fortunately, I find some comfort that he isn't brave enough to come to my mom's house. It's not just me he'll be messing with, but my mom as well.

Damn it. I had managed to put him out of my mind, to take the trip, promising myself to get lost for a while in happiness and live in a fantasy world for two days. I don't think it's going to be possible. Not with the dark clouds of guilt hovering above us. Looking up at Derrick, his innocent gesture, his want to be with me and mine for him puts all three of us at risk. I need to talk to him this weekend.

"So what do you think?"

My eyes flash to Rochelle's. Staring dumbly at her, I ask, "What?"

The group laughs, except for Derrick, who looks concerned. He steps in to save me. "Jaymes flew for the first time today. She and Ace had never been on a plane or to Vegas. It's a lot to take in."

Running my hand through my hair, I push it back. "Yeah, it's exciting too. I'm so grateful Derrick did this for us."

Rochelle's expression is kind with trustworthy eyes. I'm comfortable around her, something I'm not used to being in my regular life. Are rich people genuine or am I being played? She says, "We came up here because Dex needed to talk to Derrick about the show tomorrow night. Why don't you show me around the fancy suite."

"I haven't seen much of it. We can take a tour together." Giving the guys privacy, we walk to the windows. I've not gotten to really look at the view. I helped Ace pinpoint a few things, but standing in silence in front of these large windows, I feel like we're on top of the world.

It's not silent for long. The boys are running from one end of the suite to the other chasing each other and giggling. I love the sound of their happiness and fun. CJ is acting like a total goofball, cracking jokes as he chases them. Rochelle says, "He loves to play. He's the happiest kid all the time and will do anything to make someone laugh. He's a lot like his father."

Dex and Derrick have moved to the dining table and both have their phones out. Music is playing and they appear to be breaking down the song, note by note.

"I'm a fan of their music, and I've heard great things about Dex."

Rochelle looks my way. "Dex isn't their biological father, but he is their dad. For CJ, he's practically the only one he's ever known."

Doing a double take, I look at her thinking of Ace. Reggie. Derrick. "I don't mean to pry—"

"It's not prying." She goes on to tell me how Dex stepped in when she needed someone most. How he was the one who was there for her and the boys. We stroll from room to room, stopping to take in the view from each.

Her story resonates with me, giving me hope that maybe we'll be out from under the dirty thumb of *him*, and accepted openly and cherished as part of a family. Ace deserves a family and a man who is a true role model.

And I want that too. A man in my life for me. It's as though I've hidden myself for years. Busy as a mom, as a daughter, as a student and a worker. Life has been about working what feels like twenty-four seven. I've *survived*. But not necessarily lived.

"Jaymes?" Walking back into the living room, Derrick and Dex are standing there looking more like the cats that ate the canaries than brooding rock stars.

I go to him. I wrap my arms around his middle and embrace him. In front of Dex. With Rochelle watching. With the kids running circles around us and weaving between the furniture, I hug him, so tight. "Yes?"

Strong arms envelop me. "Will you go on a date with me tonight?"

He doesn't even whisper it. Just asks like that for everyone to hear, and my heart is his all over again. That simple. Before I answer, Rochelle drags Dex over to the windows and thus starts the worst game of *not-eavesdropping* I've ever seen played. Tilting my head up, I grin, my pants practically charmed right off me from the sweetness of his question. "I would love to. I have to warn you though, Ace doesn't eat in fancy restaurants so we might want to keep it kid-friendly."

"Not with Ace, though I'd like to take him to do some stuff while you're here. Tonight, just you and me."

"He's five, Derrick. I can't leave him here by himself."

"I actually offered to watch him," Rochelle says, "I was thinking since I have my boys here and they're all getting along so well that maybe Ace could spend some time with us. Maybe even have a sleepover."

How are these people so nice? "Who are you and how did I get so lucky to meet you?" I joke.

Derrick's playful jealousy is showing when his arms tighten reminding me he's here. "Hey, what am I?"

"A dream come true. I'd love to go out with you, but he's never had a sleepover before."

Rochelle offers, "Of course no pressure. The boys have been getting along so well that—"

Derrick adds, "Only what you're comfortable with."

"He spends the night with my mom sometimes. It's not like I have to be there every night, but he needs to feel safe. That I'm okay and he's okay."

"Do you want to talk to Ace?"

"Yes. Let me talk to him and see how he feels about it."

It's so hard to let go when being in his arms is my favorite place to be, but I pull myself off of him and find Ace and the other boys jumping on the beds in his room. "Jump to me, buddy."

When he lands in my arms, I crouch with a grunt, setting his feet on the floor. "You're getting so big, Ace."

"Derrick told me if I keep eating healthy stuff and exercise I'll be bigger than you when I grow up." I kneel down so I'm eye level, but he continues, "He said I might even be as big as him one day. That's gigantic."

"You're growing fast. I think he might be right. So, I can tell you really like Derrick." He nods, his eyes glancing between me and the other boys, anxious to get back to playing. "I like Derrick, too."

"I know, Mommy. Grandma says when you weren't single that you weren't single with him."

As much as I want to be irritated at my mom for talking about

Derrick and me with Ace, I'm struggling to muster the anger. Technically, what she said is true and the only time I've ever lied to Ace is to protect him from Reggie. I'm not going to lie about Derrick. Not to Ace. "Yes, we used to go on dates. That's when two people like each other and hang out."

"Like we do."

I smile. "Yes, like we do. So tonight Derrick wants to hang out with me and Neil and CJ's mommy thought it would be fun if you could hang out with them, maybe even have a sleepover."

"Whoa. Yes," he says, jumping up and down. "Yes. Yes. Yes. Please. Please. Please."

"I thought that might be your answer. I'll let them know." I stand and he's about to dive back on to the bed, but I grab him and hug him tight. "I love you, buddy."

"I love you."

He's so wiggly to get back that I let him loose. Standing there, I watch for a minute as the boys play, daring each other to jump off and land on their feet. "Be careful, guys." When I return to the others, I point at Derrick. "I'm all yours." Smiling to Rochelle and Dex, I say, "They're all yours. You sure it's okay?"

"Totally. We'll have a great time."

"Thank you so much."

"You're welcome. We'll let you guys settle in and come by around six for Ace. Does that work?"

"He'll be bouncing off the walls until then."

"I hear ya. With this wild crew, Dex is teaching them drums and guitar, so he's heading to the stage to let me nap. I have a feeling we're going to have a busy night."

"I think so, but I appreciate it so much."

"No problem at all," she replies.

Minutes later, they're gone and Derrick and I are left standing there. It's eerily quiet, so we sneak back to the bedroom where the kids were playing and find Ace zonked out on the bed. Derrick's hand is pressed lightly to my back, and I lean my head against the doorframe. This just all feels so good. So... *right*. That same *right*

Derrick was talking about. We've already fallen into a little bubble of comfort and I don't know if I should go with it or be leery.

My shoulders are tense and his hand slides up, massaging me. He says, "Let him sleep. If I know Neil and CJ, which I do, he's going to need all the energy he can store."

Quietly, we go back to the living room and keep walking. It's been driving me crazy not to kiss this man. As soon as we enter the master bedroom, I grab him and press him to the wall. My lips are on him, my body against his Rock. Hard. Body. "We can stay in tonight," I suggest, hopeful.

"Ha. My oh my. I kind of like you all wound tight." He slips out of my grasp and backs toward the bed. "Call me cruel—"

"Cruel."

He snickers. "I'm thinking I might tease you a bit tonight. Wind you even tighter."

Stalking toward him, I cock an eyebrow. "That would be cruel. You shouldn't be so mean."

"I'm mean now? Hmmm..." He taps his chin. "C'mere, baby." I rush into his arms. With a kiss to the top of my head, and while stroking my hair, he whispers, "Let me take you. Wine and dine you good and proper and then we have the whole night to do all the dirty, fucking sexy things you want to do. How does that sound?"

"Sublime. Where have you been all my life?"

"Right here waiting for this moment with you."

24

Derrick

SHE'S GOING TO kill me dead.

Right here.

Right now.

Rubbing up against me.

In a hotel room in Vegas.

With her hot body and dirty talk.

I pry her sexy little self off me and kick myself for asking her to wait. I'd be more than happy to fuck the night away. But that's not the memory I want her to have of our time together. Well, I do want that, but in addition, I also want to romance her and make this weekend the most unforgettable time of her life.

With the life I've been leading the last couple years, I forget she's still leading one I left in the past.

Her first flight.

Her first time out of LA.

Her first time to leave California.

Her first trip to Las Vegas.

Shit.

So many firsts. In my life, cities blur together without a second thought. I'm barely aware of where I am these days, much less appreciating where I've been.

Walking across the room, she lies on the bed and asks, "Do I get to sleep in here?"

"I wouldn't have it any other way."

"Where are you going to sleep?"

"Funny girl with all the jokes." She's laughing, completely amused. Me too. I sit at the end of the bed and take one of her shoes off and then the other. Rubbing her feet, I lean back on my elbow.

Her moan goes straight to my cock. *Fuck.* I get up and walk into the bathroom. While I readjust, she comes in. "Sorry. Didn't know you were so easily turned on."

"I think you knew."

"Maybe." She laughs just as our gazes catch in the reflection of the mirror The way she leans with her hip kicked out and a look on her face, that come-hither smirk, that used to have me begging, I see the girl I fell in love with the moment I laid eyes on her...

Reggie pulls a pack of cigs out of his jacket pocket and pops one up in offering.

Instead of taking one, I lean forward, resting my arms on my knees atop the picnic table. "You've got balls as big as San Francisco, dude."

We just got busted by Coach Thorne smoking behind the gym, scored one week of detention, and here this fucker is smoking on school property not even five minutes later. With an unlit cigarette hanging from the corner of his mouth, he says, "San Francisco isn't that big."

"And your point is?"

"Fuck you..."

I'm too busy laughing at my own joke to hear what he says next, but when he hits me in the chest, I take notice. "What the fuck?"

"There she is."

"Who?" I ask. When I follow his stare, I sit up.

Oh.

Dark hair. Almost black on this cloudy day.

Wow.

The wide eyes of innocence shining.

Shit.

Tits. Not huge, but enough to satisfy a tit guy. I guess that's what I am. I wasn't just knocked on my ass. I was knocked completely out of my orbit and straight off my axis. I didn't know her name, but Reggie did. "Jamie Grenier."

My throat felt dry and my chest hurt from the sight of her. Fuck. Am I having a heart attack at fifteen? "Give me a cigarette."

"Now you want one?"

"Yeah."

I light up—fire to the flame. My nerves settle, but my chest still aches. Then she looks my way. Reggie catcalled her and got flipped off in return. I try a different approach. "Hey."

When she realizes I'm talking to her, she replies, "What?"

"Did I see you at the mall the other day?" I never go to the mall. "I don't think so."

"Maybe over at Ernie's?" The best sandwich shop in LA.

There it is. She smiles. "Maybe. They've got the best sandwiches in the city."

Damn, I knew I liked her. And then Fate played her hand— Reggie hits me from behind. "Call her over here. I want to meet her."

It's not just an ache I feel but more in that moment, something bigger, stronger, something I've never felt before. There's no way I'm walking away from this girl. And less chance I'm giving Reggie a shot at her. No, that's not gonna happen. "Hey Jamie, c'mere."

Reggie is so excited his hands are shaking. Or it might be from the drugs he took after we were busted. Who knows? The dude is fucked up. I've known him since I was ten and he was the only kid I was told to stay away from. Naturally he was the most fascinating. Five years later, I'm almost as deep into this gang shit as him. I've learned to protect myself and my home. No one else will do it for you. We're the small-time lackeys right now, but we're moving up the ranks fast. In two years, I'll get my tat. That will be the beginning of the end of all those dreams my mom once had, but I'll own these streets. Nothing's gonna change that course now.

She walks with purpose, not afraid of us like some of the chicks at this school. Crossing her arms over her chest, she stops right in front of me—all badass attitude wrapped in a bombshell body. "What's your name?" she asks.

"Rebel."

Reaching forward, she pushes some of the hair fallen over my forehead to the side, and takes my cigarette. Dropping it to the ground, she says, "You can call me Jaymes."

I realize right then that I'm not just a tit guy. I'm a Jaymes Grenier guy. She stole my cigarette and my heart that day.

...And she's never given it back. Our eyes are still locked, both of us caught up in memories that feel more real than this life sometimes. "You changed my course."

Sadness befalls her. "You changed mine." The doorway is vacated and I'm left with the damage I've done. While she gave me her best, I gave her my worst.

Walking back into the bedroom, I find her standing at the window staring out. Her arms are still crossed and her dark hair covers half her face. I join her, our arms pressed together as we both look out over Vegas. "He liked you," I say.

When her green eyes look into mine, she asks, "Who?"

"Reggie."

I see the change. It's instant. The softness in her body hardens. The kindness in her eyes turns to hate. The patience of her usual tone is gone. "I don't want to talk about *him*. Not tonight."

"I know, but I think we should."

"Why? Why ruin this?"

"I'm not trying to ruin it, Jaymes. I'm trying to make it better.

We all have secrets and I know that mine did more damage than I ever realized."

"So this is a confessional now?" Walking to the bed, she sits at the end, her body closed off with arms wrapped around her and knees crossed. "Well, guess what? I don't want to hear it. I don't want to hear anything about him ever again."

"Please."

The plea pulls her gaze back to mine. Her breathing has changed—harshness taking over. "Fine. Whatever makes you feel better, Derrick. Go for it."

"It's not that I'll feel better. I will never feel better because of how he hurt you."

Moving higher on the bed, she grabs a pillow and hugs it to her chest. Her back is to the headboard and her knees protecting her. I can't see her face and it's killing me that she won't look up. "Just say it."

"The day I met you, he told me to call you over so he could talk to you." We can't be more than what we've been without honesty and the purest of truths, even if it hurts to reveal them. "I didn't."

"You didn't what?" she asks.

"I didn't call you over for him. I betrayed him and called you over for me."

"Oh Derrick." Her words are trapped in the palm of her hands as she covers her face.

Moving to the bed, I sit down next to her and roll her to the side so she's cradled to me. "I couldn't stop myself. I never knew what love was until I saw you that day. I didn't know what a heart felt like until it started beating for the first time for you. I know now that it wasn't my chest aching. The moment I saw you, it was my soul trying to escape to be with you." I see her struggling emotionally and hold her.

"Why are you telling me this now?"

"Because he may have liked you, but I loved you. I loved you before I knew you." With tears building in the corner of her eyes, she sits up and angles her body. As soon as one falls, I wipe it away.

"I'm sorry. What happened to you was because I fucked him over. I'm sorry, Jaymes." Her arms are around me as I lean my head on her shoulder. "I'm so sorry."

Quiet murmurs and warm breath cover my neck. "You're not to blame. I would have never been with him." She stalls and then corrects herself, "Not by choice." God, what have I done to this woman? She raises my head up until I'm looking at the face of the angel I destroyed. She adds, "The day I saw you, my heart knew I'd never survive you." Releasing a long breath, her face changes back to the one I know, the one I recognize so well—beauty and strength. "But I will survive *him*." She kisses me.

I don't deserve forgiveness or sweetness, but I receive, crave it, and am given it anyway. Rolling to the side, she manages to smile. "God, it's such a weight off, right?"

"Yeah."

"Since we're confessing, I kind of already told you, but thank you for being so gentle the other night. It was the first time since... Anyway, it meant a lot to me that you treated me with such care."

"It's how I feel about you."

"I know and I feel the same about you. One day, the horrors of our past won't haunt us any longer, but until that day, I'm glad we can be so open. It's the only way we can forgive ourselves and each other and move on."

I hadn't realized how much guilt I've carried until I saw her tears. Jaymes has always been so strong, so amazing. Knowing she was broken because of me hasn't sat well since we talked that night. Now it's her forgiveness I need. I don't deserve it. *I left her and a monster took her.* "Do you forgive me?"

"Silly man, there's nothing to forgive. Our love story was already set in motion. Our destiny was just waiting for us to meet." *Thank God.*

"I never sat at the picnic tables at lunch. We were usually behind the gym."

"I heard some guys got busted behind the gym by Coach Thorne."

My eyebrows rise in surprise. "You came to see me get in trouble?"

"Yeah, but we were too late."

"I'd say you were right on time."

25

Jaymes

MOM WINS.

I pull the pink dress from my suitcase. It's the prettiest dress I own and I think Derrick will like it on me. I hope, at least.

When I finish showering, I go to check on Ace, but stop and hide behind the bedroom wall. Peeking into the living room, Derrick and Ace are sitting on the couch rubbing their stomachs. I listen carefully since their voices are low. Derrick pokes Ace in the tummy, making him giggle, but then says, "Go for the gusto, my friend. It starts low and then builds as it comes up. Watch and learn." Derrick belches so loud that even I'm impressed. Ace is super-impressed and a giggly mess on the couch.

With a towel on my head and a fluffy robe from the closet over me, I stand in the doorway with my hands on my hips. "You're teaching my son how to burp?"

"I figured you weren't going to. Yup, we're doing man stuff out here so take your time getting ready."

The way his lips curl at the sides and the lamp's light sparkles in his eyes, he's a sight to behold. Sexier than sin and seeing him play with Ace is all kinds of goodness. Pointing my finger, I say, "Ace, keep him out of trouble. Okay?"

"Ten-four, Mommy."

I'm taking it that Derrick taught him that too.

Rochelle shows up on time to pick up Ace. We go over a few things and I tell her to call me if she needs anything or if Ace needs me. As much as I'm excited to have a whole night off, I'm also worried. He's never been away from me. Rochelle hugs me like we're old friends. "I'll take the best care of him. I promise. We have lots of popcorn, and pizza, and candy. Games and movies. So you go have fun and enjoy your night off. I remember what it's like to be a single parent and these nights are rare." Maybe that's why I feel so easy around her. She does understand. She probably understands the loneliness too.

I say goodbye to my little man and then head back into the bathroom to finish getting ready. Derrick's in the shower, but he reads me well. "He's going to be all right. Rochelle's a great mother."

My baby's not here or in the other room. He's not with me or with my mom. I thought it would be easy to let him go, but I'm finding I'm a bit too choked up to speak. Peeking out from the shower, he says, "Hey, babe."

Turning to look over my shoulder, I see wet skin and strong muscles, but when I reach his eyes, I only see concern. "You okay?"

"I'll be fine. I'm just not used to Ace being away from me, except with my mom. My friend Leah in certain circumstances."

"You don't know Rochelle, but I do. I trust her completely. I also want you to have fun tonight, so we can check in with her."

"You don't mind?"

"Why would I mind?" He dips back under the shower spray.

I take my makeup bag and dig out my eyeliner. "It's supposed to be our night and all."

"Because it's a night for us doesn't mean we pretend that he's not a part of you." He's scrubbing his hair when he adds, "Call her anytime you need. I'd rather have you relaxed than stressed and worried." Two weeks ago, my life was bleak. I functioned on little input, little sleep, little… joy. Except for Ace. But now? With a man who was once my whole life, concerned about me and the welfare of my son as well? This is heaven.

Moving the shower curtain to the side, I surprise him. "You coming in?"

"No, but I needed to see you when I say this."

With a bar of soap in one hand, he stops lathering. "All right."

"Thank you for everything. You've been truly amazing to both me and Ace and it means more to me than you'll ever know."

"Hey, stop thanking me and get in here." With his hands on the belt of my robe, he pulls me close.

Squealing I spin right out of it. "No. No. I've already done most of my makeup and hair."

With a wink and a toss of the robe, "That's okay. I prefer you naked anyway."

"Uh-uh. You chose the rules for tonight. I'm going to hold you to that good and proper wining and dining you promised me."

"You got it, beautiful."

"And don't forget the big ending." This time I send him a wink.

"I'll give you the biggest and the happiest ending you've ever experienced."

Pointing my hairbrush at him, I say, "I'm going to hold you to that."

"Kinky. I like it." He laughs.

My chest reddens just thinking about later. "I'm getting warm in here. I'm going to get dressed."

"After seeing you naked, I might be a few more minutes." I love that. I love that I can still turn him on. I don't want to know how many women he's been with all these years, but knowing it's me he's chosen? It makes me *feel* beautiful. *And cheeky.* And it's been a long time since I've felt that.

"Noooo. Save it all for me. It will give you something to look forward to." I give him the evil eye, though I'm being playful, before walking out. I'm ironing the dress when he comes out. I almost burn my dress. Wow. He has an incredible body. Toned abs, lean body, strong muscles with veins that run the length of his forearms anchored by a large silver and black watch. But it's the V made of muscles leading down under that captures my attention. The towel is barely holding on by a thread. The slightest breeze or touch could send it falling to the floor. Tempting.

"Did you notice how we've fallen back into us so quickly?" he asks.

I stop ironing again and he tugs on a pair of boxer briefs. "Fallen back quickly or picking up where we left off?"

"Both."

I agree, but it doesn't bother me at all. "I like this, and how natural it feels." Disappearing into the bathroom, I tell him, "I'll be out in a minute." He may have seen me in my undies and less, but I'm hoping to look pretty for him too.

"I'm going to make a drink. Can I get you something?"

"White wine?"

"You got it."

The zipper is tough to get up, so I put it on but leave it open in the back. Once I slip on my flats, I check how I look in the mirror, and then head out of the bedroom to find him.

I stop suddenly, my hand covering my heart in awe of the sight before me. I've never felt more grown-up than standing here looking at this man that was once the same boy I loved. With his back to me, I let my gaze linger over the man he's become. Maybe I hadn't done this properly since we've reconnected, because I'm in awe. Dark jeans, black shoes that aren't scuffed or worn out. A black button-up shirt with the sleeves rolled expose his bare arms just enough to see the strength of the moving muscles from his forearms to his hands when he takes a sip of a brown liquid I can guess might be whiskey or bourbon. I wonder if the black and silver watch is something he bought for himself or was a gift from someone else, someone special maybe. It looks expensive. Everything about Derrick Masters these days looks expensive.

Confidence stretches through the width of his shoulders. Standing at the window as if he rules the world. I'm starting to believe he rules mine again. But now I start to doubt my attire. Looking down, I don't want to look dowdy next to him.

"Wow, Jaymes," I hear and look up to see nothing less than adoration in his eyes. "Just wow."

I'm quite sure my cheeks match the shade of the dress. Holding the skirt of the dress out, I ask, "You sure?"

"More than sure." He sets his glass down and comes to hug me. "Gorgeous girl, always be mine."

"I always was."

We come together as he hugs me and my zipper slides up my back. "Tell me I'm not dreaming. Tell me you're really here."

"If we are dreaming, let's stay asleep."

"I'll happily stay in bed with you."

Tapping him on the chest, I laugh softly. "I didn't say anything about bed, and by the way, you look very handsome. Did you get dressed up for me?"

"I did," he replies, popping his collar.

A glass of wine is handed to me and Derrick toasts, "To the past and that girl I met in the schoolyard. To the present and tonight being amazing. To you and me and the incredible future I intend to give you." *I think I want to hear that every day for a while.*

"I'll toast to that," I whisper, not wanting to ruin this dream. He might be right and I'm not ready wake up. Raising our glasses, we tap them together and then seal it with a kiss.

DERRICK MASTERS IS a rock star.
Derrick Masters is a rock star.
Derrick Masters *is a* rock star.
Derrick Masters *is a* rock *star.*
Holy shit.
Derrick, *my* Derrick, well, kind of my Derrick, is a rock star.

That has never been more apparent than it is right now. Doesn't matter that I've seen him on TV, or heard him on the radio. Nope. It's when we walk through the hotel with security flanking our sides, walkie-talkies preparing security to be on high alert that it hits me. Really hits me, like straight in the face.

My Derrick is a rock star. He's famous. Everyone knows who he is.

This may be normal protocol for him, but I'm terrified. My hand is safely tucked in his. Nothing can separate the hold he has on me, which calms my nerves just a little. "Is it always like this?" I ask.

"Yes." His response is clipped, but to the point.

I don't take it as an insult. He looks like he's in a zone, focused ahead and yet, well aware of what his presence does, the commotion he stirs.

We're escorted to a large black SUV with the hotel logo shining in gold on the back panel. Everything is fancy here. I climb in and he's quick behind me. The door shuts and his shoulders drop with the release of a harsh breath. Ensuring I'm fine, his hand covers my knee. "You okay?"

"I'm okay. Are you?"

A surprised grin checks in. "I'm all good, baby. Don't worry about me."

"So that always happens—the stares and people pointing? Some asking for pics, fans calling your name?"

"Pretty much."

Sitting back, his reality sets in. "You were once Rebel—"

"I don't like that name."

"The press calls you that sometimes."

"They don't know the history. We do."

"Have you ever thought about sharing it?"

"No." Clipped. His lips are tight, his answer succinct. Turning to look out the window as we leave The Strip, I can see how much of the past still weighs on him. He may be in a different league these days, but no one can ever fully leave the past in the past. It shapes who we are in the present. He's quiet a few minutes. Sometimes I need a little peace, so I give him the same courtesy, and then he speaks. "If I could scrub it off, I would. It's a part of me. My skin. My body. My shell, but not who I am. It never was."

"You got it when you didn't see another way. There were no outs. Just big talk of dreams and following them." Resting my hand on his, I add, "But you did it. You made it, Derrick. You got out and it wasn't just talk with you. So all that back then was just leading you to greater things. The whole world loves you now."

"But I only care about how you feel." He angles his legs my way and leans in. "You think I forgot you. I didn't. I never stopped thinking about you, Jaymes. I thought you meant what you said when you told me to not look back. I looked back but you were gone." *I hate that he thought that, but it was better for him that he did.*

"I was always with you. You just couldn't see me."

"I see you now and I never want to close my eyes again for fear you'll disappear." *I won't disappear. Can't.*

"I'm right here. Right here with you."

26

Jaymes

THE CAR COMES to a stop and Derrick looks out his window. It all happens so fast that I follow his lead. The door is unlocked and then opened. We shuffle out and are whisked in a door on the backside of a hotel from what it looks like. Following a man in a suit, he speaks to Derrick as if I'm not even here. Despite my growing frustration, I remain quiet, but my thoughts spin on the matter. We're brought into a dimly lit restaurant decorated in heavy blues and golds, booths and tables. It's small and I catch the name, Hugo's Cellar at the top of a wine list when we pass a waiter.

The waiter stops and offers us a booth in the corner. It's dimmer than most of the tables and I like it. The place is busy but not overly so for being such a quaint restaurant. It feels intimate and it's definitely romantic. "Are you romancing me?" I ask, sitting in the middle of the booth so I'm close to him.

"I am. How'd you figure it out?"

Shrugging, I wink. "Wild guess."

The service is quick and attentive. We have wine in front of us within minutes of sitting down. I take several sips of mine before we just look at each other. It's been five years, but he's changed so much, the boy I once knew buried under masculine features. He was always fit and muscular, but now he commands his body instead of the reverse. His eyes tell of the life he's led. Scarred fingertips from playing a guitar instead of illegal activity. "Your hair used to be lighter, dark blond."

Smoothing it back, he says, "Yeah, it's getting darker the older I get. One day I guess I'll be salt and pepper."

"You'll look so distinguished." The attention seems to affect him and he glances down. "What?" I ask, surprised he seems shy under the compliment.

His glass is pushed forward until it taps mine. "I can't believe I'm sitting here with Jaymes Grenier."

"I'm more than a name. I'm a real girl," I tease like Pinocchio.

Deep blues drink me in and when they land on my eyes, he says, "You're more than a girl these days."

"Be careful. I might actually start to believe this is real."

"Me too," he whispers, looking away.

The waiter comes and takes our order and when we're alone, I reach over and slip my hand under his. "I'm sorry about earlier. I didn't mean to sound cold when you wanted to talk. I just don't want bombshells dropped every time we're alone. We have so much more to say to each other. I do, for sure, but can it just wait until tomorrow?"

His fingers curl around mine and he brings my hand to his mouth and kisses it. "Do you trust me?"

"Yes."

"Then let me in. I only have the best intentions when it comes to you and Ace. I will never hurt you. I will help you in any way I can, but you have to trust me. I can see you're hiding from me as if I haven't loved you my whole life. As if I'd even know how to love anyone else. This may come off as a surprise to you. It does to me. But it's also so obvious. I've never stopped feeling forever with you. We have a second chance. Please give me that chance."

"Why do you even want it? Knowing what dating me drags you

back into, why do you want to lower yourself when you're so much better off without me?"

"Lower myself?" He shakes his head. "Is that what you think? That I'm better than you?"

"You are. You proved it."

"Bullshit. Just like the bullshit reasons you gave me that day. I should have never believed you." The words are bitter as he spews them. "I fell for your lies, but I was too dumb to see the truth." When his tone softens, I dare look into his eyes again. "I see it now. I know what you did and I know you did it for me."

He's right. As much as I want to continue lying, I don't want to lie to him. Not anymore. But what could I do to protect someone that I loved more than life itself? How could I make him save himself? "I couldn't leave my mom behind."

"You said that, yes, but I know there's more to it. Your mom would have been rejoicing that you got out of that shithole, away from the gangs that were trying to take over."

My wine has become the most interesting thing I've ever seen. Avoidance is a good tactic. I think... except when you're the only two in the conversation. It gets very hard to distract him to another topic. His gaze is fixed. He's definitely not letting me out of this. "What do you want me to say?"

"Admit the truth."

"Remember when I said I will tell you anything and everything, just not tonight? Can we do that? Please?"

"Tell me I'm wrong. Tell me I'm right. Just promise to tell me the truth."

"Were you always this pushy?" I ask, nudging his knee with mine.

"Yes."

"It's all coming back to me now. Romance me. We will share all of our inner demons tomorrow. Just smile for me tonight."

A smile pops onto his face. It's fake and I laugh because he's wonderful to try for me, even if jokingly. I finish my wine and the waiter is quick with a refill. Looking around, I remark, "This place is very nice. Thank you for bringing me here."

"Remember how you used to make us sandwiches and we'd picnic in the back of the truck?"

"You gave me that guitar and we played together, making music under the stars."

"Do you still play?"

The question makes me sad. Maybe one day it won't, but knowing how hard he worked to buy me that guitar, I feel bad. "I haven't played in a long time."

"Just busy?"

I made a promise not to lie, but if I tell him Reggie took it, it will ruin what we have now. Does this lie matter in the scheme of things? His feelings are more important. I want him happy. "Something like that."

"You should play and sing. You were always way more talented than me."

I laugh. "Funny."

"Not funny at all. The truth. If you had a guitar right now, could you still play?"

"Is that a challenge?"

"Maybe."

"I can still play." I take a gulp of the deep red liquid. "Probably."

"Maybe we can play together sometime."

"Maybe."

Our food arrives. After three bites, I don't talk at all. This steak is the most delicious thing I've ever eaten. I catch Derrick watching me a few times, but I don't even care how I look to him. I devour it and the side dishes. If I could lick the dishes, I would. When my dress feels tighter around the middle, I sit back and exhale. "Whatever you want, I'll give it to you."

He chuckles. "So I feed you a good meal and now I get whatever I want in return?"

"Yep," I reply confidently.

"I'm gonna take you up on that offer, Ms. Grenier."

Rubbing my stomach, I bite my lip, then say, "I hope so." My phone chirps with a text and I pull it from my purse. It's Rochelle: **Boys are having a blast. Hope you two are.**

"Rochelle's pretty great, right?"

Derrick nods. "She's been to hell and back, but she's come out the other side stronger, not by choice, but by determination. For her boys."

I text her: **Thanks for the update. Can Ace call me for a quick good night?**

My phone rings within seconds. I slip out of the booth and answer it, keeping my voice down, "Hey buddy, is that you?"

"Hi, Mommy. We had pizza and strawberries."

"Together?" I ask, walking toward the restrooms. I stay outside the door to take my call.

"Ew. No. The strawberries were dinner. Then we got pizza for dessert."

Laughing, I love it. Hearing him makes me miss him. "Are you having fun?"

"It's like whoa, the best time. Ms. Rochelle said we can watch *Moana* if we aren't tired."

"Are you tired?"

"No. Where are you?"

"I'm at dinner. Are you okay?"

"Yeah," he replies and then yawns. "I'm good. I'm having fun."

"You still want to stay?"

"Yes. We get waffles in the morning."

"Sounds yummy. I should go, but I love you, buddy. Sweet dreams."

"Sweet dreams. Love you."

Rochelle takes the phone, then says, "Hi, he's doing great. How are you?"

"Great. Stuffed but great."

"Good. Tell Derrick I'll kick his ass if he steps out of line."

I laugh. "What if I want him to?"

Now she's laughing. "Well that's something different entirely. I won't keep you. Call or text me if you need anything."

"Thanks again."

"You're welcome. Now go have some fun and don't worry about Ace. He's a great kid and in good hands. Good night."

"Good night."

I find myself leaning against the wall smiling to myself when I get company. Derrick in all his darkness sure is a sight to behold when he comes around the corner. "Everything okay with Ace?"

"Yes," I say going up to him. "He's having the time of his life."

"That's good."

Fisting the front of his shirt, I turn us around until his back is against the wall and I'm firmly against him. "So am I."

"That's even better." Lifting my chin, he bends down and kisses me. "Do you want dessert?"

"Hell yes, I want dessert."

"OKAY, MAYBE I shouldn't have ordered dessert," I moan, leaning my head back against the leather seat and closing my eyes in the SUV.

"Don't fall asleep on me."

"I make no promises. This food coma is intense."

"Ten minutes and we'll be back, but I was hoping to take you somewhere. Can you stay awake long enough for a quick stop?"

"How can I say no to you? I can't."

Five minutes later we're dropped off on a side street. Derrick takes my hand and we hurry around the corner. "The Bellagio Fountains," I say as if he didn't know.

"Come on. It's about to start." We hurry over to a spot in the corner and he maneuvers me in front of him because of the crowds. His arms cage me in resting his hands on the railing. With my back to his front, I feel safer than I've felt in years. I love how much bigger he is than me. I love the way our bodies fit no matter which way we're put together. A loud boom signals the start of the show reminding me of times that weren't so safe...

"Get down," *Derrick yells at me.*

I'm leveled to the ground, my cheek against the sparse grass in the park. Kids are still in school, but we decided to skip. I thought we'd be making out at one of our houses, but the second Reggie found out we were leaving after lunch, he was waiting for us at Derrick's truck. "Looking good, Jamie. If you and Derrick don't work out—"

"Fuck you," I say, flipping him off.

Derrick is laughing, but I'm not. It's been a few days since I've been alone with my boyfriend and I'm starting to think Reggie's invading our party of two on purpose.

Reggie gets in the cab, but I stand outside waiting for him to get back out. "What are you doing?" I ask him.

"Let's go. We're meeting the guys at the park."

"No, Derrick and I are hanging out."

Derrick pounds the roof of the cab. "Get in before we're busted skipping out."

"Not until he moves." No way am I sitting with Reggie in the middle.

"C'mon, baby. I'll drop his ass off and it will just be us."

"No."

"Jaymes," he says, his tone firmer.

I'm about to because I want the time alone with him. I also want to have sex with him. But then Reggie says, "Get control of your woman, Derrick. She's making you look like an asshole."

I slam the door closed and start back to school, but I'm quickly caught. "Hey, ignore him and come on."

"Ignore him? He's a fucker."

"I'll happily ignore him, but will you?"

"You're gonna get us busted. Can we finish this conversation elsewhere?"

Looking back at the school, I'm surprised we haven't been

busted yet. *"Fine, but we're dropping him off first."*

When I go back to the truck, he still refuses to move, so I get in and keep to myself by putting my headphones on. If I was smart, instead of listening to EDM, I would have been listening to what Reggie was saying, the plan that was going down.

We get to the park and I move to let Reggie get out, but then he leans back in to talk to Derrick. Derrick's jaw is tense, ticking on the side, something he only does when he's stressed or angry. I'm guessing angry by the way he's staring at Reggie. The engine is cut and I whip off my headphones. "What are you doing?"

"Five minutes. That's all."

"You're kidding me?"

"Look—"

"You've got to handle her fucking mouth. The guys are talking about how pussy-whipped you are."

I know what he's doing. He's trying to turn Derrick against me. I can argue with him, but in the heat of the moment, Derrick needs to decide if he's choosing to listen to that asshole or if he's going to treat me with respect.

Derrick says, "Shut the fuck up, Reggie, or I'll shut you up. Don't talk about her like that. Ever."

My pride in the stand he took shines and I smile. So what if I'm grinning in gratification, he deserved to be put in his place. But then Derrick says, "I still have some business to handle. I'll be right back, babe."

He and Reggie walk across the park before I can convince him otherwise. "Screw them." I head in the direction of my house. It's only four blocks from here.

Rapid-fire shots sound out and I'm tackled to the ground before the loud boom sends woodchips flying around us. "Stay down," is whispered in my ear. "You're okay, baby."

...I will never forget the weight of his body on mine from that afternoon. "You're okay, baby."

"What?" The water bursts into the air as Celine Dion is piped through hidden speakers.

"You froze, your body tensed, your eyes seem to be focused somewhere far away. Not here."

"Yeah," I reply. "Just a bad memory popped up."

Derrick's arms are around me, his body molded to me from behind. "It's okay. We can go."

"I'm sorry. I had a flashback to that time in the park around the corner from our houses."

"God, Jaymes, what have I done?"

"Don't. You're not to blame any more than I am." I take his hand and pull him out of the crowd. They are so mesmerized by the fountains and show that no one notices the star amongst them. We rush around the corner and find our car waiting for us. As soon as we're safe inside, I say, "He's ruined so much. Let's not let him ruin tonight."

"What do you want, Jaymes?" And then I kiss him. He's responsive and embraces me. Our hands are frenzied and bodies anxious with anticipation.

Stopping to look him in the eyes, I reply, "You, only you."

27

Derrick

THE DOOR FLIES open and I can't pull myself away from her long enough to care that it's slamming open and just took out a section of the sheetrock. I kick it closed and keep kissing her. My shirt didn't stay buttoned once we made it into the elevator. My belt was unhooked and lost somewhere between the suite and the elevator. The fly of my jeans is hanging open and I have her dress unzipped before we reach the bedroom.

Shoes are off and the dress drops to the floor on the way to the bed. My jeans and boxer shorts are discarded while her bra joins the party on the floor. "Holy fuck, you're so damn sexy."

"Come here. I'm cold."

I reach into my suitcase, grab a condom from my toiletry bag, and toss it on the bed next to her. "I'll warm you up." I crawl up and nudge her knees apart so I can rest my body on top of her.

Her arms come around my neck and she's smiling. "I was hoping you'd say that." Her smile is so damn easy. Seeing it makes my heart hurt. I want her to always feel this safe, this comfortable, this happy. I want her life to be this easy. I don't care what I have to do, I'll do it. For her, I'd do anything.

Stealing one kiss and then another, I lower more of my weight on her. Brushing my fingers through her hair, we stop kissing. She looks shy, a little rejected, so I say, "I just want to look at you a minute."

That really brings about a natural blush that I wish I could keep there always. I'll settle for the memory. She's nervous under my gaze, not liking the attention. Sliding her hand down my middle, I catch it and bring it up to my lips for a kiss. Then I hold it, keeping her still. "What are you looking at?" she asks, whispering.

"All that matters."

The smile slips away and something else, something heavier with a thump moves in. Her heart beats against mine and without going any further I already know she's mine. Just like I'm hers.

Instead of words, we kiss, our devotion shared through touch and feel. I angle my body to the side. Moving our joined hands lower, I position mine on top of hers between our hips. "How do you like it? How do you get off, baby? Show me."

"I don't know if I can."

"It's just us. We used to know everything about each other. You've done this for me before. Do it again. Just for me."

Her fingers lower and while looking me in the eyes, she says, "Touch yourself and let me watch."

I don't normally jerk off when I have a beautiful woman beneath me, but her request is only fair. Wrapping my hand around my dick, I look down between her legs and watch as her fingers manipulate her body. "Are you wet for me?"

"So much."

Turning my hand down, I drag my fingers between her pussy lips—slowly until her breath catches. Then leave her to finish and spread her wetness over my cock as I slide my hand up and down. "I'm so fucking hard for you."

"Kiss me."

Leaning over, I kiss her how I want to fuck her—deep, possessive, passionate. "You know how incredibly hot it is watching you get off for me?" A soft moan echoes from her into me. Knowing she's close, I reach down and take her hand in mine, pulling it up to my mouth. I bite her bottom lip and pull back until it releases. Holding her hand to my lips, I lick the tips while keeping my eyes on hers that have opened. Her body moves beneath me, her breath coming out jagged and wanton.

Fuck. Condom. I've got one on in seconds and the tip of my cock is against her entrance. It would be so easy to fuck her, but the torture is too sweet to rush it. One inch enters and her lips part. Pulling two of her fingers from my mouth, I whisper, "I'll go slow every time if that's what you like."

"I don't want slow. I just want you."

Her legs bend around me and I run my hand on the outside of her thigh and lift under her knee. Sliding in, her body conforms to me, embracing me in her welcoming heat. The tightness causes my eyelids to dip close momentarily, the sensation of her overwhelming. "I'm not gonna last."

"You don't have to last, babe. I just want you to feel so good."

"I do. So good. You feel too good, baby. Too good." My body moves against hers and we find a rhythm, moving until our pleasure ignites into a flame. Thrusting faster, I pursue that dark bliss that escapes me. It's not about fucking to get off with her. It's about that bond that builds, the connection being reinforced. I want it all with her. I have it all with her. Only her.

"Fuck." My hips move on their own, my mind lost to the sensation. When she cries my name, I let go and get dragged under with her. I drop when my body is exhausted and sated. Turning my head, my nose is behind her ear, her hair tickling. The scent of her skin a mixture of sex and the last lingering notes of her perfume. She's intoxicating.

Pushing forward, I place three kisses on her neck while ridding myself of the condom in a tissue from the nightstand. Arms come around me, and I close my eyes, teetering on sleep. I rest exactly where I landed.

Whispers and the smell of heaven urge me awake. I open my

eyes slowly, the dim light from the lamp still too bright. Squinting, I see a sight to behold. With my cheek against her chest, I only see naked Jaymes. Perfection. "I wish I could wake up like this every day."

Her soft laughter rattles my head. I lift and roll off her. Running my hands through my hair, I close my eyes and then scrub over my face. "What time is it?"

"Late. Sorry to wake you. You are really heavy."

My eyes pop open and I sit up on my elbow. "Oh, I'm sorry. Did I hurt you?"

"No, you didn't, but it was getting hard to breathe."

She lifts up and kisses my forehead. "And I need to use the restroom."

Watching her sweet little ass as she pads to the bathroom, I fall back and ask, "How long was I out?"

"Not that long. Like an hour or so."

"Really?"

I hear her laughing from the other room. "Yeah, you just fell asleep right where you finished."

"Did you?"

"What?"

"Finish?"

She laughs again. Peeking out of the bathroom, she replies, "I did. Don't worry about me. I loved every minute being with you."

It's my turn to smile. "Sorry for falling asleep on you."

"You're tired. It's okay. You obviously needed it. I'm going to shower." She waggles a condom between her fingers. "Want to join me?"

I don't even bother waiting to answer. I'm up and in that bathroom in seconds. Once we're under the warm water, she's already soaping her body and I help her out by taking over. Running the bar all over her breasts, I then go lower and soap between her legs. Her breathing picks up. She's fighting it, making me chuckle, when she asks, "Do you like touring?"

"I like playing for the fans. I like the high I get." Cleaning my own body, I watch her watching me.

Her eyes are questioning but she doesn't ask what she's wondering, so I give her my answer, "It's better than drugs."

"Do you still smoke or do any?"

"I haven't in a while." Wetting my hair under the spray, I reply, "I partied. Hard. But when I joined the band, I couldn't keep doing that shit. Touring is hard on the body, but it's harder on your mind."

Turning us around, I put her under the water. While I stroke her hair under the shower spray, she asks, "What do you mean?"

I pour shampoo into the palm of my hands and start washing her hair. "I'm doing what I never thought I'd get to do—be in a band, tour the world, make money, but that's only fulfilling in some ways. Not in others."

"Money doesn't make everything better?" She almost seems disappointed.

"Money makes things easier, not necessarily better. When I meet people, I don't know if they want something from me, want to use me in some way, or if they're genuine. It's just easier to stick to those we already know."

"Is that why you invited me? Because it's easier?"

"No." I rinse her hair. When she opens her eyes again, I cup her face and kiss her. "I invited you because I never stopped thinking about you, never stopped caring about you, never stopped..."

"Never stopped what, Derrick?"

Somewhere between her telling me she was full from dinner and standing in the after of our lovemaking, I lost all reason and rationale. I need this woman. Not just tonight, but always. "I never stopped loving you."

Her hands caress my face and she lifts up on her toes. "You taught me what love was, you've shown me I can have it in my life again. I've never stopped loving you either."

The pull between us sends our bodies against the wall. I spin and let her press to my warmth while I take the cold wall. My voice is low, and direct. "Turn around."

When she does, I move her forward and drag my hands down

her arms before taking her wrists raising them up and against the wall. I harden just from looking at her—the curve of the sides of her breasts and then inward to her waist. I appreciate the way her hips curve out and then kneel down to confess the sins I want to commit against her. As the shower rains down over us, I fuck her with my mouth, my tongue taking her until her legs are shaking and her orgasm subsides, I stand up behind her. "Hold on."

Slipping the condom down over my hardness, I then push between her legs. She adjusts and I slide inside her without production, just need, just instinct to tie myself to her in every way I can. I cover her hands and thrust. "I fuck my hand imagining it's you."

Her head falls back on my shoulder, exposing her neck. Nipping, licking, kissing, I savor her. With her eyes closed, she says, "I touch myself wishing it was your hands on me."

"I'll make all your wishes come true, baby." I slide my hands down her wet skin, over her shoulders, and around to her breasts. Taking hold, I fuck and thrust, love her body like she wants, like I need. Moving even lower, I slip my hand between her legs and appreciate her clit. She jolts, sensitive to my touch, but presses against my hand.

I run the end of my nose behind her hair, and whisper, "Come for me. Show me how good this feels."

"Fuck me, Derrick. I need you. So much. Harder. Make it so I only feel you. Only you."

"Always me." I speed up and then pinch lightly.

"Always you." Her body tremors, squeezing around me.

"Oh fuck. Yes." Grabbing her hips, I start thrusting hard, her body taking and giving until I feel the rush and can't hold back. A few lingering pumps and I drop my forehead on her shoulder. "Jaymes." I release. Release everything holding me back from realizing what she is to me. Release my fears of opening up and letting her in. I release myself to her, my soul bowing at her feet. "I love you."

28

Derrick

I PROMISED HER tonight.

No questions.

Just sharing our bodies.

For me, sharing so much more.

Jaymes didn't tell me she loves me. She doesn't toss around words with that much importance without care. I know how she feels though. She told me she never stopped loving me. That's enough. For tonight, that's enough.

Sun's coming up. The Nevada sky lit up. She's been asleep on me for a few hours. The peace she's found in my arms makes me wish we could stay like this forever. She's given me the same peace. Dragging my fingers down her back lightly, I stare out the window.

The new day will give me the answers I need, but I fear what the repercussions of this new information will bring. Reggie has a hold over her. It doesn't seem he's in the picture, but he's definitely in her life.

Her phone chirps with a text. I reach over to the nightstand and grab it before it wakes her. There's a message from Rochelle: **Ace is** *crying. I've been holding him for a while, but I think you might want to come down. Suite 12447.* Glancing to the time, it's not quite six a.m.

I hate disturbing Jaymes. She's sleeping like she hasn't slept in years. Maybe she hasn't. I reply: *This is Derrick. I'll be there in a few minutes.*

Setting her phone back down, I very carefully, extra slowly extricate myself out from under Jaymes. She readjusts but doesn't wake. I kiss her cheek and then get dressed pulling jeans and a T-shirt on. Slipping on my black Adidas, I don't bother with socks or tying the laces. I just grab the room key and my phone and go.

Dex answers the door. "Come on in." I follow him inside as he continues, "He's a great kid."

"Yeah."

But then Dex stops and turns back to me. Crossing his arms, he says, "Something's going on."

"What do you mean?"

He whispers, "We found him hiding in the closet crying, but he was dead silent. Rochelle got up an hour or so ago just to check on them. CJ and Neil were in one bed. Ace in the other when we tucked them in. But he was gone. She freaked out and we searched everywhere. She found him in the closet. He wasn't afraid of her, but he wouldn't talk about why he was there either."

"Shit." I see the concern etched in his face. I'm sure it matches mine. He also looks as tired as I feel.

We start walking again. "They're in our room."

When we enter, Rochelle is sitting in bed and smiles sympathetically. Ace is curled on her lap, resting his head on her chest. Her arms are around him, but his eyes are wide open. He sits up when he sees me. "Derrick."

"Hey buddy, I came to get you and take you to your mom."

He comes running to me and my arms go out automatically. Throwing himself into my arms, he hugs me tight. I place a kiss on the side of his head before I realize what I'm doing. Damn. Like his mother, all I want to do is protect him from whatever scares him. I catch a glimpse of Rochelle whose smile was once filled with sympathy is now full of pride. Standing all the way up, I bring Ace with me. He wraps around me like a little monkey and I carry him to the door. Before I leave, I tell Ro and Dex, "Thanks for last night. We'll touch base with you guys later."

Ace gives Rochelle a side hug and fist-bumps Dex before we leave. They're only three floors down from us, so I manage to avoid being seen. Back in the suite, I ask him, "You hungry or tired?"

"I'm sleepy," he responds with a giveaway by rubbing his eyes.

"Okay." I glance toward the other room and then to the one I'm sharing with Jaymes. "Hey, go take a piss and meet me right back here."

"You said a bad word. Mommy's gonna be mad."

"Then let's not tell her, kid." I nod my head toward the bathroom. "Now go and don't forget to wash your hands." I sound like my mother.

As soon as he runs along, I go into the room and kick off my shoes. I should have put my boxers back on earlier, so I strip my pants off and slip those on in a hurry. Rushing to meet him, we both come out at the same time. Kneeling down, I say, "So, I'm going to let you decide where you want to sleep. In that room with the two beds or in that room with the one big bed and your mommy."

He rubs his chin while looking between the two options. I have to admit, this kid is seriously fucking cute. He points to the room with two beds and I smile. "That one."

"All right. Let's go tuck you in then. I have a show tonight and need to get some sleep."

"What's a show?" he asks while we're walking in the bedroom.

"It's a concert. A show." He doesn't look satisfied with that answer. "I play in a band. We play music live for people to enjoy."

"Ohhhh. What do you play?"

"I play guitar and I sing."

"Like Mommy, but she doesn't play anymore. I play guitar. I got one for Christmas once."

Now this is something I can work with, we can bond over. "Really?"

"Yeah, it's blue and white. One of the strings is broken, but Mommy fixed it with duck tape."

"Duct. T," I sound out.

"Yeah, that stuff." He climbs into bed and sits there expectantly.

So I pull the covers up and say, "Lie down. You can't sleep sitting up."

"Aren't you going to sleep?"

"Yeah. I'm tired too." I can't wait to climb back in bed with Jaymes and hold her again. This weekend is flying by too fast.

"You're sleeping here?"

"No, in there."

"My mom's in there."

"Right."

"But I thought..." Tears the size of puddles pool in his brown eyes and his bottom lip pops out.

Oh shit. "You thought I was staying in here?"

He nods, pulling the covers up to his nose. Looking down at him like that I see so much of his mother in him. Not Reggie, thank fuck. Well, shit. There go my plans. "Do you want me to stay in here?" He nods again. This is news. I'm not sure what to do, but I know I don't want him to cry. "Where do you want me to sleep?"

With a huge smile, he pats the bed that he's in. "Will you stay here, Derrick? Please?"

As much as I want to wake up next to Jaymes, this kid needs me more. "Sure." I climb in on the other side and he immediately rolls to his side, so I match his position. "Have you ever played a real guitar, not a toy?"

He nods excitedly. I think he's happy to please me. I rub my hand over his head and then pull the covers up a little higher making sure he's comfy. "Snug as a bug."

"My mommy says that too."

"You've got a great mommy."

"She likes you. She told me."

"I like her, too."

"I used to play Mommy's guitar. She kept it in the living room." As much as I'd like to say his thoughts are scattered like a kid's, I know a few adults who act the same.

It's a nice segue back to a topic I think Jaymes might be happier that we're discussing. My curiosity gets the best of me, and I ask, "Where does she keep it now?"

"The mean man took it."

I wasn't prepared for that. My heart stops beating and I find I stop breathing for a second. Trying to control my facial reaction, I fist the blanket. "What mean man?"

His demeanor is so commonplace that I start questioning what he's lived through, what he and Jaymes have had to survive. "The one that hurts Mommy."

Narrowing my eyes at him, I lean up. "Who's hurting your mommy?"

"She calls him Reggie. I hear her, but I hide in the closet and don't make a sound. Just like she told me."

Holy fuck.

Fuck.

Fuck.

FUCK.

Flopping back down, I stare up at the ceiling. I cover my face with my hands not wanting Ace to see my anger, his words ringing in my ears, *"The one that hurts Mommy."*

"Are you mad at me for not protecting Mommy?" *Oh, God. No. This incredible little man.*

My hands are down and I reach over and rub his shoulder. "No, buddy. I know you take care of her the best you can. I just... I don't know why someone wants to hurt her."

"She says for money. And drugs. I heard him say he got money for her guitar for drugs. That made me sad, so she told Santa to bring me a new one. I meant for her. She thought I wanted one for me."

Damn. This kid. He's going to be the death of me. "You did that for her?"

"She used to sing and play for me. That made her happy. It made me happy too. She has to work a lot now and has school. She doesn't smile as much."

I'm going to fucking kill Reggie. I contain my rage for Ace. He deserves to be happy. So does Jaymes. What kind of shit are they caught in?

"When I play the blue guitar it doesn't sound like the other one, but even with the duck... duct tape, she smiles."

"I bet she does."

There is so much to process through the innocence of this kid who struggles to make his mom smile. He reminds me so much of myself. I remember doing the same for my mom, through the abuse, the alcohol and fights with my father. The day he left was one of the best days of my life. When I turn back to Ace, his eyes are closed and his breathing is already evening.

Wish I could fall asleep like that. His little arm is outstretched toward me and his hand is palm up. I roll back to my side to face him and cover his hand with mine.

THE ROOM IS pitch black. Confused, I look at the clock. 1:25. I'm not even sure if that's a.m. or p.m. Much less what city I'm in.

I fucking love blackout curtains. *Jaymes. Ace.*

I sit up and feel next to me for Ace. The bed is empty so I throw the covers off and make a break for the door. Swinging it open, Jaymes and Ace look up from a game of checkers they're playing on the coffee table. She smiles. "Hello, sunshine."

"Hi," I reply, not fully with it yet. My body feels sluggish and I don't know if it's from the sexual activities all night or the tour catching up with me.

Ace asks, "Wanna play winner?"

"Sure. Just give me a few minutes, okay?"

He doesn't say anything, his attention back on the game. But Jaymes is staring at me, trying to hold a silent conversation.

Is something wrong?

Are you all right?

You're worrying me.

I love you.

I love you.

Please still love me.

I mouth, "I love you."

She smiles, though it's more relief flickering across her face than happiness. Happy. Smiles. Ace.

Fuck.

"I'm going to get dressed." I have to talk to her about everything he said to me early this morning. How do I even broach that topic? When I enter the other bedroom, I rub the bridge of my nose. I'm fucking starving and can't have that heavy of a conversation on an empty stomach. I need strength. The kind of strength she's shown she had to have to endure the life she's been living. The life where her daily worry is if she's protecting her son from "the mean man." I don't know much about what's going on with them when it comes to Reggie, but I do know that Reggie Rogers is a dead man. *No one hurts my family and gets away with it. No. One.*

29

Jaymes

DERRICK MOVES FROM one bedroom back to the one we were sharing last night. With a mighty fine itch the way he's rubbing the back of his neck. Something's wrong. Something's off. I woke up to an empty bed and Ace playing with his cars along the living room windowsill. He told me Derrick got him from downstairs and then they had to go to bed to rest for the show.

I also got a long, very excited explanation about what a "show" is and a lot about how Derrick plays guitar like we do. That part made me smile, but the rest of the story's pieces haven't been put together yet. As much as I'd like to follow him into the room and barrage him with questions, he just woke up, so I'll give him some time.

"Jaymes?"

I finish my move, my red checker jumping over one of Ace's pieces, and look up. Derrick's near the door. I get the signal to come to him, one nod into the bedroom, and get up. Maybe he's ready for those questions after all. "I'll be back in a few minutes to play. Can you watch a little TV until then?"

"Yeah." Ace gets up and climbs onto the couch. I turn the

volume up so he can hear the show we had playing in the background.

When I walk into the bedroom, Derrick is holding the door. He closes it enough to leave a crack open. It's thoughtful of him to do that so we can hear if Ace needs me. He turns and comes to me where I've stopped. "Hi."

"Hi." Then I'm hugged awkwardly, like he's forgotten how to do it. "Umm... Is something wrong?"

"Can we talk?"

"Wow, okay. Of course." I walk to the chair by the window and sit, and wait.

Sitting on the corner of the bed, he drops his head in hands and scrubs his face. When his eyes meet mine again, he says, "Have you talked to Rochelle?"

"I texted a quick thank you, but I wanted to tell her in person today. Why? What's going on? You're starting to scare me."

"Stop saying that."

"I don't mean—"

"I know you don't mean I actually scare you, but if Ace hears you he won't know the difference."

"The difference in what?"

He stands, all six foot one of him, all muscle and attitude. All Rebel. My heart quickens, a feeling I haven't had in years coming back. Love and fear mixed together. That's what Rebel was. I knew he'd never hurt me, but I knew the damage he could do.

"The difference between Reggie and me."

Now I'm standing, my arms crossed, my defenses in full-effect. "Why would he confuse the two of you? Ever?"

"I don't want to be the mean man who scares his mother."

Our gazes lock in a standoff. My breathing shallows. The dust particles glisten in the stilling air and all the wonderful from last night is lost to the past like everything else good in my life. "What did he tell you?"

The sadness. The sympathy. The way people look at me like I'm pathetic for bringing a child into this world, or worse, like I'm a bad mom. I've seen that look before. The seconds ticking by are scorching my ears in the silence and I can't take it. "Tell me." I run forward and push him as hard as I can, but he doesn't budge. So I do it again. And again. "Tell me." I keep pushing him until he reacts.

Grabbing my wrists, his hold is firm, and he stops me. "What are you doing?"

Trying to free myself, I demand, "Tell me what he said right now, damn it."

"He said a mean man hurts you." And then I stop when my world falls from beneath my feet. "He hasn't seen him, but he hears him. Ace hears him hurting you and he knows his name is Reggie. Fucking Reggie. What the fuck is going on, Jaymes?"

"Keep your voice down. He'll hear you."

"He hears you. He's not dumb."

"You think I don't know he hears? We talk about it. I know what he hears. But do you know what he hears? His mother fighting to protect him, so don't come judging me like I've done something wrong—"

"Judging you?" My wrists are lowered, the grip loosened, but not released. "That's the last thing I'm doing. I'm not judging you, but if you think I'm letting you two go back to that hellhole to be hurt, or worse, you're wrong."

"I can't leave my mom."

"Five years ago you told me the same thing, but guess what? I'm not walking away this time. This time I'm here to stay."

The fight in me escapes when his commitment is unleashed. "What are you saying, Derrick?"

"I've already said it. I love you, Jaymes. I can see how you keep that wall half opened when we're together, ready to throw it back up at the first sign of trouble. But there's no trouble here with me. Don't you see? You could have always come to me. Always."

"I came to you this weekend."

"Now I'm asking *you* to stay."

I exhale a long sigh and look toward the door. When I seek his blues for comfort, I move in, wanting to believe what he says, wanting to hide from my life and live in his for a while.

His arms come around me and mine around him. He whispers into my hair, "I'm never going to let him hurt you again."

The tears only come when I finally give in, wholly, to him, to his love, when I finally give in to hope again. He holds me while they fall wetting our shirts and he lets me cry five years worth of tears between us.

"Mommy?" Squeezing my eyes closed, I dip my head down and wipe away my tears. He'll know. Despite my best efforts to shelter him from the bad, Ace has seen me cry enough to know. "Don't cry, Mommy."

When I look at him, I raise my chin high. He looks scared as his eyes dart between Derrick and me. I kneel down. "Come here. I want to talk to you about some stuff."

Silently he comes to me. "Derrick is a good guy. I might be crying, but they're happy tears. You and Derrick make Mommy so happy."

Suspicious eyes turn jolly and trusting again. "Like when you used to play guitar."

I tap his nose. "Yes, like that."

Derrick bends down and asks, "Hey buddy, want to come to sound check with me and we'll give your mom a little time to herself?"

Arms fly into the air and he jumps up and down. "Yes."

"How about it... Mommy? Can he hang with the guys for a few hours?"

We both stand up and I lean my head on Derrick's chest. "Sure. That sounds great all around." Turning to face Derrick, I add, "Please remember, he's five. He can't be left to his own devices."

"I've got him covered. As for you, you can get a massage or more sleep."

"I've never had a massage."

"Charge everything to the room. Even the gratuity. I don't want you paying for a thing."

"You're spoiling me. How am I supposed to go back to LA after living the best weekend of my life here?" Ace is bored and runs back into the living room.

The back of Derrick's hand rubs my cheek and all the playfulness in his eyes is gone. "I meant what I said. I'm going to help take care of you guys. We can talk about it more tonight because I need to get going soon, but think about what that means to you and I'll think about what it means to me. We can come together on it. I want you comfortable with how we move forward, but I also want you and Ace and your mom safe. That's a priority."

Safe. That isn't a word I've felt since that night. Vulnerable. Weak. Frightened. But safe? I need that. Lifting up on my toes, I kiss him. "Thank you."

"You've done this all on your own. You don't have to anymore. I'm here for you and Ace however you'll let me."

I repeat, for lack of anything befitting his words coming to my mind, "Thank you. You've given me a lot to think about."

"I hope so. Now, there's a button on the phone for the spa. Just call down and make an appointment and we'll leave you to it."

I roll my eyes at myself, but I need to say it. "Thank you again."

This time he laughs. "Stop thanking me. It's my pleasure." I'm swatted on the ass as he walks away, leaving me to squeak I'm so giddy.

The button to the speaker is pushed and I choose spa from the options and am answered immediately by a sultry sounding vixen. "Good afternoon, Mr. Masters, may I book you in for a spa appointment?"

"Hi," I say, feeling squeaky still and a lot uncomfortable. Visions of what she must think when she hears me run through my head—groupie, one-night stand, hooker. I try to block the names and mortification creeping up my spine, and sound strong, like I belong.

Belong.

Looking around the fancy room, is this where I belong?

Through the doorway, I see Derrick bent down on the floor tying Ace's shoe and I know where I belong. I belong with him. But I'll take a massage first. "Hi, I'd like to book a massage in the next two hours if possible."

The accommodating voice that answered is replaced with the ice queen. "I'm sorry. I made a mistake. We're completely full today, *Mssss?*"

"Grenier."

"I see you're not listed on the room, so unfortunately we wouldn't be able to book that appointment anyway. Registered guests only."

"Hello, this is Mr. Masters. Ms. Grenier is my guest for the weekend. Can you double-check your schedule please? I can pay extra if we need to bring someone in."

"Oh. Great news. We had something open up. We can accommodate your guest in fifteen minutes. Is that sufficient time?"

With a gleam in his eyes, he says, "She'll take it. Oh, and make sure to take good care of her. Whatever she wants, make sure she gets it."

"Yes, sir. We'll see you shortly, Ms. Grenier."

"Thank you," I call out, but I think she hangs up too fast to hear.

Hovering over me, I lean back and he comes closer. "When you're with me, you're treated like a queen. Don't ever settle for less, baby."

"Perks of being with a rock star?" I run my nails lightly over the exposed skin of his neck.

"You say that as if you're the lucky one when it's me who's fortunate to have you back in my life."

"You always were so damn charming."

"What can I say, you bring out the best in me."

With his lower half pressed to mine, I raise an eyebrow. "And other things it seems. I think you have sound check, Mr. Masters, if I'm not mistaken."

This time he sighs, blowing out a big breath. Pushing up and off me, he says, "We'll pick up where we left off later."

"Promise?"

"Definitely."

Ace runs in as Derrick walks out. We give each other a big hug and I tell him to stay with Derrick. "No wandering off. Okay?"

"Okay."

"Be good."

"I will. Love you."

"Love you, buddy."

When they leave, I hurry around and get dressed to head to the spa. Before I walk out, I see Ace's toys mixed with my stuff and Derrick's shoes. It looks like a family lives here. I have to be careful of getting my hopes up too high. Derrick and I will talk later, but I love how at home I feel with him. Seriously, my heart can't take much more goodness. I want to believe it will last. I want to believe that I somehow deserve it, but I'm skeptical. Not *of* Derrick. But *for* us. For my baby boy. Surely all good things must come to an end. I just hope it's not a fiery one when it does.

Reggie

"IT'S CITY, NOT county jail. Bail me out, bitch, or I'm kicking your ass to the street." I slam the phone back on the receiver, and turn. "Open," I command.

The button is pushed, the door buzzes and I walk through with my favorite escort, Guard Derails. He's a rookie. Easy to manipulate. Easier to bribe. Especially since he uses and I'm his hookup. Under his breath, he places his order, "A quarter on Tuesday."

He's a great customer. A regular. Fuck, I'd be druggin' up too if I had to work in this place. Being busted for a pipe in a random traffic stop doesn't feel so random. The cops needed a bust; I happen to be their victim. Now I'm in for three days before I face the court. The LA scene is everything you hear it is—overpopulated. I'm banking I'll be out by morning. Two nights in and it's already getting old. Shayna is scraping money together. Sure as shit not telling her where my stash is. Bitch can use her own money on me.

My hands are freed once we reach the common area. It's small and familiar. I've been here a few times. Petty shit. They can't nail me for anything substantial. I've got too much on these dirty cops. When I walk to a table, the other inmates get up and move. My reputation precedes me. They know I'm on the verge of making a big step in the underground scene. They just aren't sure who I'm taking out to take that step. They don't want it to be them, so the keep away from me.

The TV is on. Some entertainment celebrity show. "Who gives a fuck? Turn it."

"To what?" some brave soul asks.

My silence should be answer enough. It seems it is. He's up and about to turn the dial when I see the ghost I've been chasing for years. "Turn it up."

"I thought you wanted me to turn the channel?"

"Turn it up and fuck off."

The Resistance is in Las Vegas as part of The Rebellion Tour. Last night the band members were seen at various locations around the small city. Johnny Outlaw lay low, but Kaz Fabian and his girlfriend were spotted taking in Cirque du Soleil's Love at Mirage. Derrick Masters and an unidentified date were seen briefly at Hugo Cellar's. The band performs live tonight but unfortunately, the concert is sold out.

An unidentified date.

The story has ended, but I stare at the old TV set, my fingers aching from the grip. I knew the second I saw her who she was.

The image of that motherfucker is burned in my brain. I vowed to kill him. He's always been my most wanted. But now, now he has the nerve to come into my neighborhood, my territory, fuck my woman, and mess with my family.

He's dead, but before I fucking kill him, he's going to watch me fuck the one thing he loves most—Jamie Grenier. I'm fucking pissed she lied to me. Told me she doesn't know where he is. The bitch will beg me for her life after I've finished with his. *The betrayer and the bitch*. Yeah, they're both mine.

30

WHEN I COME out of the spa treatment room, I'm led to the lounge with the hot tubs and these cool room experiences like a salt room and a chilled room. I'm also handed a cup of coconut water on the way. It's so decadent here, I wish I had more time.

In the hot tub room, I spot a familiar face. "Rochelle, hi. I didn't expect to see you here."

"Yes, Holli and I snuck away since the guys have the kids with them."

Dropping my robe on a lounge chair, I step into the large whirlpool. "Derrick has Ace."

"Yes, I saw them on their way out. Jamie, this is Holli Hughes."

The woman with Rochelle swims a little closer with a smile. "Dalton. I did change it, but I go by Hughes. I've heard about you."

"Oh really?"

"You're prettier than they let on and they said you were gorgeous."

Touching my hands to my cheeks, I remark, "I probably have marks on my face from the massage and look awful, but thanks.

You're with Johnny, right?"

"Yes." The smile on her face says it all. *She knows how much she's loved.* "How's being out on the road treating you? Or more importantly, how's Derrick treating you?"

My face heats and I try to play it off like it's the steamy room, most likely to no avail.

"He's good... We're good," I reply shyly. "It's moving fast, but it's good. We have a million things to talk about and not enough time it seems."

Rochelle says, "Well, he's so smitten that I think you'll have years to come. Not to be nosy, but how are you feeling about things? The crazy that surrounds the band can be overwhelming."

"I don't know how you guys do it. I just had a small taste last night and I'm amazed by how well Derrick handles all the attention."

Holli leans back, resting her arms on the side and kicks her feet up. "It comes with the job. They know that, but there's an aspect, their egos, that thrive on it too. Derrick's really come into his own in the last year. I think he struggled the first year, but he understands what they trade to be at the level they're at."

"What about you?" I ask.

"I owe nothing to the public because of the band. I don't owe them photos of my family or personal memorabilia. I share what I want, but I control it. I have to. No one will protect my family like I will. That goes for Dalton as well. If he's on that stage, he's fair game. When he's home, he's mine."

Rochelle is nodding, and adds, "You have a child to protect. You don't owe the press any answers when it comes to Ace. If they ask about Derrick, that's up to you what you share." *I hadn't thought about that. It must have been hard when Rochelle first started dating Dex. How fortunate am I to have someone to help me feel the way?*

"There is more to think about than I thought."

Climbing out, Rochelle wraps a towel around her and sits on the edge with her feet in the water. "We're not trying to scare you, but I know you're not used to the attention. It can be intense and aggressive. Both Holli and I have been there. If you ever need to talk to someone, we understand, and we're here for you. Just like the guys are experiencing their fame together, as the women behind the band, we share a similar experience. Have you met Lara?"

"No, not yet, but I've heard about her."

"I've known Lara for years. She's great. You'll meet her tonight."

"What's tonight?"

Holli climbs out and suddenly after seeing her incredible body, I want to remain hidden in the water until they're gone. Holli says, "The concert. The four of us are going together."

"Oh I can't," I reply. "I have Ace, my five-year-old with me."

This time Holli, standing in a bikini, towel dries her hair, and smiles. "We have two nannies to watch the kids. They're great. Ace would love it. I heard he's a wonderful boy." Walking toward the changing area, she adds, "Come on. Let's get some shopping in."

Rochelle winks. "Don't worry. I've got Derrick's credit card. Let's go spend some money."

I would ask how she has it, but somehow, I know he won't mind. He might have even given it to her. I'll find out soon enough. I climb out and start drying off because there is no way I'm missing this opportunity. I have my friend, Leah, at home, but I'd love more girlfriends, especially ones that Derrick trusts and adores, and I know he does with these two. *And they him. Perhaps I'm a little biased, but how could they not?*

"AT WHAT POINT do you throw in the towel?" Holli asks lounging on a red leather chair just outside the dressing room, where I'm trying on probably my thirtieth dress.

"I'm not sure because you guys refuse to let me." I can hear them laughing from the other side of the curtain currently dividing my nakedness from the entire fancy schmancy store. They told me to not look at the prices, but I did. Once, and then about had a heart attack and took their advice.

A black dress is shoved through the crack between the curtain and the wall and Holli says, "Try this last one on. I think it's going to be our winner."

"Why do I need a dress and heels? I have flats and jeans and blouses."

They burst out laughing again. Rochelle says, "Which is fantastic most of the time, but tonight we're going to knock Derrick right on his ass when he sees you."

I pull the skin-tight dress on and adjust the straps on my shoulders. Bending forward I cup my left boob and lift it and then repeat with my right. I back out of the dressing room and ask, "Zip?"

Holli is right there ready to help. When I'm zipped, I turn around. "Ta-da!"

"Wow." She steps back and looks me over. "Wow, Jamie. You look just... Wow. He is going to die when he sees you. Spin for us."

Rochelle comes out of her room with a dress hanging off her shoulder and tags in her hand. "I found this one—Wow, Jamie."

Holli smiles, taking pride in her work. "That's what I said. That's definitely the one."

With her long brown hair off to one side, Rochelle, says, "You look incredible. How do you feel?"

"Incredible."

They both smile.

At the counter, Rochelle slaps down Derrick's credit card. "He gave it to me and told me to make sure you spend lots of money."

"Why would he do that?"

"Because he knew you wouldn't." The clerk takes the card, the dress from me, and some lingerie the girls insisted I get for later.

Leaning on the counter, I say, "He knows me well."

"You've got a good heart, Jamie. I can tell from spending time with you and with Ace. I also know a little about your background,

Derrick's *shared* background. I'm not going to pretend to understand what you've gone through, but he says you work hard and are going to school. That's amazing. So try to enjoy the few days here if you can."

"Derrick makes it easy."

"Ace has really taken to him. When Derrick came and got him this morning, he ran right to him. It was like they've known each other forever."

"What time did he pick up Ace?"

The clerk hands the receipt back for me to sign. I catch a glimpse of the total and gasp. "I can't spend that."

Rochelle takes the pen and scribbles Derrick's name. "You're not. He is," she replies all sassy. I'm handed the dress, which is left on the hanger and a nice bag with fabric straps. I'll save it and carry my lunch in it when I return home.

Holli's already in Christian Louboutin when we leave the dress store. Rochelle says, "Derrick got him around six a.m."

I stop. "What? Why?"

Eyeing me, she asks, "He didn't tell you?"

"Tell me what?"

"Well, I'm only telling you. Please know I'm not making any judgments."

"Okay," I reply even more worried now.

She goes on to tell me how she found Ace in the closet crying. My heart hurts and I feel sick to my stomach. "I need to sit a minute."

We sit outside the shoe store. Holli is inside trying on a pair of red-soled shoes, and Rochelle sits with me. "Look, there's a story there. Obviously," Rochelle says. "If you need help, I'm here for you and Ace. I'll help however I can."

"There's no helping us. It is what it is." My son is damaged because of me. "Derrick and I spoke earlier. This is why he offered to help us. He knows some stuff." Angling her way, I say, "Ace's father is a very bad man. That's all I can say."

Her hand covers mine. "Derrick has been through a lot. I'm sure you might have heard the same about Dex. They're a lot alike, those two. Not just the past partying, but their hearts are gold and when they love, they love with their entire soul." She stands, rearranging her shopping bags on her arm. "That man loves you, which means he'll do anything for you. All you have to do is let him in."

"You make it sound easy."

"Not easy, but worth the effort." Walking toward the store, she turns back when she realizes I'm not with her. "Well, come on. Holli has ten pairs of shoes for you to try on. Let's complete that outfit."

Two pairs of beautiful shoes, a designer handbag from another store, and a sparkly clutch later, we are done shopping. I didn't bother going to the counters. I knew I'd never be able to sign the receipt. Rochelle looks at her watch. "Sound check is almost over. Let's go sneak a peek."

We work our way through the maze of back hotel hallways and Rochelle flashes her badge to get backstage. My breath lodges in my throat when we enter through a set of doors and I see the band on stage, when I see Derrick on stage. I watch, mesmerized by what I'm seeing. I've seen footage online and videos, interviews and performances on shows, but never in person. I move to sit in a seat hidden in the darkness of the arena.

I'm about to sit down, but Holli says, "We should go say hi. Dalton will figure out I'm here if I don't. He has a sixth sense."

Rochelle laughs. "He has a Holli sense."

The band stops mid-song and Dex stands. "I'm getting water. You guys figure out your riff shit."

Johnny walks to Derrick and they both start playing. Derrick says, "That's where I come in and then sing the chorus."

"That'll work," Johnny replies. "One more time."

They sync up their guitars and go through the part again. Derrick adds, "That's it."

"Hey," Holli says, leaning against the edge of the stage. "Look who I brought with me."

The three guys look over her head and right at me. Derrick's expression lights up and I love that a little too much. "Hey, babe," he says, walking to the front of the stage and kneeling down. "Ace is with Tommy."

I love that he tries to ease my worries first. "And Tommy is?"

Rochelle says, "I'll take you back to the dressing room. Dex is back there too."

Johnny lifts Holli onto the stage and they kiss under the spotlight. I'm such a voyeur, but I can't stop myself from staring. I'm not sure if it's relationship goals I'm jealous of or that their lives just seem so much easier and freer than mine. Either way, I want that.

Derrick has set his guitar down and hops off the stage. "Hey, beautiful."

"Derrick?"

"Yeah?"

I'm overtaken with emotion—I think all that shopping has made me lose my mind. This is not my world and has never been my world. Holli and Rochelle are so lovely, and although I feel bonded with them, I still feel out of my league. This is outside of my norm. I don't want to embarrass myself, but I especially don't want to embarrass Derrick. Leaning against him, I whisper, "Do you think I'll fit in your world?"

"What? Of course, but you don't need to fit in. You are my world, my love."

31

Derrick

AFTER WE BUSTED Tommy teaching the boys how to play blackjack, we wrapped sound check. Everyone went back to Dex and Rochelle's, but I stayed and asked Ace and Jaymes to wait a few minutes for me.

On stage, I unplug my electric guitar and bring in my acoustic. Holding it out for Jaymes, I ask, "Will you play for me?"

"For you?" Every reason not to flickers through her eyes, but she pleasantly surprises me when she replies, "Can I play with you?"

"Sure," I reply, grabbing another acoustic in the rack to the side of the stage.

Ace had been running around, but he stopped and sat on the stage floor. I think he knows how momentous this is.

Jaymes settles on a stool that I was using and I pull Kaz's over. Facing her, I ask, "What song?"

"Ours."

"You remember it?"

"How could I forget?"

"That's my girl. Want me to start?" I ask, watching her adjust the guitar on her lap.

"Yes, you lead."

Counting off, I tap my foot and start playing. Her part won't kick in until the second verse, but she looks like a natural sitting across from me, her fingers positioned. The first chords she plays, she nails. Not sure how long it's been, but it's like she's never stopped playing. Her sweet voice sings the melody with me, her eyes on me, but occasionally peeking over at Ace, who's grinning from ear to ear watching his mom perform.

When the song comes to the end, she strums and holds the note just like she used to sitting in the back of my old pickup truck. Clapping echoes from the audience. We can't see beyond the spotlight, but Johnny and Holli step back into the light. Johnny says, "Why are we not performing that song on tour?"

"I only perform it with Jaymes."

Holli is smiling at my girl. "Your voice is amazing," she says to her.

This time looking to Jaymes, Johnny asks, "Like I said, why aren't we performing it?"

"Me? Oh I can't tour. I'm in school and have a full-time job at a dealership. Ace is in school too."

I don't step in. She can handle herself just fine, but I see the cogs turning in Johnny's head. Wrapping his arm around Holli's shoulders, he adds, "We'll get Tommy to talk to Rochelle and see if we can work out a few dates. You think you can perform live in front of an audience?"

"I've never tried."

"Think about it and get back to us."

"I will. Thanks."

They return to the darkness and this time we hear the double doors slam closed. Jaymes jumps up, and asks, "Did that just happen? For real?"

"It really happened. A few years later than it should have for me," I say, popping a smirk that I hope makes her a little weak in the knees. "But he liked you right away. He doesn't give out praise unless he means it."

A roadie sneaks on stage and signals with his hand that he'll handle the clean up. I set the guitar back on the rack and hand him the guitar Jaymes played of mine. Ace has run around and is now running down in front of the stage. We've got to get some of that energy out. Maybe I'll take him for ice cream or a few laps around the parking garage. "We should get going. The crew needs to do some stuff that they can't when we're in the middle of it."

We weave our way back to the empty hallways, both of us watching Ace run ahead. "You still have the guitar."

I take her hand. "I use it in the show this tour."

"Just surprised me."

"I guess you were always with me, even when you weren't."

She brings my hand up and kisses each of my knuckles. "You know what I've learned most being here this weekend?"

"What?"

"You've found the family you always wanted." She's right. But she's also wrong. Until I found my Jaymes again, I wasn't complete. Now? Now I have my family. But only because of her and Ace.

"Not all of it."

LOOKING DOWN, I'M tempted to see that heart on his sleeve that he wears so openly. He used to be more protective of his feelings, not when it came to me, but when it came for anyone else to see. Along with success he found freedom. It's amazing to see the man he's become.

"I've been thinking about what you said earlier, about what I wanted, how I saw us moving forward." He's addicting. Derrick Masters is better and takes me higher than any drug ever could. Not that I ever did them, but I imagine being around him is similar. I want more, another love fix. A second chance at a life we should have had the first time.

"And?" he asks.

"I never want you to think of me as someone who used you for gain." I watch him carefully, look for his tell that he believes me. His jaw doesn't tense, his eyes stay soft on mine, so I continue, "You said you don't trust people when you meet them. I don't want to be that in your eyes."

"You can't because of the simple fact that we have a past that wasn't easy, but you loved me anyway. You loved me despite my flaws and poor judgment. You loved me for me. It's the same with you. I don't have to spend years dating you to know where your heart lies. I know you, Jaymes. I know who you are and where you came from. I know why you fight so hard to give Ace the life that you didn't get. Let me do that with you."

"I've got to be careful."

"I know. I respect that, but you can't keep putting your own life at risk to protect his. If you're gone, who does he have? Your mom? Can she protect him?"

Ace is standing at the end of the corridor, excited to push through the doors. We stop a few feet back and lower our voices. I ask, "You're taking on *his* child when you take me on. Do you understand the magnitude of that? You'll have new responsibilities to him, as a father figure, Derrick. You're still young—"

"You were younger," he snaps back.

"I don't care how he was conceived, there was never an alternative for me."

"Why is that?" There's no judgment in his tone and I don't blame him for asking. It's a fair question considering the circumstances and one I've asked myself many times, but never answered.

Looking down, the tips of my sneakers between his well worn brown Doc Martens. "I don't like to think about it because if I do, I betray Ace."

He brings me in, holding me against him. With a kiss to my head, he then lingers there. "Then don't answer it. You don't owe anyone anything when it comes to your life or the decisions you've made."

"Rochelle said something similar."

"Rochelle's heart is as big as the ocean."

"I could say the same about you."

He chuckles. "Only when it comes to you." Stepping back, he turns to Ace, and adds, "And this cool kid. Want a ride back to the room?"

"Yes." Ace comes running into his arms and that's when I see it.

I'm always seeing the boy and the man, but it's not about the past and the present when it comes to Derrick. It's about the future. "Yes."

With Ace now situated on Derrick's shoulders, they look my way. Derrick asks, "You want a ride too? That will be later." His signature smirk and a wink follows. Sexy bastard.

I sock him on the arm. "Ha ha. I meant yes to everything with us."

"You'll let me move you out of your mom's?"

Nodding, I rub where I playfully hit him, enjoying every second of being with him, Ace and Derrick and me, being together like a family. I also find it over the moon sexy that his hard muscle never even flinched. "We've got nothing to lose but more time and I don't want to lose anymore of that with you."

"Ms. Grenier, you're going to make me blush. Who's the charmer now?"

"I am. I learned from the best." Sending him my own brand of a wink and smirk, I say, "Let's go. I've got stuff to do."

"Fine. Bossy. Bossy."

Ace pipes in. "She's always like that." We open the doors and enter the hotel. We're going to have to hurry before his fans spot him, but at least I know Ace is safe sitting atop his shoulders. I may not be on his shoulders, but I've never felt safer myself than standing by his side. Looking up, Derrick's smirk is gone. Focused.

He's ready for anything. He may not claim to like any part of being Rebel but watching him now, I realize that was good training for what he was to become. *He learned to become impenetrable.*

I'm thinking those star-crossed lovers in the sky really do have a hand in our destiny. Here we are, years later, being the family we were always meant to be.

Without incident, we make it back to the suite. As soon as we come off the elevator we see Rochelle and Holli waiting outside the door. I laugh. I can already tell I'm in for some adventure, most likely, against my will. I whisper to Derrick, "I really like them."

"That makes me happy."

Holli has champagne in one hand and three glasses in the other. Rochelle looks guilty and starts speaking really fast, "So we know we promised to leave you alone earlier, but we've been having so much fun that we thought we could get ready together."

"I brought drinks," Holli adds, holding the goods up.

Derrick sets Ace down and opens the door. Once we're inside, he says, "I've been wanting to spend some time with Ace and we have a few hours before dinner, so why don't you go with them and we'll hold down the fort." Ace looks up at him and smiles. "What do you say, buddy? You want to hang out with me?"

Ace asks, "I thought you were hanging out with Mommy?"

I snort. "Different kind of hanging out, bud."

He pops his pretend collar and says, "Yeah, I could use some dude time."

My head jerks in surprise. "Dude time?"

"Derrick taught me *dude time* and to pretend I had a collar up high."

Rochelle and Holli are laughing, but Rochelle says, "Sounds about right."

Holli takes my bags and says, "We're stealing her. You get her back for dinner and prepare to die when you see her."

Ace runs to Derrick and clings to his leg. "I don't want him to die. Don't die, Derrick."

I think it takes us all a second to even realize what happened, but then I see Holli's expression fall. Heartbroken and worried. "Oh no," she says, squatting down in front of him. "I didn't mean he would die. It's a bad saying. I'm sorry. I just meant he's going to love seeing your mommy."

"He doesn't now?"

I step in and tap her on the shoulder. "It's okay." Turning to Ace, I say, "He—"

Derrick's hand rubs over the top of Ace's head, and he says, "Your mom is beautiful, Ace. She always looks beautiful. Don't you think?"

Nodding, he looks up at him, a smile appearing. "My mommy is the most beautiful. Everyone says that." I smile listening to my sweet boy. Then he adds, "Even the mean man."

The words punch me in the chest. My heart plummets to the pit of my stomach and for a split second I lose my balance. My arm is grabbed by Derrick and I'm steadied from behind by Holli. "Are you okay, Jamie?"

All I see is the fear in Ace's eyes. *What if something happens to me? Who will protect him?* Derrick's questions come ringing back. Tears fill my eyes and my hand covers my mouth hoping I can hold back the sob. I'm not sure if it's embarrassment that I have failed to protect him fully in front of Derrick's friends or that I'm realizing I will never be free from Reggie, but I snap at Ace, "Don't talk about him. Ever."

His arms tighten around Derrick's leg and tears well in his eyes matching mine. The room is quiet, no one daring to speak a word, except Derrick. "Come with me, Ace. I got you a present." He takes his hand and they walk to the bedroom. Ace peeks back over his shoulder and my heart shatters that I just snapped at him.

I gulp, and look up at the two women standing there in all of the awkwardness I caused. "Cards on the table."

They repeat, "Cards on the table."

Holli adds, "Stays between us."

Not sure why I decide to tell them, but it doesn't feel wrong to talk about it, not with them. "His father is not a good person. Think of the worst qualities you would ever want in a father and he owns them proudly. Drugs, running guns, gang activity, illegal activity, abuse—emotional and physical." Then I whisper, "rape."

Beyond the fun I've been missing in life, these women are who I wish I could be. They don't pander to the easy answers. They're strong, like I want to be. Holli, with her hands full of champagne and glasses, says, "Fuck him. He'll never come near you and that little boy again. I'll help you fight this battle."

"Me too. Anything we have to do, we'll do."

Tears fill my eyes for different reasons now. Camaraderie. Do you know those moments where you finally realize just how alone you've felt? How overwhelmed and out of control? But somehow, in Las Vegas of all places, I feel safe. I don't know these women, they don't know me, but they've taken me in. I suspect just how they've taken Derrick in too, and helped him not feel so alone. "Why? Why would you do that for me?"

Rochelle replies, "Because if Derrick loves you, which he clearly does, we love you."

And then Holli says, "The women of The Resistance always stick together."

32

Derrick

ACE IS BOUNCING in the chair while I dig through my suitcase. I can hear them talking in the living room. Although Jaymes probably shouldn't have snapped at Ace, I understand why she did. Those damn defenses of hers I've tried to keep lowered popped back up in an instant.

I don't fault her in the least. I still struggle with the same. When you've been hurt like she has or lived on the edge like I did, you're always ready to fight. Like it took me, it will take her time to change that, but I have no doubt that with enough support and love, she will be fine.

Pulling out the toy, I say, "Here it is."

He stands to get a gander. I rip the package open, and say, "This is a yo-yo. Have you ever had one?"

"No," he replies, coming closer. "What is it?"

Drugs, running guns, illegal... her voice trails off and I bring my attention back to Ace. "So you tie a loop like this and then slip it on your finger."

"Then what?"

"I'll show you. Stand back and watch the magic." He steps back. When I flick the yo-yo out and it comes rolling back in, I catch it in my palm.

"Whoa. Let me try. Let me try."

"Sure." I slip the loop on his finger. "It's all in the wrist. Quick flip and then steady."

The yo-yo just dangles above the floor. The disappointment is seen in his sad eyes. "I can't do it."

"It's okay. Like the guitar, it takes practice. I'll teach you and then soon you'll be a pro."

"And we can yo-yo together."

Laughing, I reply, "Yep, we can yo-yo together. But first, how about we go get some ice cream?"

"Yay!" He runs into the living room. "Derrick's taking me to get ice cream."

Maybe he doesn't need any more sugar. When I walk out of the bedroom, I flick the yo-yo mindlessly. "Are we all good?"

I'm only looking at Jaymes, but Rochelle and Holli answer, "Yeah, we're good."

"Go potty, Ace. Then we'll go."

When I turn back to the ladies, they're gawking. I catch the yo-yo, and ask, "What?"

After they exchange looks with each other complete with smiles and mischievous looks in their eyes, Rochelle says, "Oh nothing. We'll meet you at the elevator, Jaymes." Another all-telling expression on her face that I can't tell jack-shit the meaning of. They seem to get it though.

With Ace out of the room and the others gone, I go to her. "Don't beat yourself up. I can see that's what you're doing."

"I just, I can't. I don't want to do that to him."

"He's a happy boy. You gave him that happiness. We all fuck up. What you said was a real and raw reaction. He didn't take it personally. He was all smiles in the other room, so don't stress about it."

She's going to anyway because she cares so deeply, but maybe when she steps back from the situation she'll realize she's allowed to be human. Looking quickly over her shoulder to make sure the coast is clear, she turns to me and says, "I haven't told you everything."

Now I find myself looking to make sure Ace isn't coming. "Wash your hands, too." Looking into the softer sides of emerald, I ask, "Is this something you want to do now or later?"

Dropping her head to match her sagging shoulders, she whispers, "There's so much more I haven't told you."

"Go easy on yourself, Jaymes. You're doing the best you can. It's what we're all doing."

Ace runs in and she lifts up. "You be good for Derrick and listen to him, okay?"

"Okay."

He runs to the door, but I stop him. "Give your mom a hug, Ace."

Her sweet smile returns and she dips down into his wide-open arms. "I love you."

"Love you." Dashing for the door, he says, "I'm ready."

"Coming."

I follow him, but when I start to open the door, he says, "Give my mom a hug, Derrick."

Just the exact right thing we needed to break up the heavy. The kid's got great timing and Jaymes and I both start laughing. But when I start walking back to her, my feet slow just as my world does. Jaymes with the bright eyes and raven hair, sweet pink lips with the bow at the top. Jaymes Grenier with the sassy mouth and good grades, the girl who kept me alive by demanding my time. Standing right in front of me waiting for a hug. I hug her when I'd rather give her forever.

She owns me.

When I reach her, I take hold of her hips first and let her question me with her eyes. Her arms come up and around and I slide my hands higher to her waist, keeping the distance between us. "What are you doing?" she asks.

"Looking at you."

"What do you see?"

Life. Love. Hope. Fulfillment. Joy. Perfection. "Forever." I close the gap and run my fingers into the hair at the nape of her neck. "Close your eyes, Ace." That makes her smile, but I'm kissing her and she's receiving and then kissing me right back.

Her body is putty in my hands when she looks up at me. "That was some kiss."

"There are more where that came from."

"I hope so."

"I know so."

Ace asks, "Can I open my eyes now?" Making us laugh again.

"I'm going to take this kid out. You have fun and I'll see you later."

She blows me a kiss and then one to Ace who catches his. "Good trick, my man. The ladies love that."

A sideways glance was earned from her on that one, but the door closes, so it's all good.

We head down to the shops and past the restaurants to find the small little Gelateria. After a few minutes of explaining that gelato is Italian ice cream, Ace orders Stracciatella. I didn't even know what gelato was until last year when we toured Italy, and here's this kid ordering the most Italian one from the bunch. He makes me grin with pride.

We sit in the corner of the shop eating and talking about the yo-yo. I pull out some of my best tricks to his amazement. Eyes are on us. Whisperings heard. He looks around a few times, adept at being aware of his surroundings, but doesn't say anything. I try to keep his attention on me and enjoy our time together.

Leaning forward, I ask, "So what do you think about me dating your mom?"

"She likes to hang out with you. She smiles. That's always her tell."

"What do you know about tells?"

"Tommy told us everyone has a tell. Mommy's smile is hers."

I'm going to kick Tommy's ass when I see him next. "I like

seeing her smile too."

"Will we see you again when we go home?"

Valid question and one I'm more than happy to answer. "Yes. I'm on tour with the band for three more weeks, but then I'll be home and we can hang out again."

"I can practice the yo-yo and show you my tricks."

"I'd like that."

"Me too."

After gelato, we go to this grassy area near the pool. It's surrounded by bushes and appears to be a no man's land, or secret garden as Ace calls it. I like the privacy and the fresh air. Ace loves the freedom to run. We don't have a lot of time but I lie down in the grass anyway. It's been a long time since I felt at peace enough to do so when I'm not home. Ace lies next to me and it reminds me of the first time I met him and the first time I saw Jaymes again. It's only been a few weeks, not quite a month, but life without them feels foreign to me now. They feel like they've been a part of my life forever, their presence slowly erasing the difference.

Ace asks, "Are we moving?"

Turning my head to the side, I see the curiosity in his eyes. "I hope so."

"With you?"

I'd like that. "I don't know. What would you think about that?"

He shrugs. "What's it like where you live?"

"Really nice. I have a house and there's a pool."

"I don't know how to swim."

"You can learn."

"Will you teach me?"

Guitar. Yo-yo. To swim. It's a lot to take on when I'm used to being single, but I've watched Dex adapt to being a father. And like how it was for him, it's an easy adjustment. *That's love.* I answer without hesitation, and I mean it, "Sure."

"You're rich."

"Why do you say that?"

"Everything is nice and there are no mean people."

I roll over on my stomach and lift up on my elbows. "I'd like to say that there aren't, but you're a wise little man, Ace. You know there are bad people. But there are also good people."

"Am I good?"

"You're the best."

Sitting up, he fidgets with my watch. "Does that mean goodest?"

"That does mean the goodest."

"So if I'm the goodest and my mom is the goodest, you'd want the best in your life."

"Absolutely."

"So it only makes sense that we should live in the house with the pool."

"Ahhh. I see how you worked that in your favor, and I like your style, kid."

"I like yours too."

WE KNOCK ON Dex's door an hour before we need to leave for dinner if we want to eat before the show. Neil answers, but Rochelle is right behind him telling us to come in. Ace tags Neil and takes off. "Have you seen Jaymes?"

"In the bedroom, but I think she wants to surprise you. Let me go check on her."

Holli comes out of the room, but shuts the door behind her. When she sees me, she says, "You did good. She's smart and funny, and gorgeous."

"She was all those things before she met me."

"Well what can we say? Every girl loves a bad boy."

Rochelle peeks out from the bedroom. "Come in here." I shove my hands in my pockets not sure what to expect. Will she look different? Or the same? What have they been doing to her? The door is opened wide and now I see—my throat goes dry and my pants fit a lot tighter. This is not the same demure girl in a pink dress that showed up yesterday. This is a vixen who likes to dominate. Black dress that shows off all her sexy curves, tits pushed up, begging for my mouth, shapely legs, and fuck-me heels. "Fuck me." I mean it one way. They think a different way. Jaymes rolls her eyes, but I can tell it's only because she's anxious. "You look stunning."

"Really?" she asks, running her hands over her stomach. "I feel different."

While I come into the room, Rochelle slips out, and shuts the door behind her. "How do you feel?"

"Beautiful."

I slide my palm on the underside of her jaw and then cup her cheek. Leaning in, I kiss her gently, and whisper, "You should always feel as beautiful as you do right now." This time I kiss her not so gently. My need ravenous.

Her hands slide under my shirt and slip in the back of my jeans, pushing my hips against hers. Our panting breaths reveal our desires. Her lips are on my neck and against my ear. "Fuck me, baby," she whispers.

I spin her around and push her head down. "This dress is hot, but I want it off." I take the zipper pull and slide from high on her back all the way down to her ass and then slip the straps off her shoulders.

She steps out of the dress and I'm left with my mouth agape. Holy fuck me. With see-through lace stretched over her body, this lingerie number is about to be ripped to fucking shreds. "You look so sexy all my plans to love on you—just fuck those."

"No, fuck me, hot stuff." She walks with confidence to the door and turns the little lock on the knob. Coming back, she stands in front of me and says, "Drop your pants and sit on the bed."

I fucking move at the speed of light. With my cock on full display, I lean back on my elbows. The tips of her red nails glide over my erection and then spread the drop at the tip, coating my head before she takes her fingers in her mouth and slowly slides back out between ruby lips. "You make me want to do such naughty things to you." *Oh shit. This girl. Need. Her. Now.*

"I won't stop you."

She smiles, but I see the determination in her eyes. She's not going to be distracted from what she wants. Bending at the waist, she takes my dick into her mouth and slides down, slicking it between her lips.

Falling back on the bed, I want to close my eyes, but I can't take them off her as she takes me. She speeds up like my breath—her mouth and throat taking me slowly, but fully inside. Pausing, she closes her eyes and swallows around me and I almost shoot my fucking load. "Fuck," is muttered repeatedly and she obeys, picking up her pace. I watch with rapt fascination as she pulls my soul from the depths of my core, tighter and tighter I coil. Reaching up, I put a little pressure on the back of her head, but when she sucks me ever harder, I lose focus. Stars and darkness, Andromeda and Perseus, and midnight songs sung in the back of trucks blind me as I explode, letting her take everything she wants, everything she desires. I give my all to her. I always will.

33

Jaymes

I'VE MADE A mess of him and by the red lipstick all over his penis I can only imagine how I must look. I attempt to slink away to the bathroom and clean up before he has a chance to look at me, but I'm caught by the waist and pulled to the mattress beside him. "Don't hide. I want to see how fucking beautiful you are after making me come."

His dirty words elicit a soft whimper that I regret the second after I realize I did it. All my boldness, my empowerment from the clothes and makeup and hair is disappearing and I realize I just want him to love me for me. So I roll toward him and let him take me in—messy and disastrous I'm sure, but this is me after being together so intimately. "You're the most gorgeous woman I've ever seen. That has never changed from the moment I saw you in that short dress with the flowers on it and that denim jacket."

"You remember that?"

"I remember everything about you. You wore thick wool socks and a pair of deep-red combat boots."

"They were knock-offs. We couldn't afford Doc Martens. I found them at a resale shop for three dollars because the heel had split from the shoe. I used to use super glue to keep them together."

"I liked them on you."

She pushes against my chest. "I think you would say just about anything right now."

"You're wrong. I don't have to say stuff to impress you. I just have to be honest."

"You have me all figured out, do you?"

"No, I wish I did, but I do know that the truth goes a long way with you these days, so I won't lie to you, Jaymes."

Reaching between us, I find his hand and our fingers entwine. "When you left that day, Reggie was pulled over the same evening on an anonymous tip the cops had received." He stiffens between us, but doesn't say a word. "He wasn't taken in."

"What?"

"I won't lie to you either. Not anymore. I went by your house that afternoon, but you were turning the corner, driving erratic, so I followed you worried you had finally succumbed to doing what you swore to me you wouldn't."

"I wouldn't do heroine. No way."

"But I didn't know that."

"I told you. I gave you my word I wouldn't. Was my word worth nothing?"

"Your word was as good as your actions and you were acting strange the previous few days. I know what you did. I saw how you set Reggie up to take the fall."

"God, Jaymes." His hands slide over his face and he starts pacing. "What did you do?"

"I thought I was helping. Like I said, I thought you weren't thinking clearly."

Stopping in front of me on the bed, his words are tight. "What. Did. You. Do?"

Panic rises, making it hard to breathe. "I... I waited for you to leave and found the package under his seat. I took it and flushed it all down my toilet."

"Why?" he yells. "It was the perfect fucking plan. He would have gone down for life."

Crawling back on the bed away from him, my words come stuttering out, "I didn't know that. I, I thought, I thought he'd be released and he'd come for you."

"Instead he came for you."

Lies don't separate us anymore. Neither do omissions.

Here we are caught in the middle of the hurricane we created.

Coming around to the side of the bed, he sits next to me. The heaviness of our exposed acts weigh his throat down and I hear him swallow. "It was a good plan."

"A great plan. I just wish I would have been in on it."

"Me too."

A light knock is followed by Dex asking, "Everything okay?"

I look up at Derrick and sigh. He nods, understanding the weight of the world I've been carrying around with me all these years. Taking my hand in his, our fingers entwine again, and he replies, "All's good."

Helping me off the bed, he pulls me into the bathroom, and positions himself behind me. My makeup isn't as messy as I thought it would be. My hair is messier. But his arms slide around me and he's kissing my temple, so all that superficial stuff fades away. At the end of the day, we made a decision, took a path, and paid the price. Now, all we can do is live with it. Having that off my shoulders gives me peace. Peace I've needed for a long time.

SITTING IN A private dining room at the hotel's sushi restaurant, I look around at the four couples and Tommy. Introductions have been made and conversation is lively. I have finally met the man Derrick refers to as his best friend. This is huge.

Kaz Fabian has his own very intriguing story to tell, and so opposite of Derrick's, but I see how they get on—teasing and joking, but honestly and genuine. His fiancée and I hit it off right off the bat. Lara Kessler has been telling me how she's been decorating Derrick's mom's house and that his mom just adores me and has these photos of Derrick and me in frames that she wants to keep out even with the new décor. She says, "So I talked her into new frames."

"I can't wait to see."

She leans in and whispers, "Between us, I've heard a lot about you in the last year. I don't even think Derrick realizes how much a part of his life you've been."

"What do you mean?"

"I'm sure you know about the guitar, but Kaz said Derrick used to mumble about a James in his sleep. He thought he was referring to a man and just wasn't ready to come out yet."

"I'm surprised Kaz never asked."

"Oh God, no. Kaz is all about being who you are and supporting that. Heaven knows I went through hell and he was right there however I needed him to be. Derrick's that way too. He has the biggest heart. A little hot tempered, but who doesn't want a friend willing and ready to fight for you?"

"That's Derrick. He used to hit first and ask questions after."

"Once at an awards show he punched my ex-boyfriend just to back Kaz up." I watch as her eyes drift to something I can't see in the distance, her memories. "I think he would have punched the world if he could because of all the anger he had tied up in him."

"But?"

Her attention turns to me. "But?"

"I thought there would be a but."

Smiling, she says, "But you came back."

Into his life. I came back. "I'm starting to think there's a conspiracy to see Derrick with somebody, especially when I look around this table."

"Not somebody. *You.*"

"You're making me feel special and you don't even know me."

She laughs and sips her glass of wine. "We may not know *you*, but we all know about you. There was never going to be anyone else even if he thought it possible."

"How possible did he think it would be?"

"Don't even go there, honey. Trust me, it's a no-win situation. Just know where his heart lies now. That's all that matters."

"What if I'm as temporary as the other possibilities?"

"You sitting here tonight should put your mind at ease."

This is new information. "He's never brought a date to dinner with you?"

"No. He hasn't. This dinner, he organized."

Derrick's hand covers my thigh and begins to rub. When I look to the other side of me, he's chatting with Tommy about some equipment, but his hand continues mindlessly. He won't know how that makes me feel, warm and cared for, or how he's treating me the exact opposite of temporary. He's treating me like we do this all the time, like we're together every day. It's natural and comforting.

This dinner, he organized. I cover his hand, and hold it until he looks my way. Leaning over, I kiss him. "Thank you."

"For what?"

"This weekend, brunch with the moms, coming by that night to pick up your mom just to see me. For lying in the grass with me when I obviously made a fool of myself and tried to play it off. For bringing my textbook up to my work when we were only seventeen because I forgot it at home the night before a test." The lines soften around his eyes and it's funny, but I never noticed before. I love that I'm sitting here witnessing another stage of his life with him. "For remembering what I was wearing the first time you saw me. And for making love to me with care but not treating me like I'll break."

"Any time."

"I have one more." His hand flips over so our palms are together. "Thank you for accepting my son and treating him like he's your own. If that scares you that I'm voicing that, I totally understand, and I won't do it again. I just need you to know that I see how you treat him and I see how taken he is with you. Thank you."

"It's been my complete pleasure to spend years of my life with you. I would never pass up a chance to spend more time with you and your son. I can make you that promise, Jaymes, and keep it."

"I don't want to go home tomorrow and I don't want you to leave to wherever the band is off to. Call me selfish, but I feel like I just got you back and now you have to go away again. I shouldn't feel this way, I know, but I'm already starting to miss you."

"Three weeks and then you'll be sick of me hanging all over you, following you around like a lovesick puppy. You know, pathetically head over heels in love kind of stuff. I might even write a few love songs and serenade you. I can already tell it's not going to be pretty."

"I'll take pathetically head over heels in love kind of stuff any day over not seeing your face at all."

"We can FaceTime. And get a sitter when I come back. I guarantee you a reunion you'll never forget." My hand is brought to his lips again, a small smile locked in his kiss.

"I like the sound of that."

"In the meantime, we have tonight."

WHEN THE GUYS head off for the concert, we all head back to change clothes. There's no way I'm standing around in five-inch heels and a dress at a concert. I'll break my ankle. Jeans and a T-shirt it is!

But not just any.

I scored a band shirt from Holli. What I didn't expect to find was a gift from Derrick waiting in the suite. I haven't opened a gift all by myself in years. Usually Ace sticks out his bottom lip and guilts me into letting him open it. So I rip the paper off like it's Christmas morning and open the lid.

That sweet man.

The burgundy of the leather is pristine, the size of the combat boots perfect. I may not be fifteen anymore, but I can't believe I finally have my first pair of Doc Martens.

He is so getting laid later.

I get dressed and touch up my makeup before going to say good night to Ace, who is with the other kids and a nanny for a few hours. "I'll come get you later, but go to bed when they tell you to, okay?"

"Okay," he agrees begrudgingly, looking sad.

"What's wrong, buddy?"

"I want to stay with CJ and Neil."

"You want to sleepover again?" Does it make me a horrible person that I wouldn't mind one more night with Derrick? Mom guilt. "Did you ask Rochelle and Dex?"

"They said it was up to you."

"I think it would be good for him to try again." I look over at Rochelle and she's nodding. "We're happy to have him if you're okay with it."

"As long as you are."

"The boys would love it and I think it's good for you and Ace as well."

"That sounds like a yes, Ace."

He hugs me tight, and says, "I love you."

"Love you, too. You have a fun night and I'll see you in the morning, okay?"

"'Kay."

Rochelle meets me at the door and we walk out together. "Ready to see that hot rocker of yours?"

"More than ready."

34

"What is this life I'm living?"

Lara laughs. "It's a nice gig if you can get it."

"Dating a rock star or being the rock star?"

"Either. Want a drink? I'm going to get a bourbon and Coke."

"I'll have whatever you're having."

Holli waves me down from the far end of the hall. When I reach her, she opens the door for me. "Come in. We usually hang out until right before they go on stage."

Peeking in, the whole band's there. Rochelle and Tommy are discussing something on an iPad and Holli holds the door open for Lara after me. I round the corner and there's Derrick. He glances up, but from the delayed response he was caught up in whatever he was listening to. Standing, he sets his guitar down and takes the ear buds out. "I didn't know if you'd be here before we went out."

"I'm glad I am."

"Me too." Running his hand around my neck, I tilt back and kiss him. Even though we're in a room full of people, I don't hold back.

Now that I've found him again, I don't want to waste a second together.

Until the catcalls come.

Then we stop and laugh. I can feel my cheeks heating, but he whispers, "Ignore them. They're just jealous."

When I look back all three are kissing their guys and I elbow Derrick in the gut. "Yeah, I have a feeling they're not jealous."

Tommy says, "I am." Spreading his arms, he asks, "Any takers?"

We all laugh and it feels so good to laugh so freely, our problems left in another state entirely. Or at least mine.

Someone knocks on the door and says, "Five minutes."

Derrick gives me a quick kiss. "I'll see you out there."

"Break a leg."

I shake my ass for him, and he calls after me, "Nice shirt by the way."

Kicking my boots up, I say, "Nice boots. Thank you."

"No problem."

Holli slaps Johnny's ass and Rochelle says, "I'll see you out there. I have a few emails I need to send."

Lara hands me my drink and we're escorted backstage by a guy with a headset who's holding a clipboard. Behind a curtain and through a door, we're led to the VIP seating. Tapping Lara on the shoulder, I say, "I've never been so close to the stage during a concert before."

Standing in front of the seats, she laughs. "You do realize you're dating a member of The Resistance?"

"No. I don't think it's sunk in at all."

The stage goes black with the rest of the arena. From where we're standing I can see tiny flashing lights on the floor.

"Well, get ready."

I'm not sure if she means for the performance or for dating Derrick, which seems to be almost the same as dating the band by how close they all are.

The drums kick off and a spotlight hits Dex. Droplets fly from the impact when his sticks hit the set. His arms are sculpted and on display in a sleeveless Journey T-shirt that has seen better days. "I wish Rochelle could see him."

"She's watching backstage. She always watches his kickoff."

Not even two minutes in and he stops, and the lights go out. I hear shuffling about on stage but can't see a thing.

The spotlight comes on and Johnny is standing at the microphone. His guitar swung around on his back. He caresses the mic like he would caress a woman. Glancing to the other side of Lara, Holli stands mesmerized. He's wearing sunglasses, but I could bet money he's singing to her. It doesn't matter that thousands have spent money to see the band tonight, he only sees her.

She closes her eyes and sways to his sultry and entrancing voice, but it's not him who holds my attention. Another spotlight kicks in and Derrick joins the chorus and then Kaz. Dex starts in with a backbeat and the guitars are added.

I spend the next hour screaming in excitement, dancing, and flirting with the sexiest guitarist I've ever seen. Derrick steps to the edge several times and once while changing out guitars, he fell into a push-up and kissed me. He didn't miss a beat and Johnny laughed.

Lara screamed in excitement with me, then said, "You just won the most hated woman in America banner. I'm happy to hand the title over."

"What do you mean?"

"Derrick was the only one left. His single status gave fans hope they'd get a hookup. After that very public display of affection, you've earned it fair and square after me."

"I can't say the honor is all mine." I laugh anyway, but I have most definitely taken Derrick Masters off the market.

Looking down at my phone, a text catches my attention: ***Ace is in bed and had a great time. Have fun tonight.***

I'm so happy to hear Ace is safe and sleeping.

The band rushes off stage and Holli zooms past me flashing her backstage pass and through the doors. We're hot on her tail, just as excited as she is. She bounds toward the band. Johnny turns and just like that she jumps into his arms. His sunglasses are off his face and she's smothering him with kisses.

Lara whispers, "They are the horniest couple ever."

I'm too busy laughing to reply, but I'm competitive by nature. "I bet I've got them beat."

"Hey Masters," I call.

Derrick looks back and then turns with a damn sexy smirk on his face. "You talkin' to me."

"Sure am."

"Why don't you bring that conversation in a little closer."

"How close?" I ask with only five feet left between us.

"Close. I want to show you something."

I shrug to Lara and she rolls her eyes, then says, "Kaz, wait up."

I think Lara might have a competitive streak too. But back to Derrick and how he's kissing me with abandon in the middle of the crew rushing around us setting up for the encore performance. "Where are the restrooms?"

"This way." He shoves a door open and we almost fall inside. Shutting the door, he locks it, and then stalks me against the sink. With one hand against the wall above my head, he leans down. "What do you need, baby?"

"Remember how good I made you feel?"

"Yes, I have a red dick to prove it."

Red? Oh right. The lipstick. "I want you to make me feel the same."

"Right now?"

"Right now."

"I've got fifteen minutes until I have to be back on that stage. Get to stripping, woman."

My jeans are too tight and my boots are a bitch to take off. I do it anyway and I'm like Speed Racer doing it. Standing there in socks and a T-shirt I can't say I'm on top of my sexy game, but he sure does seem to like it. "Do you know how hot you look in that shirt?"

"I feel even hotter. Twelve minutes."

He chuckles and lifts me onto the counter next to the sink. "Lean back and spread your legs for me."

I'd like to say this was uncomfortable or awkward, but once my panties were removed, I forgot what happened next. I just remember singing the Star-Spangled Banner and seeing stars from the ecstasy.

The knock comes with five minutes to spare. "I'll just stay here with bones made of jelly. Go on. Save yourself. The world can have you for thirty minutes. Then you're mine again."

He's laughing. "I really do have to go, babe." He kisses me and it's erotic and sensual. Careful not to expose me, he slips out of the room, but stops to add, "That was dinner. You tasted so good that I can't wait to eat you again for dessert later."

My vagina clenches in anticipation. Good Lord, that man's mouth—skilled and dirty. The perfect combination.

Managing to get dressed on shaky legs, I slip my jeans on after an exhaustive search for my underwear. I have no idea where they went. Probably to the same place that only single socks go to die. Once I come out of the bathroom, all three women are shaking their heads. "You know we could hear you?"

"What? No? Hear what?" I play the innocent.

Rochelle says, "Let's go. They're already lined up to start the encore."

We start walking, but I hear Lara say, "Girl's got some lungs on her."

"No," I reply mortified.

Holli whispers, "Don't worry. We've all done it. We're just teasing."

That's a relief. *I think.*

"I lost my underwear though. I couldn't find it anywhere in there."

She says, "That's odd."

"Yeah, it sucks. I just got those today."

We find our seats again and the band starts playing one of their biggest hits, but there's no sitting when it comes to one of their concerts. I've been revived and seeing him on stage... Gah! He's so incredibly hot up there. But then he shows me why his name is Masters. He licks his lips and tastes his finger. Holli, Rochelle, and Lara all look at me. I just nod. I'm not going to deny it. Everyone can see right through us, so I'll just own it.

Hollie's arm shoots straight out at Derrick. "There."

"What?"

"I think I found your underwear."

"Where?"

"Front right pocket."

Following her finger, my mouth drops open in shock. "Oh my God." The black lace is barely showing but we see it easily. "I'm going to kill him." After I have sex with him for that. Dirty boy. I love it and I've never been more turned on by something so naughty.

He knows I know too and flashes that signature smile that makes all of us go wild.

When the show is over, the band leaves the stage and a security guard escorts us to the back again. There are lots of people rushing around, breaking down the equipment and stands. We walk into the dressing room and the guys are so quiet, but when they see us, it erupts into a room of chaos, each couple sectioning off for privacy. I grab my handsome man's face, and say, "I'm so damn proud of you. You are incredible."

With a cocky smile, he asks, "So you liked the show then?"

"God, I loved it. It was amazing from beginning to end."

Lifting up so no one else hears me, I whisper into his ear, "I need to fuck you then make love to you all night."

His arm comes around my back and he pulls me against his hard body. "Fuck. Yes."

And we did.

Twice.

For both.

35

EXHAUSTED, I LIE on the bed and watch him at the window. The lights from The Strip light up the room even with the interior lamps off. I roll to my side and tuck my hands under my head. "Where do you fly off to?"

Languidly he looks my way. All the tension from his body has disappeared. For someone made of solid muscles, he looks at ease. Peace looks good on him. "I'm not sure. I usually send Tommy a text and ask. Or not. Does it matter?"

"Yes."

He comes back to bed and we readjust until my head is resting on his legs as he leans against the headboard. "Why?" Fingertips dance across my skin, my body his instrument to create his own music.

"I want you to be present in your life, to feel the difference between the salty air of Florida and the mountain air of Colorado. Then when you come home to me, I want you to tell me all about standing in Times Square at midnight and eating BBQ in Kansas City. Is the water around Hawaii as blue as your eyes or is it more sea green? Watch the fog roll over the hills of Sausalito and then tell me how long it takes before it disappears into the ocean. I need you to experience everything you can and remember for me."

"Come with me. Come with me and let me show you how the Eiffel Tower sparkles at night. There's a little Mom and Pop restaurant just outside Rome that's worth the trip to eat their homemade pasta. And when you're in the Maldives, you can sit on the beach and forget that everyone else exists in the world. Standing at the base of Christ the Redeemer in Rio, you suddenly feel small enough to believe there just might be something bigger than us out there. Let me show you the world, my love."

"Just like Andromeda and Perseus, we can outrun our fates."

"Because they ended up in the heavens doesn't mean they didn't fulfill their destinies."

I slide up and sit next to him. His arm around my shoulder holds me close and I drop my head on his. "Guess we'll see how tomorrow turns out."

"I'm not willing to risk it. You can move into my house."

"No, I can't. We didn't take it slow, but I think taking that kind of leap might be too fast for all of us."

"I'll be back in three weeks. I want you to find a place, somewhere safe, somewhere he can't find you."

"I'm at my mom's."

"That's not safe. If he wants to get to you, he will, and you know it."

Rearranging, I turn to face him, pulling the sheet over my lap and crossing my legs. "It's not something I like to talk about, but you need to know what you're getting into when you decide if you want to see me beyond this weekend."

"There's no if, Jaymes. Not for me."

"You always were too stubborn for your own good."

"I can say the same about you."

"I need to say this, though, and I need you to hear me, really hear me. Reggie will be in our lives forever." Despite my constant wishing for his early demise. "There's no changing that." And then the floodgate of questions is opened.

"How often does he come around?"

"Not often. Every few months."

"Why does he come around?"

"Who knows? Money. To keep me scared. To make sure you're not there. Not for Ace."

"Is that why he doesn't know about me coming to your mom's?"

"He never goes over there. Like I said, my mom has made it very clear to him."

"So he has a vendetta against me. What will happen if I show up?"

"He said he'd kill you. I'm surprised he hasn't gotten a whiff of you visiting those two times."

"How would he?"

"He has guys, druggies who will snitch for a hit. The thing about Reggie is that he's the same guy you knew. He's a lot bark, but not much bite. His ego is what keeps him in charge. He's not afraid to hurt someone or worse, so no one messes with him. But he's still small-time in the grand scheme of LA."

"So when you return to your mom's house, do you think he'll come around?"

"He was arrested before we left. I should have told you. I know I'm a chickenshit to come here under the threat being lifted, but his arrest is our reprieve. He's threatened our lives so many times, I think he's capable of following through. With him in jail, I knew we could slip away and be back and he wouldn't be the wiser."

His hand warms my knee. "I wish I would have known what you've been going through."

"You don't need my troubles. You don't need anyone dragging you down."

"You don't drag me down. I love you. I love Ace. Heck, I love your mom. We may not be married, but we're family."

Not *a* family, but family. It's silly to notice such a slight variation of words but it means more than what was said. "Yeah," I say, sighing. "Family."

I scoot under the covers and lie down.

"Hey, did I say something wrong?"

"No." I'm the worst actress ever. "I'm just tired. I'm going to get a little more sleep before morning comes."

"So that's it?"

"I think so."

"You go back to that place and I go on tour and we go our separate ways or what? I'm confused what just happened here?"

"That makes two of us." My eyes are closed, but I can feel the burn of his gaze.

When I finally open mine, he asks, "What are you doing?"

"Trying to sleep."

"You know what I mean. Why are you pulling away from me?"

I don't want us to leave on bad terms and I don't want to hide how his words made me feel. Sitting up, I face him again. "Because we're *like* family, we're not your family."

"Is that what you want? You want us to be a family? I'll go down to that Elvis chapel right now and marry you if that's what you want."

"Derrick, don't say things you don't mean."

"I mean it." And by the look of determination in his eyes, he does.

"You're still drunk."

"I only had two drinks last night, so nope, not drunk."

"You're tired. You said yourself you're exhausted from traveling so much."

"I am tired. Fucking tired, but I'm not tired right now. I feel pretty damn awake actually."

Biting my lip, I analyze every little feature on his face, searching for the crack in his composure, the lie that I'll surely find. The trouble is, I'm not finding any. I actually find the opposite—the truth. "You mean it, don't you?"

"I do. I'd marry you right now, Jaymes."

"Do you understand what you're saying?"

"I do."

"Do you understand how insane it is that we're even talking about this?"

"I do."

"Do you have a fever?"

"I do. I'm hot for you."

"You can't just be hot for me. Sure the sex is great, we get along well. We always did. Ace clearly adores you, but this is crazy talk. Don't you think?"

"I do. And I still want to marry you." Reaching out, he picks me up by my ass and pulls me onto his lap. With his arms around me, and a smile that confirms he really means everything he said, he asks, "Do you think I'd make a good dad?"

"I do." Kissing his temple, I whisper, "The best dad."

"Do you think I could make you happy?"

"I do." I place another kiss on his cheek. "The happiest."

"Do you trust me to take care of you and your family?"

"I do." I kiss the corner of his mouth. "Implicitly."

"Do you love me?"

"I do." Kissing his lips, I stay, and say, "With my whole heart."

"Jaymes Grenier, will you be my forever and marry me?" I'm about to answer, but his finger presses to my lips, and he says, "Save it for the ceremony. What time's your flight?"

Okay, that was so sexy I'm melty inside. Wait... "Today?"

"Yes. Today."

"Noon."

"Perfect. You get some sleep. I'll take care of the rest."

I land on the bed with a little bounce after he rolls me off him. Lifting up on my elbows, I protest, "What? No. How am I supposed to sleep now?"

"I don't know. Try closing your eyes and being very quiet."

"Your sarcasm is not appreciated, but duly noted."

"Sweet dreams, sweetheart." He's chuckling as he walks out of the room with his phone to his ear.

The door is shut behind him, but I'm too giddy to sleep because I just said yes to marrying Derrick Masters, the first and only man

I've ever loved. Well, kind of. He wouldn't let me actually say yes, but I'm definitely not saying no.

I grab my phone from the nightstand to call my mom, but it's only three in the morning. I huff, wanting to tell someone, but damn it, why did he have to go and ask me in the middle of the night? I have too much energy to lie still. I get up and emulate my five-year-old. Yup, I jump on the bed and touch the ceiling twice before the door opens and he peeks back in.

Getting the smile that would make me say yes a thousand more times, he adds, "Go to sleep. You're gonna need it."

This time I listen to him and flop down. When I'm covered up, he comes and tucks me in and kisses me on the head. "I'll wake you in a few hours."

"What are you going to do?"

"Plan a wedding."

"You won't let me help?"

"It's just boring phone calls tonight. You can plan the fun stuff when you get up."

He starts to get up to leave. "Hey." When he turns back, I ask, "Are you sure?"

"I can give you the boring phone calls if you prefer?"

"Not about that or the planning or me sleeping. Are you sure about us, and getting married?"

Sitting back down, his body leans to mine and he kisses me on the lips this time. "Never more sure about anything in my life. Now get some rest. I don't want you yawning at the altar." With that smile back in place, he winks, and leaves the room.

I lie there in the room with the lights outside the window still shining bright like the stars in the sky. Like Derrick and me.

We're getting married.

BOLTING UPRIGHT, I exclaim, "I'm getting married."

7:56 a.m. How is it possible that I fell asleep and slept like a baby for five hours on the morning of my wedding?

"Good morning, sunshine," Derrick says, pushing in a room service cart full of food. "Hungry?"

"Famished."

He goes back out and pushes another back in. "Me too, so I ordered the whole menu and two pots of coffee."

"I might love you more for this."

Laughing, he says, "Your love doesn't come cheap."

"Yeah, you must have spent a pretty penny or thousands to appease my appetite when all you had to do was come back to bed."

Diving on the mattress next to me, he lies there like a starfish. "I did. I got a few good hours surprisingly."

I reach over and grab some bacon from a platter piled high, and then I just decide to pull the cart up like it's a TV tray. Makes getting to the scrambled eggs a lot easier. "You don't mind me just eating off the plates?"

"Nope, go right ahead."

He pours me a cup of coffee and brings it to what I am now staking claim to as my tray. "So how do you feel now that the sun's up?"

"Are you asking if I've changed my mind about getting married?"

"Might be."

"Stop giving me outs. I don't need them. Do you?"

With a mouth full of egg-deliciousness, I shake my head. After I swallow, I say, "Not me, but I'm eating like a queen so really you got me at my weakest."

"So food is the key to your heart?" He pretends to be jotting this down on his phone. "Good to know."

"It's not everyone's?"

"I think your great tits are my kryptonite."

Taking my phone, I mimic him and laugh. "So maybe I can

287

entice you back to bed for a quickie." I lower the sheet and flash him.

"Pre-wedding sex, Ms. Grenier? You know we'll go to Hell for that sin." *Yes, and I'm going to enjoy every moment of it.*

"We've already been. It's only up from here. Now come over here and show me what heaven's like."

36

Jaymes

HE TRICKED ME with food. I don't know how I didn't remember I'd need to find a dress for the big day. But when a rack of beautiful dresses showed up at our suite, it was apparent by two dresses in, I shouldn't have had the waffle.

The saleswoman from the bridal shop downstairs is kind. "Twenty minutes. That's all we need and you'll feel less bloated. You just need to digest." Lowering her voice, even though we're alone, she whispers, "Or maybe try going number two."

I laugh, wondering how many times she's tried to settle bride's worries by telling them to go poop.

She adds, "Coffee always works for me."

Annnnnnd apparently it works for me. Twenty-three minutes later, I'm slipping into the dresses with a lot more ease.

Rochelle texts me at nine when the kids wake to tell me she'll bring Ace to the ceremony, so not to worry. And it's not that I haven't thought about him and how marrying Derrick will affect him, but watching them together, Ace is happy. In fact, he's more relaxed than I've ever known him to be. Part of me feels guilty for

289

the weight he's unknowingly had on his shoulders. But I can't feel guilty about that. *That belongs to Reggie.* Should I go and *ask* Ace if he's okay with me—well, us—marrying Derrick? In some senses, yes. But, I consider my own mom and the choices she made *for* me when I was younger to help me feel safe. Wanting to be as wise and strong as my mom, I know this is okay. This decision is for us. For Ace and me. And as much as I am over the moon to have Derrick back in my life, and so thankful for all he's done to make that happen, I know Ace is happier too.

Holli shows up with more lingerie, white this time, and perfect under the dress I've chosen. "Did you just have this handy?" I tease. When I hold it up, my breath catches. "This is beautiful."

"To match the bride. Your dark against the white lace—you're a campaign dream come true."

"I don't know what you mean."

"An ad campaign. This lingerie set is from my line. I'm a designer."

"You're a clothing designer?" I ask, shocked.

"Amongst other things."

"Wait, so let me get this straight. You're a designer, you're married to Johnny Outlaw, and you look like this? I'll be honest, I can't keep up with that."

She gives my hand a little squeeze. "It's not a competition, Jamie. You just have to be you and from what I've seen, you're amazing."

"Thank you. That means a lot to me." I give her a hug and while standing there, I think of the life and friends I've missed out on from being under the watchful eye of Reggie. He's kept me down and held me back.

No more.

10:30 A.M.

My palms are sweating. I flap my arms several times to cool down. Is the air on in this place? After checking the thermostat and verifying that the air is indeed on and set to a comfortable seventy-three degrees, I realize it's just me. Even after pushing my flight back to the afternoon and going down to file for a marriage certificate with him, I'm nervous. And sweating.

I'm about to run and spritz more perfume on, but I detour when there's a knock on the door. Peeking through the hole, I see Rochelle. The door swings open and my heart bursts with pride and love and just all the wonderful things in life when I see my little man. Kneeling down, I hug Ace so tight. "You look so handsome in your suit, buddy."

I take his hand and Rochelle closes the door behind her. "I told him dapper."

"That means fancy," he says. "You look like a princess, Mommy."

Twirling for him, I ask, "Do you think Derrick will think so too?"

"No, he'll say you look pretty. He always says that."

"Does he now?"

Ace nods and says, "Whoa. This place is a mess."

With my hands on my hips, I can't argue otherwise. "Hair and makeup just left and yeah, with the food trays and stuff around, it's a mess all right."

When Ace runs to the windows to look out again, Rochelle says, "You make for a beautiful bride, Jamie."

"Thank you. Derrick did everything from the ceremony to my dress and shoes to setting up my hair and makeup for me. I definitely feel like a princess. I just wish I could do something for him."

"Do you have rings?"

"No," I confess. "I feel terrible, but I can't afford one. I was thinking we could pick one out when he gets back, something he likes that I can give to him."

"Getting married is a big step, but your anchor is love. Don't let

291

things that don't matter break the chain. I know Derrick well enough to know that he doesn't need anything expensive. He'd be happy just having you, but I'd put a ring on it if you know what I mean. So, I've still got his credit card."

"And he did tell me to charge anything I want to the room."

"I'll call downstairs and have them bring some rings up in his size."

"I don't know his size."

She sits at the desk and scrolls her phone. "I do. He once did an ad campaign for a watch company and they wanted a ring on him. Let me find the email. You just have some champagne and relax for a few minutes."

How did I get this lucky to not just win Derrick's heart but to inherit his friends, who are his family? It's better than winning a jackpot at the casino. With the puzzle pieces of life clicking into place, I'm definitely the luckiest girl ever. Joining Ace at the window, I sit on an ottoman next to where he stands. His hands are in his pockets and his brow is furrowed. "Got a lot on your mind?" I ask, rubbing his back.

"Some." He shrugs.

"Want to talk about it?"

"I don't know."

"It's a lot and very fast. Is the wedding upsetting you?"

He sits on the ottoman next to me. His gaze stays out in the distance through the glass. "What does it mean? Derrick said it means he becomes your hubsand."

"*Hus*-band, buddy. Yes. It means we become partners." Taking his hand in mine, I hold it. "We'll always be partners too. Just like always."

"So I'll be your husband too?"

"No," I reply, amused. "You'll always be my son. Look at me, Ace." When he does, I lean down a little more to make sure he understands what I'm saying. "You'll always be the best thing in my life."

His head leans on my arm. "What happens when we go home?

Derrick said he's going to Denver." Looking back up at me, he asks, "Does he not want to be with us?"

"It's not like that at all, Ace. He does want to be with us. That's why we're becoming a family so we can be together. His job means sometimes he has to travel. I wish we could go back to LA together, but he'll be back in three weeks."

Popping up, he points outside. "Helicopter."

"So awesome." I never see the helicopter because I'm too busy taking in my son. "You know, Ace, I'm the luckiest mommy in the whole wide world because I get to be your mommy."

He turns and hugs me. "Derrick said he was lucky that he gets to be my daddy." I exhale slowly, the sweet sentiment hitting me hard on that one. "Is Derrick my daddy?"

"He is, now and forevermore."

A tissue is dragged out of the box on the desk and Rochelle wipes her eyes. I'd forgotten she was there. Wiggling Ace by the waist back and forth, I say, "Why don't you go brush your teeth and go potty. We need to leave in a few minutes."

When he runs off, Rochelle sniffles. "That was beautiful and heartwarming. Ace is fortunate to have such an amazing mom."

"Thank you and thank you for being so good to me and Ace."

She stands and shakes off the emotions, but I could use a friend since I don't have my mom here and she didn't answer her phone earlier. "Am I making a mistake? Woman to woman. Mother to mother. Be honest with me."

"I think he made a mistake the first time he let you go. He's smart enough not to do it again, but let me ask you. We don't know each other well, but I get a vibe from people."

"And what vibe did you get from me?"

"You're a survivor, Jamie. I have a feeling you didn't just let him go, let him leave and then stop feeling anything for him. I see how you look at him. I see how much you care. I see the love you both share. I don't need the details, but I do know there's more to this story. The good part is, your story's just begun and it's starting with the happily ever after. So if you're asking if you should marry him, my answer will never change. Hell, yes. Derrick's a great guy. He just needed the right woman to remind him of that. You bring out the best in him. I have a feeling he does the same for you."

"He does. He's good for my soul."

"Then don't question what you already know the answer to. Just listen to your inner voice, the one that's telling you he's the one." I swear we're interrupted more by knocks on the door than anything else. Rochelle adds, "Let's buy that soon-to-be husband of yours a ring."

THE FLOWERS ARE beautiful. I'm handed a bouquet of perfect roses with the lightest touch of pink. The card read *"To match your cheeks"* and was given to me when I arrived at the private wedding garden. Derrick had more sweet surprises up his sleeve. When I peeked outside to see how the ceremony spot looked, my mom was standing there with his mom.

The moms come rushing to me and I start crying on the spot. The planner shoves tissues in my direction and the moms dab very carefully at my face. I thought it would be seeing Ace that caused the emotional tearjerker waterfall. He was just so cute and handsome, but it's seeing them here, together, and crying from happiness that does the trick.

So now, five minutes before I'm supposed to get married, I find myself standing in the bathroom salvaging my makeup. Usually when I'm happiest, flashbacks of terror come back to ruin it, but right now, as I look at myself in the mirror, I only see the good, remembering the best times I ever had were with the man I'm about to marry...

I sit up in the back of his truck and turn the flashlight back on so I can study a little more before I have to be home. "This math test is going to kill me."

"You'll ace it."

"You always say that."

"I'm always right."

I poke his side and laugh when he squirms. "So basically it's good luck when you tell me I'll ace it?"

Sitting up, he tugs the collar of my shirt down and kisses the exposed bare skin. "Yes, ace equals good luck."

I turn and sneak in a quick kiss. "Got it. Ace will always be good luck."

...The tears come fast this time as the memory brings me full circle. Derrick won't remember that conversation, so insignificant at the time, but one that I always carried with me. My mom comes in with my makeup bag and says, "Let me help you."

"We're late," I say.

"They'll wait."

While she touches up my makeup, she says, "He told me he wants us to stay at his house while he's gone. What do you think, dear daughter?"

"I think we should." We speak in hushed, conspiratorial tones. "I don't want Derrick going near the neighborhood."

"What about you?"

"You and Ace can wait at the house. I'll go back and pack our bags and hurry back. Just the basics. Enough to get us by for a few days and work out a plan."

"We'll figure it before we land. Diane wants to throw a party when Derrick returns."

Smiling, I reply, "That would be lovely."

She stands back and inspects my face. "Beautiful as always."

"Will you walk me down the aisle?"

Her sweet smile has always comforted me and continues to do so. "Of course. Let's go. I think you're ready." *I am ready, but hearing my mom's confidence is all I really needed.* She didn't question our decision. She just smiled and accepted and supported.

My man awaits. My future sealed. *Our* future sealed.

Stepping into the room that leads outside, I kiss my mom on the cheek and take her hand. "Here Comes My Girl" by Tom Petty starts playing and I laugh. "I'm ready."

Ace steps forward and grabs my hand and starts tugging. With a huge smile, he says, "Come on, Mommy, race you to Derrick."

I take his hand and slow him down. "I think we should do this together." With the two people I love more than anything in this world leading me to the man I love bigger than the universe, the three of us start walking.

37

Derrick

DIPPING MY HEAD down, I pretend I have something in my eyes. Guess it's not pretending, but tears are tough for me. You don't cry where I came from. Fame has made me soft. Nah, I think it's just made me grateful. The guys are laughing, though, and I may be wrong but when I look at my best man, Kaz seems a little choked up himself. "You sad I beat you to the altar?" I make a lame joke.

He gets it, but being Kaz, he sees through the act and pats me on the back. "It's only fair. This has been a long time coming."

It's been eight years since I saw the girl that would become my wife.

Three of the best and worst years of my life spent together. She was the only saving grace I had. The only reason I fought to stay alive.

Five years since I looked backed. Even in that time, I knew I'd made the biggest mistake of my life. I can try to not blame my eighteen-year-old self, but I knew I was wrong and living in regret for years makes this moment so much sweeter.

The music starts—some cheesy, but traditional wedding march

and everyone stands. The wooden doors to the garden open and there is the reason I'm standing here today. I will be the man she deserves. My angel floats to me in white, her dark hair flowing around her shoulders. Ace holding one hand and her mom holding the other. Her support. I hope I can bear the burdens she carries from now on. She blinks and then tilts her head down, her emotions getting the best of her. Tears escape the barrier of my lids and damn my male ego as they slip down my cheeks.

Her eyes go wide when she sees Leah standing near the altar, her friend and a confidante that I thanked for taking care of Jaymes and Ace in my absence when I called.

When her mom gifts me Jaymes's hand, I kiss both of them on the cheek before turning fully to Jaymes, my beauty. And then vows are exchanged.

"...The one who will stand by your side, the one who will stay this time. I vow to be the man your son will look up to, not in height, but in character."

Ace is standing beside his mother because he wanted to be a part of this union, just where he belongs. I fist-bump him before turning back to the woman who has brought tears to my eyes. "I stand before you, my sweet Jaymes, and promise you my love in this life and beyond because you are the only woman my soul knows how to love, to breathe, to protect, and to cherish. I vow my life, trust, honesty, and love to you evermore." I slide a diamond-encrusted platinum band onto her delicate finger. I love when I take her breath away. Leaning down, I whisper, "We'll get you any diamond you want, but I thought I'd start with the band today."

"It's perfect. More than I could ever wish for."

My muse for music, for life, for laughter, for love speaks of hardship and sacrifice—two things she knows more about than she should.

She hasn't had weeks to think these up. They are in and from her heart. *Fucking lucky man.* "...You are not just the man I love with my entire being, you are the only man worthy of being a father to my son. There is no one else I'd rather him model himself after than the person you have become, the person I always knew you to be. So with this ring, I thee wed for this lifetime and every life after."

A sleek black and silver band is pressed onto my finger and I smile, admiring the way it looks and feels. I don't wear any rings now, but I'm never fucking taking this one off. I couldn't have picked a more *me* ring than the one she chose.

I'm kind of proud of myself for holding it together as well as I have. I've avoided looking at my mom though. She'll make me cry. In a lot of ways, today is her day as much as mine. When I'm told to kiss my wife, I don't waste the opportunity. In front of friends and family and friends who are family, I kiss my wife like we're the only ones in the world. I kiss her until she's breathless, and then I kiss her again so she remembers it when we're apart.

But to my surprise, she doesn't hold back. She doesn't even worry that we're in front of the band, the moms, her friend, or even Ace. She gives me a kiss like I'm the last man alive and her life depends on it. Damn my wife's hot.

She drags that bottom lip under her teeth and then cocks an eyebrow. "Promise me you'll always kiss me like that."

"I always keep my promises."

"That you do." And we kiss again just because we can.

A SMALL BALLROOM has been set with a long table full of flowers. China settings and crystal glasses fill it nicely. We only have time for a luncheon today. The tour can't wait. Twenty thousand tickets sold out in Denver in fifteen minutes. I have a feeling they'd be happy for me, but not to the point of letting me bail a night or two to celebrate my nuptials.

I watch Jaymes. The smile is there for others, but I can see the sadness underneath. She can barely eat and isn't really drinking. I know what she's thinking, what she feels deep down inside. I feel it too. "I don't want to leave you," I whisper while everyone at the table celebrates around us.

Our hands clasp between us and she angles her body toward me, our knees touching. "You've made me weak."

"You're the strongest person I know."

"I only had one to lose before. Now I have two and my heart hurts."

"You're not losing me. Three weeks. You can come to any show, any city. You can be with me."

"I can't," she says and I hear the tremble in her voice. "I have work and school—"

"Don't work anymore. Just go to school."

"I have Ace and he has school."

"You can fly out next weekend. To... ummm... to. Oh, fuck it. I have no idea. Tommy, where are we next weekend?"

We both look down the table at him and wait while he scrolls his phone. I cover her hand and thigh with my hand, hoping I can comfort her in some way. It's not going to be easy to leave her, especially knowing that maniac is in the same city, but at least he's locked away. *For now.*

Rochelle leans across the table and says, "Chicago."

Tommy gripes and puts his phone away.

I ask Jaymes, "Want to go to Chicago?"

Ace tells her, "I want to go to Chicago," but turns to Rochelle to ask, "What's Chicago?"

Rochelle laughs. "It's a city in Illinois, but you know, I've been wanting to take Neil and CJ to Disneyland. It's been a while since we've gone. I was thinking you might want to join us and stay the weekend at our house."

His expression is thoughtful when he turns to me, and asks, "What would you choose? Disneyland or Chicago?"

"Dude, Disney hands down."

To Rochelle, he says, "Disney!"

Dex leans over and says, "Make sure she takes you on the Peter Pan ride. It's my favorite."

"Disney! Disney!"

"Ace. Shhhh. Keep it down, buddy."

"How can I keep it down? I've always wanted to go to Disney."

CJ starts in too. "Disney!"

Neil rolls his eyes. "Kids."

The table erupts in laughter and my sweet bride is finally smiling again. "So Chicago?"

"Yes. Chicago."

My flight's at four, so while the cake is being served, I excuse my wife and myself with the lamest reason ever, but it's now or never. "We forgot we haven't packed. So we're going to go do that. Pack. For our flights."

Everyone is staring at me, including Jaymes, but she's the best, so she says, "Stuff everywhere. Yes, we must go pack. We'll see you guys in a little while."

It's when the moms burst out laughing that we turn and hightail out. Her dress is beaded and tight through the body and does this fluffing out thing at the bottom. She said mermaid. Again, I have no idea what she's talking about, but I want it the fuck off her. "Can I rip these tiny buttons off in the back?"

"No!"

My back hits the elevator and my hands go up in surrender. "Okay."

She takes a deep breath and says, "You don't even want to know how much this dress cost, so there will be no ripping of buttons or anything else off it."

Back in the suite and ten minutes later, the tips of my fingers are killing me and I'm a fucking guitarist. "What are these little torture devices and why'd you pick a dress with a hundred of them?"

"They're pearl buttons and I fell in love with the dress. Don't you love it?"

I see the telltale signs of a setup as soon as she asks the question. Her bottom lip even looks a little pouty. "You look gorgeous in that dress. I just wanted it off for comparison."

"Really?"

"No, Jaymes. I want to fucking consummate our nuptials before I have to fly out of here and not see you for the next five days."

"Your sarcasm is not warranted—"

"I know and it's duly noted, but please, baby. I'm begging you. We have thirty minutes until I have to leave for the airport."

"I kinda like you begging. And trust me, I want this as much as you do. That's why I packed our suitcases earlier. I'm all yours for the next twenty-eight minutes. I'll leave two minutes for you to catch your car ride downstairs."

"Unzip me please."

My patience is gone. If she wasn't so damn sexy standing there, shit, who am I kidding? "What do you mean unzip you? I just undid all those little fuckers to get you out of this dress and now you're telling me there's a zipper?"

"Well, you looked so determined and eager to figure them out that I didn't want to ruin the illusion."

"Show me the zipper."

She lifts her arm and I find the metal bastard and pull it down with lightning speed. Smart enough not to mess with a horny husband, she steps out of the dress and stands there for me like she just walked off a Victoria's Secret runway show. "Holy fuck. How'd I get so lucky?"

And there's that pale pink blush I ordered the flowers to match. Gorgeous.

She taps my watch. "Twenty-five minutes. Time's a ticking."

Over my shoulder in a flash, she squeals in delight and whacks my ass. When I toss her on the bed, I have my breath stolen right from my lungs. *Whoosh* and it was gone from the very sight of her.

The laughter stops and she stretches her arms above her head. "What is it?"

My mouth opens, needing air. Her beauty astounds me, but it's a life of memories from the past that I see before me. My mind flashing between her lying in bed wearing white lace on our wedding day and back to her in white cotton underwear the first time I stole them and her virginity.

"Derrick?"

Twenty-two minutes and I'd happily spend them looking at her. I start on my shirt, not rushing, just watching her. A soft smile slips into place and I recognize that one—she's happy. She's in love. She's happy in love with me.

Twenty minutes. I lie down and bring her atop me. When she bends down, she kisses me.

Eighteen minutes. I take down one of her straps and then the other. "You look incredible, but we're running out of time."

She slips it off and rolls a condom down the length of my cock.

Sixteen minutes. I was wrong. I thought I could watch her lying on the bed all day. Nope. *This.* I can watch her riding me well into next week. I hold tight to her hips, not wanting to let her go. Her tits bounce as her body moves steady. Her mouth opens.

Thirteen minutes. I flip her over and as much as I want to *make love* to my wife, I want to fuck her more. So I do.

Taking her by the wrists, I slide her arms back in that position from earlier. Call me selfish, but she looks fucking amazing open for me. She lifts her legs and I place her ankles over my shoulders. "Hold on, baby." With her hands pressed against the headboard, I take hold of her body and thrust. Pounding every ounce of sensation out of us until we're left pulsing together, electrified in our connection.

Alive.

Her legs are still up when I lay my head on her chest, panting for air. Her heart beats strong, so strong and vibrant. I want to listen to it forever. I close my eyes while she runs her fingers through my hair. She whispers, "Four minutes."

I think she's fine, still lost to her bliss, but her body shakes, wracked with a slight cry. When I look up, her eyes match mine. "There's no getting around the sadness, just distracting ourselves from it temporarily. Five days."

She holds back her tears, but I see her breath jagged in her chest. "Five days." It feels as though I've only had her back in my life for five minutes. The pain I'm feeling now resembles what I felt when I first moved away. I was desperately lonely. Desperately wanted to go back and get her. But then I heard she was with Reggie, and my heart broke. If only I'd ignored her wishes, swallowed my pride, and gone to her to find out the truth. *She was trying to protect me when she sent me away, when she was the one who needed protecting.*

And now I'm leaving her again. At least I know where we stand this time. And she'll be safe. Their driver is trained in covert operations and my bodyguard when I attend events, when needed. He'll make sure they're safe. The security system on the house is operating with a guard just inside the gate. They'll be safe and I can rest easy.

"I don't want to leave. You know that, right?"

"I know." She looks toward the window and I go to the bathroom and clean up.

She doesn't have to count down. Two minutes. I go back and pull on my clothes. Sad eyes watch me and then she gets up to hug me. Her naked body as bare as my soul as I have to tell her goodbye. I feel raw on the inside, my emotions hidden there.

"I love you. I love you. I love you," I whisper, hoping it sinks deep into her skin and deeper into her veins. I want her not just feeling my love, but breathing it deep within.

"I love you."

I turn and grab my leather duffel bag in one hand and pull my suitcase in the other.

Time's up.

38

Jaymes

THE NIGHT IS so quiet up here at the observatory that I can hear traffic from a mile away. Lying in the back of his truck, I reach above my head and strum across the strings of the guitar he gave me.

"What if I gave you the world?" Derrick asks, turning my way.

Finding his hand between us, our fingers weave together. "I don't need the world. I just need you."

When I squeeze lightly, his body cringes, tensing as if he's in pain. "Are you okay?"

"I'm fine."

...I found out a few months later that he had gotten in a fight with my father the night his hand was hurt. He never told me and never complained about the pain. Not while I was at work and not that night in the back of that pickup. But I know him. It takes a lot to upset him, much less make him violent. Violence toward women is at the top of his shit list. So if he threw one punch, he most likely threw another, but my father had gone too far when he pushed my mother.

She told me one night after a rough day. Told me to never love a man like my father. To stick to the ones that are brave when no one is watching. To marry a man that will defend your mother and not need the credit. That's the kind of man that will always protect, will always put you first.

Derrick Masters always did care more about me than he did himself. Today he proved it once again.

Leah takes my hand and spins the ring around my finger. "You're like Cinderella."

Laughing, I ask, "Did I just get married?"

Now she's laughing. "You did."

I sigh. "I miss my Prince Charming."

"Maybe that castle will keep you warm while he's gone."

"Ha ha. So how did you end up in Vegas?"

"Private jet, baby. He flew your moms and me in."

"What?" I sit up, staring at her.

"Yup. Now close your mouth. You got to marry the rock star. We just got to live like one for a day." Tilting her seat back, she closes her eyes, but I see the braggy grin she can't hide. "By the way, first class is the only way to travel when you're not traveling by private jet."

"You're lucky I like you so much."

"After flying today in the fanciest ways, I agree I'm lucky you like me so much."

I snort while laughing. "I can't believe he did that for me."

"He wanted to surprise you. How romantic is that?"

"The most."

"I'm not understanding the boots with that designer purse, Jamie. Not to judge, but that is a Gucci purse. You're really doing it an injustice with those shoes."

It doesn't matter that my Docs don't go with the purse the girls picked. Derrick gave them to me and that's enough for me to feel like the prettiest girl on the plane. I don't hear the rest of what she says because my mind is caught up in my morning. I'm married.

I'm married to Derrick.

I'm Mrs. Derrick Masters.

Mrs. Masters.

Wow.

My heart quickens and I look over at Ace sitting on the inside next to my mom. They are finding shapes in the clouds and laughing. The sound is so light and free, airy without care that I wonder if this new life will seal that beautiful sound forever. No more crying in closets or hiding when the banging starts. No more coded texts to my mom when the monster comes around. *When the monster won't know how to find me.*

The vise around my chest loosens and I feel like I can breathe with ease for the first time in years. That's the best gift anyone could give me.

THE FLIGHT IS fast, which is good since it's a school night for Ace and me both. I'll turn in my resignation later this week. I want to find a replacement first and not leave them in a lurch. It's been a steady job and one I could rely on despite David hitting on me.

As soon as we land, I'm in action texting Rochelle and hurrying my mom and Ace to baggage claim. Rochelle was on a different flight but the arrival times were close. They shouldn't have to wait long, then Rochelle can get them set up in a car and off to Derrick's.

I hug Ace, and tell him, "Listen to Grandma. It's going to be late by the time you get home, so take your bath and brush your teeth. When I get home, I'll come tuck you in and kiss you good night. Be a good boy."

"I will."

Straightening up, I turn to my mom. "Rochelle will be here in the next ten minutes or so. I'm going, so I hopefully beat some traffic. You good?" She smiles at me, and as usual, I feel her strength.

"Yes, daughter. Be safe, Jamie."

"I will. In and out. I'll call you when I leave." A quick hug bonds us before I have to break away and catch a cab.

I rush to find cars for hire and catch one with relative ease considering the crowds coming out. Traffic still sucks. It's LA after all, so I make use of the time and do the one thing I've been wanting to do since we landed.

Derrick picks up on the first ring. "Hello there, wife."

"Hello, dear husband. Where are you?"

"Denver. We landed about thirty minutes ago. And you?"

"Somewhere in LA."

"Is it only me who thinks it's really fucked up that we got married this morning and now we're in different cities tonight?"

I laugh under my breath. It's not funny at all, but I'm trying not to cry. "It's messed up."

"Five days."

"Only five days and I'll be counting every hour until I see you again."

"You can be quite charming, Mrs. Masters, when you want to be."

Mrs. Masters.

And I swoon. Closing my eyes, I savor his voice, the deep richness that echoes through me when he sings, embedding itself into my soul. "I miss you," I whisper.

"I miss you more."

Flexing my fingers, I admire my ring. "Derrick, I love you."

"I know, sweetheart. God, it's so good to hear that from you. I never thought I would. When I see you next I'm going to show you how much I love you. How much having you in my life makes me so fucking happy."

"You already have. Years ago. I've never forgotten the way you always took care of me. Thank you. I know I've said it, but I need you to know that I feel it."

"I want you in my bed tonight and to call me before you fall asleep. I'll be in bed, wishing I was in bed with you, and we can fall asleep to the sound of each other."

I thought I swooned before, but this man... this man... this man. I'm so in love with him. "Next best thing."

"Yes, next best thing to falling asleep with you here." His voice returns to its regular tone and he adds, "I texted you the gate code and the house alarm code."

"Don't worry. I gave them to my mom with the instructions you gave me," I reply mindlessly while staring out the window.

"Why?"

"Why what?"

"Why did you give her the instructions?"

Shit. "Oh ummm..."

"What are you doing, Jaymes?" He sounds alarmed. *Shit.*

"I'm in a cab."

"Going where?"

I can't tell him, but I can't lie. Shoot. What to do? I panic and sit up, looking to see where I am and figure out how much time I have. "Derrick—"

"Don't *Derrick* me. You're going back, aren't you?"

"I just need to get Ace's and my school stuff and then I'll be out of there lickety-split."

"What the fuck are you thinking?"

"Don't talk to me like that."

"Your feelings aren't what I'm worried about right now. Your safety is. Is Ace with you?"

"No, he's with my mom. They're heading to your house."

"I could have sent someone over there. This isn't good. You need to turn around and go to the house with your mom and son."

"I get your concern. I do, but he's locked up. His guys won't mess with me. They just report back to him. Even if they do, I'll be long gone."

"I don't want you going there at all."

Too late. The cab turns down our street. "I'll grab the backpacks and be out and I'll call you as soon as I leave. I'm here. Five minutes max."

"No, Jaymes—"

"I love you. Five minutes." I hang up just as the cab pulls to the curb. Reaching forward, I ask the driver, "Will you wait? I'll only be a few minutes."

"Sure. Be quick. It's not a good neighborhood."

"You're telling me."

I pop the door open and hurry across the lawn and up the porch. As soon as the front door's open, I drop my purse and run to grab Ace's backpack from his room. I shove a few books he loves and a stuffed dog he likes to sleep with sometimes into the bag as well. Opening his dresser, I pull out a few shirts and shorts, socks, and underwear. I don't even know if they match, but I don't have the time to worry about it. I'm just as quick in my mom's room, scrambling to get two of her dresses and shoes for work and putting them in a grocery bag I find in the kitchen. I have plenty of clothes in my carry-on so I run to get my backpack. With both on my back, the grocery bag in my hands along with my purse, I'm ready to leave, I open the door and turn to lock it, but then I spot a folder that has my essays in it. Dang it.

I run in and grab it and then back out the door to lock it. When I turn around, I scream, the bags in my hands and my essays falling to the porch.

"Where you going, Jamie?" Reggie is pale and his eyes are curious as he takes me in. Glancing down, he says, "Looks like somewhere with all these clothes."

"It's mostly school stuff. The rest are clothes for my mom," I lie. To save my life, I lie. "She spilled something on herself at work and she needs to change."

"So you wadded the pretty shirt up in a ball and shoved it in a grocery sack? Tsk. Tsk. Surely, you can do bet—"

That little voice in your head that guides your gut, reaffirms that your instincts are correct, and keeps you safe—mine grew louder once he left after raping me. Bending down slowly, I pick up the bag, careful to hide my ring.

But it's too late.

Reggie doesn't look high. He's calculating my demise.

"So the rumors on TV are true. Rebel came into my neighborhood, as if he still had the right to—" He walks to the far side of the porch, leaving me room to run.

"Reg—" I take one step before I see the cab is gone and Reggie's friends—two cars, four guys—are there instead. *Oh fuck.*

"Silence!"

My heart sinks. I just want to get home to Ace and fall asleep to the sound of Derrick.

His glare is deadly. I don't want to find out what else he's capable of. Walking back to me, he says, "The real problem is not that he came back. I would welcome him with open arms. I would allow him to beg for my forgiveness and be my right-hand man. But that's not what he did or seems to intend to do. Noooo, he came back to take what is clearly mine and make it his." Standing not six inches from me, he asks, "How did you always manage to go unscathed in this mess?"

"Unscathed? Hardly."

I turn away, but he grabs my jaw, squeezing so hard that tears spring to my eyes, and forces me to face him. "Don't you ever turn away from me." He pushes me free and I stumble back. "Shayna says I should put you to work for me on the streets."

"No."

"No? You don't tell me no. Not ever. Here's the thing with Shayna. She's never liked you. Nope. I'm not saying it to hurt your feelings. Just stating the facts. She's jealous of you like I used to be jealous of Rebel. So I see where her hate breeds for you. But luckily for you, I see the potential. She gives a solid blow, but she's not so great in the brains. You are, but I never tested your blowing skills. I can imagine they're decent if Rebel kept you around. Oops, I meant married you. It doesn't seem quite fair that I got arrested and you got married. I'm feeling a little left out that I didn't get invited." His expression perks up. "I know. We can have another reception for you." Though I'm shaking my head no, he says, "Yes. This is perfect."

Pacing across the porch again, he adds, "We can plan the reception, but it's no good unless we have the guest of honor in attendance. So, here's what we're going to do. You will call your husband and tell him that you are with me until he comes to the party. That's it. He only has to show up and you're all his again. And don't forget to bring my son." Dipping his head down to see my lowered eyes, he asks, "Maybe I need to inspire you to make that call. See, Pinkard, back there? He's always had a thing for you."

"Give me the damn phone."

Laughing like a hyena, he mimics me while digging through my purse, " 'Give me the damn phone, she says.' " He puts it in my hand and says, "If the cops show, you're dead."

I've taken too long. Derrick will be worried. I put the phone to my ear as soon as it starts ringing. "Are you—

Reggie grabs the phone. "Hey, old buddy. Long time no talk. So, I was hanging out with your wife and we decided to have a little party. Similar to last time when I fucked her, but this time we thought—Eh. Eh. Eh. Let me finish. We thought we'd extend the invitation for you to join us. Well, that's a poor choice of words. Watch us might fit better. Yeah, I think it does. What is that you're saying?"

He stares at me, a snarl for a smile distorting his lips. "No, you've got it wrong. You left. I stayed. This is my territory and if you want something of mine in my territory you come see me. We'll be waiting." He hangs up and drops the phone in my bag. "Now all we do is wait."

Then the world goes black.

39

Jaymes

MY BREATH COMES slow, loud in my ears as I exhale. My vision is blurry when I first open my eyes, but clears as my hearing does.

"...it's a very nice purse, but she has no style. I'll carry it around and everyone will think you gave it to me." Shayna's shrill voice. I close my eyes again, hoping to escape this nightmare and wake up. But this is it.

"I did." The voice that follows is harsh and full of hate. *Reggie.* "Anything she has is mine. I wonder how much this ring is worth?"

My heart stops dead in my chest. I want to see my hand, look at my finger, but I fear I'm safer asleep. Like a spinning Rolodex, my thoughts roll out of control.

Derrick.

Ace.

My mom.

Phone.

Ring.

Pen.

Keys.

Nothing.

I've got nothing. It was all in my purse.

I've got nothing to fight with, nothing to protect myself with. *Nothing.*

Shayna's voice is close when she says, "Let me have the ring, Reggie. We'll get married—"

"Shut up. I can't hear myself think. Go clean something."

"You're such an asshole sometimes." By the clapping of her heels against the floor, she storms out.

He yells, "Leave the purse."

My foot is hit and I can hear the jingle of my stuff falling out of the bag.

Once we're alone again, he says, "I know you're awake."

I slowly open my eyes and see what I was dreading—my hand in front of my face, my finger bare. Tilting to look where his voice came from, he's sitting on a short stool near my knees.

Rubbing his forehead, he says, "Sit up." His voice is calm, unaffected by drugs, the way I remember from high school.

Slowly, I push up, the shooting pain blinds the left side of my skull and I reach to cover it, hoping pressure relieves it.

A long exhale is blown in my direction, and he says, "This ring makes us even." I'd argue, but I know it's of no use. "Rebel was my idol. He was the last person I ever expected to betray me. You, definitely." He laughs to himself. "I knew you would. That's why this whole situation is so ironic. He did and you didn't. You took his debt for that drug drop like a champ."

"I had no choice."

"You see, that's where you're wrong. You did. You had a choice, but you stood by him even when he didn't stand by you."

"What do you want?"

"This ring is a good start, but nothing you do will take away his betrayal. Did he really think I wouldn't find out? I would have done life for that crime. He wanted me gone and for what? So he could play guitar in some pansy-ass band? Fuck that." He tosses my phone at me and hits me in the arm. When it lands, the screen lights—Ace.

"Have you ever had déjà vu, Jamie? Fuck, I just had it. You look a lot like your dad."

Death. I will kill him if he continues. "Don't."

"Don't? Ha! Fuck, that's exactly what I told him, but he never did listen. Fucking drug addict. I saw him after Rebel beat the shit out of him. He came by my ma's place before she died. Looking for a hit, anything he said. I told him to go clean up. As a favor to you. I told him to go home and don't go take that next hit. Fucker didn't listen. Did you know they found his body?"

"Reggie, please, if we ever had any nice thoughts toward one another, I beg you to not finish this story."

"This is what you're begging for? I've got to give you credit. You're a lot tougher than Rebel ever was. So as I was saying, he was found under the highway. Clothes stolen. Everything gone."

Numbness has a feeling and it spreads. It creeps through the veins icing them over along the way. Sometimes it bypasses the heart leaving you vulnerable to the things that shouldn't matter. Making them matter more. My father is dead. Numb. Tears for a man that never loved me enough to raise me come forward, the ice of my heart thawing under the mess of the situation I've found myself in.

Shayna comes in and says, "I see the bitch is awake. That's a nasty bruise you got there." She crosses her arms and stares down at me from behind Reggie.

Just when I thought I could reason with Reggie, his usual disgusting self returns. "He never replied. I think there might be trouble in paradise. Fucking groupies takes time, time he doesn't have to take your call. So, how are we going to do this? We can make another baby together?"

He's pushed from behind and Shayna leaves again, the slam of a door down the hall reflecting her anger. My body convulses, rejecting even the words from his mouth, and I throw up.

"Gross. Guess kissin's out. How about me and Shayna raise *my* son? She wants a baby awful bad."

"I will die before I let you take him."

"You're gonna die anyway, so let the games begin." The stool flies out from under him and slides across the kitchen floor. I scramble to my feet but am grabbed under my arms and slammed against the wall near the door, making the door rattle. I push off his chest as he pins me. One hit to his ear shakes him, but he laughs. Lifting my knee in the space between, I keep him at a distance while I claw the side of his face.

In a hit to my left side, the pain explodes and my vision goes black. But still I fight. I fight for me. I fight for Ace. I fight for Derrick. I fight for the life I deserve. My vision is blurry as color comes back. Swinging my right, I land a hit that sends him down. With my boots, I kick him so hard that he falls the rest of the way to the floor. I kick him again before turning and opening the door.

I run. Jumping down the steps, gunfire rings out, and I fall to the grass.

"Drop your weapon." Commotion surrounds me—red and blue lights flashing. Another shot is fired after the warning.

I'm not sure at first if I'm shot or not, but I lie there frozen as police swarm the lawn and the house.

"Roll over," I'm commanded.

When I do, the officer has a radio to his mouth. "Victim has been identified."

Through the police telling me to lie there until the ambulance arrives and being lifted on a gurney, I stare into the clear night sky, searching for something to hold on to in my mind.

Peace is found.

Andromeda and Perseus.

I stay there until the paramedics arrive, decide I need further examination, and that they need to transport me. I'm lifted into the ambulance and taken to the hospital. When the doors close, I ask, "Is he dead?"

The paramedic sitting next to me doesn't make me work for it. He knows who I'm talking about. "No. He's being taken to the hospital." When I look away, he adds, "Gunshot wound. Shot by the police."

Even though I've prayed for Reggie's death many times, I don't wish for it now. Something about a life dying always goes hand in hand with sadness. It's not sadness I feel for him, it's not sympathy or respect. I'm numb when it comes to my emotions regarding him. It was always going to be him or me. I need to live for Ace. For Derrick, and for me. So sympathy is not something I can garner for Reggie Rogers.

I have no idea what time it is or even which hospital I'm going to. They confiscated my phone but called my mom for me. She must be beside herself. I'm hoping she stayed home with Ace though. I don't want him to see me in the hospital. It would terrify him.

I'm pulled from the back of the ambulance and pushed into the bright lights of the hospital corridor. I stopped listening to the medical words being tossed around when I was told I'd be all right. It was hard to decipher the other words, my thoughts fuzzier as time moves on...

Derrick is my most favorite thing to do, and watch, and listen to. No one plays the guitar like he does. He compliments me, but I've been slow to learn. Getting better every day since he gave me my guitar. I've been messing around with a song I hope to play on his birthday. Return the favor and all that. I've already got the guitar that cost more than I should have spent, but he'll do wonders with it. I just know it.

...A familiar melody travels through my thoughts, notes I cherish every time I hear them. My throat is dry when I swallow, so I cough. "Drink this."

Opening my eyes, I smile, then leave it behind. It hurts too much. "You're here?"

Derrick's hand caresses my cheek, that look of concern I hate seeing on his face ever present. "Drink first." A fire burns down my throat and I take a sip from the straw. "Why'd you have to go and be the hero?" The concern renders itself to a smile that I find comfort in. "I could have used some of that glory."

"Your ego's big enough. You are a rock star after all."

"Yeah, guess it was your turn." He kisses my head and says, "Reggie's dead."

"I had a feeling, but I didn't ask. He took my ring."

"He took my girl. The ring is replaceable. You're not."

"I just got it though."

He laughs out loud and in it I find the peace I need. "We'll get you a better one."

A nurse walks in and smiles when she sees us. "I'm glad you're awake."

She examines me, and then says, "The doctor will be by shortly." After adjusting the bed so I'm angled up, she says, "The man they brought in right before you didn't make it."

I nod. She continues, "He died in the ambulance on the ride over."

"I don't want to hear about him. Not ever again."

"I understand but I was hoping you could piece together a mystery for me."

Derrick takes hold of my hand, and asks, "What is it?"

"The paramedics called ahead for plasma for a potential transfusion. We're short, so we searched our area blood banks for the type we needed, and a nurse checked his file for next of kin. Your son Ace was—"

"No." Anger surges and I sit up, dizziness striking quick. "Please tell me they didn't touch my son to try to save him?"

The nurse and Derrick gently press me back. She says, "Everything is okay. We need to keep your blood pressure from spiking like it just did."

"I don't care about that. I care about Ace. What about my son?"

"You had his blood tested at birth? It's not that common to do."

"My mother said I should just in case there was an emergency. She had done the same with me."

"Smart. It's always good to know and most don't have that

information. Your son's medical record shows he's blood type AB."

"Yes, I know. And?" I press her like I'm pulling teeth.

She stops messing with my covers and looks me in the eyes. "The man they were bringing in was blood type O. That's not a match."

"That's not a match?"

Derrick releases my hand and rests his hands on the bed. Staring at her, he asks, "Not a match?"

"There's no way he can be his father. O doesn't make an AB in any combination."

Dropping back against the bed, I look at Derrick. "Oh."

"Not to pry, but if I can help you in any way, I will."

When Derrick turns to me, our eyes meet and the air between us stills. "What have I done?" I close my eyes, wanting to disappear, hoping to wash away the image of Reggie forever. When I open them, I say, "They told me. When I went to my first appointment. I prayed. I begged God. I wished on the stars that he was yours. But the math. They counted back and told me. There was no way."

The nurse's cold hand covers mine, but I welcome the cooling relief. "Mistakes are made. I'm so sorry this one was made with you."

"Mr. Masters, do you know your blood type by chance?"

"I have a medical card."

"If you'd like I can find out."

The humiliation of the situation makes me feel hot and uncomfortable, exposed. "I wasn't with anyone else."

She smiles. "There are no judgments here. Just science."

"He raped me." Even now, I can barely get the words out.

A gasp followed by sympathetic eyes come. "I'm so sorry."

Derrick intervenes, "You did nothing wrong, Jaymes. You don't owe us anything."

"I owe you everything." When I dare look in his eyes, they're glassy. "Ace."

Reaching over me, he embraces me carefully, dropping his head on my shoulder. As I hug this big muscle of a man, I feel his tears through the thin cotton. The nurse leaves quietly and he says, "I'm a dad."

"You're a dad." My heart aches for him and what was stolen away. "I'm so sorry."

His head jerks back and he sits down on the edge. "Sorry for what?"

"For the last five years."

"You sure know how to make up for it. I got married and became a father all in the same day. That's a damn good day."

I inhale, my breath jagged. "Stop being so nice."

Tilting his head, a small smile plays on his lips. "Nice? I'm not being nice, I'm happy to be married to my dream girl and be a daddy to Ace. But Jaymes, seeing that the fucker hurt you not once but twice is killing me. Knowing he touched you today, or ever... He's dead, so he never will again. That also makes this the best day of my life." He wipes the tears away with the pads of his thumbs and teases, "Now stop raining on my parade."

Covering his hands with mine, I ask, "Are you really happy?"

"The happiest I've ever been. First, I get the honor of marrying my soul mate. Then I find out I'm a dad to the coolest kid I've ever met." Shrugging, he laughs. "I mean, I guess we could have figured this out just by knowing Ace. We took the long route, but we got there in the end." Leaning down, he kisses me. *He should be angry. He lost the first five years of his son's life. How he can see the good in this is beyond me.*

"How are you this good?"

I'm given that signature wink and a smirk. "Oh baby, I was always this good, but I'm happy to remind you for the rest of your life."

40

Derrick

Two months later...

"WE'LL GO OVER it again when we get home. Don't worry."

Looking in the rearview mirror, I see my son in the backseat. He's in his car seat and worrying about a science project he has due in a few days. Blood types. We've been working on it all week. His attitude is better than mine considering he's in kindergarten. This private school we enrolled him in is way more advanced than the school I went to.

I can hear him singing a song that might be weird to some, but I kind of love. "A plus AB equals me."

It does.

I could get hung up about losing five years of his life, but I get the distinct pleasure of calling him mine for the rest of it. I can't turn back time, and sure as shit don't want to speed it up. I finally feel good, at peace, and since the tour ended, I even miss performing live.

The embrace of my love, my lover, and my forever warms my

arm when Jaymes reaches over and rests her hand on my leg. Tom Petty comes on and Jaymes sighs, and starts to change the station, but I stop her. "It's my favorite song."

"It's your theme song. All the girls always felt so special when Derrick Masters used to sing this song in the school parking lot."

"Is that what you think? Oh baby, you've got it all wrong. I only ever sang it for you. You're my girl. My only girl."

"Come on. You're pulling my leg."

"Nope. Full truth. I never sang it for anyone else."

"In that case." Leaning back in the seat, she turns the song up and we sing it together.

When we round the corner to my mother's house, I say, "Ace, remember what we talked about?"

"About the surprise for Mommy?"

I glare into the rearview mirror. "Nooooo. I meant you being on your best behavior. CJ said you took his drumsticks last time and wouldn't give them back. You know how attached he is to them."

Ace's face scrunches in annoyance. "Yeah. Whatever."

"Not whatever, buddy. Don't take them this time. Don't even touch them."

"But I want to play the drums. It's not fair he gets to."

My eyes flash to Jaymes. Our minds in sync. In a much calmer voice than I'll be able to put on, she asks, "Buddy, don't you want to play guitar? Daddy's been teaching you, and you play so well." She pats my leg.

"No. I want drums."

Damn. "Why do all kids want drums?" I ask rhetorically.

She answers with a laugh, "Because they get to bang on them. Don't worry, he'll come back around."

"Let's hope. I'm really not wanting to lose street cred by raising a drummer."

That makes her laugh harder. "I think your Hollywood Hills street cred is safe."

WE'RE LATE, BUT we're the guests of honor so everyone lets it slide. My mom is the first to hug me... after she hugs Ace and Jaymes. I've been relegated to third in the lineup. But third place to them is a beautiful place to be.

The wedding celebration is in full swing and Lara has given us the tour of my mom's newly furnished home, and this time no one's in a hurry to leave. She's got a new roommate. Jaymes's mom moved in a month ago. They have so much fun together.

The band is here, their families, Leah and Jose from the dealership, too. I turn him down on a "Cherry-red Ford Minivan with only 70,000 miles on it," but I like his determination. He got me once. Not going for another. I found out later that Kaz got suckered into a lime-green 2006 VW Beetle that Lara fell in love with for tootling around on the weekends. Kaz was not amused by the car or the tootling part, but he bought it anyway. For her. Apparently. But thanks to Jose, I've been given a whole lot of teasing material.

I come in from outside and see Jaymes talking to Katerina, Kaz's sister. Swerving left into the kitchen, I'm caught before I have a chance to duck behind the counter. "Derrick?"

I pop up above the deviled eggs with a plastered smile on my face. "Yes, dear?"

Her head tilts and a hand goes to the hip. Busted. "Come over here."

Deadman walking. I make my way over with a deviled egg in each hand and pop one in my mouth, hoping to not have to talk much, or avoid it altogether.

Katerina laughs. It's not her fault. Well, it kind of mostly is, but what's a guy to say to a hot chick dragging you to bed? Exactly. She says, "Jaymes is lovely. Congratulations on the marriage."

With a full mouth, I nod. Jaymes thanks her and then says,

"Katerina tells me you two used to date."

Egg bits fly from my mouth... oh wait, did she say date or fuck? The relish in this egg is crunchy. "Derrick! Gross," Jaymes exclaims stepping back, making sure none landed on her.

Katerina's laughing, but all in good fun. "Relax, she knows, but I told her that you always only had a heart for one woman—her." Turning to Jaymes, she adds, "I never stood a chance, but life works in mysterious ways. I met someone recently that I'm quite intrigued by. Kaz will scare him off soon enough so I'm keeping him a secret." She moves to leave. "Congratulations again. I'm truly happy for you both."

Jaymes turns my way, with questions in her eyes, so I go ahead and spew it, not the egg, "That's another story from the past that doesn't need to be dredged up. My favorite story is ours. Deviled egg?"

Lifting up, she kisses my cheek. "No, it's all yours. Just like me. Now about that surprise Ace spilled the beans over." She waits expectantly.

I kiss her cheek this time. "Give me a few minutes. I'll be right back."

Heading to the guest bedroom, I find the guitar where my mom hid it for me. I double-check that the scratches are gone and strum a few times to tune it again. I want it to be perfect, like her. Something about this guitar—it's resilient, like her...

"Come on, Tank," I haggle. "You know this is for Jaymes. It's something good when she's been through so much bad. Cut me a deal."

"This might have worked on me once when you were a scrawny-ass punk, but now you're a freaking man. No deals today."

"That's a lie. I was never scrawny." I slap five big bills down on the counter. "She's worth it."

He shakes my hand. "It's a pleasure doing business with you. And take my advice, learn to play the drums. Chicks dig it."

"I think I'm doing all right in that department."

"You've made us proud, man."

He hands me the guitar just as some teenager walks in. "Oh man, you sold it, Tank? I got the two hundred you wanted and everything."

I send darts with my glare to Tank. "You overcharged me?" Covering my heart, I say, "I thought you loved me, man."

"I do. I just love a sucker and his money. Deal's done, sucker."

Laughing, I look back to the kid, and then behind the pawnshop counter at the last guitar hanging there. "It's not acoustic like this one, but it's a nice electric."

"That's three hundred. I can't afford that one. It took me two months to save up for this one."

"Solid fretboard from what I can see. You play?"

"I play. You?"

"Dabble." Tank chuckles. I add, "What's your favorite band?"

"Tom Petty and the Heartbreakers. He's the best."

Smiling, I say, "Get 'im the guitar, Tank. On me."

"No way!" The kid runs to the counter with his hands out as Tank passes it over. "No freaking way." Looking at me with his mouth open, he says, "Thanks. This is the best gift ever. Thank you."

"You're welcome. Just keep playing and don't ever let anyone stop you from dreaming."

"I won't. Thanks, mister."

The music softly playing in the background is familiar. It's a song I play every time I play live. "Hey, turn it up, Tank," I say, walking to the door. He obliges with a knowing nod.

I overhear the kid say, "That band sucks," and laugh while pushing through the door. Shrugging, I know—can't please everyone.

...I cover Jaymes's eyes hoping to please her. We walk forward until she's positioned right where I want her. When I remove my hands, her mouth drops open and she runs to Ace. "Oh my God.

How did you get this?" She immediately puts the strap over her head and starts to strum as if it's second nature. "Ace? Where did this come from?"

"Daddy."

Everyone turns toward me. Yup, they know I'm Ace's dad, but this just might be the first time they've witnessed him calling me one of the two best names in the world—Daddy and husband. Rebel can fuck right off. Although, even that name has been tempered a bit. It's a remnant of a past life, but one that led me here. My own personal rebellion that turned into a transformation. So maybe it doesn't need to fuck off. Maybe I just need to see how it fits into my life now.

Jaymes comes to me. "How did you find it?"

"I went to the most obvious place. Tank's Pawnshop."

Her smile is prettier than blue skies and sunshine, and better than a stadium full of screaming fans any day. Okay, not better, okay, yes, better. For sure better. I do miss the chant of my name sometimes. Maybe she'll do it for me later. "Thank you." With the guitar between us, I bend down and kiss her. "I didn't get you a wedding gift."

"Are you kidding me? You made me a dad. Best gift ever. Hey Ace, c'mere." Ace runs over and I lift him up into my arms. "I got you something too, buddy." The troublesome twosome and mischievous matchmakers themselves, the grandmas, come outside carrying a big box. It's wiggling and eventually barks and pushes the open flap back and pops it's head up. Ace screams, "A puppy."

The kid's got some vocals. Maybe we should get him singing lessons. Beats drums. The golden lab puppy was too cute to pass up outside of the grocery store, crying in that box to get out. They had five in the litter and we got the last one. He was the runt, but I don't see it. He's a big puppy. "What should we name him, buddy?" Ace is on the ground with the dog, who is currently licking the crumbs from his face.

Ace looks up as if he's known the answer his whole life. "Rebel, like your back."

My brow furrows as I process what he just said. I glance to Jaymes who's about to tell him to pick something else, but I stop her. I wasn't exactly thinking this was how the name would fit into our lives, but the more I think about it, the more I like it. "I think that's a great name, son."

Ace smiles, and then pets Rebel.

Jaymes leans on my shoulder, and says, "Well, that's one way to turn it into something good."

Something good. A stupid tattoo doesn't define me. It came close, but it's not me. I'm the dad in the pickup line on the mornings when my wife stays up studying too late. I'm the guy who now buys tampons because my wife promised me sexual favors in return. I'd do it anyway, but I'm not going to say no to sex with my wife. Have you seen her?

Damn luckiest guy in the world. I wrap my arms around her shoulders and hold her to me. She whispers, "How do you like being a dad?"

"It's the best." Kaz hands me a beer and we tap our bottles together and drink.

Jaymes asks, "How do you feel about two?"

Two minutes later I'm still cleaning the beer I spewed on Kaz and Lara. "I'm sorry," I say, laughing.

Jaymes is laughing harder. I toss them a roll of paper towels and turn to take my wife off to the side. Once we're alone, I ask, "Are you pregnant?"

"I am."

Sweet pink cheeks, bright green eyes. My heart skips a beat just looking at her. Grabbing her into my arms, I hold her. The guitar on her back makes it a little awkward, but we manage. "I thought I was lucky before, but you just topped that."

"I was thinking you might want to name the baby."

"Oh man, too bad Rebel is taken by the dog."

"Your sarcasm is duly noted."

Laughing, I reply, "Good to know." With my arm around my wife, we start walking back toward the other guests. "So how do you feel about Spade?"

"Ha. Ha. Very funny."

"In all seriousness, I think we should wait to see what the baby looks like."

She stops in her tracks. "Then they'd all be named Winston or Maude."

"I think we've got time."

"We do have time on our side."

Before we get too far into the party again, Rochelle pulls us aside. "How does your schedule look next week for lunch?"

I cross my arms over my chest and shrug. "Good."

"I meant Jaymes. I want to go over the contract for the song and do a test recording."

"Wow, it's moving fast."

"The guys are off to Australia in a few weeks. If we're incorporating the song, we've got to get the legal stuff handled."

Jaymes looks to me. "It's your song. What do you think?"

"It's your song. It was a gift for your birthday. Anyway, it was always written for you to sing. I've seen the contract. It's a good deal."

Turning back to Rochelle, she says, "Tuesday works."

They hug and Rochelle says, "Get ready for the time of your life."

"Wait, it's only one song, right?"

She shrugs. "Guess we'll see."

Later, we leave a party of guests who were yo-yoing for prizes, but I had to steal my family away. I have more up my sleeve and it's late afternoon. I watch the sky turn from blue to orange then pinks and yellows as I drive. Ace says, "It looks like the sky is on fire," right before he's giggling from puppy kisses.

The setting sun is getting lower and radiates beauty from its core. Reaching over, I hold Jaymes's hand, never happier than this moment right here. She asks, "Where are we going?"

"You'll see."

She does soon enough, and a smile rivaling the sun shines, and she gives my hand a gentle squeeze. "I haven't been here in years.

Not since I was here with you. Is that why you bought this truck from Jose?"

"I needed a truck bed."

Our hands rest in Ace's lap, who's situated between us on the bench seat, and he couldn't be more pleased. The puppy sticks his head out the window and my raven-haired beauty smiles into the wind. I park in our old spot and we pile out. In the back, I take off the tarp and straighten the pillows. Ace and Jaymes are chasing the puppy. I bring out her guitar and set it next to mine before I climb up. Ace runs in the grassy area while Jaymes leans against the side of the truck. She's smiling when she says, "We could be arrested for trespassing."

Hopping down over the side, I land next to her. After a swift kiss, I waggle my eyebrows. "That's what makes coming up to the Observatory fun." I paid the guard off last night when I said I was going out for ice cream. I brought her three flavors home and she never asked why I was gone so long. Trust is good like that, or maybe she's onto me. Either way, it worked out.

I lift her up into the back of the truck and then chase the puppy and then Ace until he *lets me* catch him and set him up there too. I hop back up and take my guitar in hand. Ace has a kid's guitar now and is getting pretty decent. For a five-year-old. By fifteen, those wrong chords aren't gonna fly in our house. I start to rethink my stance on that as I strum. I'd rather him play guitar than drums though, so I guess I need to learn patience. He'll get there one way or another, just like his dad. I'm just glad he doesn't have to spend fifteen years fighting his way out like I did. He's slept soundly through the night since we told him the mean man died and that he'll never come around again. He'll never have to be scared again, especially not with me around. I'll always protect my family.

Rebel settles down on one of the pillows and the three of us play a song together. Eventually, Jaymes cuddles with Ace and they watch me play another. When I finish, Jaymes says, "I notice when you're home for more than a few weeks, you start missing the stage and the fans. Your name being screamed—"

"And the pulse," I add. "But I miss you guys more when I'm away."

"We can't chant your name here or we might get caught, but know we're always cheering for you, even when you can't hear us."

She looks to Ace and it seems they are in on a plan together. With their hands fisted, they start whisper chanting, "Derrick. Daddy. Derrick. Daddy."

I have to admit, this beats any concert I've ever played.

Best fans ever.

Lying down, I rest my head on her lap next to Ace who is sprawled out the other way. We don't get many clear nights here, but tonight, as if it heard my wish, we can see beyond the universe. I'm about to point out the constellations, but when her fingers run mindlessly through my hair, she whispers, "Derrick and Jaymes."

"Forever destined to be together."

Epilogue

Derrick

THE NIGHT SKY is overcast. *Bummer.* It's not raining, so whatever. I can still work with this weather. Our fingers are intertwined, but I was idly spinning her ring around her finger moments earlier. I love seeing that band on her hand.

Jaymes Anne-Marie Masters.

I'll never tire of seeing that name on documents or hearing it spoken. We've not been married but six months, but it's been the best six months of my life. The band traveled Europe over the summer. She, Ace, and I had a blast exploring the cities during the day. Our nights were completely our own or booked with concerts. She opened our shows by performing three songs live. One song was ours that we performed together acoustically. A song written when I was seventeen and in love with a raven-haired girl with tranquility found in her eyes that settled the raging waters of my soul. The other two songs were all her. Written by and sung by her, sitting on a stool in the middle of a big stage.

She's the bravest soul I know. Not because she has no fear in performing solo, but because she has no fear when it comes to

331

things and people she loves.

Her wounds healed, leaving a small scar up near her eyebrow. I tell her it makes her look tough. She says being tough makes her tired. I think it's the baby. Reaching over, I rub my hand over her round belly. A little fist or hand follows mine and I smile. Jaymes says, "You woke her up."

"I only touched your belly."

"She's already a daddy's girl."

Chuckling, I rub again. "Could be a boy. I think that's a fist I feel."

"It's probably a heel. And since we don't know if it's a girl or boy, I'm going with it's a she. I need to combat some of the testosterone in our home."

Home.

She's my home. Ace is my home. This baby is my home.

Family.

It was the missing link to happiness. Who knew? I somehow knew it wasn't the bevy of one-night stands that slipped out the next morning. To think Jaymes was in the same city, her soul waiting for mine to return... I wish I would have seen things clearer, seen through the lies she told to protect me, sooner. It took a lot of living for me to discover what I'd been searching for was here all along. I know it now. I see her and that amazing heart of hers at work, at play, at love, at life every day. It took us going through hell to find our own heaven. Now that we're here, I'm never leaving.

A guard meets us when we arrive. We're let on to the private property and I pull into the lot to park. She knows. There's no hiding the surprise now.

"The Hollywood Bowl? What are we doing here?"

Getting out of the car, I say, "You'll see." When I come around, I help her out. I grab our guitars from the back of the car and watch her smile grow. "I know."

"I know you know. You never forget anything."

"That's not true. I just remember the best of things."

Walking with a guitar in each hand, I ask, "How do you feel

about playing a few songs with me?"

Her arm wraps around mine and she rests her head on my bicep. I pop it, flexing so she thinks I'm still as sexy as she did when we reunited. I've gotten a little mushy since she got pregnant. Ice cream. I've never eaten so much as I have in the last six months. Mushy by my standards. I'll add two more days back into the current workout schedule.

The side door is opened for us and I thank the manager for making this happen. We're led to the stage and look out. The moment is quiet, the feeling mutual and overwhelming—so much has gotten us to this point. When your dream comes true, it's good to take some time to appreciate the journey and savor the reward.

I set the guitars down and get two chairs off to the side for us as my words come echoing back. *"I'm going to play that stage one day. Just you wait, baby."* I set one down for her, and kiss the top of her head when she sits. *"You, my songbird, are going to sing for the world."*

"I was right."

Her eyes flick to mine, her lips swept up in a smile. "You've sung for the world. Just like you were born to do."

"That's where you're wrong."

This time, I look her way. With my guitar across my lap, I say, "That's highly unlikely."

"I wasn't born to sing. I was born to love you, to make babies with you, to live a happy life with my family."

My smile comes, just like it always does for her. "Are you happy?"

"The happiest." She glances out at the empty seats, and says, "Not even eight years later and here we are. Your dreams were big enough for the both of us and carried us here."

Spinning my ring around, the engraved ace symbol comes to the top. "I used to think my dream was to play this stage, but now that I'm here, I realize my dream already came true the day I got busted behind the gym smoking."

"You're always so charming. Keep it up and I might believe you one day."

"Your sarcasm, Mrs. Masters, has been duly noted."

"Fine," she says, rolling her eyes. "I'm a sucker for that story. Tell it to me again." She strums down the strings and watches me.

So I say, "Hey—"

"No. No. No skipping over the good parts. Start from the very beginning."

"I'll sing instead," I say, laughing. I start playing my new song, the one where I get to sing about a girl in a flower-covered dress and a name that starts with J. I move my chair closer to hers and look into her eyes.

My forever.

She's always been my muse, but now she's the melody that plays in my heart, the one that made it worthwhile to go back to the start.

The End

A Personal Note

Huge kisses, hugs, love, and all the good stuff in life for my husband and two kids. They stand by me and support me endlessly while I write all day and into the night. I am living my dream because of them and I will forever be grateful to them. I love you, guys. XOXO

Thank you to the team who helps me tirelessly and without griping when I make enormous demands on their time and friendship. Yes, thank you for holding my hand through the tough times and celebrating the victories with me. Thank you for you being you - Adriana, Amy B., Andrea J., Annette, Cara, Heather, Irene, Jessica, Kristen, Liv, Lynsey, Melissa, and Ruth.

To my awesome group in SL Scott Books on Facebook - You are AMAZING. Thank you for being there for me and for making this group so lovely.

Readers, you are the best, just amazing for all of your support. Thank you for loving my books.

Dear Bloggers, you are simply amazing. Thank you for your time and love and enthusiasm.

Available Books by New York Times Bestselling Author S. L. Scott

Hard to Resist Series

The Resistance

The Reckoning

The Redemption

The Revolution

The Rebellion

Talk to Me Series

Sweet Talk

Dirty Talk

Welcome to Paradise Series

Good Vibrations

Good Intentions

Good Sensations

Happy Endings

Welcome to Paradise Series Set

From the Inside Out Series
Scorned

Jealousy

Dylan

Austin

From the Inside Out Compilation

Stand Alone Books
Missing Grace

Until I Met You

Naturally, Charlie

A Prior Engagement

Lost in Translation

Sleeping with Mr. Sexy

Morning Glory

To keep up to date with her writing and more,
her website is www.slscottauthor.com or to receive her newsletter
with all of her publishing adventures and giveaways, sign up for her
newsletter: http://bit.ly/1pF049r

Join S.L.'s Facebook group here: http://bit.ly/2bq2Tfa

S.L. Scott

For more information on New York Times and USA Today
Bestselling Author, S. L. Scott:

Visit her website: www.slscottauthor.com

Sign up for her newsletter: http://bit.ly/1pF049r

Join the fun on Facebook:
https://www.facebook.com/groups/slscottbooks/

Living in the capital of Texas with her family, Scott loves traveling
and avocados, beaches, and cooking with her kids. She's obsessed
with epic romances and loves a good plot twist. Her favorite color is
blue, but she likens it more toward the sky than the emotion. Her
home is filled with the welcoming symbol of the pineapple and finds
surfing a challenge though she likes to think she's a pro.

Made in United States
Orlando, FL
15 June 2022

18836839R00209